BEYOND THE BARRIERS

PREQUEL TO THE Z-RISEN BOOKS

TIMOTHY W. LONG

BEYOND THE BARRIERS

For Guy Meadows
The bravest man I never knew

"Carry the battle to them. Don't let them bring it to you. Put them on the defensive. And don't ever apologize for anything."

Harry S. Truman

PART 1

People talk about the end of the world. Some stock up on supplies. Others practice what to do, where to hide, and what to eat. Families build shelters and participate in drills. They draw escape routes, keep extra batteries, and gallons of water on hand.

They plan for earthquakes, meteors, volcanoes, and nuclear strikes. But no one guessed the true way humanity would come to an end.

Then it actually happened.

ONE

I watched the news compulsively for three or four days just like everyone else in the country. I sat on my ass and stared at the stupid television for so long that it put me off shopping until it was almost too late.

I called in sick that Friday so I could stay home and follow the unfolding madness. The media made a point of saying that people weren't going to work. I was one of them, content to be somewhere safe while civilization fell apart.

I was low on goods like fresh meat and vegetables. The bottom drawer in my freezer was filled with crumbs from some chicken crap that spilled out a few months ago. Smelled too. That freezer burn reek that never really goes away no matter how many times you clean the damn thing.

I dug out a frozen hunk of ground chuck and tossed it in the microwave to defrost. Half an hour later, I remembered it was done, and formed a half-ass hamburger out of the meat and fried it in butter. An egg and ketchup went on top. *Bon Appetit, because it may be your last meal,* was my only thought as I ate like an automaton.

I could become a survival nut--board up the place, set up guns near each window on the second floor. That way, if one of those things showed up, I could blow its heads off. Maybe I could grow a long scraggly beard and run around in my underwear, shouting about the end of the world. Now that would be a funny sight sure to keep the scavengers away for a few days.

I wonder what I would have done if Allison had still been with me. I'll never forget the day she left. She took her shit and left a big hole in my chest where my heart used to be. "Erik," she tried to reason, "it's not you. There's something wrong with me. Something that all the counseling in the world can't fix."

In the end, I tossed her bags on the sidewalk, took her keys, and removed the one that opened the deadbolts on the house. Then I threw them on the car's hood.

Her new guy just sat there like a lump. He wore sunglasses and refused to look at me, no matter how long I stared. At one point he took out his cell phone and flipped through God knows what while I stood there with my dick in my hand. Allison's face looked sad as she loaded her stuff in the back of the dude's beat-up Volvo, and then he puttered away from my now-lonely house on a stream of exhaust that reeked of burning oil.

I crouched a few feet from the little flat-panel TV I had picked up at one of those Christmas sales and chewed the food, barely tasting the lump of greasy meat.

CNN had a live crew in Portland, and they were following a pair of the dead things around like paparazzi. It was silly, yet I couldn't look away from the television. I should have changed the channel to see if there were some better coverages of the event, but I let it roll as a pretty reporter in high heels followed them, with her cameraman close behind. In the distance, a pair of camouflaged trucks rolled by, filled with armed men and women. It was so reassuring to see them on the scene that I almost cheered, like my team was winning a sporting event.

"Again. We're live from Portland. According to locals, people with the infection are now roaming the streets. Hospitals are overflowing with cases, and there isn't an empty ICU bed to be found."

Then the camera panned back to the reporter, Caitlin Perkins, as she approached one of the dead that stumbled around like a kid in shock. The guy's arms hung at his side, and his head was cocked to the left like he had a terrible neck pain and couldn't straighten up. The back of his head was drenched in blood, and his ribs showed where the shirt had been torn away.

A flashing message on the bottom of the screen advised of 'viewer discretion.' No shit. No one should be watching this, but stare on I did.

Caitlin turned to stare at the camera. "As you can see. The affected seem to have no direction. No purpose. They're simply wandering in circular patterns. We've been assured that the National Guard has been dispatched and will arrive within the hour." She turned to face the camera; face etched with concern. "I hope it's not too late."

Another of the 'affected', as the reporter referred to them, came out of the space between two buildings--a little alley that was littered with torn trash bags. Discarded objects lay in piles over which the dead woman stumbled, falling to one knee then rising again on shaky legs. A normal person would have grabbed her appendage in pain, winced or sworn, but this thing just got up and came on. A fresh stream of blood ran down her pantyhose-covered leg and onto her expensive-looking shoes. She had been a blonde and maybe a looker earlier in the day. Now she was missing most of her bottom jaw, and one arm hung by sinew and strips of flesh at her side.

It was like a movie, and I wondered for the hundredth time if I were just seeing some crazy prank put on by my friends. I wanted to run up and down the street and find those responsible and beat them to a pulp. I had seen a ton of zombie movies, and they were, for the most part, enjoyable but unrealistic. At least that was my opinion up until then; now it had changed dramatically.

Caitlin Perkins was so focused on following the dead man that she missed the woman coming out of the alley. Caitlin was tall, lean, and pretty in a confident way. The undead bitch closed in on her, looped one arm around Caitlin's neck, and tried to bite her shoulder.

The reporter recoiled in horror, stumbled, but in a no-nonsense move, dropped one knee, and flipped the girl over her back, onto the hard pavement. It was a beauty of a throw, and even the cameraman was impressed based on his gasp. Caitlin didn't look much like a fighter, but that move was perfect. The reporter fell back, landed on her butt, and then stared at the thing at her feet. Caitlin scrambled back as it came to its feet like a drunk getting up from the night after a bender.

That's when the cameraman started shouting for help and the view went shaky. He said some words that would have the FCC calling in the morning, and then the screen was filled with sky. There was movement all around as a swarm of the things descended on him. The noise that came out of the speakers horrified me. The cameraman tried to scream, but either his mouth was covered with something or, even more disturbing, the attackers were tearing his face apart. The noise of skin being ripped off was the worst.

"They're everywhere!" Caitlin yelled as she ran.

The camera fell over, and the screen came to a jarring sideways stop against the ground. The last image was the reporter running by with a couple of the things in pursuit. The cameraman's arm plopped down limply by the screen. One of the dead things dropped beside it and clamped teeth on the exposed arm. With a jerk, it tore out a chunk of skin.

Then the screen went blank, and the shocked faces of the newscasters appeared. After a few seconds of stuttering as they tried to explain what we had just seen, the speakers crackled, and the emergency broadcast signal sounded along with the familiar static screen.

I jumped to a local channel, and they were talking about the infection, or whatever it was, in calm voices. They made it seem like everything was under control, but if people saw what I just saw on CNN, they knew how serious this was. Portland was overrun with the dead.

I didn't even want to think the word let alone say it aloud, but I did anyway. It just slipped out.

"Zombies." It was absolutely ridiculous, but there it was. The dead were rising and eating people.

I took a breath and went back to the fridge for a Soda. There was a fresh six pack in the back, and they were ice cold. I popped Coke Zero open and guzzled half of it in one shot. I felt unsteady as I looked toward the ceiling while the bubbles slid down my throat. It reminded me too much of the camera's view just before it fell on its side and the reporter ran off.

I took stock of my pantry. My weekly trip to the store should have been a few days ago, but the craziness on the television had kept me indoors. I wished now I had gone when the shit started to hit the fan, but it was no used getting worked up over it now.

I walked to the front of the house and looked outside. There were no walking cadavers. But that was where the normal ended and the weird began.

The neighbors at the end of the little street were attempting to pack what looked like everything they owned into a car. A pair of children with tearstained faces came outside. The boy sobbed when his father took a big box of toys and threw them on the lawn.

I felt for the kid, but his father was just being practical. To a little one like that, maybe six or seven years old, he must have seemed like a monster. The man spun around, picked up his boy and hugged him tight, while he whispered in the kid's ear. His shirt rode up, and he had a big automatic pistol in his waistband.

A half-formed plan had been developing in the back of my mind. I picked up my keys and crossed to the living room, over our light-brown floors.

Allison and I had spent a couple of weekends installing the laminate flooring. We had worked hard, and when we were done each day, we had taken a shower together while playing grab ass and discussing how much we had accomplished. I didn't know she was screwing that guy from work at the time, or maybe the affair hadn't even started back then. It doesn't matter now, I guess.

I grabbed my boots and went back to watch more TV while lacing them up.

The reporters went on, looking at each other in disbelief as each story was told. It was the same on every channel I turned to until I came across a news chopper in the air over Portland. It was obvious events had gotten much worse. It was almost like a riot in the streets, and there were people running everywhere. The man in the chopper was talking into his mic about the level of hysteria, advising everyone to stay inside.

"Enough." I muttered as I marched to the door, locked it behind me, and started my ten-year-old Honda SUV.

I wore a light jacket to take advantage of the unseasonable warmth. I was pretty sure rain was on the way tomorrow, but when you live here, you just get used to it. I backed out of my driveway, my gaze on the pristine front lawn with its deep, green grass, plants in the front, including two shades of rhododendron right next to each other. They looked like they were about to call it a day for the next six months. The other plants were pretty well soaked from a recent deluge of rain, and hung limply as if they had given up on life in general. *I feel ya, plants. I feel ya.*

My house was a little two-story--not the brick sort you see on TV on a perfect day, with a perfect family inside. It was white, an off-shade, and it had light blue trim, which Allison had made me put on after we had moved in. I remembered that day, standing on a ladder eight or nine feet off the ground, while I ran the brush back and forth. She would come out from cleaning the inside and check on the status, like a general inspecting her army. It had been a hot day and she had brought me lemonade, freshly squeezed from organic lemons, because she claimed that organic was better for you. I couldn't tell the difference between regular or organic, and now that she was gone, I bought whatever was on sale.

I drove slowly through my neighborhood and observed curtains pulled back, with faces partially hidden in shadow. I thought I saw a tentative wave from one house, so I waved back. The streets here were calm and quiet, which was eerie considering what was occurring in Portland.

I kept the SUV near the speed limit, which was a chore since my anxiety wanted to jump out of my stomach and strangle every driver ahead of me. After ten or fifteen minutes of painful twenty-five mile an hour roads, the street dumped me out on a main drag called Arthur Road, which was had once been a highway. Now it was a worn out road with pot holes and . That drag was old and always jammed with cars. The City of Vesper Lake sprang up over the course of twenty years, and the roads were never designed to support that much traffic. Housing developments like mine became all the rage as prices near downtown Portland went nowhere but up.

It was stop and go as I competed with other cars at the stop lights, and lights Vesper Lake had aplenty. The town had sprung up what had felt like a sleepy villa of a few thousand in a matter of a decade, and no one had planned for this amount of traffic. I managed to maneuver behind a lifted truck. The driver flashed his brights and honked at me, but I didn't care. I then took off like a shot at the light and got around a few more cars before arriving at my destination.

It was time to find out just how badly the shit had hit the fan.

TWO

The Walmart parking lot was a nightmare. I pulled up in front of the store, made a spot out of the loading zone, jumped out, and locked my SUV. I wore a baseball hat on backwards, and I guess the look on my face, which was probably determined, kept shoppers from saying anything to me about my choice of parking spaces except for a diminutive and rotund woman with dark hair cut close to her face who tried to give me a piece of her mind.

"You can't park here. Hey. Hey you. You can't do that!"

I brushed past her without making eye contact or a snarky reply.

Forced air blew down from giant units above the entrance, creating a wall of cold to keep the day at bay every time the automatic door slid open. A security guard kept an eye on nervous-looking shoppers who stood in an orderly line. I didn't stop when he approached me. He was big, not as big as me, but he was overweight, and his forehead was covered in sweat.

"Sir, I can't let you skip ahead like that." But I ignored him and kept moving. The line of people behind me disintegrated as the folks who had been patient saw me take control. Making people wait in line while the world fell apart made no sense. They should have been packing people in here, getting the last of the money while they could like good little capitalists.

The guard ran back, with his hands outstretched on either side, and yelled at them to get in line, but they ignored his calls and streamed around him like a school of fish breaking up around a slow predator. I moved past a young couple that were filling their cart with fresh fruit and vegetables. The wife was inspecting each one like they were shopping for the weekend, while her husband's eyes darted around as he followed the rapidly developing run on goods.

That wouldn't last long. Fruit and veggies would go bad if the power went out in a couple of days. They should have been collecting canned goods. Things that would last for a while.

I moved briskly to the grocery shelves, but found most had been swept clean. Employees moved around in their bright blue Walmart shirts and tried to keep order, but it was descending into a chaotic situation, and had been since I walked in the door. The stuff they were talking about on the radio. The screens above the aisles were running coverage of the attacks. Some people stopped and stared, while others kept their eyes down, avoiding the images like it would somehow save them.

I found an unattended cart with a few items and glanced around for the owner. After a few seconds I put my hands on the handle and kept moving toward the back of the store. I tossed out the contents, some boxes of cookies and Twinkies, and kept moving like it was mine to begin with. My next stop was at a canned goods section that had a few remaining items on the shelves and dumped Spam and corned beef into the cart. Then I swung through another aisle and found a lone, five-pound bag of white rice, and it went in as well. There were some sardines on another aisle, lots of sardines, so I swept those up too. Better a little protein and the vitamins they would provide than pure sugar.

Gunshots from outside elicited screams from other shoppers, but I moved on. I'd heard plenty of gunshots in my life, and if a stray bullet had my name on it, well, nothing to be done about it once I was on the ground. Or deep in it, for that matter.

I ran into a traffic jam, where a guy was arguing with another guy over a few bags of Cheetos. Both men looked to be at their wits' end, and I suspected it would come to blows soon.

I moved on toward the outdoors goods, hoping there was stuff left. I found a Swiss Army backpack that featured straps and multiple pockets hanging from a shelf and added it to my collection. I hoped it had the same build quality as their knives. A good bag would go a long way, if the world did indeed go down the drain.

Then I hit the emergency section and found a pair of flashlights that you shake to charge. A small wind-up radio was next to them, so I tossed that in as well. It was lying on its side, next to a couple of opened tents, through which someone had rummaged.

I came to the hunting supplies, and found some knives in a large glass case. I looked around for an employee, but folks were running here and there, and the store looked like it would descend into complete chaos at any moment. So I grabbed a wrapped poncho and tore the packaging open. Then I unrolled it and held it to my side. I put the thin, glass door to my back, glanced around to see if any security watched, and quickly swung my elbow into the door as hard as I could.

Glass shattered behind the poncho, which muffled the noise for the most part. I took out a game cleaning kit, putting it in the bag, then a couple of Gerber knives. There was a small axe in there as well. It had a short haft, and the burnished metal finish was dull in the florescent lights.

I took one of the Gerbers out of a box and slid it into my pocket. It was a four-inch blade with a serrated edge. It felt good to have some kind of weapon with me, no matter its size. Next up was a real weapon. I passed the archery stuff and stopped at the gun rack.

A couple of years ago, the liberals tried to get Walmart to remove guns from their stores. For the most part, the gigantic company had complied, but some stores in smaller towns, like ours, had kept them on the shelves. A lot of hunters stopped here on their way to the mountains, for needed ammo and the occasional hunting rifle.

A man stopped to look at the knife rack and the mess on the floor. He was a thin guy with a Hawaiian shirt stuck to his body, and he panted like he'd run all the way here.

"What happened?"

"I guess someone got impatient," I shrugged.

"Think anyone will mind if I help myself?"

"I don't think anyone will care. Chances are in a few days, we won't care about anything except survival."

"Jesus, it's not that bad. The government's gonna reestablish order soon."

"Hey, you can't do that." An employee interrupted us as he rounded a corner aisle with a woman in tow. Her eyes roved across the aisle sign, and he was obviously trying to find something for her.

Hawaiian shirt guy looked between us, then marched off like he didn't know what to say or do. He just spun on his heel and left. I stared at the employee until he looked away.

"You got a key for this?" I pointed at the gun rack.

"Yeah, but we aren't allowed to open it anymore. The manager's worried about a riot, about someone getting a gun and shooting people." He was short and stocky, and his name tab read Patrick. Perspiration covered his face over a sheen of oil. How many hours had he been here trying to keep order? Trying to milk the last dollar out of the consumers?

"Shoot one of those dead things. That's what they're for, so get one out for me. I have money," I said.

The woman who had followed watched our exchange, then shook her head as if just remembering something, and walked off as well. There was a buzz to the air, and things were going to get violent at any moment. I didn't want to stick around that long.

"Uh."

"Just open it for a second, Patrick. Come on man. I'll even leave my credit card with you. Charge whatever you want." I took my wallet out of my back pocket, extracted my Visa Platinum, and set it on the counter. My name gleamed back at me, embossed in plastic.

He looked at it, then at me, and started to leave. "I'm sorry."

"Look, man, you know about those things, right? Do you have a family? How about a gun to protect them?"

"It's not that bad. Everyone's overreacting, right?"

"Overreacting? I just watched a guy on the news get torn to pieces. Are you married?" I asked.

"I have someone at home."

"Then do us both a favor. Open the door, take a gun and as much ammo as you can carry, and go there. Trust me on this one, pal. You don't want to be here when those things arrive. This place is going to be a slaughterhouse."

Patrick's mouth tightened and a drop of sweat left his hairline and ran down his forehead, until it dripped down his nose and onto the floor. I thought I was going to have to take the keys and that would lead to trouble. Instead, he glanced up and down the aisles, then pulled a jingling ring out of his pocket.

"Fuck it," Patrick muttered and unlocked the case.

Shotguns and rifles stared back at me. I took down a trusty Remington 870 12 gauge. Then I pulled out a Marlin .30-06 and looked down the barrel. The store didn't have the highest quality guns, but I felt a weight lift just having the weapon in my hand.

Allison hated me having weapons, and I got rid of them for her. I sold my .40 caliber pistol, which I missed dearly, and got rid of my old hunting rifle, which was superior to the gun I held now. The worst loss was an M-16 semiautomatic I had treasured for years, but I gave it all up for her, and she left me for another man. I would have done better to get rid of her back then.

"What do you recommend?" The clerk's gaze roved up and down the selection. He looked at the assortment and swallowed so loud that I could hear it from a few feet away. He even reached out and touched one or two barrels.

I spotted a Mossberg 500 shotgun and pulled it out of the case. "This will be good both up close and from a distance."

Not wanting to stand around any longer, I pulled a box of shells off the shelf and put them next to his new gun. Then I a pile of boxes for my rifles and dropped them in the cart with the rest of stuff.

"This is crazy," Patrick whispered.

"You put that gun to your shoulder you better be prepared to pull the trigger. Stay safe out there, friend," I said as I dropped a couple more boxes to my cart.

"I hope you're wrong about all this," Patrick said.

"You and me both, friend." I took my credit card when he didn't make an attempt to run it.

Pushing my cart down another aisle, I looked for some Sterno cans. When I found them, I grabbed as many as I thought I could carry. Now it was just a matter of getting out of the store.

I loaded as much as I could into the backpack, heading out of the hunting area as I packed. While I rushed to jam stuff in, I almost missed one important area. An upended rack held a wealth of camouflage clothing. I pawed through them quickly and found a large jacket. Holding it to my chest, I decided it would do all right.

People moved around me, rushing to find anything of use at the last minute. I felt like one of *them*, and cursed again that I didn't go shopping earlier. A woman eyed my canned meat, and I stuffed it in my backpack with a scowl. A man stopped and stared at the guns in my cart, asking where I got them. I pointed him in the direction of the hunting goods, then made for the door.

That's when I ran into trouble in the form of the security guy who had tried to hassle me on the way in earlier, and he looked pissed.

THREE

The guard looked even more harried if that was possible, and when his eyes fell on me and my cart bulging with requisitioned good, I thought his eyes were going to pop out of his head.

I gave him the once-over, glad to see he wasn't armed, except for a can of mace. I was willing to bet if he pulled it, I could take him down before he sprayed me. Truth was, I was in the wrong here. I could have done the honorable thing and waited in lines that stretched almost to the back of the store, while harried looking cashiers dealt with increasingly pissed off shoppers. But this could very well be the end of the world. Who cared about a few guns and cans of Sterno?

"Did you pay for all that stuff, man? Mind if I see your receipt?" He came straight at me.

"I forgot my receipt. If you hustle, you may be able to get it from the guy at the gun counter."

"Okay, I'm gonna have to ask you to put all that shit back and put it back right fucking now." He slipped one foot back in as he took a fighting stance. I studied his body language, marked striking points and his center off balance. He was just doing his job, and, in his shoes, I would probably do the same. The only thing that stopped me from taking him to the ground was a blood curdling scream near the entrance.

The only thing that stopped things from escalating was a running man covered in blood. He was dressed in shorts and had on one flip-flop, but his long sleeve shirt hung in tatters. One ear hung by strips, and a gaping wound, probably made by a large-caliber gun, opened his middle. I should have been able to see the remains of his heart through the broken ribcage.

A woman stumbled ahead of him on a pair of sandals that looked to be a full three inches in height. This put her height near mine. She had a tight body that a pink sweatshirt treated well. I took my focus off her chest and set it on the thing after her. It was one of them, that much was certain. I was shocked they were here already.

The guard reacted first by running the twenty or so feet toward the dead guy and hosing him down with a full blast of mace. The smell of pepper spray inundated the area and sent civilians scrambling.

Unaffected, the man lurched forward, and struck out at the guard who had tried to stop me.

The guard batted his hand aside, but the dead guy stumbled forward, and his momentum sent them both crashing to the ground. The guard let out a whoosh of air as he fought for his life. On top, the undead tried to bite him, but the guard struck the corpse a couple of times. No real strength to the blows--just fear and adrenaline forcing him to fight for his life.

I froze in shock. A couple of people screamed, and one man ran over to help. He grabbed the wriggling corpse by the pant waist and pulled hard.

He didn't pull the dead man very far, but the guard was able to get a leg up, wedge it between him and the walking corpse, and push. The zombie rose into the air and fell to the side.

Rolling the other way, the guard coughed as he tried to stand. A pre-teen girl rushed in to help him up. She had a splash of freckles across her face, and she was very brave. I grabbed the zombie by the scruff of his shirt and hauled him to his feet. After marching to the door, I threw him into the road. He didn't put his hands out to protect himself, struck the ground with a crunch, but rolled over and struggled to his feet.

Grabbing my cart of goodies, I pushed it ahead of me to keep the zombie away. The son of a bitch had blood red eyes, but they were empty of life.

A big blue Ford F250 truck with a frayed American flag hanging from a pole on the back of the cab, slid to a halt, and a guy in cowboy boots and a brown ball cap stepped out.

"Is that one of them dead fuckers?" His voice carried a hint of Southern, Texas if I had to guess.

"Yep. Watch out. They're faster than they look," I replied as I pushed the monstrosity back. Tired of the game, I let go of the cart. The zombie stumbled, nearly fell over, and lurched into motion once again with me in his sights. I took one quick stride and launched my right foot in a full thrust kick that nailed the dead guy in the chest, just below the wound. The sound was sickening, as compressed guts and foul air shifted around inside of the walking corpse.

It had been a while since I had thrown one of those, but it was something I had done a thousand times. Good muscle memory, or just plain luck, was with me, as the creature flew back a few feet. It landed flat on its back and lay there in a daze.

The cowboy moved around the dead guy and stared at the hole in his chest.

"Ain't no damn way that guy can be alive. No way. Looks like his heart's gone!"

A couple of bystanders wandered over to check out the thing wriggling on the ground. They stood around and more joined us. One started talking in a cold, clinical voice about the wounds sustained and why he should be dead. He was a tall man with a gray receding hairline that rounded his head like a halo. All the while, the zombie tried to find the motor skills to get back up. It snarled at the bystanders, and one of them, perhaps feeling brave, showed his teeth and snarled back. The guy held his hands out to placate the crowd and told them that he was just joking around, that he wasn't some damn dead thing.

There was a shriek behind me. I spun to find a woman in her early twenties. Her face a mask of fear, lips peeled back as she let loose a cry for help.

The man behind her wore a biking outfit including what looked like clip-on shoes that lock into the pedals, spandex shorts, and a tight shirt. His helmet sat half-cocked on one side of his head, and the left side of his face had a really bad case of bloody road rash. One arm hung limply at his side, and the opposite foot looked to be broken at the ankle. He dragged it with each shambling step. While we were distracted, the dead guy I had kicked managed to get to his feet and fall on one of the bystanders.

She screamed as the former bicyclist bit into her shoulder and pulled out a huge chunk of skin. His mouth darted back to the wound, like an animal going at a fresh kill, while she screamed and tried to push him away. It must have been the shock. Five or six of us stood around while absurdly, a woman was being eaten in front of our eyes.

I snapped out of it, dashed in, and grabbed the bicyclist by the neck for the second time, and yanked him off the woman. As he turned around, I pushed him down, not knowing what else to do. The axe was in the bottom of my cart, and the shotgun wasn't loaded.

"We need to kill him," a man said in a high voice, and I wondered if they had the balls to back up the words.

"Someone call an ambulance," the bleeding woman's companion yelled.

"No ambulance can help that sick asshole," another yelled back.

"Not him--my wife!"

"MOVE!" someone yelled, and I spun to find the guy from the big pickup truck striding toward us with a tire iron in hand. He shoved his way through the thin fence of onlookers, raised the curved hunk of metal in the air, and brought it down on the dead guy's head. It sounded like a bowling ball dropped on a wood floor. A spray of blood struck many of the people who watched in horror. I backed up, wondering again about the substance. If it carried the disease, I wanted nothing to do with it.

That was enough for me. I grabbed my cart with its treasures, gun barrels sticking out but not reassuring me. My SUV came into view, and, brother, was it ever an inviting sight. I keyed the button and the locks clicked. When the back slid up, I tossed items in as fast as possible, but grabbed the gun and a box of ammo, and shoved them in the back seat.

Glancing behind me, I spotted the man with the wounded wife pressing his shirt against her shoulder to stop the blood. He walked her to the car, one hand around her waist to help her along. He opened the door on a red compact and helped her in. Then rushed to the other side, fumbled for his keys, and started the car.

I kept watching as I worked, because I hoped the woman was okay. I also prayed he got her to the hospital, and they would be able to treat her. There was movement in the car; it looked like he was leaning over to hug her. No, it was the other way around. She was leaning in to ... oh God no!

She tore into his neck, and blood sprayed, striking the window on the passenger side. Oh holy hell – I'd seen more than enough. It was time to go.

I needed to get home and contemplate my next move. How long could I live there without enough food to get through more than a week or two at most? I could stretch the rice, and I did have a few large bags of dried beans. That would extend anything I made by providing extra protein. Not to mention extra filler.

I had a gross of expired Meals Ready to Eat in the garage that I had gotten at work. Some brainiac in the safety department had wanted them in case of an earthquake, but they had gone 'bad' in two years, and since I was formerly in the military, she had asked me if I knew what to do with them. Now I was glad I had taken them off her hands. At the time, I had thought I would donate them to a homeless shelter, but every call had come back with a curt "No thank you." The label might have said 'expired,' but I knew those meals would last a hell of a lot longer.

After tossing my goods in the back of the SUV, I roared out of the parking lot, maneuvered around a stalled car in the middle of the road, and then darted toward a side street so I could get off the main drag as cars started to pile up behind the stuck vehicle.

I drove around a minor accident, where two stressed-out drivers argued. A large SUV had backed into an old Toyota. Probably both had been in a hurry to get home. I slipped through the space, shot out into the opposite lane, and hung a hard right.

I slid on my sunglasses, because the sun was drawing low and starting to obscure my view. A pair of clouds lazed across the sky, but they weren't the dark gray normally fat with rain. These were just plain old cumulus that cast a shadow on the land as they passed.

A familiar sight drew my eye just ahead. The zombie wandered into the road with one hand up at shoulder level while the other hung limply at his side. Behind him followed a second. This one smaller and at this distance I couldn't make out if it was a kid.

The old highway didn't allow for many shenanigans, and the first one was picked off by a silver BMW that was doing at least 60. Another car swerved to avoid the beamer as it slammed on its brakes. The woman got out and ran to the body that had been tossed onto the side of the road like a rag doll.

The second undead swerved around, somehow avoided being hit by a bright yellow Hummer, and stumbled toward the girl who was making a call on her cell phone while gawking at the body on the street. Her free hand moved all over the place as she reported the accident. I could drive across the parking lot, to the little hill that separated the road from Walmart, and help her. But before I could plan how to maneuver there, the walking dead man latched onto her neck with one arm and drove her to the ground.

I pulled alongside the little road hoping I could help her, but knowing it was a lost cause now that she'd already been bit. She squirmed beneath him, even got a backward looping elbow to the side of his face, but he grabbed the arm and tore out a strip of flesh with his teeth.

The woman screamed and thrashed under him, and I felt helpless to stop the assault. The dead guy leaned over and grabbed the back of her neck, pulling the flesh up so that I could see it hanging bloody and raw in his mouth. He chewed as she started to shake, the fight clearly draining out of her.

Where were they coming from? The dead seemed content with the taste he got and stumbled up the hill toward my car.

I dragged the 12-gauge shotgun out from the back seat and felt around until I found a box of shells. I shoved one into the shotgun and pumped it into the chamber as I swung out of my vehicle.

Cars pulled over to stare at the carnage. Two people were on the ground, one was an attractive older woman who had been standing next to an expensive Swedish car. This was newsworthy stuff--the kind of thing you went home and talked about at the dinner table. "You won't believe what I saw today, honey."

I pumped the shell into the chamber, stepped up to the small rise, and aimed down the barrel. Someone shouted at me from a van filled with commuters. "Don't do it! We're calling 911 right now!"

"911 can't help that poor bastard," I muttered under my breath and pulled the trigger. The gun hammered against my shoulder and the zombie's head disappeared ... the left half at least. He took one more stumbling step, then fell, lifeless again.

Welcome home, folks. I didn't say out loud to the commuters.

I got back in my SUV, pulled onto the road, and headed home. The shakes started about a minute later.

FOUR

I clicked on the radio as soon as I pulled away. They were going on about the disease or whatever it was. Lots of speculation, but no answers. "Fix the problem," I wanted to yell at the radio. Who cares how it started? I wanted to know what was being done to combat it.

A caller came on and suggested that the government should fast track a vaccine for the infected. Right, brother. A vaccine for something that just hit in the last few days.

A young sounding guy called in next. "So, yeah, my dad listens, so yeah. He made me call in. Anyway, my buddy Roger lives in Atlanta and him and this other guy Jake got into it the other night with some zombies."

"Sorry. Did you say zombies?" The host asked.

"He did," I muttered.

"I did. Yeah. Zombies. What? You don't believe it?"

"It's a bit preposterous is all," the host countered.

"Bro. Look outside. Anyway, Roger and this other guy and his friends or something, they've been trying to get the word out in Atlanta. The whole place is coming down just like Portland. It's spreading. I heard Seattle got it too, but Twitter's suddenly quiet, like you can't even see some stuff."

Censorship. It was all getting muted so it wouldn't cause a panic.

The executives in charge of social media should have been at Walmart just now. Assholes.

It came on so fast. When the swine flu was being hyped as the next black plague, we were assured over and over again that the problem was being looked after with plenty of vaccines. Then there were the various versions of SARS that wreaked havoc. Now no one wanted to talk about solutions. Maybe there wasn't one. Maybe there was no other way except for the one I came up with that day--a full load of buckshot to the brainpan.

My temper always did get me in trouble.

I had shot that guy in anger and fear. I didn't really think about the repercussions at the time; that I could be considered a cold-blooded murderer. I would have loved to have seen the case, though, hauled into court. Have the judge ask why I killed. What would happen when I countered with, "How do you kill the dead, exactly?"

The vision of the man's head disappearing in a puff of blood and gore played over and over like an old film stuck in the projector at school. Why wouldn't it melt away?

I pulled into my subdivision and slowed down in case kids were out playing. But there was no one there, and I got that eerie feeling of aloneness once again. I pulled into my driveway and noticed that my neighbor Hector Edwards was in his back yard. I could only make out the top of his head, so I waved a silent greeting and went inside without waiting for a response.

The house comforted me after the afternoon I'd had. Then I clicked on the TV and switched the channel over to FOX News. A group of men in white lab coats were debating the effects of the disease.

"Because it isn't possible, that's why! Why are you so ready to jump to crazy conclusions like this? The dead? Really? It's not physiologically possible for the dead to reanimate in any shape or form. Utterly preposterous!" The guy had a full beard, and his face was bright red.

"Then how do you explain it? How do you explain the men and women we have captured and brought in for testing? They move on their own like automatons, but they have no respiration, no brainwave activity, no pulse for God's sake. How do you explain that?"

"I would like to see that. I would very much like to see a dead man moving around. This is a hoax. This is all a hoax!"

Then the scene cut away to an overhead view of New York City. There was no doubting that cityscape; it was like a fixture to the American public. A bird's-eye view of that city was as familiar to people as the Golden Gate Bridge or the Statue of Liberty. The view shifted as the helicopter dropped a few feet, then adjusted as a shaking camera tried to focus on something down below.

Then a voice popped in.

"Are we live?" A man came into view who I had seen on the news many times. I couldn't remember his name for the life of me. He had a blocky jaw, like an old-time movie star, and his pepper-gray hair reminded me of a politician's.

"... as the disease runs rampant. We're over Times Square now, and we're seeing what some are calling a riot. The police are struggling to bring it under control, but an anonymous source within the department has reported that many officers didn't report for duty today, leaving an already strained city stretched to the breaking point. We need warn viewers that what they are about to see could be graphic."

The camera shifted again, and then they went to an outside view that was crystal clear. They must have had another camera mounted to a strut to get such a good shot. Another helicopter shot past then slowed to a hover a few hundred feet away.

The scene below was chaos, as hundreds of people ran in the street. Some moved slower than others, and if people stumbled, the pursuers fell on them like prey.

"Oh my God." It was the first time I had spoken since I got home, since I killed the man in the street. The undead man who had been like the attackers on the screen.

Within minutes, the 'riot' had become a full-scale mob as people ran every which way. Some of those who had been attacked rose on shaky limbs, and then set their sight on the living.

A pair of ambulances rolled into the onslaught. Figures jumped out of both sides, and others slithered out the back. Some had large morgue style black body bags in hand.

The paramedics were torn into on the spot, attacked and beaten down where they stood. A pair tried in vain to wrestle one of the slow zombies into a bag. I was glad the camera was too high to allow viewers to hear the screams of pain.

"Jesus." I knew it was just a matter of time before this shit spread everywhere.

I had been chewing on an idea for a few hours. I knew that I needed a place to hide and wait out the end, and I had a good idea where I could go. The problem was that it didn't belong to me. My buddy Ray had let me use his cabin in the woods up on Mount Arrow a few times, and I was pretty sure I remembered how to get there. Ray was a weird guy, and he'd made me promise to erase the location from the GPS software on my phone. Not that it mattered now, since my aging cell phone was down to one measly bar of connectivity, and I expected it would be useless soon enough. Up in the hills I would have zero signal anyway.

I had gear, I had gas, and I had food. I could stay for a week or two, listen to my recently procured wind-up radio, and plan my next move. I looked around my house at all the things Allison and I had accumulated over the years, and I knew there was no way to keep someone out once I left. I didn't want to stay cooped up here, however, so I grabbed what valuables I had - that I wanted to come back for- and put them in big black bags. Portable hard drive and a small laptop. I planned to bring the larger one with me. I added some of my favorite CDs, some jewelry she had left, stuff I bought her. I pocketed her engagement ring, because it had cost me a small fortune. More importantly it might be useful for barter in the future.

I put pictures in the bags, along with some canned goods that I didn't want to have to try to carry. It was already going to be a long hike to his place, so I didn't want to have to carry a hundred pounds with me. Then I opened the closet, moved all the crap aside, including my rarely used vacuum, and tugged open the entrance to the space under the house.

I brushed aside spider webs as I climbed inside and pushed the bags to a back corner where the dirt met the concrete wall, and hoped it wasn't too visible. I was going to bolt up the house, but I had no illusions about how tenuous the hold on my property would become once I wasn't here to defend it with a gun, or even my fists.

I was climbing back out, knocking dirt off my shoes, when a loud knock came from the front door. My cell phone. I popped it out of my pocket and looked at the display. Allison. Didn't she have anyone else to bug? Like her new boyfriend?

I pocketed the phone and moved to the front door and looked out the peep hole. My neighbor Devon stood on the porch. He craned his neck around to peek in the window then looked up and down the street. His face was covered in sweat, and his eyes shifted rapidly as he tried to look everywhere at once. I opened the door, and he let out a sigh of relief.

"Man, I thought you left or something. Except your car's here. Is everything okay? I mean, not that you need anyone checking up on you and all. Because of the war stuff. I bet you have a million weapons in there. Probably a good thing you didn't start shooting." He was babbling, and I felt like joining him. Devon and I had hung out a few times, shot the shit, talked about our wives, and downed a few six packs of beer. He had a quick wit and a fun way of looking at the world--kind of like a schizoid who was in control of his other personalities. He could flip from dead serious to making fun of the other neighbors in an angry German accent at the drop of a hat.

His wife was pretty and genuinely nice. I remember the day Lisa stopped by after she found out Allison had left me. She said she was sorry and brought over a meatloaf. I was touched by her kindness, and shocked when she hugged me, and then had walked off with a furtive look over her shoulder.

"What do you know, Dev?"

"I know the whole goddamn fucking place is going crazy. Did you hear there was an attack at Walmart and the new Safeway? The things came out of nowhere and started attacking people. Just biting them in public."

"Where did you hear that?" News sure was traveling fast in this tiny town today.

"My wife's friend owns a latte stand, and the customers were reporting what they saw as they ordered drinks. Isn't that fucking weird? Let me get a triple shot mocha. 'Hey, did you hear zombies were eating people at the store?'"

He laughed out loud, then looked down. His eyes went unfocused for a minute, and I thought I knew what he was thinking, because I had been thinking the same thing all day. What if this was really it? The end of everything?

"What are you planning to do?" I asked.

"I don't know. I've been watching CNN all day, and it's crazy in some of the cities. But we're so far from all that, you know? I think we'll be safe here. Just wait it out, wait for the government to call in the army or national guard. All you have to do to survive is not get bit, right?"

"What about the shit at Walmart?" I didn't mention I'd been there and seen it all firsthand.

"It's probably nothing. Kids, you know?"

"If you have another place to go that's far from civilization, I suggest you go there and stay put until the smoke clears."

"I don't think it'll be that bad. It can't be." He talked until he had convinced himself. I bet he practiced the speech in his head before he came over. I couldn't do anything to convince him otherwise, and I didn't want to take the time.

"I know a place to hide up in the hills. Why don't you and Lisa join me?" I cursed myself even as the words came out. I didn't have enough supplies to feed three mouths, let alone one.

He shook his head. A strong refusal backed up by his eyes darting back and forth.

I looked over and noticed that Edwards's little import was running, and the door was cracked open. In my haste earlier to get the goods in my house and sorted, I didn't notice my neighbor had left his car idling. In fact, when I looked at his place now, I realized that his front door was open a couple of inches. But I saw him in the back yard, so he had to be home. I had seen the top of his head and assumed he was standing back to look at his yard or something.

I moved to the side of my patio, where the corner nearly butted up against his yard, and investigated the back of mine. Edwards had been working on his fence off and on for about three months, and it was almost done, but the back near our green belt hadn't even been started. I saw my neighbor come around the fence and walk toward me.

"Hey man, everything all right?" I called out.

He was Argentinian and had a slight accent, but just now, he didn't answer. We were on friendly terms, but not as close as Devon and I. Still, I considered him a friend—well, up until now. He didn't look so good. He looked gray and tired. Devon stood on the doorstep and slipped his glasses off, as if he didn't believe what he was seeing. He put them back on, and the gray man turned and stumbled toward us. His attention set on me, and he started moaning and snarling like a dog.

"Oh shit. Oh shit!" Devon's voice bordered on hysteria. He looked around at the empty porch as if searching for a weapon, but there was not even a scrap of furniture. Then he glanced over the yard.

I didn't wait around to find a weapon. Edwards was moving slowly enough that I didn't feel he represented much of a threat. Of course, I could have been fooling myself. After all, it had been a while since I was in the service, and all those fighting skills were a little rusty. I should have gone back and gotten the axe from my house, or the shotgun.

"Hey, are you okay?" I had to be sure before I did anything even though I already knew the truth.

I was suddenly light on my feet; the old moves came back like I had practiced them just yesterday. I shifted to the right, so one side of my body was presented, while my left was at an angle, so I offered less of a target.

Edwards was covered in red, like he had spilled an entire bottle of wine down his shirt. He was missing one side of his neck, and the ear opposite hung by a flap of skin. He moaned at me like he was half asleep, and a chunk of meat hung from his mouth.

Then his wife, Cindy stumbled out of the home. Half of her face was torn off. The stocky woman had always had an easy laugh and had told me dirty jokes when Edwards wasn't around. She wouldn't be telling jokes now.

"Devon, stay back," I said, but didn't look back for him, trusting he had the sense to stay in place.

Edwards shambled toward me, blood dripping from a headwound. It ran down his face and onto his shirt. His wife didn't look much better; her wounds were also horrific. I had a vision of him coming home, her greeting him at the door. Maybe he was freshly bitten, and it hadn't kicked in yet. But he died there while she dabbed at the blood and exclaimed that he needed to go to the doctor. He came back as his undead self and attacked his wife of over two decades. Now I would have to contend with them, and I didn't feel anything but shame.

He was less than two feet away when I lashed out with a side kick that swept my neighbor off his legs and onto his back. Then I was past him, and I would have administered several punches to the face, but I was once again leery of the blood. What would happen if that stuff got in my mouth or into a wound? Would that be enough to kill and change me into one of them?

Landing like that would have taken the breath away from a normal man and made him think twice about getting up, but zombie-Edwards must have felt lucky, because he rolled to his side. I kicked him hard under the chin. He flopped over and didn't move for a moment.

"Oh, Cindy," Devon said from a few feet away.

She was getting closer, and I didn't want to hurt her. I dashed behind Cindy, snatched the back of her shirt, and dragged her toward their house. She went under protest, trying to spin and snap at me the entire time. I shoved Cindy inside so that she landed face first on the floor, and slammed the door shut, and hoped her newly undead status would keep her from figuring out the doorknob any time soon.

"You should go," I said to Devon who hadn't moved an inch since the conflict had arose.

"I..."

"Shit," I said before Devon could find the words.

Edward was getting back up again, and I didn't think I could maneuver him inside the house while his wife was trying to get out.

I strode toward his struggling body, threw my leg high in the air, and then came down with the back of my boot to his neck in a downward axe kick. Bones snapped with frightening finality, and Edward no longer moved.

I leaned over and gasped for air. Then I turned from his body and threw up everything in my stomach.

That was two. Two people dead at my hand, and the day wasn't even over yet. Devon stood on the patio and watched me come up on shaky legs. His eyes met mine, and I could only read a sort of horror that made me want to turn away in shame.

"That is why you need to get out of Dodge, my man," I said and went inside to pack.

"I just can't leave it all behind. I need to think, and to process," he whispered, almost to himself, then turned and walked away.

FIVE

Three pairs of jeans, that's all I allowed myself. I took down some trusty flannel shirts from a box in the closet and jammed those into the pack as well. Then I added socks, underwear, the basics for survival and keeping warm. I had a pair of thermal underwear as well, which I slipped into a side pouch.

A few of the boxes of MREs were stuffed in the extra room, the one we were going to make into a child's room. Now it was filled with all my accumulated junk. It looked just the way it had when we had moved in, cluttered with boxes, but now there was a layer of dust because I had not been in the room for months.

I took the MRE boxes and moved them to the front of the house. Gunshots popped in the distance. There were just a few a while ago, but now they were coming more rapidly. I thought of Devon and his wife crammed in their home, and for a moment, I considered inviting them to the cabin again.

What good would they be? As far as I could remember, he had no survival skills, and I doubted he even camped out. He and his wife were the type to stay in and watch a movie on the weekend rather than go into the woods and pretend they were outdoorsy.

I had a big hunting knife. It was a LILE knock off inspired by the Rambo blade that had a bunch of tools screwed into the pommel. Part of it was serrated to use like a saw, and the rest was long and razor sharp. I tucked the sheathed blade into the back of my pants in lieu of a gun and felt a little more confident. There was nothing like a deadly weapon at your side to help calm nerves.

More pops of gunfire, so I moved everything I needed to the front door. I took a few shotgun shells and loaded four into the magazine tube, then I fed a round into the chamber and leaned the gun against the wall with the barrel pointed up.

I snatched up the Marlin, chambered a round, and set it next to the shotgun. I felt like I was more or less ready for war, but I would have felt better with my old handgun at my side.

I went into the tiny garage and looked around for some tools. I found a small pry bar and added it to my stash, along with a tool kit that was neatly organized.

All of this planning was done on the fly. I had never really considered what it would be like to flee my home, knowing that I might never return. There was a deep gnawing in my gut that I knew was fear. Fear of going out there. Fear of leaving everything behind. Fear of never being able to come home again.

I looked around my house at all the things I had accumulated over the years. Well, Allison and me. I glanced at the cheap paintings that adorned the wall; one had a large schooner breaking through a spray of waves. It could have been a bright and gaudy picture like you would see at a library or museum, but the artist had chosen a subtle palette of colors that fit into just about any room. Another fixture to leave. Yet I found myself staring at it for some time before my mind kicked back into overdrive.

I loaded boxes in the car, and every time I moved past Edward's, I tried not to look at his body. I tried to keep my mind on the task at hand, tried to ignore what my eyes would tell me if I gave them a chance. A dead friend and by my own hand. I pushed my shame aside for the time being.

I moved the shotgun to the front seat and put the rifle in the rear with my backpack. I returned to my house for another load of MREs, when I felt the eyes on me. I looked up toward Edwards's house. His wife's ghostly face, with its splash of blood, stared at me through the front window, as she walked into the glass again and again.

Jesus, Cindy.

I shuddered and grabbed the last few boxes and shoved them in the back of my little Honda. Then I went around the inside of the house, unplugged everything I could, and grabbed a charger for my cell phone and one for my laptop which had a large collection of porn. If nothing else, I guess I am a practical man.

Devon was nowhere to be found. I imagined he and Lisa were back in their house talking over what they should do. Hopefully they would use their heads and think out the situation. If it were me staying, I would have started boarding up the house first, put something over the windows so none of those things could see in. Then reinforce the front and back sliding glass doors. Finally, nail the wooden door to their back-yard shut and strengthen it with a shovel or rake against the ground.

With everything loaded, I returned to the house one last time and went into each room to make sure I hadn't forgotten anything.

Then I secured each window and double-checked the sliding glass door. A cursory glance under the house assured me the stash of black bags would not show unless someone got right down in there. I wished I had some carpet to cover the spot with, although if someone discovered the carpet, they would probably be more apt to poke around in the space. Why was I even thinking I would come back?

I went to the junk drawer I kept in the kitchen and dug around in the back. There was a picture in a simple frame, and I pulled it out. In the photo, Allison and I grinned at each other. She was in profile, beautiful, and I remembered the day when we first met, when I swore I would always be a happy man if I could just wake up to her smile every day. Long, blonde curls hung to her shoulders and framed her small face. She wore a bright green tank top that left her shoulders and slim neck exposed. How many times had I touched her there, ran my hand over her skin, and then kissed her neck as we lay together in bed.

My face was nothing special next to her fine features. Where her eyes were a pale blue, mine were brown and deep set. A scar around the right eye gave me a bit of a leer on that side, which was my good side, so to speak. The other had a scar much longer that caressed the corner of my lips, and sometimes gave me a dour look that reminded people of the Joker, or so they claimed.

Shrapnel had kissed me there during the first battle of Fallujah. I had been young then, and the firefight had scared me to death. Especially after the burning metal had sliced my face open so fast, I hadn't even realized it until the pain had slammed into me like a mortar.

Short, wiry hair that I kept close to my head. I was balding in the back, and that was okay. When I finally shaved it, I would look like a proper military man again. Didn't shave this morning, so my face looked scruffy; that reminded me to grab a toothbrush and shaving kit on the way out.

I pocketed the picture and went to the bathroom to retrieve a black bag and fill it with toiletries including a Costco sized supply of toothpaste.

My cell phone buzzed against my leg. I retrieved device from my pocket and found it was Allison again. I answered so I could at least say goodbye. We hadn't spoken much since the divorce, since it all went to shit, and I honestly didn't know what I would say to her if we did speak. It's not like I was going to wish her good luck in her new life with her new man.

"Hey."

"Hi." Her voice sounded so far away, hollow, and I could hear wind rushing past like she was on the move.

"Are you okay?"

"Yeah, some craziness, huh? I'm getting out of town and heading to my folks home down in Eugene. I hope to be there by dark."

"Good luck." I didn't know what else to say.

"Erik, listen. I never had a chance to say I was sorry and I regret what happened."

"Not saying sorry, or fucking that guy? Which do you regret, Allison?"

"Both." Her voice came in small, and I was pretty sure I heard genuine regret.

"I'm heading out too. Call me when you get there and let me know you're okay." Then I clicked off the phone and pocketed it. Why had I bothered with that last line? I shouldn't have cared how she was or where she was going. What did she expect me to do? Drop everything and go rescue her the way I rescued her the last time?

That had been a hell of a mess. Her boyfriend at the time had been a real piece of work. A sociopath who got off on locking her up all day and wouldn't let her go anywhere unless he was at her side. She had met him in college. They had moved in together, and that's when he had started to display his real side. I never asked if he had hurt her. I didn't have to. When I had come through the door, she had practically rushed to hide behind me.

He had got in my face and tried the tough guy act. I had kicked him in the shin, and then had thrown a short vicious punch into his solar plexus so fast that all he could do was grunt and fall to his knees. He had screamed profanities, wanted to know where I was going with his property. But when I had looked down at him, he had decided to shut the fuck up and let us go without any more trouble.

I locked all the doors and checked the windows one more time. I set the house alarm, knowing it wouldn't do much good if the power went out. If the police were too busy with the virus, or riots in town, there was no way they would have responded to my piddly house alarm anyway.

I slid into the little Honda and started the engine.

The sky grew dark as big puffy clouds slid into view. I backed out of the driveway, forgetting my sunglasses for now. Edwards was still dead and lying in his front yard. I had trouble looking at his body as I backed out. His not-so-lovely wife was still banging away at the window, smearing blood all over it with her hands.

I drove past ghastly faces that rose up in curtained windows, past Devon's, where I didn't see a light or a trace of him or his wife. I stopped at the end of the street and looked both ways. The road was zombie free, for now, and I hoped it would stay that way.

I suspected that it would not.

SIX

When I got back to highway 322, I ran into heavy traffic. On the worst day, it could take ten or fifteen minutes to get through the city. Today, I didn't think I would be able to make it in an hour. I pulled out of the turn lane after waiting for what seemed like an eternity, and then stopped again. A few cars had pulled over to the shoulder lane, so that was not an option. A few brave souls tried weaving into the opposite lane, but they met traffic, and had to either jump back into the correct lane or drive off the road and look miserably at the line of traffic that wasn't going to let them back in.

It took ten minutes at one light, and then ten more at the next. I drove past the Walmart I had visited earlier in the day, and the place was in full panic. People no longer stood around dumbly. Some fought back, but most ran. A man was pulled down by three of the former humans and screamed over and over at the top of his lungs for help. My hand was on the shotgun before I knew it.

A horn honked loudly behind me, and I realized the light had changed, so I accelerated to the next light and waited there as well.

They were everywhere, Men, women, and even children with blank stares, most covered in blood, some even missing limbs.

Some were missing throats, and some staggered on broken bones. One walked right up to my window and snarled at me. He had a screwdriver driven into his chest, just to the left of center. It should have punctured his heart and made him drop to the ground. Only he was already dead, or undead.

I gave him the finger, and the light changed. As I accelerated, I popped my door open quickly, which bowled the zombie over and probably made a dent judging by the 'thunk'. Score one for the good guys.

The next light was almost about as bad, but a side street called to me--one I knew well from my years of living in the little city. I shot down it into a residential neighborhood that led me to another side street. I ran parallel to the main drag for a while, but jetted down yet another street before emerging onto a lightly traveled road. It took a long time to get back to highway 322, but once I reached it, I was only on it for a few minutes before jumping onto a tiny, two-lane road. Home free at last.

I WAS on the outskirts of the Vesper Lake when something reassuring came into view.

A half mile ahead, a row of military vehicles pulled into an orderly line along the side of the road. A group of men in camouflage piled out of a Humvee, while another pair rolled pylons across the street.

After the day I'd had, it put a smile on my face to see some response from the military. It didn't matter if they were National Guard or the Marines. They could have landed a platoon for all I cared. They were here, offering some sort of protection.

I slowed down as I neared the men. I laid the shotgun in the front seat next to me, so that if anyone looked in, they would know I was armed but not an immediate threat. I considered putting it in the back, on the floor where it was less likely to be seen, but what was the point after the day I was having, and I was pretty sure others were in the same boat.

Two men dressed in camouflaged gear were in the process of maneuvering a heavy, concrete-filled barrel into place on the side of the road. A man dressed in jeans and a t-shirt jumped down from the back of a military transport. Others milled around a guy that gestured around the location. From the back, all I caught was grey hair shaved close to the skull.

As I rolled to a stop, I waited for someone to come out and challenge me. No one did, so I pulled forward until I was level with the guys moving the barrel.

"What's the word?" I called after rolling down my window.

"Fucked is the word I'd choose." One man said without looking up at me.

One of the men smirked but otherwise ignored me.

"So you guys army?"

"Something like that. We're all they could call up on short notice. Some of us didn't even have time to get our shit together, like Timmons over there--in the comfortable clothes." He gestured to the guy in the t-shirt.

I caught the eye of the tall graying older man as he came over. He moved with a sure step and didn't take his eyes of me. He wore a pair of dark brown with tan diamond snakeskin boots that gleamed in the sun. I felt like getting out and saluting, maybe reporting for duty. Some men are just made for the job of being in charge and making sure shit gets done.

He nodded a greeting as he came around the front of the car.

"Heading out of town?" he inquired in a baritone that probably boomed when the need called for it.

"I was thinking about it. Depends on what's out there."

"I'll tell you what is behind you. A whole world of hurt." He grimaced.

A couple of men rolled another barrel into place right next to my SUV. They nodded at the older man, and then looked at me like I was dirt.

"Don't mind them. We've been together for a long while." He gestured toward the men. When he lifted his head, I noticed a fine scar running from his chin to his neck.

"The name's Tragger." I stuck my hand out the window. I don't know what possessed me to try and make a new best friend. The camaraderie of the military does that. Even though I had been out for a while, it felt like the right thing to do.

"I'm Lee." He shook my hand.

Lee, huh? Was that a first name or last? His hand was strong, calloused. So was mine. We didn't bother testing each other.

"So are you going to read me the riot act now? Explain why I should go home and wait it out?"

"It's your life, son. I don't really care where you're going. My orders are to hold position here until we get other orders. You understand about orders?"

"I was in the army for a while."

"You have the look. Things are getting crazy. We could use another man with some experience. You know much about that weapon?" He looked at my gun.

"Enough. I know a lot more about some of the automatics your men are carrying."

He glanced at his crew as they continued setting up the roadblock.

"I didn't see any insignia. You guys National Guard?"

"Not quite. Let's just say we're another option the government sometimes employs."

Mercenaries.

"Must be a cool unit if they allow shoes like that." I glanced toward his boots.

"Damnedest thing. When the call came out, I didn't have to locate my regular boots. I think my wife put them in the attic somewhere. Anyway, these were the only shoes I had at hand that weren't soft." He grinned.

Fine. Lee had his secrets, and I didn't care to know any more about them. Whatever these guys were up to was none of my damn business. But a sense of unease settled over me. A feeling I couldn't quite put my finger on. I decided it was in my best interest to move along and follow my original plan to strike for the cabin.

Before I could offer a goodbye, a man ran out of the trees like he was being chased by fire. Lee's head shot up to take in the sight, then he started calling out orders. Men piled out of one of the transports with guns in hand. Some were ready, but others fumbled for magazines.

"If you want to get your hands dirty, feel free to break out that cannon and help out. Just don't get in the way." He smiled. His teeth were yellowed--probably a lifetime smoker. One tooth was missing on the left side, and it gave him a garish look.

I sat for a few seconds, unsure of my next move. These guys could probably handle a small army. Already they were taking cover where they could. Rifles lowered, and someone had the right idea by assembling what appeared to be a .50 caliber machine gun emplacement.

I could just drive away. Leave them to handle whatever was coming. I could put the SUV in D and just make for the cabin. I was just one guy, and they were many. Would my hastily procured shotgun make that much of a difference?

Lee strode away and tugged a large caliber handgun out of a holster. His boots kicked up dust as he made a beeline for the trees.

I stopped when the first thing came out of the woods. The road in this location ran straight through the City of Vesper Lake and ended in the city of Auburn before winding around to the mountains. A pair of cars came from the direction of town and swerved to avoid us. Why didn't I follow their lead and punch it?

I opened the door and stepped out of my SUV. Emptying a box of shells on the seat, I shoved a half dozen into my pockets as I followed Lee.

There was just one of the zombified citizens at first--a man in his twenties, with a halo of blood dripping from his forehead. It splattered on his bright blue Pokémon shirt, then cascaded down around a huge wound in his abdomen. This man should have been on the ground howling in pain, or dead.

A guy in a dark leather jacket didn't hesitate. He raised his rifle and shot a moaning blood drenched man right between the eyes. His body flopped back and thumped on the ground. Whatever had pulled his strings was now severed.

A few more moaning creatures broke free of the woods. The hair on the back of my neck came to attention and a chill raced over my body.

Lee coldly raised his hand cannon and blew one of the creatures off her feet.

Several more of the dead stumbled in from behind us. My gun was at my shoulder in a split second, but I couldn't pull the trigger. Shots echoed all around me. Calls of "Good shot!" and "Nice one." Didn't affect me with any sense of peace at what we were doing.

It horrified me.

A large man shambled toward me. I had no choice. The gun was low and when I fired his knee disappeared as it splattered all over the pavement. He went down hard, but he didn't stop. He dragged his body along the ground as he kept coming at me. His eyes locked on mine and devoid of any kind of life outside of the blood red haze that suffused them.

I shook as I lowered the gun and pumped a ball of pain into his head. He flopped so hard that his head bounced back up and came to rest on a smashed nose. Brain and gore stained the ground.

That was the third zombie I'd put down and the day wasn't even over yet.

SEVEN

The fight was brief but bloody.

Lee's men stopped to congratulate each other. Some kept their eyes and weapons trained on the trees. Others went over their weapons while comparing stories of shooting brain-dead people to death. I didn't feel the fire I had felt earlier. All I felt was empty. I was planning to leave, drive up the road a few miles, then throw up.

"Are you alright, son?"

Lee had come up beside me, while I stared at the body of a woman. She lay on her back, one arm at an odd angle over her head. Her other arm hung by stringy sinew.

"Yeah."

"Why don't you move out? I don't think you have the stomach for this."

"No one should have the stomach for this." My reply caught him off guard.

Lee's eyes roved over the bodies.

Back in my enlisted days, there had been an enemy that wanted to shoot me. That had justified shooting back. These were just people who didn't understand what they were doing.

"I'll tell you what. If you run into some bad shit, or you think you want to come back and join us, do that. Otherwise, it was nice to meet you. Now fuck off and all that stuff." Lee bore a grim smile that didn't quite reach his eyes.

I liked Lee from the moment I had met him, but now I pondered his motivation. Who had given him orders, and why weren't his men wearing any sort of insignia?

THE CAR ROARED TO LIFE, and, as I drove off, I caught his stare in the rearview mirror. He didn't lift his hand to wave. He didn't smile. He just watched me go.

I flipped through radio stations. Some of them were running the emergency broadcast system messages. Then announcers came on in prerecorded voices, advising people to get to safe places until things were under control. A list of buildings ran, which included schools, probably for the large auditoriums, and military bases, where people would be let into cleared locations.

I jumped around some more because I didn't care for the bad news piling up. I came across a talk radio show where people were calling in and sharing their experiences. It saddened me when a kid no more than nine or ten called in and wanted to know what to do about his father, who was sick but locked in their basement. He wanted to see if his dad was okay.

The guy on the radio was initially at a loss for words. *You and me both, pal.* He then told the boy, that he had called the police, and when the men in uniform showed up, he should let them in.

I flipped to a music channel and drove toward the hills.

The trees grew thicker along the side of the road as I drove on into the night. A fine mist of rain dropped from the sky, but didn't stick around long enough to get the car wet. I beat at it with the windshield wipers and cranked up the brights as the car hummed along the old highway. I had the window open, and the smell of fresh, clean air with a touch of pine rushed into the car. We drove this way a few years ago, Allison and I, but it looked just like every hilly road I had ever been on.

A group of motorcycles shot by. They had been drawing closer in my rearview mirror for a few seconds before they caught up and passed me. They slowed for a mile or two then sped up again. When I got to the area where they had slowed, I found a big yellow sign with a 'Falling Rocks' warning.

For the next few hours, I drove steadily upward as my car sought the top of the pass. I had to rely on my memory, and there were more than a few times where I wondered if I had gotten on the wrong highway or missed a turn off.

I lost myself in thought, even though I constantly changed the radio channel like a kid with ADD. Sometimes I tried to focus on what was being said, really said. There was a virus of unknown origin; it made people sick and most died. Within moments, sometimes seconds, the dead came back to life. It had started in Seattle, but another channel claimed the origin was Atlanta, and that it had been running rampant for a week or more before it was taken seriously. Christ! This was the stuff of nightmares and late-night B movies. I couldn't stand to think it was serious, and yet I had killed three people with my own hands in the last six hours.

I took the turn off on a road whose sign was buried in overgrowth, and that was how I remembered where to go. I had to drive slowly as I navigated up the gravel road that was pocketed with potholes. Some small, but some so wide and deep I had to drive nearly in the brush to get past them.

I came to a cutoff and found the familiar sign for a deer crossing that hung forlornly by one bolt. I took the turn and a few minutes later came to a fence with a big padlock. The fence itself was old and rickety, but the lock was shiny and no more than a year or two old. On either side of the dirt road, trees reached into the dark. There was no way I could drive around it. I shut off my lights and let my eyes get used to the dark.

The moon was out, but it was barely visible through the clouds that had rolled in over the past hour. I stared into the night and thought about my day. It ran through my mind in slow motion--the trip to the store, the dealings with Patrick, the unsure sales associate at the gun counter. I wondered if he had taken my advice and gone home to protect his family with the shotgun I had advised him to take.

I eased the car forward until the bumper kissed the gate, and then gave it a little gas. The fence, from what I had seen, was an old wooden pair of slats that someone had nailed onto much larger chunks of wood.

It may have been a better gate at one point, but now it was just a makeshift barrier that I hoped wouldn't stand up too much pressure.

I gave it a little more gas. There was a snap, and I was through. The SUV came to a stop, so I ran back to the fence and inspected the damage. The gate had pulled away on the left side and fallen to the ground. The lock was still in place, so I picked it up, set it on the remains of the old post, and wedged it between two large nails.

It wouldn't hold up in a stiff wind, but until I came back to fix it, the jury-rigged thing would have to do. I drove slowly for the next minute, trying to remember how the road curved. It was difficult to see in the dark, so I rolled down my front window and stuck my head out. When I felt like I had made it far enough around a curve for my lights not to be seen, I popped them back on and sped up the hill.

The SUV bumped over the gravel then larger rocks as I got farther from the road. Once I had a clear view, it was just a matter of maneuvering around the larger rocks and branches that lay in the way. No one had been here for a long time. I came to one large branch and got out of the car. I had to drag it, grunting, and straining the whole time, until there was a clear path. It looked more like a small tree had fallen, and it was long and inflexible.

I drove the car past it, then got out again and dragged it back to its original spot. I was being ultra-paranoid now, but I didn't know what to expect in the coming weeks. Maybe it would all end with the world back to normal in a few days. All the footage on TV over the last week had led me to believe, at least in the beginning, that the virus had been contained, and the authorities were taking care of it. Footage had leaked out on the web, slowly at first, of attacks all around the globe.

The ports and airports into the U.S. had been shut down first. A strict policy of checking every arriving passenger had gone into effect. After a day of that, they had put a stop to flights altogether.

Just yesterday I had viewed a YouTube video of a plane landing and the emergency slide opening while men and women streamed out of the plane. Some had been bloodied, and when they had reached the bottom, one had dropped her bag, turned to her companion, and torn his throat out. Then it had been pure chaos, as more of the things had gone down the slide and had poured away from the plane in a full panic.

I hadn't been able to get the images out of my head, probably because I'd watched the video at least a dozen times before it had mysteriously disappeared.

"I can't believe what I am seeing here. Now, this is live footage from Sea-Tac airport where a plane from San Diego has landed, in distress, and the passengers seem to be attacking each other. Folks, I have never …" then his voice had cut off, and one of the newscasters had been caught staring off to the side in shock. She had turned to face the camera again and, in a calm voice, had started talking about the sports world. I should have left then my house then and there.

The road ended in another mile. It came up against a copse of trees that were at least fifty feet tall. I got out and stretched, glad that I had arrived. Assuming no one was in my old friend's cabin, I had made it to my home of isolation. I took a deep breath of the cool air, which smelled like pine and upturned dirt. It was a clean smell. Earthy.

I guess I have always been somewhat of a loner, but now I planned to cut all ties to civilization for a while.

I paused and stared into the darkness around me. Trees creaked, the wind whispered, and somewhere a small creature scurried away in the undergrowth. A chill ran up my neck. I was sure I was along, but I couldn't get over the feeling that someone, or something, was out there watching me.

EIGHT

I walked straight past the road until I came to a massive boulder. It looked like a tiny mountain had fallen from the sky and landed here. It was the landmark that told me to cut right and walk about a hundred yards. I had to trust my sense of direction, which was typically not bad, and had served me well so far in making it here in the first place. It kept me in a straight line, until I heard water and knew I was by the tiny lake. My flashlight held up pretty well, although the LED light didn't seem to be as bright as the halogen I used to have. I shook it again to charge it, feeling ridiculous as I did, like I was jerking the thing off.

I almost walked into water. I stopped at the shore, then shone the light up and down the edge of the lake until I saw an upturned boat about thirty feet to the left. It sat there like a beached whale--just a curve in the dark that told me I was close to my destination.

As I drew closer, I spotted the edge of the cabin in the woods. A space had been cut in the trees, forming a square around the wooden structure. In the dark of night, they rose like giants into the night sky.

The cabin was a welcome sight after the madness of the day. I walked up the creaking three stairs to the porch and stopped at the door. I didn't have a key this time, and wondered how I was supposed to get in. This was the big gap in my plan.

I tried the doorknob, but it was locked tight. I pushed, but it was secure. I banged on it and called out "Ray. Ray. Or anyone else. I'm a friend of Ray's. Is anyone here," but no one answered.

Praying that no one tried to shoot me, I wandered around the cabin's perimeter and tried the windows. All of them were shut, but a tiny one that allowed a view of the trees from the bathroom was loose. I shoved it up and caught a pair of splinters in one hand for my effort. The window had budged, however, so I went back to the car and got the pry bar. I could have used that on the door, but I would have been left without a secure lock. Better to find a less destructive way into the cabin if possible.

It was just a matter of breaking past some old, dried wood stain, or paint, to get into the room. I pushed the window up, and found I had to turn nearly sideways to get in. I made an awful racket maneuvering into a space that was only a little bigger than my body. I fell into the room, knocking over several plastic bottles and whatever other toiletry items Ray kept in here. I hadn't seen my friend in a few years. He was an old friend of my father, served in the police force for many years. His dream had always been to live in a cabin in the middle of nowhere, but then when he finished the place, he couldn't give up his job and ended up working another half dozen years past his retirement.

I landed on the ground in a heap, and felt around for the edge of the old cast iron tub. Something he had paid a small fortune to bring into the woods. When I reoriented myself, based on my memory of the visit years ago, I made it to the door and opened it, but kept low in case someone was waiting outside to blow my brains out.

"My name's Erik. I'm a friend of Ray's. If someone's here, please say something." Then I waited a full thirty seconds before cracking open the door. I crouched down and paused for shots to echo over my head, or for a very angry person very much within his 'right to bear arms' to blow off my fool head.

No one moved in the room, and after a few seconds where I thought my heart was going to pound out of my chest, I moved into it. Shadows coated the place, like relics of the past. The room smelled of dust and mildew further reinforcing the belief that no one had been here in an age.

I clicked on the flashlight and shone it around the cabin's main room. Unlike in the horror movies, there was no masked killer waiting to slice me to pieces with a machete. In fact, everywhere I looked, everything had a fine layer of dust. Some of it sat so thick that I could draw shapes.

It was much as I remembered, but like most places you visit and have fond memories of, it was a lot smaller. There were white sheets over most of the furniture, so I left them alone for now and went into the kitchen. I found a pantry stuffed with canned goods, like jam and vegetables. I wondered when they were made. I had plenty of time tomorrow to do an investigation. First things first. I needed to start the generator, make sure the cranky thing still worked.

I propped open the front door, then I went to the car and started hauling things inside. The day had been exhausting and I wished I could crawl into my familiar and comforting bed.

I loaded the shotgun with fresh shells, pulled my new Camouflage jacket out of a brown paper bag--the very same field jacket I had grabbed from Walmart that morning. I dragged a white sheet off the couch, curled up with the shotgun on the floor near my feet, and slept until dawn.

I WOKE to a sound I had not heard in a long time. Birds. It seemed like hundreds of them were hanging outside the cabin, and all with the express purpose of bringing me back to the land of the living.

The land of the living. What an odd thing to think about.

I rose and looked around the tiny cabin to find it was just as I remembered. A woven rug lay before the fireplace. It was old but very colorful and done up in a Native American style that gave the place a distinct western flavor. A little hand-carved wooden table sat next to the kitchen. Four or five thick chunks of maple had been glued together, and figures like bears and salmon had been etched into the top.

A pair of chairs had been shoved under the table. They were gaudy, having been constructed of thick tree branches. The main area was about ten feet by fifteen feet, and the old couch barely fit. A rocking chair sat opposite, and a small glass table with magazines from the seventies lay between them. I eyed an old copy of Time magazine that had a feature piece about an infrastructure bill that had died in the Senate last year on the cover. It was an interesting contrast to the Spartan cabin.

There was a tiny room not much bigger than the small bed it housed. Allison and I had to get very close in order to sleep in it together, which had been just fine with me at the time.

I stretched and wished I had a cup of coffee. Too many years in the city made that had long made that my first morning priority. I wandered into the kitchen, which had a bright patch of light shining through the window over the sink and took another look in the pantry. There was a simple curtain covering the opening, so I slid it aside and took stock of the contents.

Jars stood in neat rows. There was jam, vegetables, and fruit. On a lower shelf, I found barley, dried noodles, and beans in larger containers. I pulled one down and checked the date on the top to find the food was almost two years old. I had my doubts that it was still good. I'm sure the dried goods were fine, but the fruit and other perishables were probably spoiled. Then again, they had been stored in a cool place, so some might be salvageable.

I found a tin marked coffee and pulled it out. A freeze-dried bag of beans was inside, and when I cut it open with my new Gerber knife, the smell hit me with its familiarity.

I dug around in the cabinets and found a hand burr grinder for the beans. There was some wood stacked outside the door, so I got a small fire going in the oven and then went out back to get water. The rear door was locked, and had a double pane window that was covered in dust. I wiped at it to get a look out the back. All I saw were trees and a patch of cleared space around a back yard.

Wildflowers grew everywhere, and the morning air was bracing, to say the least. The clouds were gone again, and as I walked to the lake to get water, I stared at the pastoral scene around me. It was like something from a painting.

Water in the pot, I managed to make coffee by dangling a paper towel filled with grounds inside while it boiled next to the fire.

With a little caffeine in my system, I spent the rest of the morning setting up shop. I uncovered everything, opened the doors and windows, and let the place air out. The smell of dust went away after a while, as I cleaned. I took everything I could get my hands on outside and pounded them.

Unloading the SUV only took a few minutes. With the hunting rifle stored, I placed the boxes of bullets on the main table so I could later get a count, then hunted around until I found some large nails and a hammer. It was roughly a mile walk to the gate and, after making sure no one could see me from the road, I nailed the plank back into place. Then I used the axe to hack some large branches and created a half-assed covering for the entrance. A cursory glance, and it would look like the road was overgrown. It wouldn't fool anyone who got to close, but it was good enough for Government work.

I aired out the bedroom, with its twin bed, took the sheets off, and washed them by hand in cold lake water thanks to a pair of hip waders I'd found in a corner of the main room.

The day flew by as I prepped the cabin, and night came soon enough. I had been so busy I hadn't bothered winding up the little emergency radio. It started after I'd spent a few minutes cranking in some juice and flipped through channels that either played music or the familiar emergency broadcast message that still instructed folks to get to secure locations. These were listed off by county in a robotic voice.

I found a radio station that was talking about the virus, but it sounded like a repeat, because they were covering the outbreak in Atlanta that had occurred almost a week ago.

I found a bottle of Scotch on a shelf, but I didn't recognize the brand. I took a pull, and it burned all the way down my throat until it hit my stomach. Then I did it again, drinking some water as a chaser.

The surface of the lake was calm under the glow of the moon. A shadow slid over it, and I chalked it up to an owl on night patrol for a bite to eat. There was nothing to listen to up here, nothing to waste my day away on, like the television. It was so easy to just veg on the couch, but I doubted days like that would ever come around again.

I thought of Allison and took another drink from the bottle. Was she okay? I popped out my cell phone, but I didn't have a signal up here. So much for checking in with her.

Tomorrow I would scout around the lake and see if there were more cabins with people in them. I would be well advised to meet the neighbors.

The bed was comforting, and the sheets smelled less musky thanks to their lake water bath. I placed the shotgun under the bed and then lay back and closed my eyes and tried not to think of all the things I should have done. I was here now. I was alive, but I couldn't help feeling like I had abandoned society.

I had nearly drifted off when the howl of something that did not seem human made me shoot up. I was half out of the bed before I caught myself. Sitting in the dark, I listened for several moments, but there were no more sounds. It was a long time before I fell asleep again.

NINE

After a night of tossing and turning, I wandered outside and got some fresh water from the lake. There was movement behind me, but a good ways off. I would guess about fifty meters. Probably a deer or elk.

Bored. I had stacked my food supplies, counted the bottled goods, cracked one open and sampled the jam. Tried a jar of pickles, and they tasted decent. I made a list of all the food then figured out what I should eat each day to get a decent mix of veggies and enough starch. I made lists of the beans, how much made a portion, and then the rice, and how much I could get away with eating each day so that I wouldn't starve. Then I planned a menu where I would be comfortably full each day.

I cleaned my clothes in the tub. Now it was barely noon, and I didn't know what to do with myself.

I cranked the radio a few times, but all I picked up was more of the emergency broadcast station with the same message as yesterday. I found a station playing classic rock songs with no commercial interruptions, which was weird. Maybe they put the place on autopilot and headed for the hills like I had.

I checked out the generator in the back shed, but there wasn't much more than five or ten gallons of fuel in a large tank with a hand pump. I wasn't sure how old it was, but the generator started on the first try and hummed along for a few minutes before I shut it down. I would rough it as much as possible and conserve the fuel. Well, roughing it in a cabin. It's not like I had to sleep outside. I broke out my laptop and played a game of solitaire for half an hour, but watching the battery drain even a small percentage drove me crazy, so I turned the machine off.

I stared at the pad of paper I had found in a drawer and the box of pencils. I couldn't find a sharpener, but my new Gerber knife made short work of it. I pulled the pad into my lap and started to recount all that I had seen in the past few days--the very journal you are reading now. How long I can keep up the writing is a mystery even to me. Once upon a time, I wanted to pursue a job in journalism. I even wrote for the school paper and dabbled in a few creative writing classes. The military had been a strong calling, even in my early years.

The days passed ever so slowly. I tried my hand at hunting, but it had been a long time. I didn't even see a hint of game, let alone get a shot at one. A lot of smaller animals raced in the undergrowth, but I was far too slow to catch even a glimpse of one.

One late afternoon, I caught a squirrel trying to shimmy up a tree. I got it in my sights and I was pretty sure I could put a hole in it, but once down I wasn't sure how to clean and prepare it. He got a reprieve for now for now. I'd once heard from a friend from Kentucky that squirrel was tough and tasted like rubber. I suppose if I got hungry enough, I'd have to find out for myself.

I tried swimming in the lake, but it was so cold I started shivering uncontrollably the moment the water reached my knees. I settled for heating a large pot of water to the boiling point then adding cold water so I could take a bird bath in the tub.

I climbed on the roof a few times and tried to get a cellular signal, but it was no use. The phone displayed no bars. Either I was too far away or there was a complete breakdown in the cell towers. Either theory was relevant. I thought about climbing a tree, but being this far from any sort of medical attention meant I could possibly die if I fell out —or at least impale a leg or arm on a broken branch.

I tried fishing with a little success. I caught a small fish that looked like a trout, but it tasted plain no matter how much seasoning I put on the chunks of meat.

And so my days passed. I wondered almost constantly if I should leave the cabin and go back to civilization. It had been two weeks, and I was starting to doubt the severity of the situation below. Maybe the military had come in and set everything right, cleaned up the infected, and shipped them off to some camp where they were being cured even now.

I had probably been fired from my job, having been gone for so long, or maybe they would have understood my actions. My manager Tammy was the no-nonsense sort, but she did have a sense of humor. I could see it now--her laughing as I told her I went to the mountains and lived like a hermit for a few weeks. More than likely she was dead and that hurt.

Tomorrow I would walk the mile or two to the road and reconnoiter.

IT WAS COLD AND GRAY. Rain threatened from the moment I woke up. I didn't have a rain jacket, so I decided to wait, and wait I did. For the next six days, it rained almost nonstop. I became so used to the sound of water running down the roof and the side of the cabin that I heard it even when there were breaks in the deluge.

I heated water one day, because I felt like the damp had soaked into my bones and took a short bath in the tub. I sang songs from memory and even put headphones on and listened to downloaded music on my phone for a precious half hour. I planned to fire up the generator in a day or two and charge all the electronic devices.

The rain let up for a few hours then set in again. I went to sleep after finishing off the scotch, but had to keep one foot on the ground to stop the room from spinning. The next day, I felt like shit, but I hauled myself out of bed and drank what seemed like a gallon of water. At least the rain was gone, so I popped a pair of aspirin and ate some food from one of the survival kits. Dry cakes of some shit that tasted gritty, but provided good protein and nutrients. The only downside was that the stuff caused terrible gas.

I had a couple of cans of corned beef hash calling to me, but I was saving them for a special day.

I would suit up and head down to the road in a few minutes.

NOTHING. That was what I saw in an hour of standing around behind a tree waiting for a car to pass. Nothing went by, not a car, motorcycle or even a logging truck. I walked out to the street, inspecting the gate first, but there was no one in sight. I wanted to jump in the Honda and head back to town. It was driving me insane—the not knowing. Or maybe it was just loneliness.

I flipped open my cell phone, and a single bar of connectivity faded in and out. I walked around the side of the road, until I got a partial bar again. Then I dialed Allison because I was worried about her. No matter what our problems had been, I had loved her at one time. The phone made some clicking sounds, followed by a fast busy signal. I tried another number, my manager at work, but got the same thing. Then I called my neighbor Devon, and the sound repeated.

I wandered back to the cabin and spent another week dreading the fact I needed to go back and see what was happening in the world.

THE COLD OF winter came on like a heavy curtain. I passed the next few weeks uneventfully.

I hunted, and finally decided to climb up a large tree and lie on a branch. I took my rifle and after what felt like an entire day of being cold up there, I saw movement. I raised the rifle and sighted down the barrel. It had a very basic scope, but I was still able to bring the elk into focus. He wasn't exactly heading toward me, but he would pass fairly close. I took a bead on his center and exhaled gently, stroked the trigger, and the rifle hammered into my shoulder.

The elk staggered and started to run, but I had hit him on target. He took two stumbling steps then went down with a "whump". I let out a "yippee" and climbed down the tree to inspect my prize. The animal was huge, and his eyes remained on mine while I approached. He took deep breaths, and a light puff of fresh snow moved around his nose where the air snuffled in and out.

I took my knife out and put an end to his suffering by slicing it through his neck. Now I had the problem of what to do with the meat. I spent the next few hours taking off the haunches, and then I skinned him as best I could and tried to bury the organs in the ground, but it was hard going with all the roots. The dirt was miserably cold, and after a while, I went back to the cabin and dug out some old plastic garbage bags. They provided a pretty poor substitute for a deep hole. Any predator with half a nose would seek them out in no time.

I didn't bag everything. I set aside the liver and kidneys for stew. I felt like a real hunter, so I took a bit of blood and drank it down. Then I had to fight to keep from gagging.

I dragged back chunks of the big animal and put them on the porch. Some of it I would turn into jerky. If the snow came on, as I suspected it would, I would bury the rest in an outdoor freezer and hope it didn't thaw out too soon.

I went back and hacked at the ribs for a while and took a huge piece back. This I chopped and broke into smaller sections, and then I let a rack of six roast near in a pan shoved a few inches from the fire in the fireplace. I didn't have much in the way of seasoning beyond salt and pepper, but they were just about the best ribs I had ever eaten in my life.

WINTER BECAME a heavy blanket of white, and I was stuck for the time being. Stuck may have been the wrong word. I could certainly head out in the SUV and drive nice and slow out of the mountains, but I thought it would be a good idea to stay in place and wait for the winter to pass. Make a fresh run at the city when all the madness was over. And so my existence ground to a slow crawl as I waited.

I went out and started the SUV. I let it run for a good half hour. I ran the heater very high, so I could get at any moisture. The car already smelled like mildew, but it was worth a shot.

I drove up and down the little driveway a few times, taking care to hit a few potholes. I wanted to shift the gas in the tank, let it move around. If condensation built up on the inside and mixed with the gas, I would have a hell of a time going anywhere.

I created a calendar on a sheet of paper and put a reminder to do this again in a week.

Days were routine, mainly focusing on what I would eat. The survival packs would only last so much longer, so I made more of an effort to hunt.

I took down a big buck and gave him the same treatment as the elk. After dragging the carcass for half mile, I freaked when I thought I had lost my way in the snow. Stupid. If a fresh dusting of snow had come along and covered my tracks, I might have frozen to death out here.

Weeks fled past and became a blur. For Christmas, I opened the last can of corned beef. I sang a Christmas carol or two and built up the fire. Low on wood, I would have to go stand in a foot of fresh snow tomorrow and chop some logs. If Ray came back, I would ask his forgiveness for removing some of his tree line. Until then, I wasn't planning on hauling wood back through the snow.

TEN

Winter wore on and in February I had just about run out of food. The last of the emergency supplies were gone, and I was down to the gristly parts of the last deer I had shot. I had backup, some MREs, and a few canned goods, but they wouldn't last a week even if I took myself to a thousand calories per day diet.

Hunting led me to sitting in a tree for three days, but not a single animal wandered by. I was aware that someone could potentially survive for a few weeks with nothing to eat, as long as they had water, but I was in no hurry to test the veracity of that claim.

I didn't plan to wait around for that, so I packed a few supplies, loaded the shotgun, and put them in the car.

I had to crank at the key a few times, but the car puttered to life. The gas had sat in the tank for a few months, and I hoped the engine would work. Moving the car once a week must have done the trick, because it slowly came to life. I sat and idled and enjoyed the car's heat. I backed out of the snow, which was somewhat melted and only a few inches thick. The bigger concern was the ice that lay underneath.

I opened the gate with a steady hand, but some of the nails fell out from my jury-rigged repairs a few months ago. Once I slid past the gate, I put it back in place and pounded the nails in with the tire iron. Then I got on a road that was pure white and lacked a single tire line.

In four-wheel drive, the SUV handled quite well. I drove out of the mountain with the radio constantly scanning for signs of life. I came across a few stations that were playing music. One had old rock on, and the sound of AC/DC soon filled the car. The other channel played classical music for which I didn't care, but I listened for the sake of listening.

What would I find when I returned to the world? The lack of news, talk radio, or online social media left a hollow pit of anxiety in my belly. I was doing my best to conserve gas, so I didn't bother firing up the generator to charge it. I tried to call Allison, but the phone gave the fast busy again. Then I tried co-workers, my manager at work. The phone clicked like it was trying to dial out, but I never got a ring from the speaker.

There was less ice the farther I got down the road, and I was able to add some speed.

I came across a small town--just a blip on a map, really. There was a gas station with no attendant. I slowed down and looked into the windows, but saw no movement. The pumps were an older variety but still electronic, and from my vantage point, I could tell they were dead. I waited but didn't honk my horn. The road was much clearer, and it was impossible to tell if anyone had driven here lately.

I moved on and came across a small convenience store, pulled into the parking lot, and stared at the front window for a moment, but like the gas station, there was no movement. Leaving the SUV running, I jumped out and walked to the front door, where a sign proclaimed the store to be closed. The inside was a mess, like someone had tried to pack the place into many large boxes that lay open on the floor. I tried the door, but it was locked. A metal gate shielded most of the door, but if I smashed it, I could probably wiggle in.

I got back in my vehicle and started up my drive again. As I hit the old back roads that got me here in the first place, I saw house after house sitting dark. I didn't want to risk someone shooting me, so I only looked. If things were as bad as I thought, there was little point in me trying to approach one.

I came out of a street and found the main drag that led back to Vesper Lake. The two-lane road was free of traffic.

I went around a bend doing about 45 MPH and skidded to a stop at a military checkpoint. There were a pair of men blocking the road, and a Hummer stood obstructing part of it.

It had been months, but I was pretty sure this was the same checkpoint I had left when it had been manned by Lee and his men. Could this still be them?

When I saw them, I felt a sense of relief. At last, I could get some questions answered. Maybe the town was under protection, maybe there was a full military presence and the whole thing was under control. I wanted to laugh with relief.

They had their backs turned to me, so I slowed down and approached at a creep, giving them time to hear me coming. I didn't want to scare some recruit into filling my car with .50 caliber rounds from the big gun on the Hummer. I rolled down the window and called out.

"Am I ever glad to see you guys! I've been hiding out up in the mountains and missed out on the last few months. Anyone want to give me the ten-second run down?"

I was holding out my ID when the first soldier turned toward my voice. He moved fast, but in an odd, uncoordinated way. I saw his eyes first, and almost dropped my identification card as I recoiled in horror. His face was slack, like he had had a stroke. His eyes were dilated, the pupils almost the size of his irises, and they were blood red. His skin color was just wrong. A dull greenish color clung to it like he was illuminated by a Christmas tree light. He didn't exactly glow; it was more of a tint that emanated from every inch of exposed skin.

He snarled at me; his lips drew back, and his teeth were jagged points. I reached for my shotgun, knowing there was no way to get it up in time before the freak shot me with the M-16 he was carrying.

His partner raised his hand and hooted into the air, then stumbled toward me. A cry to my left pulled my attention to the tree line surrounding the roadblock. From out of the thick trees and shrubs, a veritable army of demons poured forth. They had the same greenish tinge to the skin and were in a mish-mash of clothes. There were more soldiers but also civilians—both men and women. Had the virus turned them into this monstrous form? If so, it was a far cry from the zombies I had seen four months ago.

One raised his gun, but it was unsteady in his hand, as if he were not familiar with the weapon. He aimed it toward me, but his shaky grip almost blew it out of his hand when he pulled the trigger. He staggered back, and bullets stitched the air over my head. I hauled the shotgun up into my lap, chambered a round by pumping the action, and aimed out the window it at the green guy.

I slammed the car into reverse and hit the gas, but a flood of them were on the way and didn't look too interested in talking about the plague.

"Ah fuck it!" I yelled, extended the gun barrel, and blew the first soldier back into the barricade. It was flimsy and reminded me of the one I put up at the cabin.

The noise of the shot had been like a cannon in the small space. I aimed for the barrier as I put the car into drive. The things were an army behind me. I didn't stand a chance of plowing through them because they were six or seven deep, and they looked like hell itself had opened up and spit them out.

I fired again, and the gun leapt in my hand. I missed the wooden slats by a mile. Just plowed through them and the other soldier who was standing in front trying to bring his gun up. His mouth opened in a big O that might have been a scream when my bumper slammed into his midsection, tossing him face first onto the hood of my little SUV. His body made a pretty good cushion as I barreled through the barrier. When I hit it, the thing splintered like balsa wood. The guy clutched at the hood, so I hit my brakes, and his forward momentum kept him going right on over the car and onto the ground. Then a bump as I passed over him.

Gunfire behind me, and I hit the gas to get away. I had to swerve to avoid a pair of gutted cars that lay rusting in the road next to the barricade. Then I was past, and the army of howling creatures was behind me. I kept my focus pinned to the rearview mirror as I accelerated away, which almost cost me my car. I was so fixated on the zombies behind me that I missed out on the ones ahead. They also poured out of storefronts on either side, flooding the street with fresh bodies. Some howled when they saw me, while other shambled aimlessly.

I had to slam on my brakes or risk barreling into them. I rolled up my window and hit my horn over and over, hand pressing hard against the plastic device. Sweat made me slip off it, but not for long. They crowded in, and I had to drive into the mass. I pushed them aside with the SUV, but a couple climbed up top.

These weird hybrid-zombie creatures more of less looked like regular people, and they were hungry. I pushed my Honda forward, punching the gas as I tried to swerve through the mass. A pair of them came out with bars, and one smashed my rear door window and started to climb in. They both had glowing green eyes that made me want to bite my tongue in half to stop the scream that bubbled to my lips.

That was the last straw. I floored it and grimaced as the car thumped over several of the undead but somehow sentient things.

An old man in a helmet that appeared to be straight out of World War two tried to crawl into the window. His mouth was a jagged horror of broken teeth. His parched tongue hung out, but no words issued forth. I maneuvered the gun around, leveled it at the guy, and pulled the trigger. One-handed, the shotgun was heavy, and it was a struggle to raise it while steering the SUV.

The blast turned the guy's head inside out. He flopped out of the car, and the pursuers fell on the body like scavenger birds coming across a fresh kill. That gave me an idea. I rolled the car forward and avoided a stuck car that had been stripped to bare frame. I rolled down the window on my side and smashed one of the followers in the face. This time, an overweight woman in a faded sundress that looked like she should be freezing but was somehow still on her feet. She fell back, so I hit the gas a little more to get some momentum, and shot her in the leg.

Then I dropped another creeper with a shotgun blast to the gut. The green tinged maniacal creatures fell on the freshly felled buddies in a frenzy of teeth and cries of anger or hunger. This gave me room to maneuver, so I gave the SUV some gas and leapt away from the pursuers.

My hands shook on the steering wheel like I'd just bench pressed a couple of hundred pounds. I couldn't control them. My breath was fast and ragged, and it took an effort to slow it down. I didn't want to hyper-ventilate; I was already feeling lightheaded from the fight.

I needed to find a way back to the main street and get back to the cabin. I'd be damned if I was going to remain stuck in this town with those howling things. I could always hit the convenience store I passed earlier and raid whatever was left of their food.

I started to take a left onto a side street that would lead back to my house. I was here, and it seemed worthwhile to retrieve all of the things I had hidden in the space under the house. I could also gather up any canned goods and add those to my hoard.

I also wanted to check on my neighbors, particularly Devon and his wife. Maybe they were okay and holed up like I had been, but I knew in my heart that probably wasn't the case.

I thought I had lost the crawlers, but I was wrong. They poured into the street again. There were hundreds this time, and they came from the trees along the secondary road. I hit the brakes and spun around in a circle then zipped back to highway 322. I could always find another way to get to the old house later.

If I was able to get away from this mob.

ELEVEN

I got lucky when a wave of the humanoids went after something moving along the tree line, and I was able to get around them before they could overwhelm my vehicle.

Minutes later, and at great speed, I came up on the main drag, where a group of them stood on top of hulks of cars in my path. I spun the wheel to the left, hard, and took to the sidewalk, mowing down several zombies in the process. They thumped off the car's hood, and one left a trail of blood. I couldn't imagine what these people wanted, nor did I care to stick around and find out.

I was within sight of the Walmart I had raided what seemed like a lifetime ago. They were everywhere. I honked at them to get out of the way, but they just snarled at me as I bumped into them. Without risking serious damage to the car, there was no way to push through.

Not all of them moved fast. Some were slack jawed, empty eyed, hands raised, but were not as frenzied as the green ones.

A green-eye bastard threw something under the car, and there was an audible pop.

I drove as long as I could, but I was soon on a metal rim. One of them darted forward and went after a rear tire on that side. Another pop and a second tire went flat.

It wouldn't be long now. I took my hands off the wheel and jammed as many shells as I could into the shotgun. I lost count of how many rounds I had fired, and just filled until no more would go in. They surrounded the car, and I tried to keep my foot on the gas, but the weight of them combined with the flat tires slowed me to a stop. I guessed the rear window would be my undoing.

I opened the moonroof and slithered up so I could stand on the seat. One of them was climbing onto the top of the car, so I blew a hole in his midsection first. I planted my hands on the side of the car, so I would have a chance to run and not get stuck inside when they took me down. I lifted myself up and sat on the edge of the roof so I could shoot another crawler. The blast took her in the shoulder, spinning her into the crowd with a massive spray of blood. I swung my leg up and stood on the top of the car, so I had a full view of the area around me. The metal underneath me was flimsy and buckled as I jockeyed for position.

I kicked another a green eye with my size twelve boot, and then shot another in the face.

There were too many of them--a veritable ocean of the things. I wondered if I should just put the barrel under my chin and get it over with. I didn't want to get eaten by these things. So let them feast on my corpse and choke on it.

I swung the gun up and braced it against my body as a pair climbed onto the blood- and brain-splattered hood. I smiled at one--a big, full-mouthed grin--and then pulled the trigger.

Click.

I fumbled for a shell. It fell out of my pocket and rolled down the side of the car. I bashed the first freak over the head with the gun stock and was rewarded with a hollow *thunk* as he went down. I lashed out behind with one foot and caught a tall, skinny kid in the gut. He fell on his face, so I smashed his head into the roof.

Went for another shell, got it, slid it home, and pumped it into the chamber. I was surrounded on every side, and I would never get the damn thing up to blow my own brains out. One of the nasty things leapt in front of me with a howl. His mouth was wide open, but my ringing ears didn't hear him. I whipped my hand up to slash at his throat, but he teetered on unsure feet, and I ended up slashing him across the chin with the edge of my hand. I had planned to smash his throat. Another scrambled up behind me. *Well, here we go.*

A shot rang out, and I half-expected to feel a punch as it struck my body. The one in front of me dropped, then another shot sounded in the distance, and the guy I'd punched across the chin fell onto the hood of the car and almost sent me to the ground.

I spun around and punched the man behind me. A full blow with the shoulder behind it that rocked my wrist, even though I stiffened it just before impact. He flew back, and then there were gunshots all around.

"Get the fuck down!" someone yelled. I didn't need any more prompting. I dropped to the hood of my car and dug out two more shells to load into the shotgun.

Blasts sounded around me. Bodies dropped on either side, heads exploded, chunks flew, blood misted; it was a fucking war zone. I slithered into the car via the sunroof, banging both elbows and my left knee in the process. I ended up with my ass in the air, staring at the gas pedal as I tried to right myself in the unforgiving space.

The rotters outside the car were no longer interested in me, having discovered the much more accessible flesh of their fallen comrades. More shots broke up the mob, and they soon got the message and cleared the street. I forgot to turn the engine off in my haste, so all I had to do was pop the car in drive and hit the gas. The SUV squealed as two metal rims skittered over the ground, but it did move.

There was a group of men on the little ridge that lined the road leading up the rise to the big Walmart. Ironically, they were in the same spot that I had been in when I shot a zombie in the face a few months ago. That fateful day I had made my run to the store to collect supplies to hole up and wait it out.

As I squealed up the small road, I noticed that a giant metal fence surrounded the place. They stood before it, five or six of them, and laid down fire, gesturing for me to hurry up. I must have looked pretty ridiculous in my car, rubbing metal on the road, sparks flying as I tried to outrun a bunch of bloodthirsty demons.

I made it to the little road leading up the hill, and then pulled up and into a giant metal gate that they were opening for me. The men—well, men and women. As they ran, several fighters dropped to their knees and fired at will. Others dashed a few feet ahead then laid down covering fire for the others as they stood and moved through their comrade's ranks. They moved with a military precision that impressed the hell out of me.

The parking lot was a mess of cars, trucks, and even a couple of semi-trucks. They were scattered all over the place, and most looked to be in good condition. The heavy metal fence slammed shut behind me. I pulled over, but a man gestured me forward, so I steered the squealing car along a road that ran up toward the big store. When I reached the front of the store and came to a screaming halt.

I fell out of the car more exhausted than I had been since being in the Army. I left the guns in the SUV and stood up to greet my rescuers. One of them, a tall man with gaunt features and a long, straggly beard of brown and gray, walked toward me. He tugged a handgun from a holster at his waist and pointed it at my head. He stopped a good five feet away, too far for me to try any heroics like a grab and sweep. Professional all the way, or he had learned a lot over the last few months.

"Tell me who you are, how you got here, and, more importantly, why I shouldn't blow your brains out."

Things were just getting better and better.

"My name's Erik Tragger. I've been hiding out and I ran out of food." I tried to keep my voice neutral, but having a gun pointed at my face did nothing but increase my already amped up anxiety.

"That's a great story, Erik Tragger, but here's my problem. The goddamn ghouls have gotten better and better at sending in people closer to being, well, people." On the outside, he was all polite, but there was a sense of tension that told me I didn't have much time to convince him my story was true.

"Then why risk your neck for me?" I challenged him.

"We wanted your car." He shrugged.

Shit.

TWELVE

The moment seemed to stretch forever. He hadn't blown my head off yet, so maybe I could talk my way out of this. "Look, man, I've been out in the woods for months. Living on MREs and what little I could hunt or fish. I don't have the slightest fucking clue what's going on here, except some crazy green-eye things just tried to take me apart. Just look at my eyes."

I pulled an eyelid down to show that there was no green. About the only thing he would see would be blood shot eyes.

The man leaned forward and squinted, then let out a little grunt. I guess the truth in my words seemed to get through. He lowered the gun just enough, so I felt like he wasn't going to blow my fool head off. He was younger than me, but not by much. His eyes were a gray color that was hard around the edges. He had seen some crazy shit, and I knew he would just as soon shoot me in the head as have to worry about me turning on them.

"How long after the initial surge was it before you made a run for it?"

"I lived not far from here. I gave it a couple of days after it started. I was busy watching the news, just sitting on my ass and not sure what to do, when I decided to head to an old cabin my friend has up on Mount Arrow. I took all I could safely carry, stopped at this very store, and grabbed a couple guns, ammo, and some supplies and left. I haven't heard anything since then. Radios are dead, and I couldn't get a signal on my cell. "

I looked at the street, where a small mob of ghouls was creeping up on the fence.

"Like I said, pal. We only saved you for your car. We need more transportation. You? I say we just kill you and be done with it. No offense, but we've survived this long by not trusting anyone. Besides, we don't usually let creepers in."

Creeper? Funny I had thought the same thing about the zombies.

"Oh come on. Just keep a guard on me or something. I can help you out. I have a lot of training." I couldn't believe how badly this was going. What happened to returning to civilization? Coming back to a world that worked the old way—buy, sell, stay at home and stay out of the lime-light. Right now, I felt like every cold eye in the world was on me.

"What kind of training?"

"Hey, I think I know this guy," someone spoke up. One of the men moved behind the leader and squinted at me. He was stocky, dressed in black, and had a long dark beard. His eyes were hollow, lined with circles like he didn't sleep.

"You do?"

"Oh shit! Yeah, this freaking guy saved my life when I worked here. He came in when the shit was going down. He handed me the shotgun that saved my life and told me to get out of Walmart and go take care of my family. It was a wakeup call. I went home less than an hour later, and we hid until the enforcers got started. I shot ten or fifteen zombies with that gun, man. Saved my life."

I couldn't remember the guy's name, nor could I remember if I even looked at his name tag when I went storming through the store. I was happy that he made it, though, but not so happy that he and his friends were about to shoot me.

"Really? You sure you know him, Pat?"

"I'm sure."

"Pat?" I said. "Patrick. I told you to take a 12 gauge."

"I'm glad you did," Patrick replied with a tight smile.

There was a moment that passed when I felt my life hanging in the balance between life and death. Call it cliché; call it a sense of déjà vu. I had faced death more times in that one day than I had when I was enlisted and trained to take on the world.

The guy lowered the gun at last, and we both breathed a sigh of relief. He held out his hand. I found myself taking his in mine and shaking with a firm grip. We smiled like we were old friends, and just like that, the tension went out of the situation.

"You said you had some training? What kind of training?"

"I went out for Special Forces and almost passed."

"Real badass, eh? Almost passed." He frowned. "Is that like almost getting laid?"

"It's a long story."

"How far did you get?"

"Right to the end. They called me back for a family emergency, and I was offered a chance to start over. But I didn't take them up on it. Finished my tour and got out a year later so I could be with my wife."

"Did she make it?" No hesitation, no dancing around the subject. This was a different world. If I had been asked that a year ago, it would have been met with a lot of skating around the question.

"Don't know. She was my ex," I said and shrugged. "So can you fill me in on what I've missed over the last few months?"

"Not much to tell. The world went to hell and was overrun by zombies."

"I remember that part. Where did those other guys come from? The ones with the green eyes."

"The ghouls. Yeah, they're a real fucking problem. See, the zombies don't take much to put down because they're as dumb as a box of rocks. We used to make a bunch of goddamn noise and they'd come a-running, then we'd shoot them or blow them up, or sometimes just set them on fire. That was a mistake because then we had running human torches. Live and learn. We started to run out of ammo. We had to teach the survivors how to shoot with a purpose. It's surprisingly hard to get Mom and Pop to blow people's heads off, even if they are trying to eat them."

"I can image."

"There are a lot of zombies out there, but things got worse when people grew hungry and resorted to cannibalism. Hard to believe, right? But this ain't the same goddamn world by a long shot." He sighed and dropped his hood. His hair hung long and lank, and he had a halo around the top of his head where he'd lost a lot of hair. I imagined no one really cared for monthly haircuts anymore.

"See, eating people is bad enough, but then they started eating the zombie flesh--just a few at first. It changed the people that did it. Made them a weird hybrid, like they had half a brain. It didn't affect everyone that way, though. Some it just made stronger and meaner. Now they drive the army of zombies before them, like some weird slave drivers. Messy business, all those half-changed people running around."

"What's with the green glow?"

"Don't know. We think it has something to do with the virus. It changes people's chemistry, makes their blood toxic. Well, toxic in that it would change you into a damn ghoul if you got any of that shit in your system. They say it started in Atlanta and spread like wildfire. Conspiracies were swirling about some guy moving around the country spreading the disease. Seattle went to hell first. They practically nuked that place."

"Jesus," I said. "Was he, what did you call them, a creeper you mentioned earlier?"

"Creepers? Nah. Those're the people that live on the outskirts. The ones who don't want to find a group to stay with. They prefer to go solo, so to speak. We call them creepers."

Creepers. I guess I was one of them. I had been up in the woods for so long, it seemed the perfect name for the man I had become. Stuck in a cabin until I decided to creep back to society.

He turned and walked toward the entrance to the store, so I tagged along at his side.

"Those ghoul fucks were the worst. They moved from town to town gathering up survivors and converting them. They made them eat the flesh of the undead and, bam, they were changed into those things. But they ran into trouble when they got to this town. We'd already put up the fence, and the back butts up to a forest, so we made the band of metal from all the stores around. We hit up Lowe's, Home Depot. We gathered up so much chain link, seemed like we would have enough to cover the entire town."

That thing? It didn't look strong enough to hold any of them back. A few hundred storming it, and they would be overwhelmed.

Already a pack of them streamed toward the fence near the entrance. There were calls all up and down the line, and men and women faded from behind trees, rusted cars, stacks of shopping carts, piles of trash, and just about anything that could be considered a cover. There must have been twenty or thirty of them, and they were all armed to the fucking teeth.

I expected them to start opening up at any minute with all the automatic weapons. It would make a hell of a mess. Instead, the leader, whose name I somehow managed to miss, waved at someone from the roof. A few seconds later, a scratchy sound came from the same direction, like an old LP was being played. As it sped up, it became a huge siren that whined at the sky for all the world to hear.

The creatures came at a rush when the sound howled across the parking lot and echoed up and down the street. Then the sound of a generator or motor started up along with shouts from the direction of the building.

The ghouls hit the fence and started climbing over it, and then over each other. One was just about to reach the top when the leader stuck his hand in the air and pulled it down. A crackling sound erupted from the other side of the building, and a low hum that made me want to bite through my gums sounded.

The zombies stuck to the fence were fried. The fence was apparently electrified, and it wasn't that stuff they ran through animal deterrents--the little buzz that warns them to stay back. This was a full-on, nasty blast that stuck the poor fucks to the fence. They shook and shivered, and the sound of crackling energy buzzed through the air followed by the smell of burning flesh.

They cut the power a minute later, and bodies slumped to the ground. Some remained stuck, but the others, ones that managed to avoid the fence, snarled and then slunk away. The smell of cooked meat made my nose wrinkle, but it also flooded my mouth with saliva.

"They never learn."

The leader walked toward the entrance once again. I turned to Pat, the guy who had saved my life. Well, I guess it was a trade. He had a shotgun slung over his shoulder, and if I didn't know better, I would've guessed it was the same one I handed him months ago.

"Come on, Erik, I'll show you around."

THIRTEEN

The leader's name was Thomas, but he claimed he wasn't really the leader, he was just the guy with the biggest stick. He had been a detective when the world had changed and said he had been used to walking onto a crime scene and taking charge. He also said that people seemed to like that, to respect it, so when he started to organize the Walmart, they had kept him in an advisory position.

The large store had a pair of double sliding glass door entrances at the front, but one was completely boarded up. Bars had been affixed to the working entryway and a serious door made of steel was guarded by a man with what looked like a MP5 submachine gun.

Once waved inside, I found the store's interior had been rearranged so that racks formed a maze after the door. The first appeared to have been welded together to make them twice as high. I suspected seats had been especially built on the other side, so gunners could sit up there and pick off any incoming threat. Then it was a veritable maze of shelves from here on that would funnel any invaders through a killing screen.

Once we had navigated the maze, I found the area behind it to be neat and orderly. There was a section with a guard posted that had been set aside for food. Boxes and crates of canned goods were stacked high, as were giant bags of dog and cat food. Familiar brands like Purina,

IAMS. My mouth filled with saliva at the thought of something to eat. The emergency food on which I had lived for the last few weeks, while nutritionally sound, left me feeling strange, like I was buzzing. It also tended to give me terrible diarrhea.

There was a large section of tents, where everything in the store had been shoved aside and people had set up little homes. There were batches of flashlights taped together that pointed at the ceiling to provide light. A kid ran between them, picking up each bundle and then shaking it violently up and down to recharge the internal batteries. Clever.

There was another section covered by white sheets that were run up on poles or hung from the ceiling. I got a peek inside, and there were rows of cots, ten or so, with sleeping bags on them—this must have been the triage area.

"We don't have to use that much, scrapes and bruises mostly, but occasionally we get into it with the natives and people get hurt."

"Bites?"

"We don't let them in. Everyone here understands that if you get bit, that's it. In that case, most elect to take the quick way out. Some don't, and we take care of the problem if you know what I mean."

I didn't comment.

A woman joined us. She was probably in her mid-forties and had long, auburn hair. She grinned at Thomas and pecked him on the cheek. Attractive, she possessed an air of self-confidence that I found suited her.

"My wife, Ella. Although we aren't really married, since there's no one to marry us."

"We just live in sin," she said and then grinned at him. I found their affection for each other infectious, and wished I had someone. I had lived in a tiny cabin all alone for months, and I craved attention. There were times up on the mountain when I would talk to myself, going so far as to hold entire conversations about what to make for dinner, like I was some deserted island lunatic left with only a volleyball as company.

They fed me a mix of something that was warm and, I was pretty sure, made at least partially from the dog food. Not that it mattered. I was starving, and I would have eaten a raw rabbit if someone handed it to me. They seemed tense around me. A few asked questions about the early days, and whether I had seen others when I had made a run for it. They probably held out hope that some of their loved ones had escaped as I had and were also hiding out. I had no idea, I told them, then pleaded exhaustion and went to find a place to sleep.

Before I went to find a place to rest, Thomas took me aside and said, "you can explore a little. There's a place to work out if you need to stretch your legs." He pointed in the general direction toward the back of the store. "Just keep your nose clean, stay out of other people's business, and don't steal. Things like stealing get you tossed out on your ass."

"Got it," I replied.

They showed me to a cot that first night in a long dark area that was occupied by other sleeping bodies. Some laid on cots as well, while others were on blow up mattresses, or simply in sleeping bags on the floor. I lay in the dark, listening to all the other people around me, but I could not sleep. I was so used to the silence and solitude of the cabin that I found any noise pulled me back from the brink of slumber. Of course, there was more to it than that.

I kept going over the manner in which I had arrived. Standing on my car, adrenaline had jacked my system to the max as I had unloaded a shotgun at a guy who was trying to sink his teeth into me. His body had been blown backwards as the shot had taken him in the chest and turned his heart to mush. The terror in his eyes even before I had leveled the gun at him, like he was driven to attack, like someone had been pushing him on. There had been pain in his gaze, and I had responded by killing him.

I was also hurt. Bruises ached all over my body. I felt like I'd gone twelve rounds with a boxing champ. Only I was a punching bag instead of an opponent.

The ghouls were something that boggled the mind. Zombies were unnatural enough to begin with. But men who ate the dead and became the monsters I had seen simply should not exist. None of this should exist.

How had the zombie virus even started? I rose and put my jeans on, having opted to sleep in boxers and a t-shirt. The building seemed well insulated, but it was cold nonetheless, after coming out of the sleeping bag that had been like a warm cocoon.

I slipped into my boots, laced them up halfway, and then wrapped the laces around and tied them in front. I left the sleeping area and wandered. I felt eyes on me and knew there were guards. There was probably curiosity for the new guy, but no one challenged me, so I walked and very obviously avoided areas marked with 'do not enter' signs.

It was dark, but some of the flashlights had been left hanging near the ground to illuminate a path. There were port-a-potties set up along the right wall, which made it a long walk, but it kept the stench far away from the sleeping area. I passed countless bodies huddled in tents and on cots. Some moved, as people did what they had done for years when the lights went down.

A visible sentry looked me up and down, and decided I wasn't a zombie sneaking in to terrorize the store. I moved along an aisle, finding metal walls built up to hold other supplies. A whole locker that was fifteen or so feet square contained an armory of weapons. A chain-link fence had been built around the area and there was only one well locked doorway in. The weapons all looked army issue, and with the amount of fighting and chaos that had gone on at the outset of the 'war,' it was easy to guess that the stuff was probably left lying around on bodies or in abandoned vehicles. I'd love to get my hands on one of the assault rifles, but I doubted they were going to trust me any time soon.

"Keep on walking, new guy," a gruff voice said, but I was unable to locate the source, and didn't wait around any longer.

I located the area Thomas had mentioned. It looked as if it may have been a set of offices at one time. Now, there were some padded mats, dummies, and punching bags in the corners. In the center of the floor was a large, black cushioned bag with the sand or water-type base. I walked to it and pushed. It didn't budge, and I guessed they had some sort of pad underneath it so the thing would be harder to slide across the floor.

I threw a tentative punch, and then another. I looked behind me, then closed the door so I could work out in peace and quiet. I slipped my shirt off in the cold, stretched my joints and tendons. I had tried doing basics in the cabin, but halfheartedly at best. If I were going to be any use to these people, I would need to loosen up and get the old moves back.

I hit the bag with a quick set of punches, moved past, and then spun around and launched a series of kicks, low and high. I worked a style I had learned from a guy I met in Thailand years ago. I leapt up and planted knees in the pad. Then I came down and slipped boxing into my impromptu workout.

I worked a form in the air--something like a kata but with fast whip-like strikes. Within a few attempts, I felt like I hadn't forgotten as much as I thought I had. Then I worked the forms against the bag, and even found a rubber knife to incorporate into the session. I had always been good with knives--nasty things with razor-sharp edges that I could use as an extension of my arm.

I nearly knocked the bag over with a roundhouse kick, but it wobbled back to the surface of the floor with a heavy thump. Flowing from the kick into a straight punch, and then a series of close-in elbow strikes as I passed. A sudden noise from behind brought me up short.

I spun around, and a shape slipped out of the shadows of the room near the door. It stepped into the dull light from the hanging flashlights. Black hair that hung around her face in a bob. She tucked one side behind an ear as she walked toward me and the bag. Her features were fine—sharp little nose and pixie eyes that were hard around the edges. I would put her age a few years younger than mine, but she had a look of weariness that betrayed her years.

"New guy, huh," she said, as if commenting on the rain. Her body was slim and athletic. She had sculpted arms that hung out of a tank top. Not a bodybuilder's frame; she was just in good shape. I nodded at her as she walked past me toward a dummy in the corner.

"Imprinting it in your memory?" She looked over her shoulder.

I didn't know what to say, so I decided to just keep my mouth shut.

"That's okay. This is a different world than the one you left. The rules have changed, you know."

"How so?"

"All that petty bullshit--it's gone. If you like someone or something, then you just take it. Like the goddamn ghouls; they think they can take whatever they like, and we won't do anything about it."

"They're driven by a disease. They aren't rational," I pondered out loud.

"Piss on rational. They're animals, and they deserve to burn. Each and every one of them."

I didn't press her on that. She grabbed a dummy and dragged it by the shoulders, after tipping it on its side. I moved to help, but she hauled it out and stood it up so that it popped up like a jack in the box, then she swung forward. Before it could right itself, she punched it right in the throat. The model recoiled, and she launched into a vicious assault that saw the life-size man fall back under a barrage of punches and kicks that impressed me.

I went back to work on my hunk of plastic, but every once in a while, I thought I felt her eyes on me, just as she surely felt mine on her. She moved with grace and speed, her hands darting in to strike with their sides as well as knuckles and fists. She pulled out a couple of interesting moves that had her whipping her hand around like a punch, but at the last minute twisting her hand so her first two knuckles pointed toward the floor, palm up, striking with the back of her hand.

Sweat poured off my forehead and spread down my bare chest. It had been months since I worked out this hard. Certainly living alone in the woods, hunting, climbing, walking, working on the cabin, all of these things kept me fit to some extent, but there was nothing like a good thirty-minute balls-to-the-wall workout. I stepped away and looked around. There was an old water fountain on the wall, and I went to it and hit the button like an idiot.

"Do you think this is a working supermarket?" She chided me.

"Yeah. I knew but had to take a chance." I shrugged.

She tugged a bag out of a corner, unzipped it, pulled out a bottle of water, and drank deeply. After what seemed like an eternity waiting for her to finish, so I could ask her where to get some, she flipped the top closed and tossed it toward me.

I caught it, and, after staring in her eyes, which seemed to hold a mocking glint, I popped the lid and drank. The water had a slight metallic flavor, but it was wonderful, so I sucked down some more.

"How long's it been?" She walked toward me.

"Pardon?" I sputtered water.

"Since you worked out like that. You look like you know the moves, but you seem unsure of some."

"More than a few months, I guess. While I was hiding out in the woods, I didn't have much call for punching stuff."

"Yeah, I saw you get here. That was some arrival," she said, as she took back the water bottle. After chugging the rest, she tossed the bottle at her bag.

"You had a pretty good body count. Wayne put it at an even dozen, but I thought it was a lot less--maybe five. Dave from security said he bet you wouldn't even make it. But you made it. Come on, fighter. I'll find you a towel and show you the showers. You're not a fucking creep, right? There's enough of those out there."

"Not me." I assured her, but she didn't know me from Adam.

I followed her out and down a passageway that was constructed of more shelves, until we reached a section of employee changing rooms. We chit-chatted as we walked, mainly about how I came in. She asked questions about the ride, how were the roads, if I'd seen any gangs.

The old rooms were set aside for breaks, training, and changing clothes. I followed her lead by taking a bucket of water, about a gallon, and a thin brick of hard white soap that was well used, then followed her into the room. She turned to me when we reached a juncture, then pointed to the right.

"You go in there."

Of course. What else did I think was going to happen? I started to say something, but a small grin quirked her lips. I realized she had been teasing me all along. Despite her weary look, she was quite an attractive woman.

"I didn't get your name."

"No, you didn't. But I didn't get yours either."

"Erik Tragger." It was the second time in a day I had used my name in front of others. After the long, lonely time in the woods, it still sounded weird to my ears. "At your service," I added lamely.

"I see. Well, my name is Katherine Murphy, but don't even think about calling me Kat. I fucking hate that name."

"Noted."

"Good. So, Tragger, meet me at the workout room tomorrow, and maybe we'll go a few rounds."

"Same time?"

"You got a watch?"

"Yep."

"I don't, so just guess." She turned and left.

I stared after her for a while, until she rounded a corner and was gone from my sight. Water splashed a moment later, so I went into the men's side and did my best to wash away months of loneliness.

FOURTEEN

Morning came on with a jolt. I rubbed my eyes to the sound of someone banging on my metal cot. I opened them, and there stood a boy of about five foot eight. He was a pudgy child, with a sloping forehead. He hit the side of my cot with a plastic toy soldier.

"Can you stop that?"

"Travis, what?"

"Stop it. I'm tired, man."

"Travis, what?" His words were slightly slurred, and when I looked up, he was rolling his eyes up in the back of his head, looking at the ceiling and then back at me. Just what I needed. Some special needs kid to wake me.

"I like trains." He grinned. His left eye drifted to the right as he stared at me. "Travis Shill like trains."

The little guy wandered off, bumped into another cot, which brought a cry from the inhabitant. Still staring up at the ceiling, he ran off. I lay back, put my arm over my eyes, and breathed in the smell of people again. It was a long time since I had been around anyone, and now I was surrounded by them.

I sat up after a few minutes and rubbed my eyes. Glancing at my watch, I found it was close to seven in the morning. Others snored while I got up and used the bathroom, suspecting there would be a line later. I was greeted by several people on the way, but others just glanced up at me then looked away. Some bore haunted or wary looks, others just looked unfriendly and or didn't even bother looking me over.

I looked out for the woman I had met the night before, but I didn't see her.

I ate another bowl of gruel-like food that filled me up, but didn't taste so hot. The cook had put some effort into spicing it up, but I knew I was eating dog food again. There wasn't enough paprika in the world to change that.

I ended up hanging out with Thomas and a tough-looking man named James, who had a scar running across his nose from cheek to cheek. They headed to the weapons cache and I followed along, hoping to get a closer look at their arsenal and maybe borrow a decent gun. Borrow? Who was I kidding? I would probably die before I had a chance to return it.

"Is anyone properly taking care of these weapons?" I asked noting gunfire residue on more than one gun.

"Show me what you'd do." Thomas took down a handgun and gave it to me.

It was a Beretta 92F. The weapon was a standard military pistol with interchangeable parts. I stripped it in a couple of seconds, breaking it down enough to peer into the chamber. They seemed impressed. Thomas asked me to take a look and let him know how bad the damage was.

"See this shit all over the barrel?" I held it up to the light so the other two could get a look. "That's not good. This weapon should be regularly cleaned if you want it to remain ready for action."

"Ammo and mags are kept separately so don't try any funny business. Don't think you're going to pick up on of those guns and break out of here or whatever. I took a chance on you because of Patrick. Don't make me look like an asshole," Thomas said.

There were a couple of cleaning kits but one of them hadn't even been cracked open yet.

We went over the guns, and I pulled out assault rifles and inspected them. No one had done a proper cleaning, so I took the worst of them, stripped them, and cleaned them. People stopped by and looked on from time to time. Perhaps it was being back in a civilized setting after being alone for so long, but I found the company of others comforting. Along those lines, the smell of fresh oil on weapons was also comforting.

"This needs to be tested, plus, I could use some practice," I said later as I handled a military grade AR-15. Thomas had come to check on me and my progress then let out a whistle at how the weapons looked.

"Yeah okay," Thomas said.

He went around the corner and the sound of a lock rattling along with some chain sounded. A few seconds later he reappeared with a small box of rounds.

He followed me outside. The morning was chilly, and I thought I could smell rain in the air. The clouds hung around, keeping it generally gray. Around the fence, the ghouls wandered, snarling and running at the barrier but stopping short. A few zombies roamed around them as well, and when they chanced upon a ghoul, or got too close, a fight broke out.

I climbed up on the back of a truck with a flat bed. A lot of the other trucks had been outfitted with metal plates where holes were cut in the side for firing ports. Spikes hung on them--short sharp things that wouldn't provide much grip if a ghoul tried to climb up, but would discourage them.

My Honda had been parked in a different spot and now sported new tires. No one had asked for my permission to alter the ride, and I really didn't care. The old world was gone, just like my automobile insurance payment.

I stood up, inspected the gun, loaded it a dozen rounds into an upgraded Magpul magazine, and then put the stock against my shoulder. It had a red dot scope. I sighted down it, tracked one of the zombies, and then stroked the trigger. He fell, wearing the same stupid look on his face that he had before the 5.56 round entered his forehead. The shot looked to be off center to the right, so I made an adjustment to zero in the scope.

I got used to firing the weapon again and, in the process, attracted a few onlookers. I dropped a couple more zombies, then went for some faster-moving ones. One jerked to the left as I fired at him, so I only ended up taking off part of an ear.

I packed up the gun and ammo and turned to the store, intent on cleaning it and putting it back. There were about thirty or forty of the things, and they howled and snarled as I turned my back on them, so I held up one hand and gave them the finger.

Thomas stood near the entrance with his hands crossed over his chest. A couple of patrolling guards had stopped to watch me shoot, but they got back to business as I returned to the storefront.

"Did you have fun?" Thomas asked.

"Yeah. Kinda therapeutic," I said honestly.

"Now you have to go out there and clean up those bodies."

"Wait. What?"

"Just kidding. Let the fuckers rot," he chuckled and preceded me back into the store. "They'll probably have the bodies ate up by morning." He added with a lip-smacking noise.

I was beginning to appreciate Thomas and his grim humor.

Throughout the day, I had thought of Katherine and her lithe body. I wanted to work out with her, but more than that, I wanted to talk. Just talk.

"Christ. How many dead bodies do you think there are just laying around in abandoned homes?" I said.

"More than I want to think about," Thomas replied. "Hey. Keep your nose clean, as the saying goes, and I'll put you in charge of the armory. James is supposed to have that duty, but he doesn't really know shit about guns."

"I'm honored," I replied honestly.

I went to the workout room that night around the same time, and went a few with the same dummy Katherine had gone at. She didn't show up, even though I waited for close to an hour. So I called it a night and showered with the bucket of water.

The next day was much the same, except I talked to more people. The special needs kid, Travis, wandered by a few times and stared on while drool ran down his face, and tried to teach me facts about trains, but in his own way which involved a lot of repetition. After a while he wandered off to torture someone else.

I tried to be useful. I went outside and checked over my SUV. It was in the process of being modified. A mechanic with a terrible face wound looked at me and mimed that he couldn't talk. Then he stared at me. I assumed he was waiting to see if I would flinch or look away from his wound. Instead, I shook his hand and told him my name. I assumed he could hear alright or he most likely would have been zombie food by now. He shrugged and went back to work, welding a piece of metal in place.

There was some activity toward the front of the gate. Half a dozen men were gearing up, and a large flatbed truck was being moved near the entrance. The walk was brisk thanks to the early morning air. Most of the parking lot was wide open. On a normal day, back before the proverbial crap hit the fan, this place would have been buzzing with activity.

A burned out half strip mall was inside the perimeter. I made out a check cashing place and a coffee shop. My mouth flooded with saliva at the thought of a fresh cup. I could just about kill for one right about now.

A couple of men had guns at the ready. They were going over their load as I strolled up to them. I was impressed by their decorum. They were smiling, but they knew their way around their weapons.

One of the men, I was pretty sure his name was Daniel, nodded at me. He checked up on me when I was cleaning up the weapons inside. He asked a few questions about an automatic I was working on. I thought he was just checking me out and not really interested in my answer.

"Going hunting, guys?" I asked.

"We got a call--just a half message really. A few streets over, west of here. We think some survivors were trying to reach us and got trapped in a house."

I was feeling pretty useless around the camp. Everyone seemed to have jobs but me, except for cleaning guns. I wanted something to do. More importantly, I wanted to prove myself to them.

"Want some help?"

They looked back and forth, but not at me. I was probably intruding on a group that was used to working together. They didn't know the first thing about me. I might get spooked at the first sight of blood. I might demand to go back. I could run off, for all they knew. All the training in the world might have been under my belt, but it meant nothing until I had proven myself.

"It's nothing personal, man. We're full up," one of the men said.

Daniel looked me over then glanced at the other guys. Upon closer examination, I noticed one of the 'guys' was actually a woman. She turned, and with her short hair I thought it was Katherine at first. But she was younger, her face fairer. She was dressed from head to toes in full digital green camouflage gear. She popped a magazine into a large handgun, jacked the hammer back, and slammed it into a holster.

"Yep. No offense." She smirked.

"Come on. Thomas said he was okay. It wouldn't hurt to have another set of eyes, would it?" Daniel said.

One of the men shrugged, but the girl looked away from me.

An older man with a shaved head regarded me. His forehead had a nasty burn scar that ran up to his scalp. Hair would never grow there again. I didn't blame him for shaving the stubble off. He had a pair of pistols on his hips and a snub nose machine gun under one arm.

"I'm O'Connell. I don't care if you join us. Just do what I say, when I say, and we'll all get along fine. Ain't that right?" He looked among the squad. They all grunted assent, but the woman did not. She looked me over like I was a cockroach.

"Sure. I can do that," I said. Taking orders wouldn't be hard. I was just happy to be useful to these guys.

"What's your poison?" Daniel opened up the top of a storage bin strapped down to the back of the truck. I glanced in and saw a few older guns. A hunting rifle was pushed against one end. The barrel was strapped to the side. I pulled the weapon out and set it aside to assemble on the way. Then I tugged a .45 ACP out. Daniel gave a half smile at my choice and handed me a box of shells from another bin. I dug out a magazine that looked like it fit the handgun. After a bit of testing, I tucked it in my pocket to load later.

"This will do," I said.

"Now don't go doing anything fucking stupid and we won't have to fucking leave your ass out there. Cool?" Daniel said.

"Cool." I agreed.

We piled into the back of the truck. I tried to make small talk with Daniel, but he turned his attention back to one of the guys who was telling a story about facing off against a pair of zombies in an old apartment complex.

We left the safety of the Walmart walled of parking lot. A couple of men came out and moved the gate aside. This involved shifting massive concrete barriers with a heavy lifter. After we drove away, they put them back into place.

"If we run into zombies, what's the count?" One of the guys yelled over the hiss of air rushing past the truck bed.

"I'm good for five or six." The girl smiled. She checked her pistols for what seemed the tenth time.

"What's the bet for?" I asked.

"Just bragging rights. And someday, when we find a warehouse full of beer, a bunch of those" she said.

"Yeah man, Liz here owes me forty-seven cold ones." One of the men grinned.

"That's all she's got, cold ones," another guy said. The group cracked up until she drew, jacked a round into the chamber, and fingered the safety to off in one smooth motion that ended with a gun leveled at the last guy. His eyes went wide.

"Cold enough for you?"

"Cool it," Daniel said. "There's trouble up ahead."

FIFTEEN

We had left sight of the store and had been speeding down a side road. There were a few cars pushed out of the way and those contained bodies that were little more than rotted clothes and bones.

The truck came to a stop just as we entered a residential development much like my home had been situated in, but here it looked like a war zone. Houses had been burned out, and or broken into. Shrubs and blackberry grew out of control. Discarded items and looted possessions were tossed all over yards.

"There!" Daniel stood up in the back of the truck and pointed at a pair of cars that were intact. They were station wagons, and they looked to be full of boxes.

I stood up, holding the hunting rifle to my shoulder as I tried to keep my focus everywhere at once. The driver slowed our vehicle, and I leaned forward to absorb the momentum. I caught sight of a familiar car tucked between two houses, but I wasn't sure why it rang a bell. It was a newer make, and a deep shiny blue, like someone was taking care of it.

Birds called out to us as we passed. An entire murder of crows took off when Liz waved her gun in their directions.

"Crow's are good eatin'," she said without any expression in her voice. "Tastes like chicken."

"How the hell do you catch them?" I said in an effort to keep things light since we were potentially walking into a fire fight.

"Buckshot," Daniel interjected.

"Help us!" A man called from one of the houses, but I couldn't pick out exactly which one. A pair of our men jumped over the side of the truck as it came to a stop in the front yard. Two more went over the other side and spread around the truck, their backs to us so all angles were covered. I was impressed by their cohesiveness.

I jumped down and followed Liz, who seemed determined to lead the way. The two others fell in behind her. One was O'Connell. With four on guard duty and us advancing, I felt confident in my comrade's ability to react to a threat. They were good.

"Remind me why we're babysitting the neighborhood? Could just mean more mouths to feed," the guy on her left said.

"Because they're people, and we need more if we're going to win this fight." O'Connell kept pace with them and looked at the guy.

Another scream from inside made our group pick up the pace. I glanced around to check the position of our back up one more time. The driver of the truck was on the radio. He was probably assuring the compound that we were safe and sound.

I turned my attention back to the house. It was a huge three story that was probably built in the 70s. A grown over gutter draped the building. Vines had snaked their way up the side and given the place a genuinely creepy look.

Windows had been darkened from closed blinds or curtains. I thought I saw one slip aside ever so slightly, but when I studied it, the material held firm.

"Help us!" a woman yelled.

I moved over tall grass and crunched over what felt like bones. I didn't bother stopping to investigate.

We reached the house, and Liz was the first through. One of the guys went with her, while Daniel and I set up a perimeter. They had some basic hand gesture down pat, so I played along like I understood what they were saying to each other.

There was a commotion from the inside, but no shots. We remained vigilant, but didn't follow. After a few seconds, Liz called out. "We found them."

"Come on, new guy. Meet Justin."

The room was a mess of overturned furniture and ruined floor. Someone had burned a hole in the hardwood and built a fire pit in the center of the room. A pile of burned wood lay around the sides, and empty cans of food had been tossed in the corners. The walls were covered in spray painted words, but they looked like they were done by an illiterate hand. I couldn't make them out to save my life.

The others were lowering their weapons to the ground. As my eyes adjusted to the room, I became aware of other figures. A couple huddled behind a sofa, and someone poked around a corner with a machine gun.

Ah hell!

We were surrounded. Someone had set a trap, and we had fallen right into it.

"Fuck me," I muttered before I could help myself.

SIXTEEN

I glanced up at the foyer, finding another guard hanging over the side of the railing on the second floor. He had a gun trained on us as well. I might make it to the door, and for a split second I considered abandoning my new 'friends'.

Dejected, I lowered my rifle. A few days back in the world of the living and I was already being subjected to the worst of humankind. Bad enough all those creatures trying to kill us, now we had rival humans after us as well.

"What's the meaning of this?" Liz demanded.

Someone had a pistol pointed at her head. He stood close to her, but with the sunlight pouring in from the window behind his figure, I couldn't make out any features.

"The meaning of *this*? Oh. You fell for our pretty little trap. Ain't that a bitch?" That voice was familiar.

"We came to help!" Liz looked furious, with her mouth set in a hard line, eyes daring the gun to waver from her forehead.

"And help you did, darling. You helped us to some shiny new weapons, a new truck, and whatever supplies you have in said vehicle. I bet you have food out there, don't ya. Never enough food to feed all of us hungry men who're just trying to keep the peace in the new world."

That voice!

"Son of a bitch!" Daniel said.

"I'd hate to paint the walls with this one's brains." The man gestured at Liz with his gun.

"We ain't gonna to hurt you. Just fuck you over. If you run home real fast, you might be able to avoid any creepers in these parts."

A couple guys holstered their guns and patted down our crew. They took their time going over Liz with their hands. She was stiff as a board as they handled her, but her eyes were livid.

The speaker shifted to one side, and I caught a flash of brown that didn't look like military boots to me. Snakeskin. That's when it hit me.

"Lee?" I said before I could help myself.

He turned to regard me. His eyes were tired, red rimmed. They sat in sockets that were almost skeletal. I nearly took a step back when I saw the change. What happened to the man that was planning to guard his post? To protect the innocent? His motivation may have been mixed up when we first met, but this was insane.

"Do I know you?" He squinted his eyes as he considered me. He kept the gun in a steady grip, though.

"You were setting up a roadblock months ago. I thought you were one of the good guys."

"Good guys?" Lee had a slow drawl. "There's no such thing as good guys anymore."

"Come on, Lee, we're both military. Why don't you let us go, and we can just forget this ever happened. We'll leave, and you can slink back to your shit hole." Damn my mouth.

"Military." Lee spat. "Let me tell you something about this world, son. I left my family in the care of the military, and do you know what they did?"

I stared back, waiting for the answer to his rhetorical question. One of the men shifted, lowered his guard as we went through the motions of dropping our gear on the floor. I set my rifle down then slowly lay my pistol next to it.

"They left. They didn't even bother to stick around and protect them. They just up and left. Now I don't know about you, but is that any way to treat women and children? They left fifteen families in a big school gym. Deserted them. When I found my wife, my Margaret, she was dead. Eaten away. But she wasn't. See, I had to watch her get up and stagger toward me."

Lee took a few steps toward me. The space between us was only a few feet, but he made it seem immense as his enflamed eyes bore into mine. Lee mimicked the dead with his hands waving around in front as he closed the distance. His gun was leveled at my forehead. I was pretty sure he was completely unbalanced and about to splatter my brains all over the entryway.

"I just watched her walk up to me. I let her into my guard, felt her arm around my neck. She didn't smell like my Margaret anymore. Not by a long stretch." He stopped right in front of me, gun leveled at the space between my eyes. I didn't stare into it. Instead I used my peripheral vision to study his men. The rest had lowered their guard as we dropped our guns. Even the man on the floor above was no longer pointing his weapon at us.

"I held her back. Kept my hand on her neck so she couldn't bite me. I looked into her undead eyes and wanted to see some spark of life. You know what I saw instead?"

His eyes were huge as he cocked the gun.

"Nothing. I didn't see a damn thing."

On the word 'thing,' I flowed. I kept my eye on the weapon even as I moved to the right. If he fired, it would go past my forehead. My left hand was already moving. I slammed the barrel away from my face, wrapped my hand around it, and wrenched it toward his chest.

My foot swept around his legs, so we looked like we were in a weird half-embrace. If I wanted to, I could have yanked his legs out from under him with a sharp twist of my hip, but that would get me nowhere. Lee was at my mercy. I twisted the gun, so the barrel was under his chin. I pressed up, just so he was aware that I was a few foot-pounds of pressure away from putting a bullet through his face.

"Hey, HEY!" one of his men shouted.

"Tell them to back off or I put a bullet through your head!" My voice came out raw and broken. I was mad, and adrenaline was making me even more volatile. I had always trained to remain calm under pressure. Keep my head down, assess the situation, and then react. I had tossed the first two rules out, and if I kept up on this path, I was likely to get us all killed.

"You think this is some kind of television show? Huh? Think I'm going to just say the word and my men will back down? It ain't that easy, son. My boys are hungry and trigger happy, so why don't you just drop the hard-ass act and lower the gun."

"Out! Everyone out! Get to the truck. If any of the others follow, I WILL kill him!" I didn't look around. I didn't meet anyone else's eyes. I didn't wait for confirmation. With Lee still bent, back arched, I marched us to the door. He didn't struggle; he seemed to take it in stride, and even smiled at me.

The gaping spot where he was missing a tooth gave him a skeletal and quite mad grin.

The rest of the crew filed out as I stood in front of the door. Liz tried to meet my gaze, but I had it firmly on Lee. I didn't want any mistakes. If any of them flinched, I was going to kill him.

O'Connell snatched his handgun off the floor but kept it low as he went out. I backed out last. It was awkward to hold him like this and walk to the truck. Words were whispered back and forth between the folks we had left outside and the reconnaissance team, as I now thought of them.

"It's not personal." I said as I hauled him into the cab with me, then forced him to sit in front of me so his upper body faced the house.

The others dropped down low in the truck bed and scrambled for weapons. I didn't know the drivers name but he nodded at me once then started the truck.

It groaned as he shifted into reverse. He gunned the engine and we shot backward. Lee was half hanging out of the truck, and he shifted his weight, so I had to make a quick decision. Either drop him, or we both went down. I let go and he across the pavement in a flurry of curses. The truck slowed for a corner and then accelerated away but not before I got a full dose of hate from Lee. If looks could kill, I would have been six feet under.

We returned with less than we had left with, but we were alive. The driver had radioed ahead, and when we pulled into the compound we were met by a small army. The men and women came out in force. I saw every kind of weapon, including a pair of Japanese swords in the hands of a young woman with slightly Asian features, and haunted eyes.

Thomas met us as we entered through the gate.

When folks simmered down and went back inside, I was left with just the crew that had gone out on the "rescue mission." Thomas listened to the story again and thanked me with a handshake.

As we headed inside, Liz turned to confront me. Her eyes were angry, and I could understand a reprimand. I could have played it cool, given our weapons over, and maybe they would have let us go just like they said. Maybe they would have used us as hostages or even tried to get info on our forces.

"Christ, Tragger." She sighed loudly. "I'm not going to say that was a stupid fucking thing to do."

"You kinda just did."

We walked in silence for a few more feet. Daniel turned and winked at me, then sped off into the Walmart. The others kept pace.

"You know you just made an enemy, right?" she said. "Lee isn't going to forget that nor forgive you or us."

"I know." I shrugged. "But look at it this way. We're alive and maybe Lee and his men learned a lesson today."

I would have liked to report that was the end of Lee, and that I never saw him again. That, sadly, was not what happened in the coming weeks.

SEVENTEEN

I went to the gym again that night, but Katherine didn't show. I worked away some of the tension I had built up during the standoff with Lee. There was no way I would be able to sleep, as amped up as I still was, so I worked out until I was exhausted.

I had considered asking Thomas about Katherine, but it seemed prudent to mind my own business. I'm sure she had her reasons, and they were none of my concern.

The next day, Thomas showed me the communication room where they were picking up a signal from Portland on a low band radio. There had been transmissions for a few weeks, although sporadically, about the work on the city to keep out the undead and the ghouls.

They had been formulating a way to leave the compound. I was taken aback at first. They had shelter, a way to protect themselves, and they had food and water.

"This won't last forever. We've held out well enough, but the supplies you see are all that's left for miles around. A lot of people in the store don't want to be isolated anymore. So many rumors out there about the cities being free of the dead. About the government being in control. They just want a chance at a normal life."

Plans based on rumors. I wished I had a better idea on how to proceed.

The strategic exit was basic—they didn't need something with a million steps to get out. The hard part would be the distracting the dead and ghoulish. The plan called for someone to drive a small tanker to the end of town, near the barricade through which I had blasted, drawing them out and stringing them along, then detonate the truck's gas supply. The gas station in the parking lot meant we had a good bit of fuel for all the trucks, so we could spare a some to light up the day. When the ghouls went to investigate, the convoy would leave and head for Portland.

The problem was that someone had to be the bait to set off the distraction.

"Who might that be?" I wondered out loud. The other men in the room turned as one and looked at a form that had slipped into the room.

"That would be me." A familiar voice said.

I turned and found it was Kathrine. She didn't offer a smile, just a stony wall of non-emotion, just like her voice when she said she was going to create the distraction. I don't know what was more surprising, her speaking up or my next words.

"I'll go with her."

"Not necessary. We have a capable guy. In fact, it's Pat here, the guy who spoke up for you the other day."

Pat was nervous and looked away when I tried to search his eyes. He crossed his arms, and stared at the map laid out before the planners. They had a crude drawing of the Walmart compound as well as the street leading out of Vesper Lake. There was a line of cars and trucks drawn over it in red, with stick men manning guns on the back of trucks and SUVs. I saw some of the innovative things that the engineers in the group had created for the cars. Sunroofs turned into gun ports and one pump truck with a nozzle that spat gas. Probably a flamethrower, but it would also work well to lay down a stream of gas that could be lit. It would be messy and there would be flaming zombies, but what better way to create a distraction. Not only that, but heavy rain was expected the same day so there was lower risk of setting the entire town ablaze.

"I have no doubt that Pat is a capable guy, but don't you need someone with some combat experience?"

"You're looking at a roomful of men with combat experience," Thomas said.

"He can go if he likes. The more the merrier," Katherine spoke up. "Besides, I hear he did good things yesterday."

"The jury is still out on that one," I said.

"Fine. We've run this place from the start with the help of volunteers. You want to go with, be my guest. But I want to say that a guy like you is very valuable, and I would prefer if you stayed with us. We may need your expertise later."

"You make it sound like a suicide mission."

"What else does it sound like?" Katherine said.

THAT NIGHT, we met and went over the plan. Then Katherine and I worked out in the gym. She told me she had been 'busy' the last few nights and unable to make it. I took her at her word. After we were covered in sweat and walking toward the shower room, she thanked me for volunteering to go along.

"I know you'll be a big help."

"Why do you want to be the one?" I asked her, looking out the corner of my eye to see her expression. It didn't change.

"Someone had to do it. I have nothing left to live for. My children were ..."

I let her trail off and didn't say a word. I had escaped relatively unscathed. My own reason for going was the inescapable feeling that my fate was somehow tied up with Katherine's. I've never been one to believe in a god or a destiny, but somehow it felt right when I was with her. Emotionless or not, she was the first woman to whom I had been attracted in years.

"I wish I could say I understand, but I don't. I didn't really have anyone before the event, and I don't have anyone now. If I die, then it won't be a great loss. Who will look for me years from now when the world is right again?"

"Is that why you agreed to go? Some gesture of futility against an insane world?"

"No. I volunteered because I wanted to be with you."

She stopped walking and turned to stare at me.

"I'm not good at this kind of thing. I don't know how to feel, anymore, so just ..." She paused and looked past me for a few seconds. "Just watch my back and I'll watch yours."

I nodded, and we moved on down the hallway. At the shower room, we parted, and I went into the quiet space and shut myself into a stall. I tossed my clothes in a heap and wondered where I could get them washed. There was an abundance of pants and shirts, thanks to the store's supplies, and people took from it freely when they needed items. I would raid it tomorrow and find something else to wear.

I splashed lukewarm water over my skin and shivered in the cold. A little soap went a long way toward making me feel human again after the brutal workout I'd had. I was washing the last of the water away when there was a tentative knock at the door. I turned to look, and a pair of slim calves was all I could see under the door.

"Huh?"

Katherine opened the door and gave me the first smile I had seen from her. It was tentative at best, and then it fell. She was dressed in a towel that covered her body from chest to thigh. She was pale, and goose bumps stood out on her skin.

I rose and took her hand in mine and drew her to me. Her towel fell aside, and we kissed for a long time.

MORNING WAS QUITE a shock compared to the last few. I woke to a dimly lit tent and the touch of a warm body against mine in the sleeping bag we had zipped together the night before. She stirred against me, her hand over my chest, her body curled against my back. Her hand slipped down and found that I had the typical guy's reaction to waking up in the morning, so we made the best of it. Why not. We might die in a few hours.

An hour later and we had a huge breakfast of pancakes, powdered eggs and powdered milk mixed with metallic tasting water. Thomas felt that we deserved it, since we were going to have a strenuous day. At least fifty gathered to eat the fine meal. There was laughter and a hint of excitement that rippled all along the group. They were ready to move on, to get away from the constant danger, and head out to find a permanent place of safety.

For my part, a grin touched touching my lips whenever I caught Katherine's eye and she smiled in return. Thomas looked between us a couple of times, but just shook his head as if he had seen something beyond his ability to comprehend.

EIGHTEEN

The caravan assembled behind the giant store. Some had spent all night loading the trucks, which comprised some eighteen wheelers and a few UPS delivery trucks.

The tanker itself looked ridiculous. It was covered in flowers on one side. Someone's weird sense of humor at work, I suppose. The Walmart must have had a lot of cans of paint. This seemed as good a use for it as any. It had a lot of weight, and they had welded on a scoop like you see on the front of a train engine to move things off the tracks.

There was a lot of activity behind me. I was more concerned with inspecting my newly tricked out Honda. It now had a set of galvanized metal plates over the windows with holes cut in so I could see out the front and sides. The sunroof had part of a big oil barrel on top of it that latched from the inside. I could stand up and use a handgun, but a rifle would never fit. The windows had been removed on either side, and the slots would provide firing ports.

The plan called for Pat to ride with Katherine, and I would follow close behind. If we ran into trouble, I would slow the car and take out any threats. Thomas produced a couple of hand grenades, one of which was phosphorous--nasty stuff. Got into the skin and kept burning because it didn't need oxygen. Two were frags, and there were a couple of smoke grenades. I was leery of the last, because it would just confuse the field of battle.

A pair of 'tanks' would escort us to the end of the street and provide covering fire as we ran with the horde behind us. One had a fire nozzle on top, and the other bore a couple of hard-looking men armed with hunting rifles. Our snipers.

A side gate was opened, and Katherine roared out of it, into the icy morning in the souped-up wrecking truck. On the back was a large gas tank filled to the rim with a mixture of premium fuel and soap flakes. There was a canister of compressed air under it that would inject the mixture with enough oxygen to make the explosion count. It would all come down to timing.

I followed close behind as she made the first turn then got onto 322. The horde of zombies was on us before we were half a mile away. I put the car in park, slipped the metal cover off the sunroof, and popped up with one of the AR-15s from the back seat. I aimed down the scope and loosed a magazine of shots at the wave of dead coming my way. A few dropped, but at this range it was hard to get many headshots. Some took rounds in their appendages and chests. One was shot through the neck, and fell sputtering a black blood that oozed more than flowed.

I dropped into the seat and roared off with a fresh ocean of the things behind. After another half mile, I stopped the car and tossed a fragmentation grenade at the onrushing creatures to make sure I had the attention of every one of them. It exploded in their midst as they screamed toward me, tossing bodies and parts of bodies into the air. A small puff of smoke and asphalt rose behind me as I sped off again.

The wrecker was approaching the barrier, so I took the opportunity to apply more damage. One more frag grenade joined the fray, and I emptied another magazine into the horde.

I roared up to the wrecker. It was stopped near the barricade. She had to maneuver around the rusted hulks of trucks and cars I cursed just a few days ago. In one case, she barreled through one because it was sitting catty-corner, blocking the road. She came to a halt, and Pat was already moving. He slithered out of the door and shut it hard. He moved on top of the cab and went to the giant white tank. Maneuvering the air hose into position, he fastened it to the bottom.

I screeched to a stop and came out of the cover shooting. They were still a hundred or so feet away, but I dropped them one after another by taking careful aim and stroking the trigger gently. I set a box of magazines next to me and burned through them until the assault rifle jammed. I tossed it in the back, grabbed another one, and kept shooting.

Behind me, Katherine was also on top of the truck, and they were feeding hoses into the tank. She yelled something, but I couldn't make out her words. I fell into the seat and spun the car around and backed into the truck, touching my rear bumper so they would be able to get in when the thing was armed. I popped back out of the turret and opened up with the gun, calling to them between shots.

"What's wrong?"

"Goddamn thing won't start. Everything's working, but I can't arm the explosive."

"Fine, we'll do it by hand." I pulled a grenade out of my stash. "Catch!"

Katherine looked at me like I was insane, but I mimed throwing it to her twice, then threw it for real. She leaned over and caught it in both hands and shot me a dirty look.

The horde drew closer, so close that I could pick out their faces from this distance. Rotted filth, demented demons. Most wore the visage of tortured humans, but some seemed to revel in their new state and wore bones woven into their hair. There were hundreds of them, just as we suspected, and they were still pouring out of the buildings and side streets.

"We don't have much time!" I yelled.

"Are we supposed to blow ourselves up?" She should be hysterical, but she sounded mad that I didn't explain the plan. Well, it wasn't much of one.

"Just pull the pin. You have about seven seconds to get clear. You'll both jump on top of the car and hold the fuck on for dear life!"

I watched as Pat took the grenade and studied the side of the tank, probably looking for a place to put it. "Dropping it in the tank would be best. It'll spray gas everywhere!" I yelled.

Faces appeared out of the trees to the right of the truck. I kept my eyes on Katherine and wondered if they had a chance now. I couldn't let her go like that, and in a quick decision, I determined that I would either save her and Pat or go out with them in a massive explosion. If I ran back to the caravan without them, how would it look? Besides, what did this new world have to offer me? I had seen its best, and its best wasn't much to look at. Survivors huddling together waiting for something to happen. Well, this was something.

I popped off a few more rounds, got back into the driver's seat, and took out the machine gun I had been saving. I closed the turret, so none of them would crawl on top of the car and fall inside.

The M249 was a machine gun that sprayed an impressive amount of ammo. I had a box of ammo magazines, and one was already loaded.

I ran to the truck and clambered up the side, banging both knees in the process. With adrenaline pumping I felt alive for the first time in half a year.

They closed in from all sides, screaming, slathering, and snarling. Dozens of dumb zombies wove between them, but for the most part, it was the faster ghouls I had to contend with.

I opened up with the machine gun and obliterated the first line of creatures. They fell under withering fire. Blood, sinew, and chunks of flesh exploded out their backs. I spun to the right and dropped more of them then changed magazines.

"What's the holdup?"

"Damn pipe won't budge. I can't get the oxygen to come out."

Without the air being force fed into the tank, we would never have our explosion. All that gas in one place was a terrific chance at a bomb, but without air, it was likely to fizzle until it reached 750 degrees. We had rigged a couple of hoses into water nozzles designed to give a wide spread of the air. When it bubbled into the gas, we would have our accelerant.

"So the grenade won't do what we want?"

"It'll accelerate the explosion, but we need to get the gas moving to get the full effect."

"Shit!" I said and emptied another magazine.

They were at the truck, and Katherine pulled a handgun and popped a pair in the center of their foreheads. I shot at them in earnest as they clawed up the side. She got on top of the cab so she would have a wider view of the field of battle. The problem was that the things were closing in on the front as well.

"Ah fuck!" I yelled.

He kicked out as one clawed up the side, but it caught his leg and bit at it. He was wearing double jeans like the rest of us, and a pair of thermals under that. Hopefully the ghouls couldn't bite through that much fabric. He kicked out again, and it fell back into the crowd. Then he drew his gun and shot the next one in the face, but there were dozens more coming. We had about three seconds before the rush arrived.

"Shoot it!" I yelled, and then fired off another magazine of ammo. The machine gun was meant to be mounted on a bipod and shot while lying prone. Firing it meant constantly fighting the upward pull of the gun.

"What?" Pat called back. I looked behind me, and Katherine was changing magazines.

"Get to the car, Kat!" I called.

"Don't fucking call me that," she said, and a smile quirked her lips. She was breathing hard and flushed. She was enjoying this, the danger. She and I would make a fine pair if we survived. The chances of that were pretty slim. I tried to swing the gun around and use it judiciously, but there were just too many of them, and in the way were my two new friends.

Pat fell down as three of them grabbed him.

I tossed the machine gun at one crawling up the side of the truck and dragged my 9 mm out. I studied the valve then put the gun close to it, angling it away from the tank. Then I fired, knowing that there was every chance I was about to detonate the fuel.

The gunshot rang out, and the valve turned an inch from impact. I kicked it with the heel of my boot, and the thing moved. I kicked it again, and this time was greeted with a burst of air. Gas spewed out the top as the air bubbles mixed with the noxious fluid.

Katherine had reached the car and crawled into the driver's seat. I picked up the egg timer with the wires running out of it and pounded it against the butt of my gun a few times. It started ticking. We had about 45 seconds to get the hell out of there.

Pat managed to unsling the shotgun from his shoulder, turn it at the undead horde and fire a blast, but there were too many, and they dragged him off the car. He screamed and thrashed as they tore at him.

I yelled out for Pat, but it was too late. He screamed and fought with everything he had.

Katherine gunned the engine, and several of the leering ghouls latched onto the side, so she shot them in the face. I leapt onto the hood of the SUV, cursing myself for leaving the goddamn lid closed. I held on for dear life while yelling at her to just take off. She started to back up, but we hit a patch of the things. I looked behind, and there was an army of them coming at us, just as we had hoped.

They swarmed, but in the distance, the convoy was almost out of the Walmart parking lot, so we had done our job. The truck with the snipers was in hot pursuit so they were now out of the fight, not that they'd been much use considering how quickly the ghouls moved. The snipers could just as easily hit us, as one of them.

There was no way we could get through that press of bodies. We would have to go the other way. I banged on the top and yelled as loud as I could, "Just go for the open road. It's our only chance!"

A ghoul grabbed an arm, and another latched onto my ankle, as Katherine gunned the engine. I shook off the one on my foot, but the other one had somehow wedged his foot in the side of the car, and he was really stuck. His face was a nightmare of scars and damage, his eyes the same luminous green as the others I had seen.

"Die," it hissed, then snapped at my hand. I jerked back, twisting my forearm in a violent downward motion to break free. He snapped at my exposed fingers again, and I punched him in the face for his effort. My right hand held onto the turret for dear life, using the small slot they had cut in it. The metal was dirty and jagged, and I felt it bite into my forearm with each movement. He was about to make my life a lot worse than having lockjaw.

He slithered onto the top of the car as Katherine swerved around the last of the barriers. It seemed like my whole life the last few days had been made up of barriers, from this one, to the fence, to the space inside the store.

I pulled myself to my knees and held on with my left hand as she punched the engine. We must have been going thirty-five or forty miles an hour. The wind whipped past me, and the smell of clean, cold air filled my nose.

A blast behind me drew my attention, even as I punched the ghoul in the face and snapped his arm with a vicious knife-hand strike to his forearm. He howled in fury, so I hit him in the nose, and that took a lot of the fight out. Dust rose in the air, but it wasn't the explosion I had expected. If the rig didn't go up, it might make for a bad escape for the refugees, but at least they had a head start. The sound had been familiar, though, and I wondered if ...

He stood up on the doorframe. His foot was most likely in the slot they cut in the galvanized steel panels for me to shoot through. I planted my right foot, and then thrust my left in front of me in a kick that caught him in the chest. He fell back with a scream that was drowned out by multiple loud thumps. I hazarded a look over the side of the SUV. His foot was still stuck, but his upper leg and body were completely gone.

The latch popped, and I slithered into the seat next to Katherine. She shot me a wide-eyed grin, which clearly showed how amped up she was at the escape. She was wallowing in the danger; she seemed made for it.

"So what happened to the tank?"

"I don't know. But that small explosion might have been Pat." I took a deep, shuddering breath, and the shakes set in. I had been running on pure adrenaline for the last few minutes, my body guided by instinct more than logic.

"Pat?"

"He had the frag grenade I tossed you. I think he blew it up while they ate him." I shivered.

"Poor Patrick. He was a brave man." She sighed.

"He was a good man. I owed him."

"Now what do we do? Wait a while and try to ..." She jerked forward as a massive, orange blast of light lit the daylight sky. It didn't take long for the sound wave to reach us. I looked behind me, through the hole in the metal over the rear mirror, and was greeted by a tiny mushroom cloud as the huge gas bomb exploded. We were probably three quarters of a mile away when it happened, but she hit the gas anyway, accelerating around the cars and trucks abandoned on the road.

Katherine pulled over a few minutes later, and we got out to watch the smoke as it rose into the air. The explosion had been massive, and some of the trees along the road had caught fire, but just as anticipated, a drizzle set in and dark clouds rolled to the west. Soon this entire area would be blanketed in rain and that fire wouldn't go far.

I crawled into the driver's seat, and we talked over our options. We could go back to town and attempt to follow the caravan. We could go back to the Walmart and hide until help came back, or we would go to the cabin and do our best to survive.

Torrents of rain arrived as we reached the abandoned store I had seen earlier. Was that just a few days ago? We stopped, and I chased off a couple of mongrel dogs. The door was locked, but the glass in it was shattered. I held a pistol in front of me and called out that we were friendly—and alive.

The store was empty of any goods, but something in the back caught my eye. The floor had an old wooden section that creaked when we walked over it. Except for one spot.

I felt around the edges until I found a hidden latch. It snapped open, and I lifted a cleverly built hatch.

We found a lot of canned goods in the small space, so we loaded them up. I found some bags of flour, as well as a few large canvas bags of rice and dried beans. I wondered what happened to the people who managed to collect this much food and never eat it.

There was another hidden door in the floor in the storage room, which led to a room with an old TV and radio. I took the radio and raided the supplies, which consisted mainly of powdered milk and cereal. It was a weird combination, but I was betting I could live on Cheerios.

We made it to the cabin before night. It was raining hard--a sheet of turgid water turning the night a gray that pulled at my view and made it hard to see. We had some slow going for part of the ride, because the windshield wipers had been removed to make room for the metal plates.

The first night, Katherine and I spent an hour heating water to near boiling and pouring it in the old tub. But it was worth it. She said she hadn't had a proper bath since the epidemic began.

The barricades were down for now--the ones that had hindered my life for the past half year. The barricade at the city, the barricade to my existence, and, so it seemed, the barricade to my heart. I joined her in the tub, and told her I was glad she was with me.

I wish I could say that we lived happily ever after, but wasn't a fairy tale, as Lee would have said, "not a fairy tale by a long shot."

PART 2

NINETEEN

I woke to the sound of thunder in the middle of the night. The rain that had set in the evening before was gone, but the sounds of the gods bowling across the heavens tore me out of sleep. I clutched at the warm body next to me and concentrated on her name. Katherine, not Allison. Allison had been years ago--a lifetime to me. She had been my first true love—and, I thought, the last—but things did not work out the way we planned. I think it was my choice of careers. After Special Forces, I got into security because there wasn't much else for a guy like me to do. Personal escort had been my favorite, protecting minor celebrities, and those with a lot of money and no common sense.

I moved on to consulting, but the pay wasn't that great, and I was frequently gone for up to a week at a time. I missed my wife during those days, but she didn't miss me as much. It was a guy at work who did us in. I remember plotting to take him apart. I had a romantic vision stuck in my head. I would confront him, push him, and when he snapped and took a swing at me, I would separate his arm from his shoulder. Then I would break his jaw, leave him unable to beg Allison to come back. I spent hours and hours plotting. The play ran in my head, but I wised up after a few days and realized it was no use. It would just make me look like an animal to her, plus it was a great way to end up in jail.

Katherine had a gentle snore that was almost soothing after I'd spent so many months in this place without a soul to talk to. Her auburn hair was a mess in the moonlight, but I didn't care. To me, she was the loveliest thing I had ever laid eyes upon. I longed to lean over and kiss her neck, but I feared waking her. Instead, I lay contently next to her warm body, and breathed in her scent.

Damaged: that was a good way to describe her. Even though she had given herself to me, I could feel a gulf between us. It was as though I stood on one side of a stream, reaching out for her, but she remained on the other side, holding back as if she had a secret. I wanted to ask her about her life before the event, but I was afraid of the answer. She was with me now, and I didn't want to hear about a past love. Perhaps my reluctance stemmed from my problems with Allison.

I changed my mind and touched her after all, running my hand over her shoulder, which was bare and pale against the dark flannel sheets. The day had been warm, but nights in the cabin were cool. Thunder rattled across the sky again and shook the roof. Rain started to patter down once again, and I noticed that Katherine's snores had stopped. She rolled over to face me in the dark, her eyes luminous in the pale light, like a cat's eyes.

"When did that start?" she whispered.

"About five minutes ago. I'm surprised you slept through it for that long."

"It's beautiful."

"The thunder?"

"After being in that enclosed space, large as it was, with all those people, I can't believe how much I missed the sounds of nature. We don't live in the Pacific Northwest because we want year-round sun. We live here for the beauty of the rain."

"And here I was bored out of my mind with no one to talk to the whole time. Why didn't I meet you on my way out of town back then?"

"That fickle bitch fate likes to mess with our lives."

I leaned forward and kissed her. She met my lips, but it felt almost perfunctory, and I wanted to ask her what I was doing wrong. She went through the motions, but something was on her mind.

"Well, thank you for coming back with me. We should really talk about what the hell we're going to do now. I don't want to face an army of those things again, but I want to get to Portland."

"Christ," she sighed heavily. "I remember the first time we ran into them, during the whole initial zombie thing. It was bad enough that we had to put up with these groaning, moaning bastards with no brains that wandered around like lost kids. Alone, they weren't that scary. I mean, you could see them coming a mile away and put a bullet in their skulls. It was around the third week that we felt like we were getting a handle on them. Masses were rounded up and taken away in trucks while we watched. Hometown militias sprang up, and helped take care of problems, if you know what I mean. We still received occasional messages from our political leaders, but they were growing more and more terse."

"Weird. I know what went down, but I never pictured the world would end like that. I guess I expected us to go to war with a heavy hitter and we take each other out with nukes."

"Not morbid at all," Katherine's lips quirked up. "It wasn't really the end. I mean, it isn't now either. It's like a bump in the road. Do you believe in evolution?"

That was a funny question. I wasn't exactly a liberal or a conservative, yet I couldn't say that I was a religious man either. I needed explanations for stuff; I needed to see things to believe in them. The idea that there was some god sitting above me constantly judging my actions and planning to roast my ass in hell if I screwed up didn't make sense. Then again, neither did the dead walking around.

"I think so. People have been changing for thousands of years, getting taller, losing their need for wisdom teeth, stuff like that."

"And the ghouls are the natural offshoots of the zombies. The virus that reanimated the dead and created the mindless things, well, it affected the living in strange ways. It made them like a half-zombie hybrid."

"What started it all? I got a few hints and half stories from Thomas."

"No one's really sure. Lots of theories but no answers. Some said it was a swine flu vaccine that went wrong, others whispered it was a CDC lab in Atlanta that was doing some shady stuff, and one of their scientists spread the infection on purpose. Some said it was terrorists. Some said it was a comet strike stirring up weird stuff in the air. Space spores or something. We spent that whole first week listening to the news channels with talking heads, discussing, theorizing, but we never heard a real cause."

"Someone has to know."

"Maybe it is a form of evolution--a shifting bacterial infection that found a way to get rid of us. AIDS didn't work; the black plague tried it; Ebola was a huge success. Don't get me started on the Covid variants. Maybe all those antibiotic-resistant monsters got together and figured out a way to kick our ass."

"I like your ass right where it is." I pushed myself against her as the rain came down harder than before. It rolled down the side of the house and splashed on the ground, making an ocean of noise.

Lightning lit the sky, and a glance out the window showed tall skeletons in the form of the trees surrounding the cabin. The air felt like it was charged. All those ions bouncing around from the flashes of light in the sky made my hair stand on end. Or maybe it was her shifting against me, under the covers, in that tiny bed.

"Is that right?"

I pushed the mess of hair off her forehead and kissed it gently. She offered me a smile in return. Those hard lines around her eyes softened for a moment, and I felt a genuine sense of affection.

"What did you do before?" I asked. We didn't really talk about who we'd been before the incident. I think it was a byproduct of our current situation. I believe that, on some level, we were avoiding the 'before' because we wanted to concentrate on the now and not on our old lives. Those were long gone.

"I was a teacher. Social studies were my specialty, but I also taught girls' volleyball."

"Makes sense. You fight like a teacher."

She laughed at that, and I grinned at her in the dark.

"I used to study a lot of martial arts. I took some kaji-kempo, and then some other stuff so I could work on my aggression issues. I had..."

I let it hang. I could hear her breathing in the dark, and she stiffened slightly against me.

"You don't have to tell me."

"It's okay. I was hurt once by a man, and I swore that would never happen again, so I learned how to take care of myself."

I stiffened under the blanket. "I'm sorry," I offered lamely. I found I couldn't let the tension go.

"It was a long time ago. Anyway, I learned how to fight, and I never feared a person again. Well, until I saw the zombies and how much damage they can take before they go down."

"Evolution again?"

"Something like that. The ghouls seem feel pain, and they fall if you shoot them in the head, but a wound just pisses them off. Some are smarter than others, and some seem to be in control. The ones that came at us at the barricade were driven by one of the smart ones. You may think I'm crazy, but we had a theory that the smart ones used some sort of mind control."

"You're kidding, right?"

"They seem to be able to put the ghouls into some sort of hypnotic state. They whip them into a frenzy, and they go crazy for blood. Did you see how they attacked us?"

She was right; they didn't act like the zombies at all. Of course, I only had a few days' worth of experience with the things, while she'd had months. I suppose a form of hypnosis wasn't that much of a stretch. Look how far it got Hitler.

We chatted for a while longer, and she shifted under the blankets against me but didn't seem interested in lovemaking. I was just happy to have her with me, so I didn't press it. Her body was warm against mine, a feeling completely alien to everything I'd known for the last few months. I wrapped my arm around her and, sometime in the night, found solitude in sleep.

TWENTY

Morning came in with the same overcast gray. I struggled up to a sitting position and noticed she had put on a shirt sometime during the night. Katherine slept soundly while I rose and donned shorts and a tank top. The night may have been cold and rainy, but the day was already heating up. My watch was in the kitchen, and I was surprised to see it was after nine. When I was at the compound, we usually woke around seven, but at the cabin I was used to sleeping in--an indulgence I hadn't allowed myself in years.

I dug out some coffee we'd scrounged from the convenience store and built up a fire in the stove. Water boiled, while I used my old method of suspending the grounds in a wrapped-up paper towel and letting it sit for a while. The water passed through my crude filter as it cooked, and within fifteen minutes, I had a fresh pot of Folgers. I grabbed a box of cereal, Lucky Charms, popped it open and sat down to enjoy breakfast.

She came out of the bedroom a half hour later and joined me. Her long legs hung out of the shirt, and she curled one under her body as she sat down. I felt a rush for her--a burst of emotion I could not readily identify. It was a combination of giddiness and warmth, and I wished I could put the feeling into words.

She smiled when I brought her a cup of coffee.

"Cream or sugar?"

"Neither. I'm used to drinking it black. We had a whole section of coffee saved up during the setup phase at the Walmart, and it was almost as closely guarded as the guns."

"Priorities and all..."

I was still getting used to drinking coffee again, having been without it for a few months. I got a quick caffeine buzz today because the brew was dark and very strong. I expected her to turn her nose up at the stuff and tell me it was too thick, but she took a sip, and then another without comment.

She mixed some of the powdered milk with water from a pitcher on the counter and poured it in a bowl with the cereal I was eating. I watched her move around the kitchen looking for things, and I pointed out where I stored items. If I expected her to comment on my place-ment, I was in for a surprise, because she accepted what I had done and went along without a word.

We ate in silence, glancing back and forth between our food and each other.

"How did you find this place?" she asked.

"It was a friend's. I stayed here once with Allison, and it seemed like a good place to hide out while I waited for the world to go to hell."

"Who's Allison?"

"Ex. We came here about two or three years ago and stayed for a week."

She didn't comment.

"So what would you like to do today, honey?" She tacked the last word on with a hint of sarcasm that got a grin out of me.

"I'm concerned about food. The main reason I left the cabin was because I was out, and the stuff we picked up on the way back won't last long. We need to figure out how to survive."

"I have a few ideas."

"Oh yeah?"

SIX LONG STICKS poked out along the lake's edge; bobbers of pinecones and chunks of wood hovered on the calm water while we sat and watched. A bucket of fresh water stood next to the poles in case we caught anything. I had my doubts. During the months I had spent here, I had caught maybe seven or eight fish.

I had also dressed in jeans and left the tank top on. A thick shirt I'd picked up at the Walmart hung unbuttoned. She didn't have any clothes to speak of. Everything she owned had been left behind in the store. The plan had been to rejoin the caravan as it moved away from the city. We didn't count on getting caught in the mess at the barricade.

I tried not to think about the fact that she had thought she was on a suicide mission when we had set out to blow up the tank of gas.

So she wore one of my shirts like a dress and looped a piece of rope around her waist, and a pair of my pants that were too large but she rolled up the pant legs, while hers soaked in a tub of water with a little bit of soap. She and I had set the fishing poles, then dragged down the little chairs from inside the cabin and set them on the wet ground. The legs had sunk into the mud, but we were content to sit on rickety chairs as long as we could watch the poles.

We spoke a little, but for the most part, we just stared at the water. The gulf that separated us was in full effect again, and I wondered if it was I who was holding back.

"Penny for your thoughts," I offered.

"Penny isn't worth much these days."

"It wasn't worth much a year ago either." I smiled.

"I don't know what to do. I'm used to being busy, organizing, teaching the others to fight. I'm used to cleaning, rationing supplies. There isn't really much to do here."

"Except me," I said with a wink.

"And there is that. I know there's an attraction, but I'm a few years older than you, Erik. I can't have kids anymore, and in this new world, we need to repopulate, to replace the numbers we have lost."

"You think I'm gonna run off with someone younger than me just because she can have babies? That's just plain stupid, Katherine. I like you. I like being with you."

"For now. I am a sad and empty woman. I loved the world more than anything, and then the world took away everything that meant anything to me. I hate it now, and if I died tomorrow in a battle with the ghouls, who would remember me? No one, and that's just fine with me."

"I'd remember you for the rest of my life," I said, my voice choked with emotion.

"I'm sorry. I'm just trying to be practical."

"Damn your practical. I'm happy to be with you for as long as you'll have me." I stood up and went to her, took her hands in mine. They were slim and cold, and I felt the edges of the hard calluses on the sides. Leaning over, I offered an awkward hug.

"Got one," she yelled and slipped away. She grabbed the pole with the bobber that had been tugged underwater and hauled out a hard-looking little fish that resembled a catfish. After pulling it up, she ran her hand along the head to hold down the fin, then she took the hook out of its mouth and put the little guy in the bucket.

"Huh." I considered the fish as it swam in circles looking for a way out. We had dug out some worms and grubs and put them in the empty breadbox, so we would have a fresh supply ready all day. The hook went back in the water, and she took a seat to watch the poles. That was how we spent our first day together.

It was coming up on the warmest part of the day when she stripped off her shirt and tossed her panties at me. I hung them on the back of my chair and stared at her body in the daylight. She stepped into the water, having moved the fishing poles aside, hooks removed and stuck in a branch so we could find them easily.

"Goddamn that's cold!" She shivered and hugged her chest.

I shrugged out of my shirt and let my pants join hers. I followed Katherine, and when my feet hit the water, I gasped. It was warm out, but this was very cold water. She flashed a smile at me then moved deeper, so the calm surface came up to her knees.

"Come on and catch me." Some of the tension went out of her, and I followed. She dashed one way as I closed in, and then the other way when I reached for her. She stepped back, and I moved after her. Her eyes gleamed in the fading light, and I felt a rush of emotion for her once again that was hard to explain.

I sank to my ass and my pride shrivel up between my legs. She splashed water at me, and I splashed back. A pair of birds flitted across the surface of the water behind her, then fled to the trees. I wished I had a way to catch them.

Her nipples were hard as little rocks when I caught her and pulled her close. We kissed, and I held her to me so she couldn't get away. The water settled around us, and I thought about making love to her right there, but suspected it was too cold to try, though things below hinted that I was up for the challenge.

"You caught me. Now what are you going to do with me?" She said.

"I guess you're mine now. I think I get to do whatever I like. I mean, as long as you, you know, want me too," I finished lamely.

"That stuff I told you about was a long time ago, Erik. I trust you."

"I'm glad."

I stared past her at the far shore because I thought I had seen movement. A shape that was vaguely manlike moved into the woods, but maybe it was just an animal. I stared for a long time, and she turned in my arms to follow my gaze.

"What is it?"

"I thought I saw something. Probably a deer."

"Hmm, let's go inside where the animals won't see the things I am about to do to you," she purred.

"Wait a minute. I get to do what I want."

"Right. Same thing."

As we left the water I stared at the spot again, and I swear I felt eyes met mine.

TWENTY-ONE

S hadows moved across the wall after I lit candles in the dark. There were a few of them left, and I felt like it was the right thing to do--a romantic gesture. She stretched on the bed as I moved around the room with the lighter.

Earlier we had hauled in a half dozen fish Katherine had helped catch, and then split them and fried them in a bit of olive oil I had saved. There were spices in the cabinets, things that had expired, but they tasted fine. Salt and pepper with a dash of powdered garlic that was so old it was turning white. The fish were delicious, and we ate a couple of them. We boiled beans and ate them with the fish, and when we were done, I soaked the pan in some water and took her back to bed.

We lay together again as I tried to find sleep. Her hand was draped across my waist this time, and every once in a while, she would flinch, like she was nodding off. I wanted to sleep, but my mind was on all the things that had happened. Spring was on the way, and I was pretty sure we would be able to live on the stuff we caught here. Hunting would turn up some deer, and we would have meat, but we wouldn't have any produce--no vegetables or fruit. We had some powdered milk, but not a lot, and the calcium would be sorely missed.

Unless we could find some fruit, I worried about us getting scurvy, the way sailors used to when they were at sea for lengths of time. Lack of vitamin C might be worse than lack of anything else. We may have to venture out and try to find an old off the road drug store that had multi-vitamins.

I started to drift off as well, but something drew my eye to the window. The moon made the outside world murky at best, but the lack of outside light meant there was nothing to reflect off the glass in the cabin, so I had a good view out the window directly across from us. We could have constructed some sort of curtains, but there was no need for privacy out in the middle of nowhere.

Shadows drifted--diffuse shapes that eluded trees and ringed the cabin like silent sentinels. My eyes were drawn to a copse far away. I could just make it out in the dim light, and I could also make out a shape that I thought had green eyes, which stared into my own. I gasped and sat up in bed, clenched my eyes together then stared again, but the shape was gone.

"IT WAS PROBABLY a deer plotting to set a trap for you," Katherine said the next morning.

We were enjoying breakfast, such as it was. She sat across from me, having woken earlier, and made coffee and some flat but delicious pancakes. We didn't have anything to make the things rise, and she used some Cheerios, ground up, to make the mess stick together before baking them in the oven. The coffee was strong, and I enjoyed several cups.

She wore one of my shirts again and nothing else, and it looked a hell of a lot better on her than on me.

Katherine cracked the windows, so a breeze rolled through the cabin and out the open door. I thought of the shape I had seen the night before, but discounted it as not being real. We were too secluded to attract one of those things.

Then again, why hadn't I run some sort of snares or alarms? Bottles hanging from twine might be just the thing to give me a heads up. I would have to scour the cabin for items to use. There are probably enough bottles left over from the preserves to make something. The biggest problem would be covering the entire area around the cabin.

I tossed the rest of my coffee back, wandered to the back window, and stood there for some time. The trees made it hard to see far, so I crouched down to the level where I'd been when I saw the figure and stared for a long time. I found the copse and watched it. Birds flitted from tree to tree, and I heard the unmistakable call of a hawk as it soared somewhere over the woods. It was green, pastoral, and I felt at ease once again. The sense of normalcy, the comfort of having Katherine with me, sank in, and I smiled at my imagined apparition, then went to join her in the other room. The smell was all Pacific Northwest. Trees and fresh dirt. Moisture in the air. Everything just as normal as it should be.

"No monsters?" She sat on the chair, legs crossed demurely while she sipped her coffee.

"Not that I can see."

"Then come and kiss me."

THE TRAIL WAS hard to pick out. I had been this way a few times while hunting last year, but it was far from the lake, and I didn't think I would have much luck hunting here. Now, with food being scarce and necessary for the two of us, I would settle for cooking squirrels if I was fast enough to take one down.

I was dressed in my jeans and a long flannel shirt. She wore her jeans and a shirt of mine belted at the waist. Katherine had to roll up the sleeves, and she wore one of cabin owner Ray's camouflage caps. She followed behind me, hunting rifle pointing at the ground. I had my trusty 12-gauge in hand and one of the handguns in the waistband of my pants.

"I think it was near here," I said as we eased through the low vegetation. I was still trying to convince myself I hadn't seen anything at all-- just a trick of the light, a ghostly mirage brought on by mist and the low moon.

The air was crisp and clear, and the smell of evergreens was pungent. There were fallen pinecones to crunch across, wild blackberry branches to step over and push aside. Too bad it wasn't closer to summer. With the coming crop of berries, we could solve our vitamin C problem and have a sweet treat. She kept an eye on the ground, because she wanted to find some tubers and cook them.

I dropped to my knees as if I knew what I was doing, looking for footprints or broken vegetation near the ground. Nothing stood out, so I moved around the spot, but still nothing caught my eye. I didn't really know what to look for anyway. I was far from a scout. In fact, if a game trail jumped up and bit me, I wouldn't know what to do with it.

"See. It was nothing," she said as she moved behind me.

"I know, but thanks for humoring me."

"No problem. Maybe all the living out here alone for so long got to you. I'm just glad you aren't running around naked in clown paint yelling that the cavalry's coming. A person needs companionship."

"Well, I have you now. You'll just have to stick around for a while and make sure I'm not crazy." I grinned at her. "I was thinking of creating an alarm. Just some fishing wire with bottles. It would alert us if something was trying to get to the cabin."

"Good idea. There's a lot of land to cover. How're you going to differentiate between game and a green-eyed asshole?"

I shrugged. She had a good point. We should be so lucky as to have a buck wander near the cabin and alert us to his presence. He might as well show up with a dinner bib on.

Later I took to my old hunting spot with the rifle jot lucky when a deer wandered along the path. We dragged the whole thing back to the cabin and butchered it. She even sipped at some of the blood, so I joined her. When I looked up at her, I recoiled. She reminded me of the ghouls we'd fought just a few days ago with the blood dripping down her mouth and chin.

I shuddered and looked away.

WE CUT UP THE MEAT, and then she showed me how to make strips, so we could smoke them. I made a fire outside, and we used an old barrel lined with small branches to chamber the smoke. We put as much meat in as we could, and let it sit outside all evening. We had fresh steaks, and then I made a stew with some of the meat and rice. It wouldn't last long. In fact, none of the meat would.

"We can't stay here," I said.

"I know. We have no way to refrigerate stuff, and if we don't cure the meat before smoking it, we run the chance of getting sick. We would need a lot of salt for that."

"Do you think we should go back to that store and see if we can find some?"

"It's worth a try, but I think we should try for Portland."

I had to agree with her. The thought of staying in the cabin was one I found hard not to love. I wanted to spend as much time as I could with her. I wanted to make her happy and show her how much she meant to me now that she had rescued me from loneliness. She stared into my eyes in a challenging way. I think that if I'd said no, she would have tried to go without me.

"I think so too. It's a good idea to go soon, since we may have wiped out a lot of those ghouls from town. We can probably zip through that barricade, or what's left of it, and then set out after the group."

She leaned over and kissed me, but I caught a hint of sadness in the gesture. I looked away, because I was reminded of Pat's sacrifice at the barrier.

We buried the remains of the deer a quarter mile from our home. I went out with an old shovel while she straightened up the cabin. I put all the parts in an old, black plastic bag I had been using for various functions and dragged it away. The thing had a hole in it somewhere, so it leaked a trail of blood behind me. At first, I tried to flip the bag over, but it was overloaded, and I was afraid it would break. I tried to cover it up by kicking leaves and pine needles over the stain, but I knew it was useless. A predator would smell the blood from a mile away.

I found a patch of ground and went at it with the shovel. It was hard, and there were a lot of roots in the way. I had to really work at it, but it felt good to stretch my muscles. At one point, I found a thick root and went back to the cabin for my axe. I tugged it from under the edge of a bench on the porch. When I looked in the window, I saw Katherine with her back to me. She was standing in the kitchen, staring out the window. I watched her for almost a minute, but she didn't move. Then her hand went to her forehead, and her shoulders move up and down before she brushed at her eyes.

I walked back to the hole and finished with some judicious use of the sharp blade. I found it very hard to put myself in her shoes, to imagine losing my entire family to those things. I knew that it made her a bit of a wildcard. During the battle at the barricade, Katherine had been gleeful while she had fired into the ghoul ranks. As we had driven away, she had swerved to hit some of them with my car.

I looked up, because I had a strange feeling between my shoulder blades, like someone just ran a feather over my skin. I'd had that feeling before, a few times, when the action had been hot in Afghanistan. Ducking had usually been the thing to do, reacting to the strange sixth sense that we humans had when being watched.

I spun in a circle as I studied the thick vegetation. It was probably Katherine coming to get me for help with something, but I knew in my guts it was something else.

TWENTY-TWO

"Is that you, Katherine?"

Nothing.

I walked around the spot and looked toward the cabin. I sighed, dumped the bag in the hole, and pushed dirt over it. Covered in sweat, I slipped my shirt off, just as I heard movement in the distance. I snapped my gaze up and could have sworn I saw a man walking away from the site, a good fifty feet away. Goosebumps burst out all over my body, and I reached to the back of my pants for the gun.

Only I had left the gun at the cabin.

I should have gone back and grabbed a weapon, gotten Katherine, made sure it wasn't her I had seen. I should have done a lot of things, but instead I picked up the axe and walked toward the place where I had seen the shape. I moved as quietly as I could for a man in size 12 iron-toed boots, which wasn't very quietly at all. Branches and twigs crunched under me, as did pinecones and green needles left to rot.

A pair of birds shot out of the woods ahead. I gasped when they took flight but kept my cool. If I had my shotgun, I might have dropped them and had roast bird tonight.

There was a small clearing ahead, and I stopped to look around, turning in a full circle. I listened when I didn't see anything, just stood in place with my eyes closed, but nothing ... wait. Was that a keening sound?

It reminded me of a dog or something, maybe caught in a trap. As much as I had traipsed over this area, it was still possible that I missed a snare left by a hunter. If it was a raccoon, I wasn't sure what I would do. I'd probably have to kill it rather than face getting bitten trying to set it free.

I moved toward the sound, which came from the direction of the sinking sun. The bright light blinded me, so I shaded my eyes with one hand as I crept up on the location.

I came upon a man dressed in rags who had become ensnared by a tree trunk. His hair was disheveled and full of twigs and pine needles. How long had he been out here? His jacket was green, which explained why it had been so hard to see him. It wasn't camouflage, but the color was just the sort of green to make a person's eyes slip past it in the woods.

"Are you okay?" I asked in a low tone already knowing that he wasn't. He turned and his vacant eyes met mine.

The zombie moved slowly and moaned at me. His face was a nightmare of wounds, I guessed from walking through the woods and getting his face scratched, or maybe he'd been attacked by animals. I supposed if you don't feel pain, you don't really care about twigs whipping against your face and body.

I shuddered at the thought, then I got a look at his mouth, which was dry and covered in old blood. This contrasted against the blue lips and jagged, yellow teeth. He continued to turn and shuffle at the same time. He keened in that tone I had heard earlier, taking it for an animal. The analytical part of my brain pondered how the thing could make noise like that when he clearly wasn't breathing. His jacket was open, and his shirt was in shreds. He even had a gaping wound in his gut, and out of that horror fell a mass of maggots and things that would haunt my sleep that night. He tried to stagger forward but remained caught. I backed up and wanted to run. I wanted to go back to the cabin and forget about what I had seen. I wanted to run screaming, then come back with one of the assault rifles and blow this horror away.

Instead, I unlimbered the axe. I held it in two hands and regarded my opponent. Though it offered no real fight, I had to kill the thing on principle alone. When I was back in Vesper Lake, I had been fighting for my life. Now I was just doing preventive maintenance. It had to be done for our safety; I would put a rabid dog down the same way.

I lifted the axe high above my head. The back of it was flat, and I hoped it would splatter less if I hit him on the temple, and then crushed his skull while he was on the ground. I lowered the haft in a horizontal plane to the ground, watching him raise one arm toward me like an automaton. Then he tugged forward, and with a rip, the man's jacket tore as he staggered toward me.

I swung too late and hit him in the shoulder, which pushed him to the side. He spun nearly around with the impact, but turned again to come at me. I backed up, stepped on a fallen branch, and stumbled backward. Reaching out with one hand, I found nothing to catch me, so I had to take a few steps to recover. He came at me, eyes livid and teeth bared. He moaned, and the remains of his jagged teeth and torn lips were the only things I managed to focus on.

If he touched me with those teeth, I would be dead before I could curse him. Just a bite--that was all it took. I would have enough time to fall over before he was tearing into my flesh, and in the event I managed to fight him off, I would still have the wound to contend with.

Giving in to gravity, I fell back, landing on my ass in a heap. I rolled to the left as quickly as I could, dropping the axe in the process. Before his hands came up to grab me, I was back on my feet. I pushed his arms down then thrust him away. As he spun to the right, I planted my boot in the small of his back and kicked him back the way he had come.

I panted hard from the rush of adrenaline, from the sudden exertion, and from the fear that was ripping at my brain like a bird of prey. I looked for the axe, but it was lying in the brush, and I was frightened of going for it. I didn't want to take my eyes off him for even a second. I kicked him again, harder this time. He was driven into the tree, and, as he staggered away, he went down. He made no attempt to break his fall; he just flopped over like a rag doll.

Staring up at me, he cocked his head to the side and went for my right leg. His teeth bared in a rictus that looked plastered in place. This thing wore one expression, and that was anger.

I lifted my boot and smashed his face. The second one caved in his head. He still flopped his hands around and kicked at the ground like a struggling animal. The third kick cracked his skull like a giant egg, and soft brain matter flowed around my foot, so that I slipped and almost fell down for the second time that morning.

I staggered back and rubbed the bottom of my shoe on the soft vegetation, as if I could wipe away the guilt of what I had just done to the man. I wanted to throw up my breakfast. I wanted to run back to the cabin and hide in the bedroom for the rest of the day.

I backed away from the twice dead corpse.

"God have mercy, and all that," I muttered.

I turned away and went back to the hole I had dug and finished the job. Pushed dirt over the remains of the deer, stared at the ground for a few minutes, looked back at the place where I had crushed a man's skull.

How in the hell had the guy found this place? Was there another cabin nearby? Were there more of them? I should have taken a moment to walk the area and check for them, but I needed a gun for that. I wasn't eager to engage in hand-to-hand combat again anytime soon.

"Fuck," I swore as I realized I now needed to dig another hole.

I returned to the cabin, and Katherine was herself once more-- composed, cool, and relaxed, except for the tightness around her eyes. How I wanted to ask her about the sadness that had come over her, about the pain that made her hold back, but I was too afraid of the answers to those questions.

Sighing, I went to collect a gun and some ammo. I told her what had happened in the woods, and she agreed that we should sweep the immediate area. I took one of the handguns, a .40-caliber pistol, and checked the load. The magazine was full, so I tucked it into my belt and loaded my shotgun with as many shells as I could shove in there. Then I tucked a few into my pockets.

She took a 9 mm to cover me, slinging the hunting rifle over her shoulder. I wished we had another shotgun, for up-close work if we needed to fight. The spread would be devastating with both of us shooting. She held the pistol at her side as we left the cabin. I wished I could lock it, but we had never found a key. It was silly. The thing that had attacked me in the woods was surely a lone incident, a lone man—zombie—lost in the woods, and I just happened to stumble upon him. Maybe he had lived somewhere nearby, another cabin or lodge, perhaps.

Maybe he had some vague recollection of the area and was just lost. He was probably the same shape I had seen the night before.

We walked outside the cabin and established a perimeter a hundred feet in every direction. The day was cool, which suited me just fine. I was too amped up to deal with heat today.

We found—nothing, and I was more than a bit relieved. We went back to the cabin, both exhausted after stomping over the vegetation, through bushes, and over piles of needles. She held a compass and was good with the device and kept us on the perimeter at all times. Katherine would point back in the direction of the cabin with a grin every time I looked worried about how far we had gone.

We passed the car, looked it over, and then walked to the road as the last part of our reconnoiter. I hugged the bushes while Katherine stood back and covered me. Unmoving, I kept an eye on the entry for a few minutes. My focus roving around, I listened and watched, but I didn't see anything out of the ordinary. With a heavy sigh, I turned and smiled at her, so she joined me at the gate.

"I hope he was the only one."

"Me too. I don't want to go through that again."

"You've killed them before. What's the big deal?" Her voice was as dead as the thing in the woods I had smashed into the dirt. I regretted the killing, but she seemed blasé, as if taking a human life was the norm.

"I did, but that doesn't mean I liked it."

"You get used to it."

She spun on her heel and walked up the road toward the cabin.

TWENTY-THREE

That night was much as the last, except we talked about where we should go next. They had put some gas in the Honda at the fort, but it wouldn't last long enough to get us around the mountain from this side. We would probably have to head back to Vesper Lake and try to get through the city. I was hoping that if we could keep up enough speed, we would be able to just zip through the tiny town, and then get on the freeway and follow the caravan before a horde figured out where we were going. They should be in Portland now, enjoying the good life. I bet it was all smiles, flowing beer, and plates of hot food. *Or at least something to eat,* I thought as I chewed on a hunk of dried deer meat that had a strong smoke flavor and nothing else.

We lay in bed, side by side, my head near her ear. Her hair frizzed out, probably from not having any sort of conditioner. I tried to imagine what she had been like before the event, but I had trouble picturing her as a classic soccer mom with a minivan and kids in the back.

"When we reach a place with more people, I'll understand if you want to leave me and find someone else." She spoke softly into her pillow, barely above a whisper.

"I don't want to be with anyone else," I assured her, tugging her naked body closer to me under the sheets. She was so soft and warm under the blanket that I wanted to stay this way for a week.

"I can't have children," she reminded me after a quiet moment.

"I don't care. I don't have any, and never put much thought into the idea of having them anyway."

"But it would be irresponsible, Erik. How many people are dead out there? We need everyone to help repopulate the world. I don't have a place in that world. I can't contribute a child."

"Katherine, you aren't a breeding machine. No one is. Life will return no matter what and no matter who I want to be with. I don't want to run around and bang rows of girls in the hopes of getting one pregnant. There will be plenty of horn dogs up for that job." I tried to make a joke of it, but she didn't laugh.

"It's not funny. All the children are dead, so many are just ... gone. We need to have more, and I can't help. I had cervical cancer, but Frank didn't care. He and I had two already, and we were happy." She sobbed into the pillow, and I held her close. It was the first time she had mentioned the name of one of her family.

I didn't know what to say. I was going to tell her I loved her, and I think I did. I certainly had strong feelings for her, but was it enough to overcome this ... this insecurity? Her body shook, and she pressed her head deeper into the down pillow and tried to stifle the sobs. I wanted to tell her everything would be okay, but there was no way to know that with certainty.

"Kat, I ..."

A pair of green eyes stared into the window from less than twenty feet away.

"Oh fuck!" I stifled the exclamation at the last second. I was out of bed in another second, and into my pants before the glow disappeared. Snatching up the shotgun from where it rested near the bed, I checked the load while I was getting into my boots.

Katherine came to her feet, and the blankets piled around the middle of the bed, while she stared at me like I had seen a ghost. I *had* seen a ghost, or a ghoul, to be precise. And the son of a bitch was right outside the cabin.

"Ghoul," I whispered, and she dropped down to find her clothes. I tossed the gun on the bed, shrugged into a shirt, and buttoned up the top. I glanced outside as I moved, watching for the green thing in the bushes, but it was gone.

I raced to the front of the cabin with Katherine close behind. She didn't even question; she just grabbed the handgun, popped the magazine and double-checked it was full, slammed it into the piece, and then slid the top back to load a round. She followed as she performed the movements, all smooth, all by the book.

I checked the windows, ducking low as I did so, but I sucked in a breath and stood up. Those things didn't use guns; they attacked en masse and didn't care for the consequences or losses. They were one step above mindless zombies--the monsters that had started the whole event. I hoped it was just one of the damn ghouls. I didn't know how we would defend against a hundred of them. It had to be one, just like the zombie I killed in the woods earlier. It had to be a single ghoul, lost and alone in the woods.

Maybe I was just seeing things, just imagining the man with green eyes, the shape in the woods, and the impression of someone watching me with Katherine in bed. With a tight grip on the shotgun, I strode to the front door and slid it open.

I had the irrational dread that they would overrun us, take us, eat our flesh, or change us into them. The details on the ghouls had been scarce, but Thomas had told me enough to scare me. He told me about how the things had become smarter, how they had seemed to be making plans and following through with them. How they drove the first zombies before them like an army. An army of the dead.

I aimed the gun in the wan light, but all I saw were half shapes-- shadows of things that were barely visible in the three-quarter moon. The trees around the cabin made it twice as hard to see, rendering it darker than it should be.

I wanted the darkness now; I wanted to fade into it and hunt the monster down. It was just a dead man who would soon have no head. They didn't have any special powers, and they certainly didn't possess strength beyond that of a human. What they did have, from what I had witnessed in my few skirmishes with them, was a rage that went beyond anything I had ever seen before. Soldiers on the front line didn't even act that insane. The ghouls had shrugged off wounds, gunshots, kicks to the head, and came on more pissed off than before.

"Where are you?" I whispered to myself as I panned the gun around the area.

I heard Katherine moving behind me on the porch. I risked a glance back, and found her leaning against a post that supported the porch roof, so she blended into the darkness like part of the cabin.

She blinked, her eyes bright white against the dark.

Turning, I took a step toward the woods and stopped right at the edge. I stood as still as I could for a few minutes, but I didn't hear any movement. I was prepared to admit I had been seeing things; one of those dreams you have in the day when you close your eyes for a few minutes. I had probably slipped into that half realm of half-sleep and didn't even realize it. But as I prepared to go back to the cabin, there was movement.

It was to the right, so I swung the gun that way. Then movement to the left. I backed up a step and panned the gun around me. Whipping my head around, I tried to focus on one sound, but movement in front of me threw me off.

Katherine gasped behind me. She had taken a step down the stairs and stood on the bottom one, staring away from me, into the darkness. Following her gaze, I saw a figure move into the moonlight. It was a woman in torn clothing, and she moved like she was injured. I ran in that direction, gun locked against my shoulder.

"Hey, hey! Don't come any closer." I knew the words were stupid right after they came out of my mouth. She was a zombie--had to be. Living people didn't move like that. That slow, shambling half-stagger like a drunk trying to look sober—but less coordinated.

I didn't get a chance for further inquiries, as Katherine pulled the gun up to eye level, aimed, and put one right between the woman's eyes. She stopped as if in shock, then sank to her knees and fell face forward into the dirt.

I spun around as something crunched across the grass, catching sight of an enormous man with no shirt, who moved in slow motion. He was dressed like a farmer—overalls on, suspenders half off his massive frame. His mouth was missing its jaw, and ribbons of flesh swayed from his head, just like they did at his open gut. I followed my girlfriend's actions by raising the gun and blowing his head off.

No matter what you think about me from reading this tale, I take no pleasure in killing. I flinched when I did it. I don't think taking a life is an action that anyone should ever contemplate, let alone perform. But it was necessary, and the fact that they weren't exactly alive helped propel me along the path to becoming a mass murderer.

His head half-disappeared, and he fell backwards as the buckshot threw him off his feet.

Katherine's gun popped a couple of times behind me, so I spun around. She was contending with a pair of zombies that came out of the woods. From what I saw of them, it looked like they were on a hiking trip before they died. An older man and woman, both covered in blood. He stooped as he staggered, and, despite missing an arm, his backpack remained on one shoulder. He carried it low, like some bizarre hunchback.

They both dropped, and I had to back up as three more came out of the woods toward me. Curse the night. It made them almost impossible to see unless they were right in front of us. I fired low, intent on at least hitting them if I couldn't make a headshot. I was backing toward the cabin, gun level, and I knew that Katherine had my back. The gun fired again, this time twice, and one more of the things dropped.

I moved toward her, toward the sounds she made as she lifted the gun and fired. At one point, I thought I was right next to the cabin, but I was much farther away than I estimated, and I took a look back. I met her eyes, and they gleamed in the dark. While I hated killing the people in front of us, she loved it.

Then I swung my attention back as more of the zombies came at us, and behind them came a flash in the dark of green eyes. I aimed in that direction and sprayed with buckshot, even though he was about forty feet away. I didn't really stand a chance of killing him, but I would settle for a wound, maybe a lucky eyeful of shot.

"In the cabin," she yelled, and I turned and hit the step. Then I reconsidered. If we went inside and a huge flood of the things arrived, we would be stuck, forced to defend four sides against them, because as soon as the windows broke, they would be on us. If the dead things weren't driven by the ghoul, I was pretty sure we could disappear in the cabin and they would go away, not bothering to look inside.

"Let's get out of here, Katherine. Let's get in the Honda and go!"

"Where are the keys?"

"Kitchen. Right next to the stove in the big wooden bowl."

"Okay."

She dashed through the open door and stumbled. Then something fell over. At least five of them closed in on the cabin, but I was busy shoving shells into the shotgun.

"How many more shotgun shells do we have?" I yelled at the door. Rifle loaded, I put it to my shoulder and shot one of the things in the throat, which punched it off its feet. I jacked another shell in, lifted the gun, aimed carefully, and took a zombie's head off.

The darkness was getting to me. The blasts of the gun stole my sight away each time I fired, and there was no time to recover before I had to fire again. I stayed at the foot of the stairs and waited patiently for Katherine. I heard her back into something else in her haste. We didn't really put things anywhere with any logic, and I cursed the poor planning. Usually, I was much better at that kind of stuff, but I wasn't seeing the future as brightly as I should have. I should have been better prepared. Should have, could have, and would have—no use in dwelling on mistakes.

"I can't see!" she yelled as she threw things around in the dark. The gunshots had to have stolen her eyesight as well, and it would be a while before she had her night vision back. I'd have given about a million dollars for a pair of night vision goggles right about then.

One was almost on me when I shot him in the chest. At least I think it was a he. The figure was just a blur in the dark. It moaned, deep and long. I spun to my right and dropped another one. Some of the shot went wide, taking one of the zombies behind this one in the leg. That zombie fell and started crawling toward me.

"Got 'em!" she yelled. I wondered if she'd gotten more bullets or the keys or both. She came dashing out, just in time to drop a zombie dressed in bright orange sweats that helped her stand out a little in the dark.

Katherine handed me a fresh box of shotgun shells. I dropped to a crouch, and dumped the container on the ground. Big shells went everywhere, and I scooped them up, putting them in my pockets as fast as I could. She covered me, ejecting a magazine, and sliding one home in one quick motion.

"Let's go, Erik!" She yelled and shot one of the zombies in the face. There had been a trickle before, but now there were a dozen more. I took off, her holding my hand and covering me as I ran for the car. There were a few ahead of us, but it seemed like most had been headed toward the cabin.

A few more raving creatures appeared as we ran in the dark, but for the most part, it was a clear path. We dodged a pair that stumbled past, and then I shot one in the face when he drifted in front of us from a section of the road.

The Honda was just ahead. I could make out its shape as we ran. We put on a burst of speed. The car was soon surrounded by moving forms. We were in even deeper trouble. I raised the gun and shot one that was shambling in our direction, but more walked toward the vehicle.

Katherine must have followed my focus, because she emptied the magazine in the thing's direction, then slammed in a replacement just as quick as a whip. She had one hand on me, on my shoulder, so I was guiding us in the dark. I had to rely on the poor moonlight as I pounded over ground covered in gravel and bits of wood. One wrong move and we would be eating dirt.

A shot rang out, and Katherine stumbled against me. She let out a cry. I slowed and turned to see if she had tripped on something, but she was holding her arm. In the moon's faint glow, her eyes showed shock.

TWENTY-FOUR

"What happened?"

"Shot! Someone fucking shot me!"

"That's not possible. Those things can't use guns."

"Well, someone in the woods has my number, because I've been shot." She groaned and stumbled against me.

"Shit!" I ran ahead and fired off a few blasts, dropping zombies as they staggered toward me. The smell of gunshot and blood was heavy in the air. The undercurrent of pine and spruce couldn't disguise it. I wondered if I would be smelling blood tonight in a more intimate way. My own blood, as my flesh was torn from my body.

I hugged Katherine to me as I stumbled into the back of the SUV. The barrel of the gun clanged against the top of the vehicle. I had half a mind to dive in the back, grab the M249 and open fire.

A crash behind me told me they were in the cabin. Stuff smashed against the floor. They weren't my things, but I still felt a sense of loss at the intrusion into our lives, into my new home.

I groaned and maneuvered Katherine to the passenger side seat. One of the bastards came out of the dark, so I lifted one leg and kicked straight out, smashing the undead man in the chest with about two hundred pounds of pressure. The kick was under control, yet panic rode my body like a wave. I felt it cresting in my chest and threatening to bubble to the surface. I knew how to react to it, how to hone and form it into nothing but pure violence.

I was around the car in a flash as she slammed the door shut. From the other side, Katherine fired once, groaned, and then fired again. I was in the driver's side seat in a pair of heartbeats, and I slammed the door in one of their faces. A man about my age, who was missing an eye and all his teeth. From his gums hung strips of flesh that flapped when he opened and shut his mouth like he was chewing on a tough piece of meat.

I shivered at the dreadful image, then thrust the door open and into his face. He fell back, and I slammed the door closed again. Katherine clutched her shoulder with one hand as she grimaced and tried not to cry out in pain. I took the keys from my pocket and found the familiar Honda key with shaking fingers. It slid it in, and I waited for the inevitable part of the movie where the car wouldn't start. It always happened when two people were in a vehicle and creatures were closing in, but this time we were greeted by the small but powerful engine kicking over. I turned on the headlights and gasped at the mass of zombies.

The front of the car was not covered by metal as the windows were, and I wondered if I would be able to make it through the dead. I counted three of them directly in front of the car and at least five or six more behind those.

I swallowed, pushed the panic down again, and directed my energy toward a cool and calm violence--something at which I was becoming very good. I eased the car forward until the bumper pushed into the first pair of monstrosities, then gave it some gas to nudge them. One spun away to the right, but the other went down in an uncoordinated mass of limbs. I drove over him, his body responding with a sickening crunch. I pressed on, one body at a time, until we had pushed aside or flattened all before us, but a quick glance in the rearview mirror revealed a couple of them in pursuit.

They weren't moving fast, but they were interested only in us, and I couldn't help but feel like they were being driven toward us. I noticed green and felt the urge to grab the machine gun, pop the top, and lay into him. I couldn't risk it, however; not with Katherine bleeding next to me. With every bump, she groaned, and more than once cried out in pain. I reached over and put my hand on her leg, but she didn't respond to my gestures.

We made it to the gate, and I ignored it, assuming we would never return, and this time punched the gas. I took out one more of the zombies and smashed through the wooden planks as if they were kindling. The green aura faded behind me as I swung the car to the right, so that the ghoul was no longer in my rearview mirror. I set my speed at thirty-five and, when the road was clear, took it up another ten miles per hour. I hadn't gone this way and didn't know what to expect. I had driven toward town before, and that didn't turn out so well, so I went the other way. I had no idea where this led, except deeper into the mountains.

"Are you okay?" I asked.

"It hurts," she whispered

I drove on as indecision gnawed at me. After another mile, I pulled over to the side of the road and had a chuckle at myself--at my old habit of getting out of the way. No one was going this way except us. I bet I could have stayed there for a day and not have spotted another soul in an automobile.

"Let me see." I turned on the overhead light, which barely illuminated the interior. It was dim and dull, as if the light bulb were going out.

"Just drive," she said softly.

Turning, I took her bloody hand in mine. I pulled it down gently as I stared into her eyes. She held on at first, gripping her sweatshirt like it was her prized possession. Then, after a very brief battle of wills, she gave in and let down her guard. I tugged at the shirt as gently as I could, but she winced and gasped as I touched the wound.

Her pale skin was marred by the puncture. It puckered out above her shoulder blade, and I worried about fragments of bone exploding from the shot and causing more damage. I tugged her forward and verified that there was an entrance and an exit wound, so at least the bullet wasn't stuck in her. How the hell had this happened?

"Did you see who shot you?" I reached for the glove box and found some old paper towels. Probably left over from the last time I cleaned the car, months and months ago. I tore off the first few and threw them in the back, then folded one into quarters and pressed it to the wound. She cried out and moved to push my hand out of the way, but I batted it aside.

"I'm sorry it hurts. I'm concerned about the blood loss, so please keep these packed close." I tried to sound reassuring, but even a wound this small could be deadly. She needed antibiotics, a doctor, stitching at the very least. I would settle for a vet right about now.

Portland. The name rang in my head, and I knew that was where we needed to go.

"No," she said.

"What?"

"I didn't see who shot me, but it couldn't be one of those things. One of the zombies. It had to be a ghoul, which means they are getting smarter, learning our ways."

"They used to be us. I would say they already know our ways." I folded another paper towel and put it over the back of the wound, then carefully slipped her shirt back over it and put her hand on the wound. "Hold that tight."

She settled back in her seat and held the improvised bandage against her shoulder. I flipped through the glove box and found an old bottle of Advil. I wasn't sure if it would thin her blood out, but a couple might at least take the edge off. I rattled the bottle in her direction, and she gave me a half-smile. Opening the lid, I asked her if she wanted two.

"Give me four."

Nodding, I handed them over, and she dry swallowed the pills. I grew thirsty watching her suck them down. I would have given anything for a glass of ice-cold water.

Starting the car, I looked back the way we had come. If I went forward, we might drive for hours before I found a way out of the gorge between the mountains. If I went the other way, I knew we could make it back to Vesper Lake, but I was sure it would be just as bad as the last time I was there, when the things almost got me. Now I would be with someone who was wounded, which meant keeping a constant eye on her. I couldn't count on help from the Walmart crew; they should all be long gone. I would have to get to town and find a back way out of it without attracting too much attention.

"I think we need to head back to town, pass through and either catch up with the caravan or get to Portland and meet up with Thomas and the rest of the Walmart crew."

"How are we going to get out of there without the things tearing us apart? I know how many there are, and how much they want our blood. There's no way, Erik. No way."

"I'll have to find a way around," I said, glancing at the gas tank, which was about a quarter full. I was sure we could get there, and then maybe halfway to Portland. We would have to stop and fill up somewhere. I was thinking that we could drive around and find a trucking station, maybe a car dealership. They always had gas on hand, and we only needed four or five gallons to get us there. The problem was that we could well run out before we found a place to fill up.

"It's dangerous."

"So is letting you bleed to death."

"I won't bleed to death. It's slowing now; the paper towels are helping."

Leaning over, I kissed her. Her lips were cold, and she was tense from the pain. I turned up the heat and put the car in gear. After doing a one-eighty, I punched the gas. The metal plates on the outside of the vehicle rattled and groaned as I sped up.

We went past the road that led to the cabin, and I glanced up it, but in the dark I couldn't make out anything. There could be fifty of them and I wouldn't know it.

I kept Katherine's gun at my side as I drove up the freeway. I was still concerned about things on the road—abandoned cars or rocks, people, zombies, or even ghouls--so I kept the speed down. She sat beside me, in silence, suffering. I set the gun in my lap and took the wheel with my left, then put my hand on her leg to comfort her. I could feel her staring at me, and when I looked over, she was watching me in the pale light. Her eyes were almost luminous, and I felt very deeply for her in that moment. I felt that I should tell her how much I cared about her, but I was afraid she would not return my feelings.

Out of habit, I turned on the radio and scanned the channels. I found the station that was playing old songs again, and I was surprised when she sang along with Rock and Roll Hoochie Koo under her breath. Having been hurt before, I knew how it felt to want to keep your mind on anything but the pain. I took a knife to the arm once in a brawl in a place I'm not supposed to talk about. Oh hell, who am I fooling? No one gives a shit about that stuff anymore.

TWENTY-FIVE

The road was lonely, cold, and desolate. A chill seeped through the windshield in icy mockery of the car's heater. I wanted to reach out and touch the glass, feel the dread that waited on the other side, but I kept my eyes on the road and ran along at a steady speed. When we were a mile or two from town, I took a left and went down a main road that ran parallel to the highway. I slowed down but kept my high beams on.

The road was draped in a curtain of trees. They were already starting to encroach on the asphalt, and I figured that in a year it would be completely overgrown. The road itself was covered in branches, leaves, trash, and the bones of things I wished were animals. There were also corpses pushed into ditches and hanging out of cars. In some cases, it appeared people had died in their vehicles, or their heads were blown off while trying to get out. It was all a harsh reminder of the fate we had escaped.

Coming around a bend, I realized I was close to the highway again. I shut down the high beams and slowed. I tried to weave over the road in an attempt to pick out any ghouls, but it was bare, with the exception of trash and a couple of abandoned cars. A door on one car stood wide open, and an old, skeletal hand draped over the broken window frame. I avoided looking at it, slowing the car further as we came up on the site where we blew up the fuel truck.

I eased the car to a stop and left the engine running. Grabbing the assault rifle from the back, I opened the door with a quick glance behind then slid outside.

The car's engine purred along as I stepped onto the cold asphalt. The metal frames the engineers had put on the vehicle rattled gently, and I realized that when I was at speed, it probably sounded like a Mack truck from the outside.

I wished, once again, for night vision goggles, but I might as well have wished for an army at my back. I slapped the rifle's stock to my shoulder and crept forward.

The night was cold, and it felt like a thousand eyes were on me, just waiting for the signal to run in and tear me limb from limb. Mindless things ripping my flesh apart in an attempt to find some sort of life in my blood--the life they lacked.

I was about ten feet away when the headlights from the Honda revealed that part of the road was gone. Parts of the truck—a skeleton really--lay in a heap, like some god had picked it up and slammed it into the ground. I studied the road, and even broke out my small pocket light to walk the perimeter of the blast.

The hole wasn't deep, but it was immense. I could imagine the volatile gas rushing out, as air fueled it into an explosion that mushroomed and swept anyone near it into the inferno. Sure enough, there were bodies everywhere--most looked like charcoal caricatures of life.

Most had arms outstretched. It was the blast wave that swept over them that made their arms fly up.

As I walked among the bodies, one of them moved. It was a subtle twitch that almost made me empty a magazine into it. Its mouth was open, and its eye sockets were black and crisped, while its lips pulled back over teeth covered in soot. The head jerked, and I almost screamed. Then the rat, upon sensing me, left the body it was gnawing on and scurried into the night. I watched the animal speed away and had a crazy thought. What if the zombie virus affected them?

Taking a deep breath, I tried to ignore my heart, which was beating a staccato pattern of desperation against my chest. It felt like it wanted to rip itself free. I backed up to the truck, and a howl in the distance set the hairs on the back of my neck at attention.

I slid back into the car and found a gun pointed at my head. Katherine had her pistol drawn and, ignoring the wound in her shoulder, kept that barrel just as steady as I had ever seen her hold it.

"How's the road?" she asked as she lowered the piece.

"Fucked."

"What's plan B?"

"You're assuming I have a plan. I think we'll head for my house. I have some supplies stashed."

"Oh good. I always wanted a nice man to take me home. I hope you have a giant bottle of Vicodin."

I reversed the car, turned around, and took a side road.

We pulled into a scene I had not expected. Granted, it wasn't the idyllic neighborhood where kids play, families stroll, streets are clean and swept, lawns mowed, trash cans left on the curb. Still, it was far from the chaos I had anticipated.

When the world went to shit, I thought for sure there would be roving gangs of people banding together, going house to house as they looked for supplies. My old neighborhood had barely been touched. Sure, there was crap in the streets, but for the most part, it was clean. There was no graffiti, no bodies in the streets, and no houses torn apart.

It had been months since I had been in this part of town. I took a turn, hoping it would look familiar. Instead of finding a block I knew, I found another endless row or cookie cutter houses. The sky ahead had an odd, orange glow. I rolled down the window and stuck my head out as I slowed to just a few miles an hour. It didn't help my view but it brought the smell of smoke.

Something was on fire, something big. I stopped the SUV, and the door groaned from the added weight of the metal armor as it opened. After stepping out, I walked a good ten feet to see if I could make out what was burning. I couldn't find the source, so I got back in the Honda.

I rolled forward very slowly. With the headlights off, the orange glow was my beacon. As I made the turn, I came into view of a house burning out of control. Cars were parked all over the front. One was a huge military transport that I thought was a Stryker.

Shit! This was not what I needed right now. Katherine was hurt. I needed to get to the old house and find my bag of supplies.

I was about to back up when a familiar figure came into view. He was standing on the sidewalk like a conquering general. The burning house lit his frame from behind. Tall, gaunt, and bald. The dead give-away was those damn snakeskin boots that gleamed in the light of the fire.

It was Lee.

A pair of bodies lie on the ground. One of his men was going at one of them. I let out a gasp as I recognized what was happening. They were raping someone. The person on the ground fought, but didn't seem to have much strength. She screamed and reached for the other person, but they didn't move.

So this was what had become of Lee. He was letting his men rape and pillage like it was the middle ages.

"What's happening?" Katherine had her eyes open, and she looked to be in a lot of pain.

"Remember Lee? The guy I have had a few run ins with. He's here, and his men are raping a woman."

She sat up then groaned.

"Stay still." I leaned over to check her dressing.

I placed my hand over hers and pressed. She winced and sat back in the seat.

"What are you going to do?"

I wasn't even sure what I was planning. I had half a mind to shoot Lee. The gun was in my hand, and I would stand a pretty good chance if I stood up and opened the turret.

There was laughter from the men. At least a dozen, maybe as many as fifteen, stood around watching the show. It made me sick, but what had I expected to find? People living together in harmony while the zombies were kept at bay?

I swore quietly then sat back in frustration. Slipping the car into gear, I rolled forward until I was a good twenty-five yards from the house. Reaching into the backseat, I came up with the assault rifle.

"Don't." Katherine snapped.

I stared at her for a few seconds in the pale light, then looked at the men and back at her. What could I do? I was one man and they were so many. It wasn't fair, but I was helpless to stop what was going on.

"Hey!" One of the guys had caught sight of me. I should have backed up when I the chance.

TWENTY-SIX

Guns were pulled and leveled in my direction. With the armor plating, I was somewhat protected, but a stray shot or ricochet would kill me or Katherine just as easily as a direct shot. If I used the turret, I probably wouldn't even get the gun out in time to fire back.

I tossed the M-16 in the backseat and drew my .45 as they came towards me. I backed up, but a couple of them broke into a trot. Then, to my horror, the military transport slid out and blocked my path.

"Shit!" I cried. Katherine had her gun out. Her eyes were wide open.

I would have to go through them.

Indecision made me hesitate. By then, they had stopped in front of the car and several automatics were pointed in my direction. Lee didn't seem to think I was any sort of threat. He strolled toward my SUV like he was out for a Sunday walk.

"Fancy car you got there. What say you get out and my men and I will let you live."

"Fuck you, Lee!" I yelled out the open window.

"Oh. My reputation precedes me. Well, ain't that something. Come on out of there, son, and we can chat. Whatever I did to you, I can let bygones be bygones." He smiled from ear to ear, like a politician at a rally.

"I should have killed you when I had the chance," I said.

He stopped and stared, squinting as he tried to make out my shape in the dark car. I had a small advantage there.

That gave me an idea. If I hit my bright lights and gunned it, we might have a chance.

"You," he said.

"That's right, me. Name's Tragger. We met a few months ago. Back then, you seemed like a man that had all the answers. Now look at you. A thug. A looter. A rapist. How does it feel?"

"Feel? I don't feel any more. So just take your high and mighty ideals and shove 'em up your ass."

"You've fallen a long way."

"You don't know the first damn thing about me, son. But you are going to learn. Gonna learn the hard way."

I leveled the .45 in his direction. I might have been able to kill him, but it would mean I was a dead man.

Just then, a shot shattered the night. I ducked down in the car. Katherine let out a little yell and waved the gun around, trying to find a target. Another shot, and then Lee's team started shooting into the darkness.

I looked for Lee, but he was on the run. Tugging the .45 up, I took aim, but he disappeared behind a beat up Suburban. I fired anyway to make him think twice about his life choices.

There were shapes all around. They came out of the night like wraiths. I felt a chill as one passed the car. He was dressed in dark overalls and had an AK-47 to his shoulder. I made out strong Latino features.

The dark Suburban roared to life and took off. I pointed my gun and fired off a few rounds. The back window shattered, but the car disappeared around a corner. The men ran into the night, and the vehicle behind me roared off.

Free to move, I hit the lights and backed up as fast as I could, angling the car into a driveway. Slamming the gear into drive, I shot out, down the street, and fled.

I had half a mind to circle around, hunt down the big Suburban, and take care of Lee. A man like that couldn't be allowed to continue his reign. But who was I to police the new world? It wasn't my business. What he had done was horrible; what his men had done was worse. They all deserved to meet a grisly end.

Right now, I had to take care of Katherine.

I punched the gas and accelerated away from the battlefield. Coming around a corner a bit too fast, I had to slam on my brakes to avoid running into someone standing in the street. The tires screeched and Katherine cried out in fear, as I came to a stop a few feet from the shape

From a distance, it had appeared to be a person. When they turned to look into the bright lights, I saw that it was one of the dead. It was a pitiful thing. An elderly woman with long white hair hanging in her face turned to regard me. She moaned around a half of a jaw, and then shambled off into the night.

I hit the high beams and crept through roads I had not seen in months.

There was a line of trucks just ahead, as though a convoy had arrived and circled the wagons. I came up on them and slowed to a stop. Slipping out once again into the night, I moved away from the safety of the car. I played the rifle over the trucks and felt like scratching my head in confusion. How the hell did the road get blocked? My house was a mile or so up the road, and I would have to climb over the blockade to reach it.

A motor started up, and then a burst of light shattered the darkness as high-intensity beams ripped the night apart. As they came to life all around me, I shielded my eyes. I felt like a deer caught in massive headlights. Like the world had just turned on a gigantic sun. I backed up one step at a time as I tried to train the rifle all around me.

The car door behind me slid open, and I knew without a doubt Katherine was behind me, watching my back. Noises from ahead; movement and the clink of metal on metal. Whatever this trap was, I had fallen for it, hook, line, and sinker. I tried to shield the light, but all I managed was to warm my palm.

I worried that I had found a group of Lee's men. If he had made it here, I was a dead man.

"What the hell is going on?" Katherine yelled.

Before I could reply, a voice came from the barricade of cars and trucks. "Lower your weapon and identify, or we will shoot you."

I just about dropped the gun because I had no doubt she would shoot. She and whoever was with her.

I lowered the rifle, but I didn't drop it. Still backing up, I was determined to jump in the SUV and get out of here. Whatever little fiefdom these people had set up, I was not interested in getting to know them.

"Stop moving or we will shoot!"

If I turned and made a dash for the car, I could be there in a few seconds, but even a ten-year-old with decent aim would be able to pick me off.

Stopping, I faced the blinding light. "My name's Erik Tragger, and you're blocking the way to my house. I just want to get some stuff and leave."

There was movement, but I couldn't tell what was going on. I was going to climb out of my skull at this rate. I did not like standing in front of these people with no protection. If they opened fire, I was as good as dead, and Katherine would be next.

More clanking around, and I wanted to make a run for it. Fuck this. Then an engine started, and a truck backed up to make a small space. A slim figure came out of the gap and walked toward me.

"Erik?" A female voice called out almost softly.

"Yep."

Her voice played with my senses, and I saw someone from the past. The way she spoke and moved reminded me of Allison, but that was ridiculous. There was no way she could have made it to our old home together. The last time I had talked to her was almost a month before the incidents started happening. I felt my heart swell at the thought of her, of what she had meant to me at one time, and the crushing anger that had burned for months after she had left followed. It made a powerful contrast.

"Alli ..." and I stopped, because I knew it wasn't her.

"It's Lisa." She stood a few feet from me, dressed in a jumpsuit made of some thick material that zipped all the way to her neck, as well as a scarf that covered her lower face. Still, I almost backed up again when she stepped to me and put her arms around me in an embrace.

I Automatically returned her hug, and stood as she sobbed against me for a full ten seconds before I realized who she was. My neighbor-- Devon's wife.

TWENTY-SEVEN

Katherine leaned against me as I helped her out of the Honda and walked toward the barricade. Once we were past the wall, the truck started up again and pulled forward to close the gap. The lights were easy to bear from this angle, and I was able to appreciate the simplicity in the design. With the trucks and cars facing out, it made a much harder barrier for the zombies to get through. In fact, with enough firepower, this place could hold out for a good long time.

Behind the vehicles was a series of fences with concrete barricades up against them. From a tactical standpoint, it reminded me of the Walmart, where a killing maze had been set up. The people here didn't have enough fencing to encircle their location, but they did the next best thing by staggering sections so the zombies could not get in.

I followed Lisa in and glanced at the faces on either side. There were at least twenty people that I could see, but none who looked familiar. They appeared like us--tired, dirty, and sore. A woman leaned on her gun as she tried to stay upright. I wondered what they had endured over the last six months. I heard whispers and tugged Katherine tighter to me.

"Where did they come from?"

"Lisa knows him."

"She does not look good at all."

An older man looked me up and down, nodding to himself as if I met some criteria. I gave him a half shrug in response. The low hum of a smaller generator kicked in, and dim lights lit the houses behind the barricade. It seemed like my life was coming down to what barricade I was able to hide behind at any given time. Many had wished for a new world, but I didn't think this was what anyone had in mind.

Lisa spoke with someone in low tones behind me before she ran to catch up with me. She looped one hand in the crook of my arm as another person came and took Katherine.

"I can't believe you're alive," she said, and I heard a strong hint of relief. I could only imagine what she and Devon had gone through after the zombies showed up.

"Where's Devon?"

"Gone," she said simply. "What's wrong with your ... friend?"

"Katherine. She was shot by one of those ghouls."

"They don't shoot. They only direct the undead things to do their dirty work."

"Well, someone with glowing green eyes did a good job of learning how to fire a gun," I said in frustration. I didn't want to talk about it; I wanted to get Katherine fixed up and out of here. This fiefdom was fine and dandy for them, but I wanted to go in pursuit of the caravan and hit Portland as soon as possible. I was sick to death of living in fear and living on the run.

"We have medical supplies and a nurse. She has done some amazing things, even though she isn't a doctor. She can take care of her. We've had good luck getting people patched up."

Lisa guided me to a house; I think it used to belong to Mark Wilson, a neighbor with whom I was never very friendly. He seemed like a nice enough guy, if a bit aloof. The door was open, and they were helping Katherine down a hallway to what must have been their triage room.

"Have you been here since the shit went down?" I asked.

"We tried to leave once. Devon wasn't sure what to do. He wanted to wait for some instructions from the government, or at least someone who seemed to be in authority. We waited and waited for at least a week after you left. One night, the power went out, and we sat in the dark. The next day, we wandered around the neighborhood, but it was so empty. It seemed like most of the neighbors left shortly after you."

"Who was still around?"

"Well, Mark didn't leave either. He had a hunting rifle, and he took the doors off all his upstairs rooms and nailed them over windows. He tried to build a fortress, but that was in the early days, and we weren't organized like we are now." Her tone was almost shy. Her hair was once a sheet of auburn curls that hung over her face when she laughed. Now it was a lighter color, and it was straight. I realized that hair that looked so natural was an act, just like the act kept up by the other survivors around us.

"I'm so glad to see you alive. I have seen some horrible things--some not too far from here. That was you at the house that was on fire, wasn't it?" she said. "We almost shot you, you know."

"That was your people?" I asked in surprise.

"We weren't going to get involved." She stopped me with a look, probably reading the shock in my eyes. "We try to stay out of the way. When it became apparent you were going to start a shooting match, we decided to spook the other guys."

"Lee's men," I said.

"Who's Lee?"

"Long story. Let's just say he's a bad man. I wouldn't be sad to see him dead." I sighed.

"Is that his first name?"

"Come to think of it, I have no idea."

Lisa studied me, but didn't pursue the matter. I was sure we would have time to talk about it later. I was on edge, worried about Katherine. I'm sure Lisa was aware of my constant glances toward the room Katherine was in.

Lisa had a new bearing about her. She was no longer the shy house-wife that used to giggle at my jokes when she and Devon had stopped by the house, before Allison left me. She had come into her own, and I was willing to bet she was the one who had yelled at me earlier.

I found an unoccupied La-Z-Boy and took a seat. She came around and sat on a beat-up couch that was probably once a fine leather sofa imported from Italy, if I knew Mark.

I glanced down the hall and wanted to pursue Katherine, wanted to be by her side when they worked on her, wanted to be there in case they had some bad news. One of the men who had helped us out came back and nodded at me.

"Nurse said she is gonna be all right, man. She's lucky that bullet went in and out clean. She's gonna stitch her up and they'll give her some antibiotics. We don't have a lot, but we can spare some for a neighbor."

He was light skinned but had a slight Hispanic accent. He carried a shotgun over his shoulder and was dressed like the others--jumpsuit with a scarf tied around his neck. I liked him right away for reasons I couldn't pinpoint. I was pretty sure he was also the man I had seen pass the car when they spooked Lee's men.

"I'm Scott Martinez, by the way." He offered his hand, and I shook it, noticing he also wore gloves.

"The outfits must be protection from the biters."

"Smart guy. We should keep you around." He grinned.

"Thanks, I think."

"Now this is nothing personal, man, but I'm gonna have to ask you to take your clothes off."

"Excuse me?"

"Gotta check you for bites, man. Like I said, nothing personal. It's a brave new world, brother. We don't stand on modesty much."

"What, here?"

"You want a private room, amigo?"

Lisa had a churlish grin on her face, but tastefully turned her head to the side to give me the illusion of privacy. Stripping down to my skivvies, I shook my head. They were old and torn, and I felt ridiculous in them. Scott gestured, so I held my arms out and spun around.

"Not the tighty whiteys, I hope," I said.

"If a zombie bit your ass, you got bigger problems. You're cool."

I frowned as I put my clothes back on, while Lisa fought back a cough.

He wandered back outside, and I was left alone with Lisa, who sat back and studied me.

"Is that how you greet every survivor?"

"If I didn't go out for you, you would have been stripped and spread eagle on the ground before you were even let into the perimeter."

I liked how she used words like that, like she was in the military. This was not the sweet but simpering Lisa I had met a few years ago.

This was a confident woman who was used to giving orders and having them followed.

I took a seat in the La-Z-Boy again and tried to look relaxed after doing the striptease. She studied me, and I studied her in return. She was still pretty, but she had the same hard look to her eyes that Katherine had. I hoped she was doing well in their care. I couldn't imagine she would be too happy with their methods of inspecting for bites.

"I thought the bites were fast--like the movies. You get bit, you die and change. Come back as one of those dead things."

"It used to be that way, but the virus has mutated. In some cases, it can take days to make its presence known. The ghouls have sent in more than one survivor who didn't even know they were going to change. Those things are too smart by far. We need a plan to kill them all."

"I think I know what you mean. We had trouble too. It was like they were driving a bunch of the zombies to kill us. They seemed to have a strange power over them. How can a virus do something like that?"

Sighing, she sat back. She put her hands in her lap and looked small all of a sudden. If I had been close to her, I probably would have patted her hand in a familiar gesture, like one friend does for another.

"We don't know much—just theories and rumors. There was a lot of talk of a bad swine flu vaccine, and then others said it was the regular flu shots. Then there was a rumor about some experimental gas in North Korea that got out of hand. None of it makes sense."

"Understatement."

"Yeah. What have you been up to? You look like you're in good shape."

I had been hoping for answers, but like the other survivors, these didn't know anything either. I wanted to pound the chair in frustration, but what good would it do? Would it even matter, knowing how the cursed virus started? It would just be one more thing to file away for a rainy day when we were all old and retired from zombie hunting--if we lived that long.

I had done more thinking along the lines of food and supplies. The stuff in stores wouldn't last forever. We would need to start farming, raising animals, taking care of crops. How could we do that when the world was overrun by the dead?

"I hid out at a cabin until I ran out of food. Then I came back and hooked up with a bunch of crazies holed up at the Walmart."

"Oh them. We have been in communication a few times. They wanted us to join them, but we were happy here."

So there was dissension in the tiny fiefdoms after all.

"You didn't want to join forces?"

"We worked hard to build this place. We brought in generators, a tanker full of diesel. We have semis full of food lined up. We brought in a truck filled with water bottles, and we're doing all right. When we need more stuff, we go on recon and get what we need. We didn't need them trying to bring it all to them."

"They had a pretty nice setup. Very secure."

"We have a nice setup."

I had to agree. They had a defensible position and they were well supplied. If overrun, they could always pile into the trucks and make their escape.

As if to punctuate my thought, a gunshot broke the still air outside. Another followed. From the blasts, I guessed it was an AK-47, which had a very distinctive sound. I would have loved to have gotten my hand on one; they didn't look as nice as my assault rifle, but they were a lot more reliable. The damn things had been used in wars all over the world for decades and were built like tanks.

"Shit," she said and jumped up. I followed her out, but I glanced back down the hallway through which they had taken Katherine. Lisa saw my look. "I'll be out there when you're done. As soon as you can, ask around about a jumpsuit. They're pretty good protection, and your clothes are a mess."

I thanked Lisa and turned to go check on Katherine.

The hallway led me to a kitchen, where a respectable triage unit had been set up. A pair of tables draped in white made up the beds. They both appeared to be padded. There were a couple of kitchen chairs in a corner, and a whole counter full of tools and medications. There were syringes and a box of sutures, piles of gauze and bandages. This place was ready for war.

Katherine sighed as the nurse slid a needle out of her arm. She smiled in a goofy way at me, and I wondered what kind of painkillers they had given her.

"You know something, Erik? My life was a lot simpler before you walked into it."

"If you're getting romantic, then I'm all ears."

I went to her side and took her hand. She was still cold, but the woman attending piled a sheet and a quilted blanket on her. Katherine's shoulder was exposed, and the paper towels had been pushed aside. The woman took the same syringe, wiped it and Katherine's skin with alcohol, and then administered a couple of shots to the area. Katherine didn't even seem to notice.

"She's floating on a sea of morphine right now. She may get sort of loopy."

"I'm Erik. Thanks for the hard work, Doc."

"Oh I'm no doctor, but I'm the next best thing. I'm a nurse, used to work in a facial reconstruction office, but I have all the chops."

She was dressed in the familiar jumpsuit, but she had a white strip tied around one arm, which reminded me of the corpsmen I used to see in old World War II movies. She was tall and thin with strong Asian features.

"I'm Maddy," she said and gave me a short wave in lieu of a handshake.

"Hi, Maddy."

"I'm numbing the area. I don't have a lot of morphine, so I have to use it sparingly, but I do have a few bottles of Lidocaine. Same stuff they use at the dentist."

I was familiar with the drug. I once had a small procedure to remove a cyst, and they shot the area up while I tried to relax and play it cool.

I looked away when she got out the blades, but she seemed confident with them in hand. I found a chair and sat down so I could see Katherine from the right side but not view the work. The smell of alcohol filled the room.

"You're not exactly a romantic guy, but you'll do, I suppose."

"I have my moments."

"You do. But you usually have a big knife or gun when they happen." Katherine said.

"Who shot you? Did you see anything?" I asked for the second time that night, wanting answers. I refused to believe that one of those ghouls was capable of picking up a gun, aiming it and firing. In my mind, the ghouls may have been smarter than the zombies, but they barely had motor skills. There was so much I didn't understand about them.

"I think it was one of those guys with green eyes. I don't think a regular human would be hanging out with them."

"Are you sure? Did you or the others ever see one holding a gun or weapon of any sort?"

"Nah, but they always stayed pretty far away from us. They seemed intent on just corralling or directing the dead bastards."

It didn't make sense, but who could make sense of any of this? The dead were back, and they ruled the world. We were now the minority, and our existence was a big question mark.

She started to say something else, but drifted off into la-la land. I stayed by her side, and, sometime during the night, my mind drifted far enough away for me to fall into a deep slumber.

TWENTY-EIGHT

I rocketed out of sleep like a sled barreling down a mountain, or such was the impression my dream left on my mind. In it, I was at the cabin, and it was covered in snow. We were surrounded on every side by the dead. After running out of ammo, Katherine had an idea. She dragged me to the rooftop, where we had a sled like the one Santa used. He was one of the zombies now, a jolly fat man in red. Red the color of blood. He waited for us and he was hungry.

We got into the sled and left the top of the mountain at high speed. We flew over a freeway, skidded onto it, and kept on going until we ran into a swarm of ghouls.

Something loud banged outside, and even in my half-sleep state, I recognized the AK-47 again. I came out of the seat and whipped my head around in search of my shotgun. A shooting pain rocketed down one shoulder. I had somehow fallen asleep in the wooden chair, and no one had woke me. I had been left exhausted as soon as my body stopped running on high-octane adrenaline. The night had been a blur. The escape, the fight, the flight, and then meeting up with Lisa and her crew of holdouts.

I rubbed my eyes, but they were so dry they felt like they were coated in sand as if I was rubbing tiny grains into my pupils. After a minute, I stood up and went to check on Katherine.

Drugged or not, she was used to living on edge, and her eyes popped open, hand moving toward a nonexistent gun, the moment I entered the area. She saw me, and a flash of confusion was washed away by a genuine smile. It touched me; I won't lie. I had spent a lot of time with her, and I was attached, but she was still very reserved around me. The concern she had brought up about not being able to bear children meant little to me. She could take her common sense and piss on it, because I wanted to be with her no matter what.

"Morning, sunshine," I said and kissed her lips. She was warm to my touch, as I pushed some hair out of her face then took her hand in mine.

"Hey, you."

Her shoulder was bare where the wound was covered in fresh, clean gauze.

"How are you feeling?"

"Like I'm on morphine. I feel a bit lost, and my body's warm. I'm glad you're with me."

"I don't see you as the romantic type. You're more of an action girl."

"I wasn't always like this. I used to be a mom and a wife, and I was happy. Sometimes I don't like what I've become. Then my anger returns, and I know it's a pipe dream."

I didn't know what to say. I liked her candor and her toughness. I liked how she could turn into a sexy woman when she wanted to, and how she could tell me what she wanted and how she wanted it.

I was on safe ground with her, which made me content.

Another shot rang out. A hunting rifle, this time, was my guess. Then another, and I was itching to get outside.

"I'll be back."

"Okay. Don't forget me." She squeezed my hand. "Thank you, Erik, for everything. I don't think I ever told you that, and I meant to."

I had the urge to hug her, but her recovering body probably would not take too kindly to it. After planting a kiss on her forehead, I left the room.

In the living room, a pair of people I didn't know leaned over a map. They glanced up as I entered. The woman, an older gal who had a matronly look, eyed me up and down.

"Bathroom?"

The man pointed toward the other end of the hall.

"In there. If it's too full, use the bucket on the side to pour just enough water in until it flushes, then stop."

It stood to reason that simple things like water were hard to come by, and there would be the constant need to get more. In the cabin, we had an outhouse in the back that was a simple hole in the ground, and it had served well enough even if it had stunk to the heavens.

After taking care of business in the dark, I left the small room and went outside. The sun was high, and if I had to guess at the time, I would have judged it just before noon. I hadn't worn a watch in months. What was the point? I didn't have to go to work--no appointments. I didn't have to worry about what time to watch shows on TV, when to cook, or when to wake up. Our brave new world had precipitated a lack of technology, and in some ways, this pleased me. I would have liked about a half hour a day on the Internet, but even that need was fading with time.

The circle of cars and trucks made quite the impressive barrier. They were parked so close together that the only way into most of them was through the rear window or trunk. A group of large SUVs created a sort of gate. A couple had open hatches, and I was betting they were the getaway plan.

One of the bigger trucks, an enormous vehicle that looked like something one would see at a monster rally, was idling. Wires ran out of the hood to a box, which in turn was connected to a bunch of car batteries. So that was how they got portable energy. Just charge the batteries every day, and with enough jury-rigging, I supposed you could run a light for a few hours with a DC convertor.

On top of the truck was a man in the same type of jumpsuit the others wore. He had a rifle pressed to his shoulder and was lying prone, watching the entryway to the neighborhood with a pair of binoculars. I stared down the road and saw a body in the street. It was too far away to make out many details.

A large hand clapped my shoulder, and it was hard not to reach up, clamp my hand around it, then turn and put its owner in a shoulder lock. Living away from people had made me an edgy fucker. I looked over my shoulder into the grinning eyes of Scott. He had on a camouflage cap like hunters wear, but the same jumpsuit and scarf from the night before.

"Hey man. Up at last?"

"Barely. I feel like I slept in a wooden chair all night. Oh yeah, I did."

"We got beds. Just ask next time."

"Next time I won't be dead on my feet, and I will."

"Don't say dead on your feet around some of these guys. They're likely to take your head off with a Louisville Slugger."

I smiled at his grim humor.

I saw my car out beyond the barricades. "Should I bring that in?"

"Unless you're leaving. We weren't sure. Nice work turning a Honda into a tank. Some of the guys were checking it out earlier. That turret is great. Too bad it doesn't have a weapon mounted in it through a big hole. That would be badass."

"You don't care if we leave?"

"Why would we?"

"I don't know. I figured you would have a big recruiting speech for newcomers. Put the love of Jesus in us."

"Shit, man, you can come and go. We aren't some outfit that makes people drink the Kool-Aid. We have enough problems as it is. Besides, if someone wants to stay, they have to show that they're useful. Are you useful?"

That was a good question. I could strip and clean guns, I knew some military tactics, and I was good at hand-to-hand combat, but having been out of the mix for four months meant I missed a lot of the action while I was stuck up in the cabin. The men and women around were much better zombie slayers than I was.

"I don't know. I can fight, and I can teach people how to grab zombies behind the ears and drive their knees into their rotted faces."

Another shot called out like a cannon blast, and I couldn't help but jump, but so did Scott. We looked at each other and chuckled.

"Target practice." He pointed at the guy with the hunting rifle plastered to his chest on top of the truck. "The stupid things must be able to smell us. A few wander by every day, so we take them out. No sense in letting a bunch of dead fucks loose."

"Ever see any of the guys with green eyes?"

"Nah, not much, they're too smart. They used to lurk around, but now they mostly come out at night, and only when they have an army behind them. But we have a lot of firepower, and we're well protected, so for the past few weeks, they've stayed away." He sounded convinced of this. After what I saw in town, I wasn't so sure.

"How many other communities around here are set up like this?"

"A few. We know where they are, and we trade stuff sometimes, but we remain autonomous. There isn't a lot of mixing. Maybe it's a trust issue. You'd think at the end of the world people would start trusting each other again."

The kid was doing pretty well with the gun, but he was jerking the barrel up with each shot. I watched and wondered how much ammo they had to spare that they could do target practice.

"You set for ammo?"

"We have enough for now, but it won't last forever. We got a guy who keeps track of all the rounds. He could tell you more. Why?"

"Because the Walmart might have some ammo. I don't think they could carry out the massive stockpile. They're in a big metal cage in the center of the store. I know how to get at them."

"They gonna give the stuff up for free? I doubt that."

He didn't know.

"They left almost a week ago. The place is empty now. They might have buttoned up and left some supplies. We should make a run before someone else does."

"Why are they gone?" He looked confused, but he also looked like he was calculating, thinking of what a boon that would be, then his face clouded. "See, I like you, Erik. You seem like the kind of guy that says stuff straight the fuck up. I can respect that, especially in the new world. But it's kinda suspicions that you show up and want to lead us to an armed compound."

Oh.

"You have the wrong idea, Scott. I wouldn't dream of it, but I see why you would be wary. You can go with me, and we can scout it out. I was at the store for a while, but they bugged out, headed for Portland. Did you hear an explosion about a week ago?"

"Yeah, it shook the ground. We thought a nuke had gone off somewhere. I know it sounds stupid, but being cut off means we gotta rely on what we see and hear, and that was a ways off, so we automatically feared the worst."

"That was me and Katherine setting off the distraction, so a caravan could get out of town and drive to Portland. We rolled a gas truck away from the Walmart and made a lot of noise until the things were all around us. One of our friends died, but we managed to get to my car and make our escape before the truck went up. We probably took out about a hundred of those bastards."

"Huh."

"Then we hightailed it back a cabin up in the hills. We hid out until we were found by those fuckers with green eyes."

He didn't have to say a thing; I could tell by the way his brows drew together. How would I feel in his shoes? Would I just trust someone who showed up and claimed to know things about outside events? I wouldn't; no one in their right mind would. And why did I care anyway? These guys were doing just fine without my help. They had built a small, fortified city here. They didn't need me.

"We really do need to follow our friends back to Portland. Maybe in a day or two. I have a bunch of guns back in the car. Maybe I could give you one for your hospitality."

"We can always use more ammo especially with guys like Junior there getting in some practice."

"Fuck you, man," Junior shot back from atop the truck.

Scott laughed and shot his friend the finger.

We had a few boxes of shells, but I needed to hang onto those if we were going to be on our own soon. Then again, without these folks, Katherine would be in pretty bad shape. It would be nice to go back and get more from the store, but I would need to convince them. Maybe a show of goodwill would help.

"I'll give you a hundred rounds of seven point six two," I said, watching his eyes. He knew what that was all right, and he nodded.

"We can use it."

"Great. Now look. Why don't you go with me? Just a scouting mission, and if it looks too dangerous, we'll head back. No fuss, no muss. Katherine is here just in case."

"We don't take prisoners, man."

"Fine, then she stays here as an ambassador of goodwill."

He laughed at that and then, with a pat on my shoulder, he left and went into the house. I stood in the road a mile or so from my house and looked down the street. If I got to the other side of the barricade and I was extra cautious, I could be there in about fifteen minutes. I decided to take the chance, wanting to know how the neighborhood had fared.

I slid over one of the cars by jumping on the hood and then over the roof. A couple of men watched, but they didn't try to stop me. My car started up easily, and I drove it off the road and onto the sidewalk, in front of an old Volkswagen van that was turned sideways. A wall of bricks was built up under the chassis so no one could get under it.

After taking a couple of boxes of ammo from the car, I loaded my pants pockets with a couple of magazines, then strapped a beat-up Colt .45 under my arm. Once I slung the AR over my shoulder, I must have made a sight. If they really didn't care about me coming and going, then I was going to do both.

I stared down the road in the opposite direction of the barrier where a pair of rotting creatures shambled across a four-way intersection. One turned to regard me, and then veered off. The other kept going. It was about twenty-five yards away, or so I surmised. I swung the rifle up to the crook of my shoulder and took aim. While I wanted a headshot, I would settle for the neck. It seemed like a round to anywhere near the brain-stem or brainpan stopped those things in their tracks. A shot to the body just forced them to fall over, and they'd just get back up. I had yet to nail one of the guys with glowing eyes, not counting the slaughter at the roadblock. Who knows how many of these things we took out last week.

Flipping the safety off, I exhaled and stroked the trigger. The shot echoed around me as it left the barrel. It struck just off center, and a puff of pink and gray mist exploded outward, then the thing dropped in its tracks. It fell to its knees and toppled backward. The other zombie paused in mid-step, turned to look at its companion, then dropped to all fours and went for its ex-buddy. She took a huge chunk of cheek in her mouth and ripped upward. I struggled to keep my stomach calm while I fired again. The feasting monster fell forward, and they lay there like lovers.

Mission complete, I headed back the way I had come.

"Nice shootin', Tex," one of the men called out. He was older, gray around the temples, and had a pair of thick glasses on. Licking his lips, he spit to one side.

"Thanks."

"I don't think you killed the second one. It's still twitching."

I looked back, and sure enough, the other was trying to move one hand away from her body, like she was crawling under barbed wire. Putting the ammo on the ground, I slid over one of the cars--a red Ford that looked to be at least twenty years old. I took to the street, which was bathed in pale light thanks to the early morning sun. It was red and pink where it bounced off clouds. I was reminded of an old saying from my father: Red in the morning, sailors take warning.

The only red I was about to see was blood.

Over the last few months, I had faced a number of these things and walked away unscathed. I fought them with guns, knives, and even hand to hand. They had been faceless monsters that I killed with impunity. I had slaughtered them--there was no other way to put it. These monsters that used to be men and women but were now mindless killing machines.

Now I had the chance to get close and study one. I took the handgun from the back of my waistband and checked the safety. Sliding the chamber back a quarter of an inch, I checked to make sure there was a bullet in it. Once I clicked off the safety, I approached the undead.

It was pitiful. The woman's dress hung in tatters around her body. Her legs looked like fat sausages, complete with a thin layer of casing to hold everything in. Her skin was nearly translucent, and the stuff under it looked putrid and rotten. As she crawled, it jiggled like congealed fat. She reached for me with a clawed hand that grasped in slow motion.

Her hair was coated in grime and blood. Her eyes were dull, white, and one was rotted in the socket. The other swiveled as she tracked me moving around her. Her chin was covered in blood, and chunks of meat hung out of her mouth.

Even as she reached for me, her mouth closed over a hunk of her companion's neck. I grimaced and took in the rest of her body. I don't know how she died; if it was the bite or if she was killed and came back.

"You gonna kill that thing or ask it to dance?" one of the men yelled.

Kill it. How do you kill something that's already dead? I crouched down on the balls of my feet and touched her arm. I didn't want anything to do with her, and I really didn't want any physical contact, but curiosity got the better of me. She was cold to the touch, and there was no blood flow under her skin. No pulse. Breaking my grip, I took a step back, lifted the gun, and blew her brains all over the road.

The walk back to the barricade took longer than it should have.

TWENTY-NINE

After delivering the ammo, I decided to hoof it to my old house. It was less than a mile, and I had the daylight to my advantage. I walked around the perimeter until I got my bearings and determined which way I had to go. Though I had driven these streets many times, they had changed now. The houses were still there, lined up in perfect rows, but they were also overgrown, as shrubs and trees grew any which way, they wanted to without man to interfere with them. There were no cars in the street, except for the dozen or more that made up the perimeter.

Most homes had their doors and garages wide open. I imagined the group here must have gone over every inch looking for supplies. There were things tossed aside in yards--empty boxes, cans, and bottles. Now-useless electronics lay everywhere. It was easy to guess that panic had set in and people had run from the rapidly approaching horror, then the opposite had occurred as those who stayed had turned to looting.

The air was much cleaner now. Maybe it was the lack of exhaust or the effect of all the flourishing plant life. It was going to be a warm day; that much was obvious from the already thickly mounting humidity.

Scott caught up with me and walked by my side. I glanced at him. He had an almost gleeful look on his face. I found it infectious and grinned back, which felt good.

"Where you goin', man?"

"My house is less than a mile from here. I'm going over there for a minute. I need to pick up some things."

"You know it's probably looted, right? Or like falling to pieces, or some shit. Some people aren't so nice."

"I have a stash. I'm pretty sure no one has found it."

"Well, I can't let you go and do a dumb thing like that by yourself. I'm going with you."

Not for the first time, I wondered if he was mentally unbalanced. Then I laughed out loud. We were all unbalanced.

"What's so funny?"

"Nothing, man. I'm just glad for the company."

"Well, all right. Let's go on a quest and shit. I get to be Frodo."

"You're definitely a Sam. I think I should be Frodo."

"But I have more common sense," he said. "Like I would never go out into this crazy world alone. You need someone at your back at all times."

"Fair point." We headed for the line of trucks.

———

BIRDS FLITTED HERE and there and chirped at everything. There were massive flights of crows and other birds that had to be scavengers of some sort. I bet the seagull population near the water had exploded in growth.

There were blue jays with their angry chant, screaming at each other and probably at us as we interrupted their conversations. I looked up as a hawk called out from where he circled far above. The world had gone to the birds, literally.

Scott was a good companion. He kept his focus everywhere as we walked through the wreckage of the neighborhood. There was a pair of scorched houses that were just burned-out husks. One was a large two-story with a gated entryway. It reminded me of the house from last night.

I wondered how many times the same story had repeated itself over the course of the last few months. How many houses were torn apart, families dragged out and killed. How many survivors were there? I hoped Portland wasn't a disappointment. I didn't think I could live like this forever, unless I found a safe community like this one to live in. Maybe that wouldn't be such a bad idea. Then again, how long would it be before the groups started fighting each other for control? How long until the food ran out? It wasn't like we could grow anything. A field would be a terrible place to work--a wide-open target—like farming in the middle of a giant bullseye.

A flash of movement in the street ahead caught my attention, and I had the gun to my shoulder in a heartbeat.

Scott reacted in the same manner. He carried a shotgun--big Remington with a pump, and worked it like a pro, head swiveling with the gun as he walked forward.

It was an old car behind which someone was crouching. I moved to one side of the street, and Scott moved to the other. Houses were closer together here, and smaller--town homes that had very little room and even less space between lots. With all the shadows they cast, it would be hard to see anything coming out of them until it was too late.

Scott scooted forward. He had the close-range weapon, so that afforded me the opportunity to cover him with the M-16. A shape moved at speed away from the car, running like it was on fire. It looked like a kid, but it was in the gap between two houses before I could even wonder if the apparition had been real.

"Damn creepers," Scott muttered when he joined me.

"Hey man. I was one of those until a few days ago."

"Really? You do look kind of creepy."

"Maybe they don't know they can just walk right up to you and say 'Hi, I want in.' You live on the run long enough, and it becomes hard to trust anyone."

We walked along in silence. I looked over at Scott to find his eyebrows drawn down, as if in deep thought.

"Yeah, you're right, but we can't exactly put out a welcome sign. We only have so many supplies."

"I know, but how long can that continue? What are you going to do when you run out, and you're ranging out from the hub for hours at a time just to find some canned food? I'm surprised you all have lasted this long. I'm serious. If you want a fighting chance, you need to take some trucks over to Walmart and clean that place out before someone else does. Or move in. The place is like a fortress with an electrified fence."

"We might talk about that later. Right now, we got this quest to complete. What's so important that you have to get to your house?"

Our voices echoed up and down the street, and I had to wonder if many creepers were in the surrounding houses, watching us--if they had guns trained on us. The hair on the back of my neck stood on end, and I took a deep breath to calm my nerves. Four months away from humanity, and I was already scared to go looking for it.

"Just some stuff I should have brought with me--that's all. Mainly a picture of my ex-wife."

"Hope that shit is better than a memory. We stick around out here too long, and we're gonna be a memory."

We were on Callow Street and had to cut over a block when we ran across an old accident. It looked like a semi had run into a UPS truck and both vehicles had been shredded. Chunks of rusted metal were everywhere. I didn't want to climb over the wreck, so I led him instead to an old pasture that ran catty-corner to the street. We took to it and passed more than one cow corpse. Someone had shot the things and left them to rot in the sun. They did not smell pretty at all. Not that the pasture would ever have won an award for its stench of old cow shit prior the apocalypse.

We slogged over land that was being reclaimed by tall grass. There was some skittering, as small animals dashed here and there in the undergrowth. Probably mice or rats, or the occasional snake. Those little critters must have been having a field day now that they were free to repopulate without rodent killer and giant lawnmowers tearing up their world.

The housing complex in which I'd lived was just ahead. The old fence that bordered one of the farmer's lots was still there, and I thought I could see my house, but it was so close to the overgrown weeds and blackberry bushes that it was hard to be sure from this angle.

The fence was an old chain link job that some cheapskate had built about fifteen years ago. It was sagging and rusted in spots, and I remembered where the greenbelt grew close to the field. Here I could slide in between the shrubs and the metal barrier.

I went first and couldn't help but snag my shirt on the fence, which set it tinkling. Scott reached out to touch it to muffle the sound. He followed, and just like that, we stood in my neighbor's back yard. I drifted to the window that investigated his kitchen. It wasn't that long ago that I left him here, his dead wife banging at the window. The house was dark, but I saw a pair of rotted legs sticking out of the hallway that led to the living room. I slid along the side of the house and lowered the gun as I got a view of the street. Here, I felt very exposed, even though I was less than a mile from my new friends.

The street was clear, and I breathed a sigh of relief. My house looked much like the others we had passed. The door was open, and my possessions had been scattered across the front yard. Pots and pans lay in a heap near a burned spot. It looked like someone had used the yard as a camp and cooked something there.

I looked past it, at Lisa and Devon's house. It was a ruin. Burned to the ground.

I pointed at the house and made a cup with my hand like it was binoculars. He nodded, and I hoped he understood that I meant for him to keep an eye out.

Slipping around the corner, I kept my gun high and went to the front porch.

The first thing I noticed was that the shrubs were a mess. The rhododendrons, of which Allison had been so proud, were nearly dead. They hung in clumps of miserable brown that looked woven into the weeds that were taking over the rest of the bushes. The grass, like all the lawns in the lots, was now measured in feet instead of inches. I felt like I was walking through a field and not a yard. If I laid down in the stuff, I would be all but invisible to any casual observer. This gave me some tactical options if this little jaunt went to shit.

I walked up the concrete steps and onto my porch for the first time in nearly many months. My furniture was gone, and it wasn't hard to guess that the burned marks in the tall grass were all that remained of those possessions. I crouched down by the door, which wasn't open but was ajar. The window facing out had the blinds drawn, so I had no idea what I was walking into. I slung the assault rifle over my shoulder and drew my handgun.

The living room was murky when I pushed the door open. Shadows cut through the blinds at the rear of the house. Dust hung in clumps from the corners, and each had a small population of spiders with webs spun and ready for prey. The carpet, once light gray and pristine, was covered in dirt, wrappers, empty cigarette packs—I think one pile was human feces. It was hard to be sure; it might have been an animal, but no matter what it was, I knew that someone or something had used my living room as a bathroom. I had to maneuver over several similar piles until I reached the kitchen.

I kept my weapon raised the entire time as I searched for anything living in my house. Standing at the kitchen entryway, I stared at the mess for a full minute before my mind could comprehend what I was seeing. Everything Allison and I had collected was either on the floor or smashed on the counters—dishes, glasses, cups, and coffee mugs. Pots and pans were strewn about as though at a garage sale. There were cigarette butts on the floor, and wrappers from food all over the place. The refrigerator was open, but it was bare of anything except a pile of green gunk in one vegetable drawer that looked like some mad scientific experiment.

I had to step over the remains of an expensive set of China. Beautiful plates I asked Allison to take when she moved out, but she had refused.

The family room was just as bad as the rest of the house. My LCD TV lay on the floor with several holes through the back. It appeared someone had used it for target practice. I wished I could meet the people who trashed my house.

I lowered the weapon and turned in a full circle to take in the mess. I wanted to break something, wanted to smash my fist into anything that would shatter.

Something thumped loud enough to shake my already rattled nerves. I walked to the bathroom next to the living room, past what had at one time been a nice couch. Now it was a ripped-up hunk of leather that needed to be burned. Rats has probably made it a home.

The door was slightly open, so I pushed it the rest of the way with the barrel of the gun and kept my focus everywhere at once.

Nothing. Just an empty room. Something scratched near the front of the home so I moved in that direction. When Scott slipped in with his big Remington extended, I nodded at him. I motioned with one hand to tell him to slow down, then put a finger to my lip and pointed upstairs.

He shot me a thumbs up and took point. I stared at the closet where access to the house lay. Looking at the closed door, I decided to check there first. No sense in leaving an opening unexplored before going upstairs.

Putting my hand on the wood, I almost jumped out of my skin when something hit the door hard enough to shake it. As I stepped back, I raised the handgun.

I took a deep breath to calm my nerves, but it did no good. My hand was shaking from the scare. Taking another breath made it stop. Scott stared at me with big, round eyes, like he had seen a ghost. I reached for the door again, and he shook his head.

Closing my hand on the knob, I jerked it open, and stepped back just in time to avoid being bowled over by a shambling horror.

THIRTY

I t was hard to tell how long the creature had been in the closet. Its body was covered in rotted skin, and its eyes were nothing but dried-out white orbs. It stumbled forward, and I drilled it through the head with one shot then another before it could acknowledge the blast. The second bullet went through the bridge of its nose and exploded out the back of its head. Blood and congealed chunks that looked like Jell-O splattered the wall.

The body slumped back and fell into the closet. I still had to get in there and open the access to the space under the house. I didn't want to have to crawl over a floor slick with blood. Grabbing the man by his ankles, I pulled him back and away from the tiny room.

Scott looked like he wanted to throw up. Maybe he wasn't used to the up-close stuff. I offered him a mad grin and set the man's feet on the floor. He was just as rotted as the woman I had killed in the street. His eyes were off center where the bullet had punched through his forehead, and he was covered in dirt and blood. He had green streaks all over his clothes, like he had crawled through the grass to get there.

I wanted to sweep the rest of the house before I went under the house. No sense having one of those things come downstairs while my ass was hanging in the air. I wished I had brought a flashlight. When I opened the door to the garage, it was hard to see anything in the murkiness. No movement, but it looked to be just as wrecked as the rest of the house.

I went upstairs on the balls of my feet. The doors were wide open except for one--the bathroom. It was odd to creep through my own house. It felt empty and alone, and I felt failure pressing down on me. The failure of a race that had given up the fight and decided to huddle together in tiny enclaves.

I had to pause and take a deep breath to steady the pounding of my heart. Was that all we were? Rats scurrying around, trying to carve out a better barrier to hide behind?

I poked the gun in each of the two bedrooms and the bathroom, but they were clear. Dressers held nothing but dust. My old clothes were gone. No underwear or socks. I had been wearing the same pair for so long that they were getting holes in them.

We went back downstairs, and I got on my hands and knees and tugged the small doorway open. It was just a big square of wood with insulation attached to the sides so it would form a seal. There was no way to determine for sure if anyone had been in here, but it did not appear to have been touched. I hung my head over the side and tried to get used to the darkness to see if anything or anyone was in the space.

I waited for a full minute, but there was nothing alive there. I crawled in, slithered through the dirt to the place I had left my stash of goodies, and grabbed the bag. I hauled it back out with me and dragged it and myself up. As I moved back, my feet hit the legs of the corpse, and I just about let out a scream.

"Well, what is so important that you had to drag us here?"

"You tagged along," I pointed out.

"Mainly in an advisory capability." Scott said with a slight smirk.

Smiling, I opened the bag. I took the laptop out and set it aside, as well as the portable hard drive. Taking the picture out, I slid it from the frame and set it on the dirty carpet. Allison would have gone insane if she saw how badly damaged the floor was. No amount of professional cleaning would restore it to its original condition.

There were cans in the bottom that clacked together, and when I pulled them out and set them down, Scott just about started drooling. He stared at them and at me.

"Why not?" I popped the lid on the pineapple chunks. It had a little ring on top for easy access. Grinning, I took a sip of the juice, which was nirvana. I had eaten whatever could be thrown together for the last day, and the stop at the Walmart saw me wolfing down dog food gruel that tasted like crap. Nothing but meat at the cabin. I couldn't remember the last time I'd had fruit.

I dug a couple of pieces out and handed the can to Scott. He didn't waste any time taking a sip, then rolled his eyes back like he was having the best sex of his life. He ate three or four pieces as well, but he chewed on them slowly, one at a time, so he could savor them. The can didn't last long, but we enjoyed every second. I still had mandarin oranges, peaches, and a can of refried beans. I tossed him the can of beans.

"What, 'cause I'm fucking Mexican you give me the beans?"

I just about spat out the bit of pineapple.

"Come on, man, how about those peaches? You got two cans."

I laughed and handed him one.

"Thanks for coming with me." I said. I felt a friendship forming with him. He was a good guy with a sense of humor, and I could see that he would be a great guy at my back and vice versa.

"Better than nothing, man."

"Gives you nasty gas."

"I don't need much help with that."

He laughed.

I laughed at his face, which he had screwed up as if he were deep in thought. Before I started cracking up for real, I slipped outside, but stopped dead in my tracks.

It couldn't have been the creeping around; it had to be the gunshot that drew them. Whatever it was, we had a serious problem. About twenty of the rotted things were closing in on us.

"Ah fuck me!" Scott whispered behind me.

THIRTY-ONE

I guess the mission had gone too well so far because now the shit hit the fan. We'd only had one of the zombies to contend with, and it was locked in the closet for so long it was probably completely brain dead—if it even had brains. Being stuck in there for a long time couldn't have been good for it. It basically fell out, and I finished it off. The ones in front of the house were much different.

They wore tattered clothing, the ones that were dressed. Some only had on tops or bottoms. There was a large woman with a gash running across her forehead and dried blood caked all over her face. She wore the remains of a pair of corduroy pants, green but covered in refuse. Her shirt was missing, and her breasts were shriveled things that looked like big raisins. Next to her was a man in a full three-piece suit that had seen better days. I expected it to reek of mothballs if he got close enough--that and rot. They were all rotted; some were falling apart. It was a pathetic group that had their eyes set on me and Scott. A feast for the dead. I didn't plan on being dinner.

Dropping the bag, I started popping the creatures one at a time. I aimed and took care that I had each shambler in my sight before I stroked the trigger. Scott wanted to run; I could see it in his body language. I had him pegged in the corner of my eye, but he stuck by my side, which raised his status quite a bit in my mind. It was easy to give in to panic and make a run for it, but a true soldier did the best he could with what he had. And we had each other's back

I brought another one down--a child this time. A kid with long hair that moved faster than the others. He or she was already halfway up the driveway when I took it in the throat. It stumbled to a halt as half of its neck disappeared in a spray of gore that I hoped to forget.

More were on their way in their shambling mass. We would have to make a run for it after all. At least they were slow, but if one of the ghouls was around, it might use its strange influence to push them at us.

I took to the tall grass with Scott right behind me. It was tough going, as we had to high-step it over the mass of green that was taking over the front yard. I hauled ass around the corner and came to a stop as more of the things came out of the greenbelt surrounding the yard. There were dozens of the shambling creatures, and they all had hungry eyes set on our flesh.

Even if I could find a place to shoot from, we didn't have enough ammo to take them all out. We couldn't call for help. Now if I had asked about those, it might have been the genius move of my life, but I was so convinced that the little communities were keeping the zombies at bay that I got hasty and didn't plan well enough. Shit!

I stopped in my tracks and stared at Scott. "Can we run through them?"

"It just takes one bite, man, and when they start dragging at you, I've seen people brought down by three of the fuckers."

I popped the first few that were closing in on us. One fell with a neat hole between its eyes. Another lost the side of its head but came on, so I shot it again, and it fell in a heap.

I looked around desperately and spotted something I didn't expect. A splash of red in the tall grass next to my rusting lawnmower. It was near the house and within easy reach. I let out a yelp as I spotted it and ran to grab it. It was still heavy, like it was at least half full. I wasn't sure how long ago I had used the stuff, so I wasn't sure if I had left it in that state. Still, I supposed with all the cars lying abandoned, folks had no problem finding enough fuel to keep their cars running. What did they need my piddly can for?

The top was one of those pop-off caps that allowed the can to breathe, so it might have been full. For all I knew, with the fumes pouring off for the last half year, it could be half water. I didn't have time to worry about it. I jerked the cap off and splashed the fluid all over the ground in front of the ones coming out of the greenbelt. I splashed it in high arcs that cascaded in a beautiful display of rainbow that coated a few of the dead.

Scott turned and covered my back by bumping three or four booming rounds of buckshot into the monstrosities on the side of the house. We were surrounded, and I had doubts about us escaping. There was no way to get through them unless I burned a path, and that was what I intended to do. If it came to it, I would lie down and put the handgun to my head.

I dashed, avoiding as many of them as I could while laying down the line of fire. I didn't have a lighter, and I hoped Scott did.

"You got some flame?"

"I don't smoke."

Oh shit.

He ran to my side and stared at the horde before us. He looked at the grass, at the gas-drenched zombies, and then at me. Grinning, he lowered the gun, then took a step right up to one of them—a man missing half of his left arm and most of one cheek.

"Hello, asshole. Welcome to the bonfire." Then he fired the shotgun into the ground at the dead guy's feet. The resulting blast ignited the grass. The gas had become vaporous, and the flame spread quickly. It was probably just my imagination, but I swear the zombie went from slack-faced to horrified in a half-second. It turned to move away from the flame but was consumed. It howled deep in its throat--an almost forlorn cry that stilled the day.

"We need to move!" I yelled at Scott. He didn't need any further prodding and launched himself at the fence. We had to leap over the spreading flames, and I was scared that my pants would catch fire. I ran for it, but the blaze was spreading rapidly. It was also saving us, because the things were staggering away from the flames. There were a couple of them standing near the fence. Scott and I came on like a pair of linebackers. I hit one with my shoulder and barreled into a man around my age or maybe a few years younger.

Another zombie snagged me from behind. Hand on my shirt but there was no grip and I shook it loose. I kicked back and got a satisfying thump against a body. A glance over my shoulder told me it had been pushed back into the fire. It stared at the flames that licked at its cotton shirt, then shrieked and ran right into the rotting thing behind him, a woman in her sixties if she was a day. Then it was chaos as the zombies became the prey—a prey to fire. We were used to being on the run. Now it was their turn.

Scott kicked one in the chest. I slipped behind a zombie and pushed it toward the rapidly spreading flame. The guy was so rotted that his skin caught on fire instantly, and the smell of sizzling bacon was in my nose. I was disgusted at myself for the way I practically drooled.

The reek of smoke was all around us, and I risked a glance back at the house. The yard was in flames, and it was only a matter of time before the fire took my pride and joy and burned it to a cinder. All the memories, both good and bad, all the stuff we had collected, all the house payments I had made toward our mortgage and property value, all my equity, gone the day the world went to the dead, and now I was going to baptize that old life in fire.

I drew my handgun and shot as I ran. The big shotgun boomed beside me, and I lost the hearing in that ear for a few seconds, but it splattered one of the things like a bucket of gore tossed against the fence. The zombie's flesh hung from the chain link, making it look a slaughterhouse. Part of its head and something I was sure was brain matter also hung there. I wanted to be disgusted, but I had no time to think about it, no time to consider the human life that was splattered all over the place.

Smoke everywhere, and it was hard to catch my breath. We hit the fence with the flames behind us. It was the only route now, as they ran in pursuit of us. I scaled the chain link and did a neat flip that had much more to do with fear than acrobatics. Landed on my feet, and felt the impact blast up my legs. My left knee almost buckled, but I ran on regardless.

Dead ahead, dead and toasted behind. They were coming from both sides, but it was hard to tell which were after us and which were running from the smoke and flames. I fired at one that was snarling at me and caught it in the shoulder. He fell back, but not for long. I had to shoot him again, and, even running, I was able to put the bullet through his head at less than ten feet.

"Ghoul!" Scott shouted from my left. I followed his wide-eyed star.

Sure enough, just to the side of the herd of zombies was one of the green-eyed creatures, and he did not look happy. With pasty, white skin, he was a real waxen nightmare of old and dead combined with something resembling a human.

I developed a new plan that didn't involve escape. I hadn't run into anyone who had a clue what these guys were up to. I wanted that green-eyed bastard in my hands, wanted to drag him back to the barricade and find out everything I could, even if it meant blowing his brains out to see what was in that head.

"Erik!" Scott called, but I shot another zombie in the face and raced toward the ghoul. I was still a good thirty or forty feet away when it caught on that I wasn't interested in just getting away.

I had to shoot another zombie, then I ducked as one came at me with arms open wide like it wanted a hug. I turned my run into a flying front kick that was just as pretty as you please and dropped the big zombie in his tracks. The boom of the shotgun behind told me the guy wouldn't be getting up again.

Then there were a pair of them ahead, but I was dry. I didn't have time to pull the assault rifle over my shoulder, and I was too close. By the time I got it up to my cheek to aim, the other would be able to close in on me and get a bite, so I tossed the handgun and drew my big knife.

With the blade touching the inside of my forearm, I held it in a reverse grip, then came in with a slash that took one of the women across the throat. It was so fast that she didn't have time to react, and she fell back gurgling. The second one managed to loop a hand over my shoulder and pull me in. Her mouth was rancid, like old meat with teeth stuck in it. She looped her other hand around me, but I batted it aside. The knife was at my side, so I dragged it up, slashing into her stomach and tugging upward. I would like to say there was a splash of warmth, but it was anything but. I'm sure her intestines spilled out, but they felt like a bunch of cold snakes that wanted to wrap around my arm.

She didn't seem to mind the wound that would have brought a normal person to her knees and left her bleeding to death. She held onto me like a vice. I hit her a couple of times with my left hand as I tried to dislodge her, but she wanted a piece of me. She snapped at my face, and I barely got my hand out of the way in time to avoid the bite.

I pushed her away and ripped the knife up. The blow was quick, and I think I cut through most of her forearm. She loosened her grip enough for me to get the knife out. When she tried to bite me the next time, I had my blade ready and cut her across the face, taking part of her lip off in the process. Then I reversed the blade and, with a whip like motion, drove the knife into her temple as hard as I could. It went in cleanly, and she dropped like someone had cut her strings. I dragged the knife free as she fell and caught sight of the green-eyed ghoul. His eyes met mine. He snarled like a dog then turned and tried to run.

"Where the fuck do you think you're going?" I yelled.

I hit the ghoul from behind with a kick to his lower back. He stumbled forward and hit the ground. He managed to get one hand out, but it snapped with an audible pop. I wasn't messing around. Reversing the knife, I slammed the pommel into his temple. He tried to rise again, so I repeated the blow. The second one collapsed him.

The zombies had no brain, no pulse, no life. They were the walking dead, as improbable as that sounds. They were an abomination--a thing that should not exist. They were an offense against nature. These ghouls were worse; they were like the dead, only they had a brain of sorts. To my surprise, the ghoul beneath me was moving. His lungs rose and fell as he breathed.

What the hell were these things?

THIRTY-TWO

With the unconscious and stinking ghoul between us, we made our way back to the camp. We had to drag him, and at first, I didn't like the idea of his filthy skin touching mine. I was on the right and Scott on the left. The closer we got to the base, the more I wanted to put a bullet in this thing's brain and leave him to rot.

Scott didn't say much; he just grunted as we dragged the man. He glanced at the ghoul from time to time, and then at me. I didn't offer any thoughts. I wasn't even sure what had possessed me to capture the creature. A ghoul. I supposed that if I were a bastard, I could torture this thing. I didn't relish the thought; I had no desire to do it. I had met people who could do it. I had met men who would grin and shake my hand, maybe clap me on the shoulder, and then go on to their torture devices.

My hand was on fire where I had brushed the burning grass. Adrenaline had helped me ignore the pain, but now it was back. My palm felt rough, and I was pretty sure there were blisters. I hoped the damage was minimal. It was hard to see, though, because my right hand was covered in soot. I wished I had a container of ice-cold water I could pour on the burn. And while I was wishing for stuff, I wished I were on vacation in the Bahamas with no zombies around.

"You guys have anything to drink back at the camp?" I asked Scott.

"A little. We got some cheap whiskey, the kind that comes in plastic jugs, but we save that shit for special occasions. Some days I would kill for a shot of tequila."

"Drink of choice?"

"I'm Latino. What the hell do you think I like, Bud Light?"

"Name like Scott, that's real Latino."

"Mom thought it would be cool if we had names that fit into American society better. My sister is named Mary—or was. I don't know if she's alive. I have a brother named Sean, and it's spelled with an E-A just like Sean Connery. I think she liked his James Bond the best."

"Who doesn't?"

The thing between us stirred; his legs kicked. I considered smacking him upside the head again, but I was worried about killing him before we got back. We were across the field, and, when I looked back, the smoke was rising into the sky. I wondered how much of my old block I had just torched. At least the houses were spaced a few dozen feet apart. My yard was separated from Edwards's by a stone path that led back to the greenbelt. I think the community had once thought of running a full walking path behind all the houses, but it never happened.

"Hold up. I'm worried about this thing waking up and biting one of us. Does the virus spread the same with these ghouls?"

"I don't know, man. I think they ate some of the fucking dead flesh and the virus mutated in them or something. I haven't heard of one of them biting anyone."

"I'm not taking any chances."

Yanking out the knife at my side, I used it to cut off the ghoul's sleeve. We had to drop him, but he barely stirred. He smelled like rot, just like the zombies, but he had an undercurrent of something like old fish. His arm under the sleeve was white with massive patches of gray. He had open wounds that oozed pus, and I didn't want one of those sores touching my clothing. It was bad enough having him between us.

I used the sleeve to gag the creature. It opened one eye, which blazed a shade of green. I wasn't in the mood, so I drew back my arm and punched him in the temple. He went down like a sack of potatoes.

THE BARRICADE WAS BUZZING when we got back. Men and women, armed to the teeth, patrolled the tops of cars and the perimeter. The air was filled with the shouts of the community as they came out of tents and houses.

"It's Scott. Hold up!" My companion yelled as we approached. He raised one arm and waved it. I looked behind me at the mess we had left, but all I could see was a column of smoke slowly rising in the early morning breeze. The sky was crystal clear with the exception of a few light puffs of cloud.

People had long worried about the impact we had on the environment. That we were going to destroy it. One thing was for sure: Humans were a dying race, a breed that was bound to pass on like so many that had come before, but the earth would still be here long after.

Lisa was on top of a car, staring down an automatic barrel at us. My skin crawled as she drew a bead on me. I wondered what she made of the ghoul, wondered if she was thinking of blowing us away just for hauling it back. Trust was hard to come by nowadays.

She would be right to kill him and us. I wondered if I would do the same in her shoes. I realized what a mistake it was to bring this thing with us. I should have ended him when we were back at the house, but this was an opportunity to study our enemies' leaders. What sort of information could we learn?

"What the fuck is that?" she yelled as we drew within fifteen feet.

"One of the ghouls."

"What?" Coming off the car, she slid to the ground with a neat slide down the hood.

She came at us with assault rifle raised, stopping a few feet away before she lowered it to her waist. The gears were spinning--I could see it in her eyes as she considered what we had brought with us. This was a great opportunity; she had to see that.

"You can't bring that ghoul in. Lay it out and take care of it, then drag the body somewhere. I don't want to see the thing."

She turned to leave.

"Wait!" I set the unconscious creature down on the ground. Scott leaned over to help, then straightened and stretched until something popped in his back.

"Heavy mother fucker," he grunted.

"What? You think that thing is going to come in here? Maybe we can feed it, give it a room to stay in? Maybe we can ask its name and treat it like family, the way we did with you and Katherine last night?"

She had a point, but the tactical advantage had to outweigh the risk. We could learn so much from this ghoul. We could find out how they controlled the zombies, how they lived, where they lived, and how many there were. I was afraid to admit that the ghouls might have some sort of organization, that they might be living in groups and communicating, like we did. If that were true, then we would need to find and eliminate them, because they would certainly be unwilling to peacefully share the world with us. They would want to destroy us—or worse, gather us up like they were farming cattle.

"We need to find out if they're organized. We need to learn everything we can. Don't you have a secure room where we can keep him while we gather intel?"

"Gather intel? Is that another word for torture?"

"What the hell does it matter if we torture this thing? It's not even human."

"I can give fuck all about him. I don't want him in the camp."

Lisa had worked very hard to maintain this enclave in the midst of hopelessness. She had been a beacon for the survivors, given them a place to gather and live together as a family. They relied on each other. They protected each other, and I had no doubt that each would sacrifice himself or herself for the others. It reminded me of the military, and that was why I felt so attached to them after only one day. I couldn't betray them, but I didn't want to lose valuable information we could learn from the ghoul.

A scream from ahead drew my attention toward the end of the road. There were a couple of zombies headed in our direction. A loud moan filled the air and lifted the hair on the back of my neck. I looked down at the ghoul, and his eyes were open and glowing.

"Are you doing that?" I wondered how intelligent he was.

"You will die," he hissed in a burst of foul breath that made me want to turn aside and throw up.

I looked back, and there were more of them. They were filling the street, heading in our direction. I considered the ghoul--this man that used to be human but was now some sort of monster. Who was I to become judge, jury, and executioner?

"Call them off or I'll blow your brains all over the road. You want to die?" Pulling my handgun, I pressed the barrel to his head.

"I'm already dead ... just like you. You just don't ... know ... it."

His speech pattern was a mess. He could only choke out a few words before wheezing.

"Fuck! How do you do it? How do you call and control them?"

"Why are you still... among the living?"

White rage filled my vision. It tore across my eyes and filled them with hatred for this thing. He was human once, like me, like all of us, but he had no humanity left. He was worse than an animal. He was a demon that needed to be put down.

I held his collar as I kept his head off the ground. Dropping him, I stood and blew his head open with a pair of rounds that turned the concrete red and gray, like a bowl of putrid spaghetti had been spilled.

More moans filled the air. I did a full turn as I took in the hordes that were closing in on us. I saw five or six coming in every direction, with more behind them. A shambling army of rotted dead that walked like living men and women. Their cries and snarls filled me with more rage. This was not supposed to happen!

"Call everyone back!" Lisa yelled.

A pulsing sound ripped through the air, like they had routed a semi's air horn into an air raid siren. Houses opened on all sides, and people came streaming out and into the street. They were strapping on clothes, packs, guns--it was a perfect example of organized chaos. There must have been thirty people, who would put the population of the enclave at something like seventy. Would it be enough?

Scott grabbed my arm and tugged at me. I stared at the ghoul on the ground as the light left its eyes. The body didn't even twitch; it just lay listless like it had been on a morgue table for days.

The rage washed over me, but I used it rather than let it take over. I had met men who would go blind with rage in the heat of battle and make mistakes. Blind anger was a powerful tool, but it could lead to mistakes.

Forcing down the adrenaline shakes, I took a deep breath, then another, before focusing on the zombies coming at us. Men and women with horrible wounds that no longer bled. Strips of flesh hung over rotted clothing as they came after us.

Lifting the rifle, I stared down the iron sights at a man dressed in a suit. His tie was still pulled up tight, but most of his shirt was missing. I put one in his forehead, and he fell back without a sound.

I walked as I shot, my gaze sweeping with the end of the gun as though the weapon were some sort of strange eyewear that allowed me to see the dead. And when I saw them, I dropped them. I fired fast, exhaling as I squeezed the trigger. Most fell with one shot, but some took two.

A voice called to me, then two, but I ignored them and fired. The voice in my mind was counting, and when I ran dry, I was already reaching for my back pocket for another magazine. The old one went into my waistband, and the other was slapped home without a look. My gaze never left the things coming after me.

They snarled and groaned as they moved in on us. There were no tactics; all they cared about was getting a piece of my flesh. I was probably fifteen or twenty feet from the barrier when other shots started to fill the air. Bullets buzzed past--angry wasps that tore holes in the air and passed with a brutal blaze through the zombies.

A group of three left the safety of a bunch of overgrown rhododendrons when they saw me. I spun to my right and coolly dropped two of them. The third zombie was too close for a shot, so I snapped my foot up in a front kick to the thing's chest. The kick was cool and coordinated; I exhaled as I struck, and every muscle in my body tightened on impact. The blow snapped ribs, but the zombie merely fell onto its back and, after a couple of seconds, started struggling to its feet. I turned and dropped a pair that had gotten too close, and when I spun around to kill the one that I had kicked, a bullet ripped from my right and tore its forehead open.

Looking back, I found Scott with his shotgun. He pumped a round in and fired at nearly point-blank range at a pair that had been closing from my right. One fell, so I dispatched the other. She was probably in her sixties and dressed in rain gear. It was easy to imagine she had chosen the thick clothing to protect her from bites, but she was missing most of one hand. They must have started there when they turned her into a meal.

I shot her in the head and then started to fall back. I was not done with the fight, but I needed to get to the other side.

"Let's go!" I called to Scott, but I didn't stop to see if he heard me. I ran for the line of cars and jumped on an old Ford, landing with a boom that probably left a dent in the hood. In two breaths, I was over it and sliding to the ground, then through a line of defenders.

Zombies parted, but it soon became a tangle as I strove to get around the combatants. Guns in all forms came out as the zombies came on. From all sides, they poured out of the woods and into the streets. They came in pairs and then in tens. It was the worst scenario I could possibly imagine, submitting my newfound friends to this horror. They came covered in blood, some fresher than others. Some had only strips of flesh left, and some were missing limbs. One poor woman in a jogging suit was missing part of her face; she was no longer 'juicy,' that was for sure.

Reaching the other side of the compound, I slid over another car and into the street. I dashed for my Honda and flung the rear door open. The M249 came out, as did an extra pair of magazines.

The gun was heavy, and I would be better off getting to cover so I could mount it on something. At this range, I would be far from accurate.

None of that mattered. I wanted to blast these things back to Hell.

THIRTY-THREE

The gun was a terrible pounding that tore open the day like a plane was flying overhead. It jerked back against my shoulder, so I leaned in and fought the recoil as I sprayed a healthy dose of .223 rounds into the oncoming creatures. Parts flew off with sickening ease. Bodies fell back as the bullets hammered into them over and over. One would almost call it a bloodbath, but there wasn't much blood.

Long before I was ready to stop, the gun ran out of rounds, so I dropped the giant drum and tossed it in the back of the truck. I slammed another magazine in and let out a fresh burst. The chatter of shots came from behind, but there was also the sound of engines starting up. One, a very low rumble, sounded like a big diesel engine.

I glanced over my shoulder to see an army of men and women setting up lines of defense. It looked like something out of a textbook on how to defend a line. Some lay on top of trucks and yammered away with assault rifles. Some, like Scott, had dropped the big guns and were going at it with handguns. He had what looked like army-issue .45s in each fist. He spun and shot, moved and shot, and when he shot, something fell.

It was a massacre, plain and simple.

But they kept coming.

The first car to leave was a beat-up station wagon. It had someone in the back, and I suspected it was Katherine. Another car swerved around it and, with a roar, shot into the lead. A couple of other cars came after, then a big wrecker inched along around them. I kept glancing back to see how the warriors were holding up. Gunshots echoed everywhere. The ringing in my ears settled in and would be there for a while.

Scott came to my side as I unloaded a fresh magazine. He had one gun under his arm while he reloaded. He slapped a magazine in, then repeated the process.

"What's the plan?" he yelled.

"Staying alive."

"I didn't ask if you could dance, man. I want to know if you have a fucking plan to get the hell out of here before the place is overrun."

I didn't have a plan besides killing as many of the zombies as I could. I had brought them here, and it was my duty to get rid of them.

The gun hammered to a stop, and the last recoil left my shoulder feeling sore. My ears rang, but the sound of the dead rang louder than any shots. They came on, slipping over bodies, and they fell among the corpses. Moving corpses among the still corpses--it was a nightmare. All I wanted to do was run away screaming. My flesh crawled as I watched the zombies clamber for me.

Scott continued shooting them, but we were seriously outnumbered. More cars were starting up, but I wasn't ready to leave just yet. I dug in my pockets and pulled out the keys. "We can take my car." I tossed the keys to Scott.

"I look like a fucking chauffeur?" he said and tossed them back.

Catching them, I grinned. He grinned back and shot one in the face. There was a splatter of blood that was nothing more than congealed red, like the blood that pools in the bottom of a container of leftover meat in the refrigerator. I grimaced and tossed the M249 in the back of the car. My trusty shotgun was on the back seat, so I tugged it off the floor and checked the breach. Picking up a box of shells, I stuffed it into my pocket. I could kill a few more while the survivors made their escape.

They were all around us. I emptied the shotgun and started to reload, realizing we would not have much time. They were ten or fifteen feet away, and I could pick out details. Things I wished I could not see. The empty eyes, faces covered in blood. Some gray, others pale and white. Listless features on moving bodies. And behind them I caught the sight of green eyes that burned into me--seared like fire. I saw one pair then two, then several others popped up. And they urged the undead on.

I had a new target.

I emptied the shotgun and reached into the back of the car for the hunting rifle. It was on the floor, and I didn't have time to check its condition. I opened the front door and used it as a brace to lean my body against. Then I lifted the gun, slid the bolt back, and watched a round fall into the chamber. Lifting the gun to my cheek, I took careful aim.

They were about fifty feet away, and they had their hands out at their sides as if corralling the zombies. One gestured, and a group stepped forward. I waited until he gestured with the other hand, and then I blew his brains out.

"We need to get the fuck out of here, man!" Scott yelled from somewhere behind me, punctuating his words with a shotgun blast then another.

I spun around, and he was almost swarmed. He staggered to the SUV and got in, slamming the door shut and popping up in the turret. He squeezed the gun between his body and the opening, then turned away from me and shot a pair.

I had to fall back, but they closed in on the other side. Now my way to the car was blocked. I fished the keys out and called out to Scott. He turned to see my wide eyes, and I threw the keys at him. He nearly dropped the gun as he made to catch them, but he managed to snag them in one hand. He stared at me, and I could not read his eyes. I wanted to tell him to take care and to watch out for Lisa and Katherine, but it seemed unnecessary.

I slammed the butt of my gun into the face of one of the zombies, and it fell away with a crunch. There should have been a spurt of blood. I was afraid that the only blood I would be seeing anytime soon would be my own.

The rifle was empty, and I didn't have time to load, because they were everywhere. I spun away from the car and kicked one in the chest, then I swung the gun like a bat and laid another one out.

A small space opened, but I felt hands reach for me. The stench of the dead and rotting made me want to puke my guts out. I tried to breathe in the mass, but it was damn near impossible. I knew it was panic eating at me—an absolute dread sinking into my gut like a dark night. I had no escape. The SUV was ten feet away, but it might as well have been a mile away for all the good it did me.

I swung the gun hard into another zombie, and the stock came loose. Goddamn cheap Walmart rifle. More cold hands. Drawing my knife, I went at them with my own version of teeth. The blade was a crescent of death that I used to slice my way free. There were so many of them, but I might buy myself a few more seconds. The clothing might hold up against a small bite, but it wouldn't if one set into me with intent.

Hands. Rotted breath. Moaning. Cries. What would it feel like when they tore me apart? I should have saved a bullet for my own head.

Then a space opened, and one of the green-eyed bastards stood ahead of me. I dove for him, but something came down across my back like a lead bar. While I staggered under the blow, I still launched myself at the fucker one more time. I just needed to close in and sink my blade into his throat. Then another blow, this one to the base of my skull, and the lights went out like someone had covered the sun. My knees hit the ground and sent pain rocketing up my legs. I tried to get my hands out to stop my fall, which was the last thing I was aware of, except for one hazy thought. At least I wouldn't feel pain when they tore me to pieces.

PART 3

THIRTY-FOUR

Reality was the bitch I didn't want to deal with. I came to it unwilling, tried to ignore it, but there was a ringing in my ears that wouldn't let me be. Pressure on one side of my head made me feel like I had a cold and needed some medicine. I needed some Oxy while I was at it, because my whole body felt like a punching bag, or the remains of one tossed into the trash after a lifetime of faithful service.

The smell of dirt, mud, and old leaves filled me with a sense of peace. That came into sharp contrast as I tried to blink away flashes of light. It was like I had stared at the sun and paid for it with the aftereffects burned into my retinas.

I lifted my head, but the pain made me pay for that little effort. A pissed-off demon bashed around in my skull. It screamed over and over for me to just give up and lie here for eternity.

Reaching up, I felt around the back of my head, which revealed a huge lump to my questing fingers. My shoulders hurt when I moved; they felt pinched and sore right in the middle of my back. Where had that blow come from?

My head was in a fog. The last thing I remembered was the battle at the barricade. My half-suicidal attempt to take out the enemy while my new friends got away.

Some of my vision returned after I blinked, but only on one side. My left eye continued to throb in time with my heartbeat. A blast of darkness that almost cleared soon fizzled out again. I shook my head, but that only made my brain rattle around and hurt even worse.

I rolled to my side and then onto my stomach, managing to get one arm under my body and push myself off the ground. My hand crunched against leaves and wet foliage of some sort. When I gripped at pressed grass, I felt something slither across my fingers.

After I rubbed my eyes, my vision started to come back.

It was cold, wet, must have been close to morning. I got a glimpse of my hand and grabbed a piece of earth to reassure myself it was still there. Then I looked up at a scene of horror.

I would like to say it was some sort of hallucination brought on by the blow to the back of my head. I would like to say it wasn't reality, but a bad dream. But the place in which I woke was all too real.

I was in a large cage complete with rusted metal bars. It looked like someone had taken over a farm of some sort and put people in the cages instead of animals. There were other large jails, some just chicken coops, but those had kids in them. I got a glimpse of grungy faces cowering together. They shifted around when they met my eye with a nervousness I did not find reassuring.

Another giant cage to the right was filled with folks--men and women in various states of dress. Some looked familiar, but I couldn't be sure if they had been at the camp with me. I sat up and leaned my head forward so I could rest it against my fist, arm crooked and set against my knee. The effort of getting up had all but exhausted me.

I looked up again, and this time I saw the sky. It was red like blood, and I had to wonder if there was something wrong with my sight. The clouds rolled by but had a pink tinge that made me think of the end of the world. They were late to the party, since they missed the end by about six months.

I had a feeling this was the end for me, because I was in a cage, and it was rare to keep things locked up like this. Either I was a prisoner, or I was food. Couldn't be much else. I struggled to a sitting position and heard a cry behind me.

Turning, I found a girl lying on her side, sobbing. Her body jerked in big movements that made her look like she was having a seizure. She wore a jumpsuit like I had seen at Lisa's camp. It was gray, and she had her sleeves done all the way up. Near her was a man who wasn't moving. I could only see the back of his head, which was caked with blood that matted his black curls. That had to be Scott.

It was warm, must have been morning, but I felt a chill deep in my bones. I wondered how long I had been on the ground. Cries from all around came in at an alarming rate, as my head struggled to equalize the pressure on either side. I crawled slowly, like an animal in pain. My back ached, my head hurt, and my shoulders felt like they were carrying an extra passenger between them.

I looked all around me to find the place was a nightmare. A home to misery.

Dirty faces pressed to metal bars. So many people, and all of them in misery. I heard screaming in the distance, but it was too far away to pick out a location. There were shamblers walking around, zombies in various states of decay that stopped to look at the men, women, and children in cages. How the hell had we ended up here?

I went to Scott and found him covered in filth. I looked down at my own shirt, the flannel one I had worn for months, I found it was in equally deplorable shape. I felt Scott's neck and found a pulse. Breathing a sigh of relief, I turned his head. His face was bruised, and when I checked the back of his head, the lump there had dried blood on it. I hoped that neither one of us had a concussion.

I pulled Scott's head into my lap as I sat near his body. Brushing away his hair, I pulled back his eyelid to see if his eyes were dilated. I had no fucking idea if that was how you checked someone this damaged, but I had seen it on television dramas. What else could I do?

He shuddered, but slept on while I continued to hold him like a child. I did feel very protective of my new friend, like we had done and seen a lot together even though I had known him for less than a day. I hoped he would come around.

Outwardly I was calm. Inside, I was an inferno.

Rage was building inside me as I sat and considered my circumstances. Away from Katherine, carried here with my friend, thrown into a scene from hell. I had to get out of this cage. Then there were those around me being treated like Jews in Germany during World War II. How many times had I seen a documentary and raged against the injustice to humanity that had taken place? Here it was in the flesh, and I was likely to die in the middle of it.

There was a curious lump near me, and I reached out to touch it. The mass was a piece of meat, and when I pushed it, a bit of blood drizzled out. It was disgusting, and when I foolishly put my finger to my nose, I smelled the stench of decay. There was another lump, and when I pushed at it, I realized that it was the end of a human arm.

I recoiled and dropped Scott's head, which got a reaction out of him. He reached up to touch his bruised skull, but his eyes remained closed.

That's when the voice came and sent shivers up and down my spine.

"Eat. Become us." It was raspy and deep. I turned slowly to confront one of the green-eyed men about whom I had been so interested in learning.

I didn't have any words for this thing that was supposed to be a man. It was no person; it was no creeper. It was a monster. I had seen too many of these things driving the zombies on. On one hand, I wanted to crush his skull. On the other, I wanted to ask him why he did what he did. What did they stand to gain?

He was dressed in a pair of jeans that were surprisingly clean. He had on a long-sleeved flannel shirt. His hair was long and black and was a rat's nest. Perhaps this emissary dressed just for me. I wished I were out of the cage so I could offer a proper thank you, just before I took him apart with my bare hands. I had held one close not too long ago, and I knew they were just as fragile as regular men.

"What are you?" I ran my hands through my hair, but the action made my head throb. The pain pissed me off even more.

"We are you. Only better." His voice rasped and paused between statements.

"Better? You're better? You're a fucking monster!" Yelling didn't improve my pain.

The thing stared at me for a long time without blinking. That was odd. His lips parted, and I thought he was about to stick his tongue out and waggle it like a child. His lips did not curl up or down. No smile, no frown. His brow did not move. He was a walking, talking corpse. I wished once again that I were outside this cage so I could finish his transformation.

"You will join us... As will the others in the cages."

"You expect to change everyone in this camp by making them what? Eat some rotting piece of flesh? You are out of your mind."

"Not everyone... Only you few."

"What about the other people? What do you feed them?"

He didn't respond. I stood and went to the metal bars and pulled at them. This ignited a ripple of pain across my shoulders that made me nauseated. I had to sit down and collect my thoughts for a moment.

It was just as I feared. The people in the cage had been used for feed. At the end of it all, we had become livestock to the monsters we had created. I had to get out of here. I had to free them somehow, but who was I fooling? This wasn't some action movie or adventure book where the hero had all the answers. I was far from heroic. I was just a man caught in a bad situation. The fact that I didn't have a gun to shoot my way out was going a long way toward me being as useful as a wet kitten.

The ghoul turned without a sound and wandered away. His steps were mechanical, and he had about as much emotion in him as a rock.

I regarded my companions. The young girl's eyes were open, but she stared blankly at me. Tears streaked the dirt around her face. She sniffed and her body shook, and I tried to imagine what it was like to be a child caught up in this madness. She couldn't be more than fourteen or fifteen. She should be surfing the web, looking at Facebook, hanging out with her friends, going to music lessons after school, prepping for college. She shouldn't be locked in a cage like an animal.

Holding one arm out, I put my hand up I started whispering to her, because I didn't know what state her mind was in. "It's okay. I promise not to hurt you."

She stared at me, and then seemed to withdraw. Her eyes clouded, and she clenched them tightly shut. Then she curled up into a ball and shook as great wracking sobs took hold. I nearly wept at the misery before me.

I considered the situation. I didn't know shit about girls her age. All I did in my teens was chase them. Now I needed to be someone quite different, so I moved to her, creeping across the ground ever so gently.

When I reached her side, I sat down with my legs crossed. The ground was cold and wet here, grass pressed down by the bodies that had been in here before us. At least I assumed that was the case. I reached out and shoved aside the chunk of meat that was left near her head, shuddering in revulsion. I couldn't even pick out what part of the body it had been. It was just meat, like something left over from cattle.

I wanted to douse my fingers in acid to clean them, but I stuck out a foot and kicked the chunk across the cage where it rolled over and over until it struck a bar.

The arm was a mess. It was covered in blood, with the exception of the hand. So, like a weird handshake, I took the arm by the fingers and pushed it away as well. I couldn't get it far enough away, though, so I picked it up and slung it under my side, flinging it away so it struck the bars with a hollow clang. Scott groaned and curled up into a ball, the ground crunching under him as he moved.

I reached over and gently touched her shoulder, just leaving my hand there for a moment then patting her. I didn't want to push my luck, so I lifted it and tried to talk to her again.

"Hey, can you tell me how you got here?"

I tried to appear as non-threatening as possible, which may have been next to impossible. My normally short hair was in need of a trim, and after the lack of baths, it probably hung long and lank. I hadn't shaved in days, and I'm sure my eyes were hollow and rimmed with red. I had slept the sleep of the injured, not the sleep of the tired, and I was paying for it.

My eyes were raw, felt like sand had gotten into them, and I wanted to rub them. I really wanted to put my face in a pail of cold water and revel in the feeling. A bath would wipe away the filth of the past few days.

I patted her shoulder again, but she recoiled from me like I burned her. I backed up a few inches, but sat so my chin was on my fist. She stared into my eyes, and it appeared that she came to some kind of conclusion.

"I don't know. There was the fight, and people were running every-where. Mom said to hide in our truck, but when I got to it, there were a bunch of the monsters around it."

She sounded so young. Her voice quavered as she spoke, and I barely resisted the urge to reach out and touch her again.

"Were you at the camp with Lisa and the others?"

"I don't know Lisa. We were up from the center of town, in the Vesper Wood area. About thirty of us. Mom said we were going to move on soon, but it kept getting pushed back. Said there were a lot of sounds out there, a lot of noises, like the things were getting closer. They raided our first camp, but we fought them off."

I let her talk.

"We had a lot of guns, but this time they came late at night. They were silent, and they just walked over the cars and barricades. By the time the alarm went off, there were too many of them. We tried to fight, but they swarmed the camp."

Smart of them--quiet and at night. I tried to imagine a less organized group than the one I had been in. How long had it taken them to grow complacent and lax in their patrols? As the batteries wore out, had they been forced to use less of the flashlights? Maybe they didn't have enough fuel to run generators all night. This required a lot of organization. Lisa's group was always on guard. That is, until I came along.

Of course, that had been my fault. Bringing the ghoul there had been a terrible mistake. I should have killed the green-eyed bastard when I had the chance. Should have left his head split like a melon and returned to camp. What did I gain? I had the picture of me and Allison and some fruit, but that was all gone now. All gone and me with it, because I was sure I would die sooner rather than later.

Darkness all around. That was the new world in which we lived. It was devoid of life and love; these things that had been human were washing away the old world and recreating it in their own rotted image. Their lack of humanity and love was appalling. How many had gone to church? Worked as cops, maybe doctors and nurses? Or just Joe Everyday who gets up for work and kisses his kids and wife goodbye, only to become one of these things.

"Gotta get out," I mumbled and realized she had stopped talking. I seemed to have drifted off and was muttering to myself. The girl was staring at me with those big eyes that bored into my head like a drill. My vision swam, and all I wanted to do was lie down and sleep for the rest of the day. Just put my head down and call it. After a midday siesta, everything would make sense again.

A voice in the back of my head screamed it was bad to let someone with a concussion sleep, but I silenced it with a loud "shhh" that may have come from my mouth and may have come from inside. Either way, it silenced the voice and I laid my head down on the filth and slept.

I didn't dream.

THIRTY-FIVE

It was dark when I came to. Jerking upright, I reached for my mouth. A line of spittle rolled down the side of my face. It felt like a bug, and that freaked me out. As I rose off the cold ground, I may have let out a little cry. My head still hurt, as did my throat and back. I shivered violently and curled up into a ball. It was so cold. The earth beneath me was hard and unforgiving as it leached more warmth from my body. I shivered again, and my body took that as a cue to shake all over.

Scott was having a similar reaction, so I went to him and wrapped my body close to his. We may have been strong men, but I should have done this when I first woke. No attraction, no ulterior motives. I just wanted to get warm. The girl watched me from the opposite corner. Her dirty hair covered her forehead, but one luminous eye held my gaze. It didn't blink for a long time. She shook just as we did. Lying next to Scott, I put his hand over my chest and pulled him tight. To the girl, I gestured, and after a while, she rose and crept to me, snuggling into the crook of my body, but when I tried to put my arm around her, she stiffened. I laid it on my side, parallel to the ground.

No bugs chirped, no crickets called, and no animals moved in the underbrush. The only sound came from the zombies as they wandered around the camp. Sometimes I would hear them approach the cage and rest a hand or a forehead against it. They were probably staring at us like we were prime rib. I rolled my head to the side to stare at one who leaned forward, blood and gore leaking out of his mouth. Most of his forehead was missing. I gave him the finger, rolled back over, and went to sleep.

IN THE MORNING, things were no clearer, least of all the sky. Clouds had rolled in overnight. It was overcast and gray, reminding me of a fall day. I went to rub my eyes, but one look at my filthy hands dissuaded me. The girl stirred against me. Quietly I tried to extract myself from the little sandwich we had created, but my movement woke her. She turned her head and, for a moment, the filth covering her features made me think of the ghouls that stood outside our cage. I sat upright, and she scrambled away from me and into the corner.

"The fuck?" Scott's voice came from behind me. He stared at me with huge eyes that looked none too friendly. I looked between the girl and him, and I couldn't help it. I burst into laughter.

"You think this shit is funny?"

"The look on your face is. You should see it."

Scott scowled and turned away, then he rolled over and sat up. He looked the way I felt--haggard and worn. The girl pressed herself to the edge of the cage and watched us from underneath a curtain of hair. She cried gently, mewing like a small animal. How long had she been in the cage? Yesterday she was barely coherent. Yesterday she was much as she appeared now. Small. Lost. Sad.

Another minute and she seemed to recognize me. Sleep probably dulled her mind. It had dulled mine, not to mention the effects of hunger and thirst. She gave me a half smile and slid across the ground to me. I held my hand out, and she shook it.

"Nice to meet choo," she mumbled, and I nearly broke into tears.

"Just 'cause we slept together don't mean we're engaged," Scott shot from behind me. I turned to regard him, and he had a big shit-eating grin on his face as well. For the first time since the attack, I felt like I was among friends.

AN HOUR PASSED where we spoke in low whispers. The girl's name was Haley, and she was seventeen. She told me a bit more about the area in which she had lived, and even spoke of her life before the coming of the zombies. She was not the typical teenager who was filled with angst and taken to brooding about being misunderstood. She participated in a drama class at school and had even acted in a few plays.

We sat together, the trio of us. Haley smiled occasionally at one of Scott's jokes. It was a strange feeling to be happy in this cage where we should be huddling in misery, but it was like an unspoken bond had formed that would not let us succumb to despair.

Zombies walked past us, and sometimes one would stop and stare. A well-dressed man—except for the blood and missing ears, stopped in front of the cage and watched us for a long time. Scott tossed him one-liners: "What ju staring at, Pedro? What's wrong? Zombie got your tongue?" He picked up clumps of the earth and tossed them at the cage. One flew through the bars and smacked the dead man in the face, but the corpse didn't even acknowledge the blow.

For the last insult, Scott approached the bar, unzipped his pants, and peed all over the dead man. Haley had the good sense to look shocked. She turned her head and covered her eyes, but she was giggling.

Scott did a nice job of covering the man in urine, then he zipped up and took a seat with us once again. It was good to have some levity, but the gnawing hunger in my gut was getting to be a real problem. I was having pains that made me clench my hands and hold my stomach. Sometimes I shook uncontrollably, and sometimes I wanted to grab a chunk of dirt and stuff it in my mouth. Anything to fill that void.

Inspecting the cage took Scott and me all of two minutes. It was tall, rounded on top, but covered in a plastic material to keep some rain out. I stuck my hand out the bars by the metal door, but I couldn't tell what kind of lock held us. I stretched and cranked my wrist around. It was no use. Whatever held us in was out of reach, which made me stomp the ground in frustration.

"I tried that the first day. The lock must be in the center of the door. I couldn't reach it," the girl informed us, then went back to staring at nothing. I scowled at that.

Scott and I went over the entire cage again, but we could find no easy way out. Maybe if we had some kind of torch or a hacksaw. Sadly, all we had was some rancid human flesh.

Later in the day, we sat together but didn't speak. Rain drizzled down, and the sky was dark gray. One of the ghouls walked to our cage and tossed a couple of chunks of meat inside. I eyed him—make that her —but refused to look at the meat.

She was tall and thin, with hands that hung like emaciated sticks. Her fingers were long, and some were missing fingernails. Her skin was the same mottled off-color of the other ghouls. Her eyes glowed green just as those of the other ghouls I had seen, and she was a nightmare. Her skin was sunken, her cheeks barely existent, for her cheekbones were so sharp they looked like they could be used for weapons.

She didn't speak; just shook as if she were laughing, and then walked away. The zombie wore a faded t-shirt with bearing Elton John's face, which was a strange contrast to her nightmare visage. A pair of canvas-style pants hung around her bony waist.

"Come back with some Wendy's next time," Scott called out and flipped her the bird, but she didn't acknowledge him.

I snickered at his comment.

"Goddamn that woman is butt ugly." Haley giggled at Scott's joke this time.

"She was probably a bouncer before the world changed."

"Nah, man." Scott shot back. "She was a porn star. I bet she used to shoot three or four movies a week."

I laughed at the image of that ugly thing ever being attractive. Then I worried that we may have crossed a line by discussing porn in front of the girl, but she didn't even blink.

"I think she used to be a coffee barista," Haley offered.

"She'd scare off the customers." Scott scoffed, turned his head, and spit out of the cage. It sailed through the bars and smacked a passing zombie in the leg.

"You're making an art out of it," I told him, half expected him to start throwing feces at the zombies, which would be just about the ultimate in irony. Look at the humans in a cage throwing their shit at a bunch of undead.

"I might run out of spit soon. Hope it rains."

"We're going to die in here, aren't we?" Haley whispered.

I went to her side and draped my arm over her shoulder, wanting to tell her that everything was going to be okay and that I had a plan. The problem was, I had nothing. Not only was I out of ideas, but I was also so hungry there was no way we would have the strength to fight the undead off if we did get free. All they had to do was wait outside for us to eat the rancid zombie meat or die of starvation.

"You're a brave kid. I respect that you have survived this long, so I'm not gonna bullshit you." I took a breath. "I don't know. I honestly don't know. They never open the cage, so there is no way we can attack or run. We don't have any sort of tools to get through those bars."

To make my point, I walked up to the bars and struck one with the meaty part of my hand. They rang hollow, which made the girl's face drop. I hated to be the bearer of bad news, but I truly saw no hope in our situation.

The bars were thick, at least an inch around. They must have originally housed some sort of small animals, maybe even monkeys.

"There has to be a way." She sighed and stared out, up at the clouds. They had grown thicker, making the day even darker. Now a crackle sounded from far away, and a blast of lightning lit the sky. It was a full twelve seconds before we heard the thunder, and sure enough my two companions were counting.

The rain started coming down harder. Sticking my hand out, I let some run over my palm in an attempt to clean it. I rubbed it against the inside of one pant leg, then stuck it out again and caught enough to sip.

Haley and Scott joined me, and for the next hour, we drank our fill. After the negative turn our conversation had taken, all at my doing, it was pleasant to return to happier thoughts.

WE PASSED the night in silence, huddled together, shivering from the cold as rain pelted down. It ran into the caged area and soaked the ground, wetting our clothes making sleep impossible. We kept the girl between us, but it was only for warmth. I needed her and Scott just for warmth.

Lightning continued to blast the air around us. I may have dozed a few times, but not for long. Somehow Scott slipped into sleep and even snored.

I was so hungry. It was at least three days since I'd last had food, and I was starting to daydream about every meal I had ever eaten. I remembered a day when Allison and I had gone to the city and stopped at a burger joint. I'd had a fish sandwich that dripped tartar sauce all over the plate, so I had dipped my onion rings into the mixture. How I wanted that meal again. I would even settle for one of the poorly cooked deer steaks from the cabin.

Kicking the cage in frustration, the lashing blow made me fall on my ass. I was weak, but the force of trying to put my foot through a metal bar was oddly therapeutic.

We were going to die here.

THIRTY-SIX

For a long time, I sat staring at the dark clouds. The rain grew heavier, and I didn't have anything to do but watch it. Rain. Wet ground. I followed the tiny rivers of water that were forming. They rushed in every direction, but some were coming at the cage. I knew that if the rain didn't let up soon, we would be sitting in a puddle.

Water flowed around the bars, and that was what caught my eye. I got to my feet and walked to the place I had kicked. The bars went deep into the ground, and I suspected they had some sort of thick cap to hold them in. But the mud around them told a different story.

I grabbed hold of the bars and lifted straight up. I almost broke into tears when they budged. It wasn't much, but I could tell that we had a chance. Why didn't I think of this before?

After waking Scott, I furiously whispered my plan into his ear. He was sluggish, but after he stood and stretched, we took a shot at the cage. He was out of it, judging by the way he came awake, rising slowly and shaking his head. I'm sure he felt the way I did, which was exhausted. But how else would we ever get out of this place if we didn't try to move the cage?

We both squatted, wrapped our fingers around the bars at knee height, and on the count of three we lifted. Scott and I kept looking over our shoulders and peering into the night, expecting the zombies to take notice of us at any time, but luck was on our side. The ghouls were doing whatever they did at night.

After what seemed like forever the cage gave a sucking sound as the bars came out of the mud. The bars came up about an inch, but we set it back down. We could lift the cage, but not high enough for either of us to get out.

"Lift it a little higher and I can fit. I'll figure out the lock and go get keys if I have to," Haley said.

"You wouldn't leave us here, would you?" Scott asked.

"No way. I actually like you guys. You make me laugh. Plus, if I help you guys out, I think you might be able to protect my lily-white ass from those things."

Scott chuckled appreciatively. At her humor, I hoped. She may have been aged from the terrible life we were forced to live, but Haley was still just a child as far as I was concerned.

"Come on. We don't have all day!" Was this the same girl who was shivering and wrapped in a ball the first night, afraid to get too close?

"If you can't get us out, you have to promise to get out of here. Just run, and don't look back," I said.

Several emotions flickered across her face, but she nodded once.

In the pouring rain, it was hard to see if any of the creatures were nearby. I hoped for the best. Scott and I lifted the cage as much as we could. We had to strain and reach down, letting go with one hand each time so we could grip the cage a bit lower. At last, it was about a foot off the ground, and my arms were trembling. I didn't think I could hold it much longer.

But just like a snake, Haley bolted to the tiny opening and slithered out on her stomach. So there was one advantage to being this starved. In fact, she looked like one of those Hollywood starlets that ate a bowl of peas for dinner.

We lowered the cage as quietly and as slowly as we dared. I wanted to drop the damn thing, but I was afraid it would sound like a bunch of bells ringing. We managed to set it down with just a few grunts. When it had sunk back into the earth, I breathed a sigh of relief and sank down next to Scott.

The night folded around her as she scurried away. Eventually she came back around and looked at the lock, then at us. After she tugged at something, she disappeared. Scott and I waited for a minute, sure that she would reappear. A form walked toward the cage, but it was hard to tell if it was Haley. As the shuffling steps drew near, we both knew it was one of the dead.

It was a man this time. He was dressed in a gaudy red velvet shirt with blue pants. He looked like some ridiculous troubadour. Probably worked at a Mexican restaurant and was caught in the mess in his uniform.

"Friend of yours?" I asked Scott.

"Hey, fuck you, white boy. If I had a gun, I'd put him down with a single shot, Latino or not, bright puffy red shirt or not. Although I give him points for style. It's hard to pull off that ensemble."

Clapping my hand over his shoulder, I suppressed a chuckle. It was odd to think I had known this man for a very short time, and yet he was now my best friend in the world. He was currently my only friend, and I felt a fierce need to protect him even though he was more than capable of taking care of himself.

"I hope she comes back," I said.

"You don't think she will?"

"Would you?"

"For you? Nah, I'd rather haul ass out of here and take my chances in the woods all alone. Of course I would, dumb-ass."

"Yeah? Well, I'd let you rot. You smell like death."

"You're one to talk."

Scott walked over to the other side of the cage and stretched his hand out. He came back with the arm I had tossed aside the night before. He took it to the bars where we had lifted the cage and held it out to the zombie, hand first, like he was offering a handshake.

"Hey. Take this and fuck off." He waved the hand around. The zombie didn't have very good motor skills, but he managed to take the arm and sink his teeth into the rotted flesh. Then he wandered away with the morsel hanging out of his mouth.

"Do you blame me for this?" I had been afraid to voice this question, but it had gnawed at me since the day I awoke in a cave.

"I don't, man. There were too many of them. They had that planned for a long time. The green guys are getting smarter." He didn't turn around, just kept talking into the night. "We noticed them changing a month or so ago. Getting more coordinated."

"It was me that brought them. I should have killed that ghoul when I had the chance."

"Coulda shoulda. No way to change that shit now. We knew it was going to happen 'cause it's happened to other communities."

I sighed and stared into the darkness.

We waited for what seemed forever, while the rain continued to hammer down. We discussed how to get the cage lifted long enough for the other to slip through, but I was already so tired I could barely lift my hand to my head, let alone hold the cage up long enough for him to slip out.

I sat down in the mud and thought about the meat they would offer in the morning. Should we give in? Give up our humanity? At least I wouldn't be hungry and cold anymore. It would also give me a chance to see what they saw, feel the world the way they felt it. In a way, I felt sorry for the damned things. It wasn't their fault. History was littered with tales of people eating the dead. It was a shame that we were being hunted to extinction by the 'better' humans. *We are you. Only better.* The ghoul's words came back and chilled me to the bone.

To tell the truth, I would rather die than eat the rancid flesh. I would rather sit here and starve to death than become one of those things. Sighing, I leaned back against the cage. The rain had died down a bit, and the cover kept my back from getting more drenched. There was no way I could lay on the cold wet earth.

Scott sat beside me but didn't speak. Weary, I laid my head back and closed my eyes. Without the girl here, we didn't seem too concerned about huddling for warmth like we did before.

I was drifting off when a hand landed on my shoulder, which made me jump away from the bars. Heart pounding in my chest, I came up in a fighting stance, despite my foggy mind.

It was the girl, and she looked scared. Her hair was pushed back behind her ears, and her face was washed clean, so at least the rain had done some good. A bar sat in her hand—just a hunk of metal. I crept closer to her.

"I couldn't find any kind of keys. There's a lock, but it's dark, and I can't see how it works." She was standing by the door, feeling it with one hand. Metal clanked on metal, but she moved it gently.

"What are you planning to do?" I spoke.

"Not sure. I thought I could hit the lock, but I don't want to alert anyone. Maybe I can wrap the bar in something."

"Good thinking." Scott unbuttoned his shirt and slipped it off. He handed it to her through the base of the cage, then stood shivering. His skin should have been dark, like he had a tan, but he was just as pale and white as me. I was probably paler. Glancing down at my hands and forearms, I realized that if I had red eyes, I would make a pretty good albino. I laughed at that thought, and Scott looked at me with a quizzical expression.

I was losing it.

She wrapped the bar in the shirt and then took a tentative swing at the other side. I couldn't see what she was doing, but the sound was like thunder. It was softer with the padding, but to me it sounded loud enough to wake everyone in the camp.

The people in the cage across from us were on their feet, peering at us. They looked like desperate refugees, like something out of a movie about the Holocaust. The feed pit--that's what they were in. If we got out, I knew I would have to take them with us.

She hit the door again, and a zombie wandered by on the other side of the cage. Scott thought fast. He dashed to that side and quietly called to the creature. It walked up to the bars, and Scott kept the dead man entertained by making faces and hand gestures.

If it wandered to the other side, we were screwed, unless she was quick enough to bash in its head.

"Shit!" she whispered. Another clang. This wasn't working.

"Describe the lock to me," I said.

"It's not a lock. It's just a bent piece of metal. The sides are away from each other, kind of like a Z. I can move it, but not far. There's some kind of bolt or something holding it shut. I tried hitting the bolt, but it didn't work."

"How thick is the Z-shaped piece?" I kept my voice calm and low in the hope that it would soothe her. I didn't want panic to show, even though I was about to go out of my mind with fear.

"Not very thick. But it is pretty hard."

"Can you slide the bar between it and the door?"

"Oh!"

She handed the shirt back. Metal scraped on metal. She groaned, then there was a snap and she fell back. I pressed on the door, but it didn't budge, which made me want to scream! Glancing over at Scott, I found he still attempted to keep the zombie's attention, but it kept trying to wander off.

Then there was a grating noise, and something hit the ground with a thunk. Pressing on the door again, I found it opened on noisy hinges.

THIRTY-SEVEN

"Help us!" someone called. The others in the cage across from us had their hands pressed between the bars. Dirty hands and dirty faces--just like us.

I slid out of the tiny opening, and when I saw Haley, I swept her up in a fierce embrace. As I held her tightly to me, she sobbed in relief. "I thought I could sneak into a shack and find a key. But the guys with the green eyes were in there. I was lucky I didn't get caught."

"You did great, Haley. I'm so proud of you."

Scott dashed to the side of a cage and whispered to the inhabitants. It didn't take long for them to catch on. Three or four of them lifted the cage, and others slithered beneath. It was dark, and rain still drizzled down, making it hard to see for more than a few feet. The others looked to be in bad shape. I was concerned that they would be hard to separate from the dead if it came to a fight.

When I joined the group, they stretched out fingers to touch me. I shook hands, but we remained silent. Then, like wraiths, we moved to other cages and lifted them or broke locks. Some picked up weapons and took out any of the wandering dead. Thumps in the nights, no cries or groans, just bodies falling to the ground.

If one caught wind of what we were doing, there was someone to put an end to them. The sound of 'thunks' and metal grinding on metal were all I could hear. It was so hard to keep from running. Every extra noise had me on edge, biting my lip and fearing we would be caught.

Within moments, the dead lay all around us. Some of the living had their eyes set on the small housing spaces, and they had a hollow look, like they were already dead, or they expected to die. I grabbed a guy by the upper arm and hissed in his ear.

"If you go in there, you'll raise an alarm. They'll bring an army down on us." The man was large, grim. He was covered in blood, and I wondered whose it was. Rain pelted his bald head and ran rivers down his hard cheekbones. If I saw this person from afar, I would have suspected him of being a zombie.

"They killed my son. They dragged him out and butchered him like he was cattle. He screamed the whole time. The next day they killed my wife. For that, I want to kill every one of those abortions." His voice was choked with emotion, but his eyes were flat black orbs.

"Listen to me. It's suicide. If we get out of this, we can come back when we are better organized. We can come back with guns, and we can hunt them down. Cleanse this place."

The man stared at me for a long moment. Scott joined me, and his eyes were filled with concern. He touched my shoulder and motioned for the woods a few hundred feet away. Haley was at his side. She tried to smile, but it was halfhearted.

I was scared too, and wanted nothing more than to run, but I felt the need to get these people away from this death camp. I was sick and tired of being on the run all the time, but what choice did we have? The moment we woke up the ghouls in this hive, we would be dead. Hundreds of zombies led by ghouls would make short work of our group.

I looked at the dirty faces of young and old, men and women. We were a pitiful sight. Some had open wounds and wouldn't survive much longer, but they would at least have a chance. If we went in blazing with what few weapons we had, it would be over before it started.

"Pass the word." I gathered the man and Scott close to me. "Once we're free of here, we'll come back with weapons and a plan and burn this place to the ground. No one will ever fear this place again."

I couldn't tell if they believed me or not. Maybe they just wanted a shred of hope to overcome the desire to kill. I had the very same feelings, but I suppressed them and focused on getting us out of here.

There were nods all around, and before they could even finish passing my words back, I was on the move. I grabbed Scott, and we took off for the woods. We tried to stay low, but it was hard to see in the dark. We moved across the ground, hiding behind what cover we could find. Stacks of wood and rotted enclosures provided a slim hope of staying out of sight.

Rain continued to pelt the survivors. Everyone was slow and sluggish, including me. I felt like I was beaten down, and I hadn't even started in the woods. Glancing up at the moon, I tried to figure out where I was, but there was barely a splash of white through the heavy clouds.

It was almost impossible to see anything ahead of us. Scott seemed at home moving at night, staying out of the line of those things' eyes. It wasn't easy, but someone who paid attention could do it. We had to be aware of our surroundings at all times. We had to be ready for the creature that stumbled around a corner. And it was just such a creature that almost proved our undoing.

Scott moved ahead of the group, while I hung back and kept an eye on the survivors. There were fifteen or twenty of us, and we were all worn to the bone. The others in the cage—I didn't know how long they had been there. Each was filthy and smelled as bad as me.

As I helped an older woman to her feet, someone grunted ahead.

Scott grappled with someone in the dark, so I dashed ahead and found it was one of the dead. A man about my size, missing the top of his skull. He was dressed in rags and reminded me of one of the caged people we had helped free. I went after him, but I was so weary it was hard to put one foot in front of the other, let alone think about fighting.

Scott went down, and I was there to help. Grabbing the zombie by the pants, I hauled him off. It was like picking up a ton of potatoes. The zombie swung his arm back, but I batted at it and pushed him aside. I reached for Scott, but recoiled when he stuck his arm out.

"I'm not fucking bit."

"Are you sure?"

"Oh, I'm sure. I would know if I got some skin ripped off."

The guy was trying to get back up, so I pushed him down by driving my foot into his ass. He went flat and cried out in a low moan, but started to move again soon after. I grabbed Scott by the arm and helped him to his feet. He brushed at his soaking wet clothing lamely.

Scott stepped on the back of the man's head. I have seen a lot of pain and suffering since I returned to the world, but there was something sickening about the way the zombie's head was crushed into the dirt. The way it mushed and the bones ground together.

Scott looked rather pleased with himself. I blew out a breath and moved on.

Staring back at the camp, I felt rage flood my body. Maybe it was from the death of the undead that I had just witnessed, but I wanted nothing more than to go back and annihilate the camp. If I had a big enough gun, I would have done just that, even if it meant me dying.

The woods were a canopy of misery. Sounds came from all around us as the rain continued to pelt us.

Haley was waiting for us a few dozen feet away. She gave me a questioning look, but I shook my head. We pressed on, me in the lead as I tried to be a leader. I had no idea where I was, and there wasn't even a moon to follow. How long had I been in the cage and never thought to mark the passage of our one orbital body? Or maybe I had, and hunger and exhaustion had simply stolen away my memories, made me weak and confused.

I struck out between a pair of trees that led down a slight hill. At the bottom, we came across a stream. I almost wept in relief; at last, water!

I ran toward it but slowed when I nearly tripped over something on the wet ground. Under the leaves and fallen branches, something crunched. As I drew close, the darkness played tricks on my eyes. Studying the ground, I thought I saw bones. They had to be branches or sticks, but it must have been the stress of being around all the dead things that did it to me.

The smell was the second hint. It hit me like a weight, as the scent went from clean rain and forest to the rot behind us.

As I closed in on the riverbed, I tripped on something and went down. I stuck my hands out, but I still hit the ground hard. The breath whooshed out of me, and when I got one back in, I regretted it. Slowly, I looked around the place where I had fallen, a few inches from the edge of the water. It was littered with bones.

Scott gave a low groan, as if in pain.

We huddled close to the water as we fought to catch our breath. I stared at the slow stream as it meandered by, wishing more than anything I could drink from it. The bones of the dead were everywhere. Chunks of meat and rotted tissue made a slippery surface for us to navigate.

Sounds to the side, near the break in the woods, caught my attention. A voice hissed at us. I turned to regard the approaching cluster of people. They stared at us, and I stared back. Scott must have recognized one of them, because he rose on shaky legs and approached them. They talked quietly. It was still dark, but I saw his head turn toward the stream, then toward us. He shook his head. The group of three moved off.

"Friends?" I inquired when Scott rejoined us.

"From another enclave. We used to trade with them. I can't remember names but one of the guys was familiar. They are going deep in the woods. Lick their wounds. I don't think they want company."

If we all stuck together we would make a lot of noise crashing through the forest, surely making ourselves a larger target for the ghouls to track, but what choice did we have? Though tired, barely able to rise to my feet, I crept off into the night and away from the water and its filth. One drink from that stream would have probably been the end of us.

THIRTY-EIGHT

As we trudged, I went over old training exercises and tried to apply them to this situation. We were outnumbered, so guerrilla tactics would be best. Stay light and mobile, scope out the enemy, and only engage when we had the advantage. Strike one. We had neither the advantage in weapons nor the ability to hide and move, for we had no idea where we were.

We had nothing in the way of weaponry, but like all good primates, we could scrounge up clubs or staffs from fallen branches. My focus swept the ground as we staggered through the woods. I finally found something useful: a heavy stick about three feet long with a large knot in the end.

It was just in time too, as a walking corpse stumbled from between two trees. I moved toward it, so I was no longer in the light. He or she was still a few feet away, but I had to be sure. It could be a refugee from the camp--someone like us who spent days or maybe weeks in captivity and was now trying to survive.

The weird preternatural glow to the thing's eyes gave it away. Not quite a ghoul, but still brighter than the dead we had encountered thus far. I didn't need any further prompting. I swung the stick around in nothing approaching a graceful manner. The club came up in an arc that stretched from my knees to my shoulders, driving the heavy end into the zombie's head.

It went over without making a sound and didn't move again. Panting in the dark, I stood over it and worked on catching my breath.

There was nothing quiet about our steps as we crashed through the forest. We took to the woods and let our fading adrenaline drive us along. I didn't have much left, and I couldn't imagine they had much more than I did.

What I wouldn't give for a hot bath, a bottle of ibuprofen, and a six pack of cheap beer.

We moved for as long as we could before Haley begged a break. I panted beside her until I caught my breath again. Then I put my hand on her shoulder in what I hoped was a comforting manner. She reacted by covering my large hand in her cold slim one. Her eyes were large and glistened in the dark, as if she had been crying. I stood like a big dumb oaf, wondering if she wanted a hug or something.

She sat down on a log and stared back in the direction from which we had come. Scott dropped down beside her.

I sat as well, even though I was afraid I would never be able to get up again. I picked the most uncomfortable-looking section of the log, leaned over, and tried to catch my breath. Scott did the same next to me, as did Haley. She was having trouble breathing, but when I looked over at her she was still looking away, back toward the camp we had fled. I wondered what her thoughts were, but I kept mine to myself.

A bunch of black bulbs caught my eye. Reaching down, I pulled one up and studied it. I was tired and couldn't afford to make a mistake, but we needed something to eat. After turning the mushroom around in my hand, I popped it in my mouth.

Scott looked over and gave a gasp as I chewed. I shot him my best grin and pulled up another one.

"Are you fucking crazy, man?"

"It's okay," I assured him. "Black Trumpet is an edible mushroom. We need the protein."

He looked at the 'shroom then touched it with his tongue. Scott recoiled, but then he stuck it in his mouth and chewed, keeping his eyes scrunched the entire time as if he were indeed eating poison. I would have thought a survivor of one of the worst events in the history of the human race would have a bigger pair and expressed my thoughts. I was dog-tired but didn't want to miss a chance to rib my friend. It was all in jest, and I thought it might take the edge off our situation.

"Whatever, man. I bet I can whip up some dog shit tacos you wouldn't look at twice," he countered. Haley looked on but didn't say a word.

Her face was paler than I remembered, so I moved my hand to touch her forehead to check for fever, but she moved aside before I could make contact. She sat back, away from us, and wedged herself into the crossing of two large tree trunks. I tried to meet her gaze, but she didn't let me. Instead, she closed her eyes.

I didn't blame her. I was cold and tired too, but we had to stay alert. It wouldn't hurt to let her keep her eyes closed for a few minutes.

Movement to my left. I caught the shadow of something just as Scott jerked his head to follow it. We might not have had weapons, but that didn't stop Scott from picking up a large branch. He put it over his shoulder and gripped the haft with both hands. If he was anywhere near as exhausted as I was, he might get one solid swing out of the hunk of wood.

I dropped into something close to a combat stance and got ready to fight if I had to. Lucky for us, it was just one of the mindless zombies who wandered by. Its bald head passed between a break in the branches and then moved on. I exhaled as quietly as possible and wondered if the things even had decent hearing. For all I knew, the undead were deaf mutes that relied on something else to sense those around them.

I was so tired that I started daydreaming about men in white coats who surrounded a pair of zombies bound in shackles. They poked and prodded, and one even used a pair of pliers to snip off a fingertip. The thing moaned and groaned but didn't acknowledge the pain.

Shaking my head, I snapped out of it. Was there a place in the city where they made a study of the dead? Was there a clinic that was looking for some sort of cure? The government had to be in control of something. They had to have a plan. Was this how the human race was meant to die out? In a flash of undead that devoured the world? I refused to believe it.

I reached down and urged Haley to her feet. She sighed as I helped her up, then looked at me with blank eyes. I tried to look reassuring, but it was a struggle that she didn't bother to acknowledge. When I reached to touch her head again, she did not pull away. She was hot, like she was running a fever, probably from all the running. Not to mention living in filth and cold for days. I shouldn't be surprised she was getting sick. When was the last time she had eaten?

"Let's roll, hombre," Scott said.

I tugged Haley along behind me, and her tiny hand burned in mine. We headed in the direction I hoped was away from the camp. The rain fell again, and it just added to the misery. I stumbled over a fallen branch, then slid across a pile of leaves that gave out as I stepped on them. My foot got stuck every time I squished over a mud hole. My shoes were a mess, but at least I still had them. They grew heavier and heavier as they accumulated more and more gunk.

I ran smack into someone or something and threw a halfhearted punch. It was a jab with little force behind it and, of course, I missed by a mile. The figure stumbled back and held his hands up. He hissed at me, and I dropped my arms to my sides. Another survivor.

"It's me, from the cage. Name's Jack."

I remembered him from not so long ago. He was the one who wanted to go back and destroy as many of the ghouls as he could in a suicide mission. I stretched out one exhausted arm and placed it on his shoulder. Somehow, I managed a nod that I hoped was somewhat friendly.

"Nice to meet you, Jack. Welcome to the boy scouts from hell."

"And girl scouts," Haley muttered.

He gave a sharp chuckle at her gallows humor. Scott slid up beside me and studied the man in the dark.

"Where are the others you escaped with?" Scott asked.

"I don't know. We took off together, but I got separated and back-tracked. I think there's a road around here somewhere. Seems like when they brought us in, we weren't too far from some houses or maybe a farm."

"A farm? Hiding out there would be appropriate," I said.

"Huh?" Scott looked at me like I was crazy—again.

"Like the old zombie movies. People boarding up houses and hiding out while the dead figure out ways to get in."

"You are one morbid mother fucker, you know that?" Scott said.

I shook my head and pointed into the dark. How much longer until light? If the dawn arrived, we might have a better chance, but the dead would also have a better chance at finding us. Stepping away from the men, I assumed they would follow, while I let my instincts guide me toward who knew what.

THIRTY-NINE

The sound of birds tweeting all around us was reassuring. It gave the air a sense of normalcy, as if we were on a camping trip and not running for our lives. For the past hour, we'd made our way through the woods, hoping we weren't going in circles.

Jack was a big man, but he seemed to have more energy than either of us. He crashed through whatever we came across with a sense of purpose, like he was on a mission. I admired his drive, since mine was all but gone. When was the last time I'd had a real meal? The few mushrooms sat in my stomach and made me queasy, because they demanded company. But the night held little in the way of relief. I came across another patch of mushrooms, but I didn't recognize them. They taunted me, and for one crazy minute, I imagined them sautéed and placed atop a massive porterhouse steak.

We sat with our backs to trees on a slight incline. I wanted to close my eyes and sleep for a few hours, but I settled for drifting off, then shaking my head when I had waking dreams. The thought of dozing off was tantalizing. It would be so easy to just let it go and drift off for a while, but there was no telling what all was out there or if they hunted us. An hour ago, we had heard a scream in the distance. We looked at each other with wide eyes. My back broke out in goose bumps.

We were tense, expecting them to come upon us at any time—a

horde of the undead intent on either dragging us back or simply eating us. I didn't think I had the strength to last much longer.

Then I heard someone talking.

I put my hand on Scott's knee, and with the other, I motioned for him to be quiet by putting one finger to my lips. He opened his eyes and stared at me like I was a stranger. He was probably just as foggy as me.

I motioned toward my ears, but I didn't know if he understood, so I did a little movement with my hand, the thumb and first two fingers coming together as if I were casting a shadow puppet on the wall. Scott shook his head again.

Then a branch snapped nearby, and the voice came again. I couldn't make out what he was saying, but it was male. Maybe it was a survivor. Maybe it was a ghoul. I held my breath and rose ever so slowly to my feet.

A shape drifted nearby; it rose in the gloom then slipped away like a shadow. I took one step after it then another. A second shape followed not too far from the first. They moved in a direct line--not confused at all. I knew the sort. These were either military or trained individuals.

A flash of camoflauge reassured me of my assessment. I had to be careful, very careful. If they were tightly wound, they might shoot before asking questions. I knew I would.

"Scott. Do we have any dry wood for a fire?"

My voice echoed in my ears like I had just shouted in a deserted warehouse. Scott just about leapt out of his skin; his eyes went wide as he stared at me.

"The hell, man?"

"Go with it." I made a rolling motion with my hands, hoping my gestures would guide him.

The shape didn't move for a few seconds, and I imagined a gun coming up to take aim at my head or Scott's. I play-acted as best I could, which probably wasn't very well. Leaning over like I was scrounging for wood nearly made me fall flat on my face. I pushed aside some leaves and brush, the ground cold and wet against my hand. There was an earthy smell, and it made me think of my body buried in its depths. That was how I wanted to go out--not in someone's stomach.

"Don't move," a voice said to my left. He was good; he had moved from his location with barely a sound.

I hoped he didn't mean it, because I put my hands up and then slowly straightened my back. When he didn't shoot my fool head off, I decided that maybe he wasn't as trigger happy as I had assumed.

"Someone there?" My eyes darted around the dark space as I searched for his form.

"You know I'm here. And you know I have a gun pointed at you, so stop the dog and pony and tell me just what in the fuck you're doing out here?" The voice was gruff but sounded young, based on the timbre and the way it wavered ever so slightly.

"Okay, but can you lower the weapon and show yourself? There are four of us, and one is a young girl. You're probably scaring the crap out of her."

"Sorry. For all I know, you're one of them, or working for them, and this is a trick."

"No trick. We just escaped the zombie camp back there." I motioned in the general direction from which we had come, but to be honest, with all the walking and confusion, I could have been pointing in the opposite direction.

The man stepped out of the woods. He was tall, lanky, and held his gun like a pro. I took one look in his eyes, which were hard, then I looked at his rifle. It was a very nicely kitted-out AR-15 with short stock, laser sight, probably fully automatic. He could cut us down in a split second.

The man was probably twenty-five or so years old. His clothes were in good shape, and his shoes weren't polished, but they were clean except for the fresh mud caked around the soles.

Jack rose beside me, with Scott on my other side. The man looked from face to face, and I wondered how we appeared. He didn't betray any emotion, but we had to be in bad shape. It was nearing dawn, and the breaking light of morning had revealed Jack to be a bloody mess. His face was red, and his clothing was covered in crimson. Scott wasn't too bad off, but the days in the cage were rough, and his clothing was dirty and drenched in water. He stood shivering like the rest of us. This is a test of the typing

Haley peeked around my side. Her face was dirty, and her dark hair looked like it would make a good bird's nest. Mud and small sticks caked it, making her look almost wild.

The man looked from face to face and settled on Haley. I motioned for her to stay behind me. I was judging our distance, considering how far I would have to move to close and get my hand on the gun. He stood about eight feet from me, and his legs were spread, so he had decent base from which to fire. If I made a grab, I doubted I would have a chance. Even if I could get close and knock the barrel aside, there was a chance the bullets would hit some of the others in my troop.

We stood in silence for a while longer, and I felt like, once again, my life hung in the balance. I wondered if it would be best to just give up here and now. A bullet to the head seemed more desirable that hanging out in the woods, being hunted, waiting for death every moment of the day. Despair was something I had faced before, and it was something I faced now.

I grinned at the kid, and he relaxed.

"You're one sorry looking bunch."

"We just got our asses kicked, tossed in a cage, and then left to die. Been in that place for almost a week," Scott said.

"We heard there was a ghoul camp around here. Let's go talk to the old man. He'll know what to do." He lowered his gun, looked around the area, and motioned for us to go ahead of him. When we passed him, he didn't level the rifle at us, but he did keep it at the ready.

"Old man?" I asked.

"Our leader. A lot of the men in our troop owe their lives to him," the man recited this like a litany. His eyes lit up with something approaching religious reverence. "He even brings in some of the creepers. That's what you guys remind me of, you know. Creepers. With any luck, he'll be willing to help."

I knew this kid's sort. Didn't have a plan until he joined the 'corp' or army and found a purpose in life--like killing other men in faraway places or protecting the country from terrorists. That had been the ultimate slap in the face as far as I was concerned. It was bad enough that thousands of our guys died in the jungles of Vietnam to protect the world from communism. The 'war on terror' had been much more nuanced, but I felt defense contractors had come out the ultimate winners.

I knew this firsthand because I had joined up thinking I would make a difference. But the war dragged on, and I was lucky enough—although at the time extremely bitter—to get out while the getting was good.

"Is he close?" Scott looked around, as if the mysterious leader were about to pop out from behind a bush at any moment.

"Near enough. That way." He pointed with the barrel of the rifle. "I'm Andrew, by the way."

We did introductions.

"I don't know if I can make it. I'm really tired, man," Jack said.

He was in bad shape, probably the worst of us. All that blood, was it his? His eyes were bloodshot and shone with an angry glint as he looked back at the man with the rifle. Not too long ago, he had been in a cage, expecting to be eaten. And before that, he watched his family being dragged away and slaughtered. I wondered if he were even sane.

"We have food and water," the soldier said.

Jack looked between him and me, then grimaced and pressed on.

We marched into more misery.

FORTY

The break in the woods came much sooner than I had thought it would, and I never would have found it had we proceeded on our prior path. Not even a quarter mile from our resting spot. As we stepped out of the close-grown trees, we stumbled into a small creek. It ran parallel to the nearby road, but it wasn't the first thing I saw. That vision was reserved for the military-grade vehicles pulled up alongside it. I went down with a splash and had a vision of the bloody water we had seen a few hours ago, but some of the stuff splashed in my mouth and tasted like heaven. Instead of hauling myself to my feet, I drank my fill as I lay shivering in the water.

It was warming up, but the night and captivity had taken their toll. I still felt chilled to the bone, but at least I was out of the woods. The risk of hypothermia had gone down considerably. Now that I was in the stream, all I wanted to do was lie there and drink until I was sick. I wanted to throw up a gallon of water and then drink again.

My stomach clenched up as the cool water hit. Then I did feel like throwing up, but settled for a long, loud burp. As I sucked down water like a fish, I kept my eyes on the men and vehicles around us. A couple of guys had stepped out and trained their weapons on us. A nice mix of old and new barrels leveled in our direction, but the kid with whom we'd come out of the woods must have said something, or made some sort of motion, to assure them we were no threat.

Scott staggered beside me and dropped to his knees. He rinsed his hands as if he were at home getting ready to do dishes. Then he dipped his hands once more and scooped up some clear water to drink. He sipped slowly, something I should have done, since I was cramping up.

"Fuck me." Jack sighed and leaned over to sip near me.

The line of military vehicles, minivans, and trailers roared to life. I even saw a Stryker. It was moving, but it had seen better days. Someone had taken spray paint and tried to camouflage the sides, but it looked more like a six-year-old's finger painting than a military transport.

A couple of Hummers surged up the road with men poking their heads out the top as they manned the machine guns.

Men jumped into their vehicles, which quickly roared to life. The smell of exhaust tore at the early morning air.

A man stepped out of one of the Humvees and strode toward me. I was still on my knees, so the first thing I saw were his boots. Diamond patterned snakeskin. I cursed under my breath. As soon as he saw me, it was over.

"You guys look like hell spit you out. Bunch of creepers I bet." Lee spoke the word like it was poison.

My hair hung to the side and hopefully shaded my face, so I glanced toward him. Would he even recognize me with the week of beard and filth caked on? The only time he had seen my face was at the military checkpoint almost half a year ago, then again at the house they tried to trap us in. At that time, I was clean-shaven.

Lee strolled toward us then stopped beside Jack. I kept my head down and tried to act like I was breathing hard, which wasn't too far from the truth. I wanted the appearance of a man that was too tired to get up and shake hands.

A group of geese picked that moment to fly overhead, honking as they passed. A flight shaped like a V that swooped away from us. A couple of the men popped off a few rounds, which scattered the birds but didn't hit any of them.

"How many of you are out there?" Lee asked.

"Not sure. They had us in a camp back in the woods. We just escaped a short while ago. Probably another twenty or thirty back there.

But we need to get out of here. There's a shit load of dead in the woods," Jack said.

Haley stayed away from Lee. She was behind Scott, and didn't look to be in much of a hurry to be noticed. Her face was pale and dirty, and she looked like she was a few years older. It was the weariness, the constant danger. It had to have worn on her worse than on us. Then again, I didn't know what she had been through in the past six months.

"Who's the kid?" Lee pulled his gun. He had the barrel in the air, like he was going to shoot a bird out of the sky. Now that would have been an impressive sight.

"She was trapped with us. They kept us in a cage, and she helped us escape. Her name is Haley, and she's very brave," I spoke up, feeling fiercely protective of the girl for no reason other than our companionship. I had never had kids and didn't know how to talk to them or relate.

One of the men approached and whispered in Lee's ear as he lowered the gun. He squinted as the man spoke, looked toward the woods, and then back at us.

"Looks like you stirred up a hornets' nest. A bunch of bodies seem to be heading our way, and when I say bodies, I think you know what I mean. You all aren't about to do anything stupid now are you?"

Lee turned away and talked to the other guy, giving orders that I couldn't hear.

Scott leaned close and whispered in my ear.

"You looked like you'd seen a ghost when that guy showed up. History?"

I kept my voice low. "He's a renegade military prick. I kinda kicked his ass a few days ago."

"What the hell are we going to do when he recognizes you?"

"I hope he doesn't. He'll probably kill us."

"Fuuuuck," Scott let the word hang in the air.

Maybe we could sneak to a truck, crawl in the back and steal some food while the military guys were distracted by the crawlers. Then we'd be able to sneak away at the next stop. It was a shitty plan, but it was either that or remain here and wait for the dead to find us. I doubted he would let us join his group. This was the same man that set a trap for my friends. These men were thieves, murders, and rapists. If I could fool them for a few minutes and get on board a vehicle without Lee noticing me, I might be able to get my hands on something useful, but I didn't think I could stomach being so close to them.

We were on an open stretch of road, and it would make us perfect targets if anything came out of the woods. Across the double-lane road was a fresh copse of woods into which we could crash and try to hide. I didn't like either option, but maybe we could join up with the men and get away later.

"Are you okay, girl?" Lee had his full attention on Haley.

She stared at him but didn't say a word. She wasn't shaking anymore, and I was glad she was coping with the cold better than I was. She probably had more practice at it.

"Haley?"

She turned to regard me. Her eyes were darker now, lined in red--bloodshot and desperate. Had her eyes always been that color? I thought they were hazel, but now they were just black.

"Are you okay?"

She looked at Lee and took one step back.

"What the hell?" Scott took a step after her.

Lee took a pair of long strides, brushing past me.

Lee grabbed her arm as she put it out as if to push him away. He took her wrist and yanked her to him.

I went red with rage. What was he doing? If they had burned a family out of their home just to get their food, what was he going to do with a sixteen-year-old girl? Surely the entire world had not descended into anarchy. There had to be some humanity left.

"Let me go," Haley roared. She struck at Lee, but he deflected the blow with one hand like he was swatting a fly. He leaned over so he towered above her head.

"Let her go, God dammit!" I said, trying to get to my feet.

At my cry he turned and looked at me--really looked this time. Then his face darkened. Storm clouds filled his eyes, and I could tell I was about to meet an early end. I hoped fate hadn't planned for us to make it this far only to be shot down like dogs. I wasn't planning on lying here and watching something bad happen to one of us, especially not Haley. She had come back when she could have run, could have left us. In fact, we told her to, but she still came back for us. Without Haley, we would still be in the cages.

"Erik," she cried and looked at me. I met her eyes. They were filled with ... something that wasn't fear. They were brighter than before, like she had changed contacts. They had been dark, but now they were brighter and partially green.

"Hello, Tragger. Nice to meet you again, son," Lee said in a low voice.

FORTY-ONE

I gasped for breath as I struggled to get to my feet.

"Let her go," I said with as much force as I could muster.

"I'll let her go, alright. Then you can join her. This little bitch is becoming one of them, and if you were paying attention, you would have known that. But you know something?" He paused for dramatic effect. "Even if she wasn't turning into one of those ghouls, I would still do this. Because I owe you."

Lee pointed his gun at her head. I screamed from the ground and rose, but someone pushed me down. Thrusting my hand out, I found an ankle, hooked my hand in a claw and yanked. The man cried out in pain and nearly fell over. There was one other man near me, and he had a gun pointed, but I didn't care. I planted my hand flat on the ground and shot my foot out. It slammed into the other guy's shin, knocking him off his feet. In case he fired, I slid to the right.

The soldier went down, and I struggled to my feet, but I didn't have anything left. Lee moved fast. He slid to his left, boots shuffling over the wet ground with a whisking sound. He had Haley's arm in hand and dragged her along with him.

"Stop!" he yelled, pointing the gun at my face.

If I were on my feet, I might have had a chance, but from my position on the ground, I would be dead before I could try to knock the gun aside and go for a strike. It was suicide, but I didn't see the folly of my action. All I knew was that I had to rescue Haley before Lee did something to her.

One of the guys I hit came back to his feet, and he was not happy. He pointed his gun at me, jabbing it in my face. The other guy rolled on his back, still clutching his shin. "Ah shit, man, that hurt. That fucking hurt!"

"Don't shoot him," Lee ordered the guy with the gun pointed at my chest.

The man looked at Lee, then at me, and snarled. He flipped the gun over and jabbed the butt into my gut, and I went down hard. My breath went out, and I couldn't catch it again. Jack moved toward us, but the guy swung the gun at him. He stopped and held his hands out.

Lee stared at me for a few seconds, while Haley struggled to get away. She snarled and pulled at him, but he held her just as firm as if she were tied to him. His face was unreadable. If he was trying to tell me something, then I didn't understand the message.

The next event would be burned into my brain for as long as I live.

Lee pushed Haley down. She fell back on her behind and stared up at him with something approaching rage. Her eyes were bright, and something should have clicked in my head, but all I saw was the girl who had helped us.

The gun boomed across the silent morning. A few seconds ago, the birds had started to call to each other again, making their plaintive cries, each struggling to be heard. I also wanted to be heard. I wanted to scream my rage, wanted to yell against the injustice, but all I could do was sit there, defeated, while Lee put a fucking bullet in the girl's head.

She was gone, and I think part of me fled with her.

I stared, unable to think, unable to even make a sound. I was in shock, but it faded to white-hot rage in a few seconds. In that time, something happened.

The dead had arrived.

I backed up on my ass as an army of the things broke from the cover of the trees. They lurched and drooled blood as they set eyes on the living. Lee turned his gun on the nearest and fired. One of the zombies spun to the right but recovered, turned to face us, and lost the back of its head to a bullet.

There were five, no ten—there were fifty of them. They moved toward us, intent on our flesh. One of the ghouls broke from the trees and paused to study the scene. I looked at him and knew it was the same bastard that had taunted us at the camp. He snarled when he saw me, then his eyes went to the girl's corpse.

Scott helped me up, and we backed away. I was filled with rage over Haley's murder. My body and soul hurt, and I was angry and exhausted.

The undead came on and were killed. The men and women around us moved with precision as they fell back to their vehicles. One of the campers had only one door, and they ran for it, covering each other as they entered. I wished I had a gun in my hand, but I was so exhausted that I probably wouldn't have been able to lift it.

I studied the soldiers dumbly, wondering if any had been at the ambush last week. They moved like pros now, not like the heartless scavengers that had tried to take our weapons and gear.

Scott and Jack got to their feet. We were forgotten, left behind by the men with weapons. They were swarming their vehicles, firing as they went, but they didn't get all the undead.

The ghoul obviously had some time to plan and act. His line of zombies moved from the other side of the road. A canvas covered truck left, with a female soldier half hanging off the back. She tried to grab a hold of the back of the Jeep, but missed and fell off. One of the men reached for her. He had a frantic look on his face, as the driver gunned the engine and the car took off, only to smack into a pair of dead, knocking them to the side.

Lee was clinical. He moved backwards, covering his crew. He fired slowly, accurately, and when he ran out of rounds, he just as calmly dropped the magazine into his hand, put it in a pocket, and came out with a fresh one.

There were too many of them, and they were everywhere! The moans of the dead chilled me to the bone; their calls for us, the living, made my heart race. We had come so far, so very far in the night, and we were back where we started.

We stumbled, and I fell first. One of the soldiers had gotten turned around while he sought targets, and we all crashed together. I fell on top of him, and I didn't even think about my actions. The gun was there, on the ground, and I picked it up. It was a small-caliber handgun, but it would take out the dead just as well as a hand cannon.

"Get the fuck off me!" the man screamed.

Jack grunted and fell back. Scott was first on his feet and pulled me up. The guy struggled to get up, but the strap from his rifle was wrapped around his shoulder, and he fell flat again.

I should have just left him, but I offered my hand, and he took it. With Jack's help, we staggered back toward one of the vehicles. It was surrounded by the dead, but the guy with the gun started shooting. I dragged the pistol up and put one in the side of a creature's head. It fell off the back of the car with one hand clutching the guy it had been trying to bite. The man struggled and pushed but was dragged off the back. His screams were furious.

Lee called orders as he made it to the large trailer. Guns sprouted along the sides where the windows had been. There were slits in the sides, and metal plates slid out of the way to allow more guns to point outward. Shots rang up and down the road as the vehicle lurched forward and smashed into a couple of the dead that were trying to climb to the roof. They groaned as the big RV pulled away and ground them into the dirt.

We made it to the side of the military vehicle. It was surrounded, but we cut down a few in front. Scott moved like a man possessed. He had a look on his face I hadn't yet seen on him. He was mad--beyond rage. Swearing, he jumped into the car and kicked one of the dead away from the driver's side. He picked up a small machine gun, looked like an MP5, and jacked the chamber back to make sure it was loaded. The zombie he had pushed off the side of the truck was replaced by a black guy with part of an ear and cheekbone missing. His mouth moved like he was talking, but he was probably imagining meat between his jaws.

Scott stuck his boot in the guy's chest, and calmly held him back while he took the magazine out of the gun, as the dead man peered inside. Satisfied, he jammed it home, raised the gun, and blew the thing backward with a tap to the head. Scott didn't waste ammo. He aimed and fired--one shot per zombie. Aim, fire, shift. Aim, fire, shift.

"Let's go, man!" Jack screamed. He plopped down in the back and tried to look everywhere at once.

There was a large-caliber machine gun mounted above us and I planned to put it to use if I could get up there.

The soldier with us jumped in the back of the car beside Jack and fired as fast as he could, but we were surrounded. Scott sat down and handed me the MP5. "There's only a few shots left. Make 'em count while I get us moving!"

He cranked the keys, and the truck roared to life. I held the gun in unsteady hands and shot the zombies as they came at us. Another truck roared past us, with one of the dead hanging from the back while the gunner on the big .50 caliber tried to take aim. The driver turned, pulled a pistol, and shot the thing in the face, but his car was pulled to the right, and he clipped our truck then ran off the road, into the bushes. They were swarmed in a matter of seconds, and their screams went on for a long time as they were eaten alive.

"So sick of this shit," I muttered as our vehicle lurched forward. One of the dead was just ahead, so I stood up in the tiny space, held onto the front windshield, and shot him in the head. Scott swerved slightly, but we still pulped the zombie.

There were at least a dozen more of them ahead, and we didn't have enough momentum yet to escape. If we were going thirty or forty miles an hour, we might have been able to barrel through them, but we were at a crawl. Scott punched the gas and knocked a few zombies of the way. The soldier with us stood up, changed his magazine, and opened fire at the zombies ahead of us.

We made slow progress through the human barrier, and we met with more and more resistance. The dead surrounded the car and reached for us, clawed at our flesh. The stench of rotted meat was disgusting. I couldn't decide if I wanted to shoot them or throw up. The rotted dead were everywhere, and I was once again struck by how obscene they were. The things were an abomination.

I shot as many as I could until we were able to break free. I was already starting to feel better, a new reserve of adrenaline welling up from beneath my exhaustion. Every muscle ached, but I was in my zone now. I had a weapon, and we had a vehicle.

As we broke through the last of the dead things, Lee caught up. I heard a thump and glanced behind, taking my eyes off the enemy for a split second. Lee was flopping in the back of the truck, trying to climb onboard with us. He had his upper body over the back of the vehicle and strained to get in.

The man who had helped us get to the truck leaned over the back of the seat to help Lee. His upper body hung to one side, one leg dangling over the edge of the spot where the rear door should have been. One of the zombies got lucky. They grabbed his foot and tugged, pulling the poor bastard off balance.

Another latched on as Scott turned and pointed his gun. I could tell that he wasn't going to get a good shot, though, because one of the soldiers was in his line of fire.

I shot one of the zombies in the face when it got too close, then I leaned between the seats and offered Lee a hand. He seemed surprised. He had his other hand in the back, gun over the seat as he fought for purchase in the bumpy ride. His camouflaged shirt rode up to expose a burned wrist and a tattoo of a devil surrounded by a yellow flaming pentagram. Instead of taking his wrist, I grabbed his pistol.

We lurched ahead, free of the zombies, and Scott put the pedal to the metal as we screeched up the winding road. There were a few of the dead on the road, but Scott did a good job of avoiding them. I admired his resolve not to smash into each one like a piñata, which might have damaged the truck. The last thing we needed was to be stuck.

"Let go of that gun!" Lee yelled, but I ignored him and pried it loose. Jack held onto him so he couldn't get into the seat; his legs hung over the back of the truck like zombie bait. I didn't care if one of them took him. I was just as likely to put a bullet in his skull after what he did to Haley.

"Scott, pull over as soon as we're free. Lee and I are going to have a little chat."

"Does the chat involve tossing his ass off a cliff?"

"As much as I know we need to keep other humans alive, it is pretty tempting."

Lee stared daggers at me. If he had the gun, I was sure he would have shot me right about then. The scar that ran up his cheek was livid as he ground his teeth together, and I swore I could smell the stench of death on him. How I wanted to shoot him and be done with it.

"At least let me sit in the seat like a big boy. I hate having my ass hanging out for the zombies to latch onto."

"Do you think Haley felt that way, too? Think she'd like to be sitting with us, instead of lying in a pile of blood, you son of a bitch?"

"Hey, son, she was changing into one of them, and you know it. Everyone knows that when the eyes go green, you shoot. We don't need any more of those ghouls in the world. They're already convinced they're stronger and better than us. I did her and you a favor. It's time you recognize what's right in front of you."

"What's in front of you, Lee, is a fucking gun, and it's pointed at your face. Do you really want to keep justifying killing the girl that helped us escape? A girl, Lee, a seventeen-year-old girl!" My hands shook with rage as I lifted the gun and pointed it at his forehead. My finger fell across the trigger, and I wanted to apply the pressure it would take to fire the bullet into his smirking face.

"You going to shoot one of your own? Are you going to shoot a survivor?" he challenged me.

"Is that the same choice you've offered the people you dragged out of their homes? The people your men raped and killed?"

He didn't even acknowledge my questions. He just stared at me like I was speaking a different language. I hated this man, and I barely knew him.

"Do it," Scott said.

I glanced over, and Scott's eyes were just as livid as my own. Jack looked between us, but I couldn't read his expression. Maybe, like me, he was exhausted and sick of running.

"Scott, pull over, please," I said, deciding I couldn't kill Lee. As much as I wanted to, he was right.

Scott came to a halt and took the MP5 from my lap. He looked at me and winked. I guessed he was letting me know he had my back no matter my decision.

"Get out," I said simply.

"You gonna just shoot me here, and leave my body for the goddamn zombies? Takes a real man to do that, you know--to step forward and take care of business. It takes a man with guts. You sure you're up to the challenge?"

"Get out of the fucking truck. NOW!"

Lee stared at me for a while, shook his head, and then slid out of the back seat.

It was much quieter here, a mile or so from the death and destruction. There were a few birds chirping, and noises from the bushes surrounding the road. A lazy cloud picked that moment to drift over the sun, setting the road on fire as diffuse light scattered across the ground, faded, and then reappeared.

I pointed the gun at his face and thought about all the reasons I should let him live. He was one of us, as disgusted as I was with him. He was a human, and we were an endangered species. I thought of all those who had passed into the night since the uprising of the dead, saw their faces, and felt a sense of loss.

Would one more death change anything? Then I pulled the trigger.

Shock registered on Lee's face as the hammer smacked against a dry chamber. I stared at him then at the gun. With a cry of fury, I tossed the pistol into the bushes.

I reached across the back of the seat, grabbed him by the collar and pushed. His precarious position, ass in the air, meant he had no purchase. He flopped off the truck and landed in a heap.

"I hear the dead are recruiting. Go fucking join them."

"Coward. Come back here and face me. This ain't over. Come back here!" he screamed as we drove away. He was on his hands and knees, with his hand pressed to his stomach.

He was right about that; it was far from over, but that was all later.

FORTY-TWO

We drove for miles until we came to the outskirts of Vesper Lake. The road was blackened and scarred, and the same husks of cars I had grown used to were now faded shadows in the pale light. We needed a place to hole up, but the cabin was too risky this late in the day. The drive would take at least an hour, and I didn't trust our gas supply to get us there.

Every once in a while, the radio squeaked, but I didn't take time to figure it out. Scott fiddled with it and changed channels. He listened and sometimes spoke into the old CB speaker, but he didn't get a reply.

We pulled off on a dirt road, which we followed until we came to an old farm. The house was blackened and gutted, but we found a barn in the back--more a slaughterhouse than anything else. The sign out front informed us that they sold quarter and half slabs of beef. I was so hungry I was pretty sure I could devour one if it appeared. I wouldn't mind a juicy steak cooked over an open flame.

We did a quick reconnaissance, but the place had been long deserted. The remains of a man, or woman, in overalls, lay outside of the building. It didn't twitch, so we left it undisturbed. There were no animals left, and the gates around the place were wide open. We didn't bother with the house; it was obviously empty. The roof was partially caved in, and one side had disappeared in the flames.

The place we called home for the night still bore the stench of things long dead. There was a bucket in the corner filled with a dried-out collection of organs and intestines. It was so desiccated flies didn't even buzz around it. I took it outside and tossed it as far away as I could. Then I slid the long door closed and latched it with some bindings I found over one low wall that was probably used as a waiting room prior to slaughter.

Jack sat in the back of the truck with his head drooped forward, chin on chest, as he snored like a locomotive. He was still covered in blood. I looked over the remains of my own clothing and thought of how much I would give for a change right now. My week in the woods and the cages had not been kind to them. My pants were nearly dry, but they were hard to move in. They were crusted with old salt from my sweat, mud from the woods, and all manner of things that I must have brushed into while on the run. Sniffing the shirt, I smelled my own stench; not a hint of Haley to be found. I hung my head and sighed.

"Yeah brother, I'd cry too. You smell like shit," Scott said. He had the same quirky grin as always, and I almost embraced him right then and there. It was my fault he was stuck here with me, but he took it in good spirit, just like everything else. I hoped someday I would be able to make it up to him.

"What the hell do we do now?" I said.

"I don't know about you, but I would love to get some rest, and then call in an air strike on the bastards that kept us in that cage. We left a lot of people back there."

"I know, but the army and air force are long gone. At least I think they are, unless you know different."

"I'm not sure. There were rumors of military survivors rebuilding in some cities. I heard the military had a safe city built up around Pittsburgh, but who knows if that's true."

I went to the truck and rummaged around. There was a cover over the back, from the seat to the bumper, and there were boxes secured under the seat itself. After popping the latch, I sucked in my breath. Scott came over to look at the contents and whistled at the haul.

"Who the ..." Jack jerked up and nearly fell out of the seat. Scott and I chuckled and welcomed him back to the land of the living. He rubbed his eyes as he crunched over the straw-covered ground and joined us. His eyes went wide.

Food!

I found a bottle of Gatorade. It was full of water—clean, clear water. In a few swallows, I drank it down, not caring that it was warm. There was a case of the bottles, and we made a serious dent in them. There was no question about reserving some of it. We weren't on a deserted island; we just had to scrounge for our meals, and when we found them, it was in our best interest to enjoy every bite like it was our last.

Then we tore into a box of Cliff bars. I ate three before I came up for breath.

We looked through the other boxes and supplies, stacking and sorting, compiling and discussing. There were enough supplies here for a half-assed plan that was forming in my brain, but we needed to do it right. We needed to plot, and we needed to trust each other implicitly. I needed help, for I couldn't do it alone. As I stared from face to face, they must have known what I was thinking.

There were boxes of weapons and ammo, from handguns to fully automatic machine guns. Trying not to grin like a maniac, I ran my hand over the neatly stored weapons. I was familiar with some of them, while others were foreign or had unusual designs, but they all had one thing in common. They were good at delivering death.

As night drew close, we left off counting our haul. We sought a place to rest and pulled loaded weapons close. I found a few smelly old blankets, rotted things that moths had been at, but they were better than nothing. Scott got in the passenger-side of the truck and reclined all the way back, while Jack stretched out in the back. His feet hung over the side. He looked like a big baby bump under the green blanket, and he snored like a train once again.

I withdrew to a corner of the building and curled up on some straw. It wasn't that comfortable, but it was better than the cage in which we'd been kept.

Tomorrow would be a new day. Tomorrow would be filled with hope. It would be a fresh start for us, or it could be our last day. But it would be new, and it would be filled with death. I was no longer content to be herded and chased, nor would I be compliant to the will of the ghouls. I was no longer at their mercy or at the behest of the dead. I would take the fight to them.

FORTY-THREE

It might have been morning, or it might have been night. I woke in a ball of pain that started at my scalp and ran to the tip of my toes. The smell of the old place assaulted me, as did snoring from across the room. I went to stretch, but my limbs ached so badly I let out a hiss of pain.

The image of Haley flashed through my mind: her head snapping back as the bullet entered, the look of fear on her face. There was something there that I didn't understand, and I wondered for the first time if Lee had been right. Had she been in the process of changing into one of them? Did she eat from the undead flesh while we were trapped in the cage? While she was out and looking for a key, had she been captured, and force fed?

These thoughts made me toss and turn as I tried to come to grips with reality. My mind became a haze of pain and regret, fear and loathing. It became a cesspool of the darkest things in the human nature. It made me bitter, and it made me hate.

It was red hot--a seething mass of energy that lurked beneath my skin, aching to get out. I tried to sleep, to ignore the sounds of the world around me, the smell of death and rot that permeated the air. It was hard, hard to ignore everything that had happened over the last few days and months. The cabin, Katherine—oh my God, Katherine. I wanted to get back to her more than anything, wanted to protect her, to love her. She was scarred, and so was I, but together we could forge a future. I was sure of it.

First, I had to take care of something. I was tired of being on the run, fighting for my life. I was going to bring to the dead what they had brought to so many of us. I was going to put an end to every one I could find, and then I was going to burn them from the face of the earth, if it was the last thing I did.

I rose, my legs popping as I groaned. I probably had a lack of potassium, and it was making me weak. My body was trying to keep up with the torture, but it was hard pressed. There were more protein bars, and it would have to do. At least they would fill the void in my gut.

How many boxes of Cliff bars were left in the entire world? With the U.S. overrun by the dead, how long did it take for the factories to shut down, for the grain and supplies to stop flowing? How many cargo ships sat off the coast and waited for something to change?

I wished I had a cup of coffee--a big twenty-four-ouncer that I could nurse until it was the perfect temperature then guzzle for the caffeine. I found the next best thing in some energy drinks that were stashed with the rest of the supplies.

I ate a dried-out protein bar and washed it back with a pair of Red Bulls. They were the sugar-free kind that left a weird aftertaste in my mouth, but the chemicals, herbs, and heavy caffeine hit me like a brick, leaving me buzzed before the first one was gone. The second one was just gravy.

After pulling stuff out of boxes, I sorted and categorized. There was an arsenal here, and I planned to use it all. Guns, bullets, grenades, even some empty glass bottles that would make great Molotov's. Fill a bottle with fuel, stick a piece of cloth in, light it, and watch the Z's crackle, pop and burn. Bye bye, bastards.

"Why do you have to start that shit so early?" Scott mumbled. He slid beside me and took in the food and drink. I could tell he was in just as much pain as I was.

"About time you got up, princess. I was about to send a toad to wake your ass up."

"Am I the toad?" Jack sat up in the back of the truck and rubbed his eyes.

I looked between the two, looked closely at their eyes, and felt sorry for doing it. They weren't changing into ghouls. These were my friends, and I would protect them from any harm. They would never eat of the dead, nor would I. I would die of starvation first.

"You're something, but I don't know if I would go with toad," Scott said.

"Good to know I'm loved."

"Yeah, those things out there would love to munch on you." Scott chuckled.

We ate a few more protein bars and compared the taste and texture to sawdust, then discussed the merits of a few beers with breakfast while we sorted the gear.

I found a jacket in one bin that was a little worn and a bit tight over my frame, but I was able to slip into it. The thing had an impressive number of hooks and pockets; I would be able to hang all manner of gear on it.

Scott dug around in the glove box and came out with an old manual for the machine gun mounted on top of the beat-up Hummer. He started going over the device, and even fed some bullets into it from a large ammo box.

"Want me to shoot?" I asked?

He smirked at me and shook his head. "No fucking way, partner. I'm going to be all over this thing when we bring it."

When *we* bring it, eh? I was planning to ask them to stay here while I went, but from their faces, I could tell that was a mistake. There was no way they would wait here while I waltzed off with our only transport and a will to die for my new cause.

I checked the perimeter next, something I should have done to begin with but didn't have the energy for. It would probably serve us right if we were ambushed.

The farm was a few hundred feet off the main drag, so I doubted we would be disturbed. I checked as much of the place as I could, and even went to the wide-open front gate to check for footprints, but the only fresh signs I saw were the marks from the truck.

A dog barked somewhere in the distance. It sounded big, like a lab or German Shepherd. Birds made a cacophony in the woods for several seconds and then quieted down. With so many humans gone, it was no wonder they were returning and probably multiplying like flies.

I walked back to the slaughterhouse and noticed an old well to the side. It was partially covered with a fallen tree about sixteen feet tall. Looked like a small maple to me, but the leaves were all dried and blown away. Pushing the husk aside, I checked the pump. It was old, and there was a block on it--a piece of metal that slid into a latch. With a screech I pulled it out, and the handle moved. There was a tap that was covered, but I couldn't move it. I went and found a rock and hammered it a few times until it came loose. Take that, primate ancestors.

I worked the pump for a minute before yellowish water came out. The wind picked up and blew some of it on me. I backed up, but there was no smell of rot, just rust. I went to the other side and pumped until the water ran clear, then I did my best to rinse my hands clean.

On the tip of my tongue, I tasted a bit, and it was as sweet as honeydew. Scott stared at me from inside the slaughterhouse, and I gestured for him to come over. He tasted it, whooped, and then drank some. We took turns sipping the water until Jack came out.

"Well you're just full of surprises, Erik." He grinned at me.

"I just fired it up. I didn't dig the thing."

"You're still my hero."

Jack didn't stand on ceremony. He walked around until he found a bucket and dumped out whatever the hell was in it before. After he rinsed it out a few times, he stripped out of his clothes. Scott and I looked at each other, and his eyebrow quirked up at the corner as the larger man dropped his drawers.

In the chilly morning air, he filled the bucket with water then dumped it over his head, while we pretended to look at everything but his unabashed nakedness. Not that I had a problem with the human form; it was just weird. He shivered, howled at the cold, and did it again.

"God damn, I'm alive."

After he went back inside to get dressed, I shrugged at Scott and did the same thing. The water stung like an electric shock, but I felt almost reborn after the icy cold washed away my fear of the day to come.

FORTY-FOUR

We left an hour later, somewhat clean, and more or less refreshed. I had a full stomach, and the energy drinks were doing their best to eat away the lining of my stomach, but I was more buzzed on caffeine than I had been since the cabin. The morning air had burned off to reveal a warm Oregon day. Clouds pulled back, and the sun roared down like an angry god.

"Any idea how to get there?" Scott asked from behind the wheel. He'd driven yesterday, and when we got in the vehicle, he jumped in the driver's seat like he was made for it.

"We head back the way we came. The turnoff was about three miles down the road. I remember a big burned-up husk of a crew cab on the side of the street. Then we visit Haley and find our way to the camp."

Scott was silent when I mentioned her name. Had he become as close to her in the cage as I had? I felt an odd sense of loyalty to her memory, even though I had only known her for a day or two. I had thought of her as a kid sister. Someone I would have been happy to listen to when she was troubled at school, but she was gone.

"Do you think he was right?" Scott asked.

"Doesn't matter. He shouldn't have done it. Asshole." Jack leaned forward.

"I should have killed him when I had the chance."

"Maybe, but he is one of us. Good or bad, he's still human," Jack said.

"Bad, man. That was the same guy that dragged a family out of their home because they wouldn't join his cause. We had enough whack-jobs in the day. We shouldn't let them run around like that."

"Who are we to judge?" I wondered out loud.

"Fuck that, man. This is a new world. A world that sucks, sure, but it's ours, and we have to shape it, or we're dead. We'll all become creepers like those things. Do you want to wander around like that? I sure don't. Not me."

"I don't think we should have the power to decide who lives and dies."

"Really, Erik? Then what the hell are we doing now if we shouldn't be judge, jury, and executioner?" Scott shot back.

"He's got you there, boss." Jack said, leaning back and putting his hands behind his head as he stared at the sky. He hummed a song as we drove on.

Scott did have a good point, but this wasn't simply about judging. This was about eradicating a cancer from the earth. This was about vengeance. This was about taking out every one of those undead bastards, so they never again held people against their will. I would err on the side of humanity when it came down to it.

We took the turnoff and drove past the spot where I'd tossed Lee out on his ass. There was no sign of him. I might have had a change of heart and put him down after all.

It wasn't much longer before we came across the battle scene. Most of the bodies were gone, but there were spent shells all over the ground.

We sat in the idling car for a moment, staring at the spot. Haley's body was still lying there, alone, next to a puddle of water that had been my salvation for all of two minutes. I got out without a word and went to her. She looked pathetic with her face to the side, one arm over her head, the other crooked against her body. Her legs were splayed open, so I pushed them together, but resisted the urge to touch her. There was a familiar smell to her--that rotted stench like fish guts left in a bucket. It could have been from the cage; we might have all smelled like it.

I skirted the area with my rifle held low, but nothing moved in the woods, even when I moved into the trees a bit. Scott and Jack dragged branches to Haley and covered her as best they could. We didn't speak as we got back in the truck and drove off.

———

"I THINK this might cut into the camp. The road hasn't seen much use, but I have a feeling it is in that direction," Scott said. He was pointing at the dirt path. There was a mailbox that read 'Johnson,' but it hung at an angle off the post like someone had run into it with a car.

We had been up and down the area, over and around the back streets, and while we had escaped the ghoul camp at night, I was reasonably sure that we were in the right location. I jumped out of the truck, puffing up dust with my beat-up boots, then moved to the edge of the woods that rose in a low fence around the pathway.

I would have given just about anything for a suppressor for the gun. It was an older AR-15, much like the gun I used back when we were at the Walmart, but this one had seen a lot of use. Half a dozen magazines weighed me down, and I planned to use as many of them as possible.

"I'll take a look. Hang back for a second. If you hear gunfire, come in with guns blazing."

"What if a bunch of boy scouts are camping in there?" Scott grinned.

"Then come in singing Kumbaya, mother fucker." I faded into the tree line.

The woods weren't as dense as I remembered, and it would be about my luck to have chosen the wrong location. I crept ahead, feet placed softly, gun raised, as I tried to not step on any branches or into holes. Light streamed in from breaks in the trees, but, for the most part, it was dark and gloomy. It smelled fresh, the wet earth and trees. There was no stench of the dead carried on the wind here.

I did my best to head in a westerly direction. I had affixed a tiny compass I found in the tip of a survival knife to the stock of the gun, and I followed it west. When I came to a fallen tree, I had to lower the gun to slide over it. As I came up from a crouch, I caught movement ahead.

The ground here was covered in pine needles, and each step was a crunch that sounded, to my ears, like I was stepping on bubble wrap. I kept expecting a group of the dead to swarm me as I crept toward them.

It reminded me of the day I came across the zombie in the woods near the cabin. Katherine and I had been together then, and I was fiercely protective of her, even though she would have likely picked up an axe and buried it in the thing's head as fast as I would have.

The zombie was near the ground, low, and it was grunting. I assumed it was a man from his frame. Big and blocky, but bent over. If he wasn't a zombie, I hoped it didn't stand up too fast and end up with a bullet in his head.

With my thumb, I snapped the safety off. The click was so loud, I was sure everyone in a one-mile radius heard it, but the guy kept on doing whatever he was doing.

I drew to within a few feet of the man before he pulled up from the ground long enough for me to get an idea of what I was dealing with. It wasn't even male. It was a woman with a bloated body, grunting over a prize. Her mouth was covered in blood and viscera; she chewed a mass of congealed matter while blood leaked down her chin and onto the ground. The sound was disturbing, like hearing a bear chew on a hunk of flesh.

She drew back, showed her teeth, and moaned. I kept my cool and shouldered the weapon. Reaching to my waist, I retrieved a long machete that had turned up at the slaughterhouse. It was stained red, but not from rust. I suspected they put animals down with it, probably with a slice across the throat. The most impressive thing had been the edge. It was almost sharp enough to split a hair. It did a good job of lifting the hair off a patch of my arm.

She moaned and snarled, but I wasn't in the mood for zombie bull-shit. I didn't give her a chance to turn around and stand up. Instead, I moved forward and stepped to the side, so the overhanging tree wouldn't stop my blow, then I buried the blade in the side of her head.

Adrenaline and the rancid aftertaste of energy drinks made me want to throw up. The sound was like hitting a cantaloupe with a knife. It sank in deep, and when I tried to withdraw it, the damn thing stuck.

I held on with both hands as her body spasmed. Still, to this day, I do not understand why massive damage to the brain kills the creatures. They are already dead; removing a limb just makes them mad. But for some reason, when you put some lead—or a blade—in their brainpans, they go down like a sack of potatoes.

It was the same for this one. She hit the ground and didn't get back again. I got a glance at her prize, which was a leg. The end had been partially eaten away, but it was still dressed. Male or female, I couldn't tell from the shredded foot that was just a mass of gore hanging from the end.

There was a pair of zombies wandering near the edge of the woods, but I avoided them and moved farther along the perimeter. Within moments, I found what I was looking for.

By the light of day, it wasn't nearly as ominous, but it was still the camp, and it still looked like a scene of hell. The cages lay like discarded hunks of metal, and some still housed inhabitants. We might have missed them during our escape, or they might have brought more people in during the night.

I came in at the wrong angle, and now I couldn't see the little shack where the ghouls hung out. I would have to kill any that got in my way as I burned a path of destruction through the maze. Caution would be needed, and Scott and I had already discussed that. I didn't want any of my fellow humans dying. Some might even be from Lisa's band of survivors, and that would weight heavy on my already addled mind.

The only deaths I wanted to cause would help finish the job that God started with these things. I wanted them all on the ground, no longer moving.

The strangest thing in that strange day happened. A plane buzzed overhead. It was a small Cessna--something I hadn't seen in a good long time. The tiny craft dipped low, slowed, and scanned the camp. I crouched down and took aim, just in case. But what in the world was I going to do? Shoot down a potential ally? If it held friends of Lee, then that might be a different story, but I doubted his ragtag group could muster up a pilot and organize flights to find him. It was only fifteen hours or so since I had kicked his ass out of the truck.

What did the airplane signify? Was there an organized base of some sort nearby? Maybe they were getting ready to fuel bomb the sight and I was about to join my enemies in a massive pyre.

Some of the dead paused in their aimless ambling. They looked up and considered the propelled bird, and then moved along again. I marked five or six right away and began to build up a map in my head. The topography of the piece of land left minimal cover. Lucky for me, I wouldn't need it. Our plan was simple. I would provide a distraction to draw in the Z's, start cutting them down, and then the guys would come in and take care of stragglers. Once we had most of them gathered close, it would be a slaughter.

That was the plan, but I knew from past experience that no part of a plan went as intended once that first shot was fired.

I skirted farther into the trees as the plane roared away into the distance. The wind shifted, and I got a whiff of the dead, the dying, and the rot of those left in the cages. Some had been forgotten or refused to do the bidding of the ghouls. Lifeless bodies clutched bars or lay curled up. One, a woman, judging from her frame and remaining clothes, clutched a child to her chest. Her body was wasted, head covered in pus and scabs. Her desiccated arms latched onto the smaller person in a death grip. The child, who appeared to be about three, squirmed in her embrace. His eyes, green and glowing, shone with malevolent intent. I shuddered and moved on.

There was a group of them standing over a still body. They had torn off most of the person's flesh, one arm, and part of a leg. I counted seven or eight of the things and decided it was a good place to start.

Slinging the rifle over my back, I checked my two handguns. I patted each magazine on my chest as I confirmed where everything lay. On each shoulder, a pair of green eggs sat. I had taken the time on the ride over to wrap the metal parts in strips of cloth, so they didn't clink when I moved. Two came free in my hands.

The pin came out with a click that sounded as loud as a gunshot in my head. Well it was too late now; I was already moving away from cover to deliver my first volley.

FORTY-FIVE

With a large stride, I came out from behind a huge oak and swung my arm forward. The grenade flew in an arc that fell just short of the undead. After I popped the other pin, I moved one step closer. This one landed just to the side of one of the zombies. It looked at it, but nothing stirred in that brain. Nothing to tell it to move, jump, or just get the fuck out of the way. It stared at it like a curiosity.

The first explosion ripped the air in a ball of hate and high-speed shrapnel. I was already behind the large tree, trying to make myself as small as possible. Pieces of metal accelerated by the explosion whizzed past me, as did chunks of the dead. When I peeked around the corner, a scene from a nightmare greeted me. Some had been blown apart, while others had lost limbs and were still moving on the ground. There wasn't much blood, owing to their strange physiology, but they still came apart just like normal humans.

One, bereft of its legs, crawled away, so I shot it first. Gun up, forehead sighted, the stock hammered into my shoulder as I put the thing down. Then I aimed and fired until I had finished most of them off.

I moved farther along the camp perimeter. The zombies were on the move, too, looking for the source of the explosion. They came off the ground, rising like ghostly apparitions. They moved in slow motion at first, but faster as they sensed something was up.

How could the dead sense anything? They might have reacted to sound or to the explosion, but they couldn't see me. Still, I felt like they were looking right at me, like their eyes were burrowing into my soul.

It was the ghouls. They had to be stopped. I had to eradicate them and free their hold on the masses before me.

There were a few, then there were a couple more, then dozens of them. They came at the woods with their lumbering strides, slack jaws, and empty eyes. They came in their masses with the stench of the earth surrounding them. Flies buzzed around them in clouds as they feasted on blood and any exposed viscera they could find.

I moved from tree to tree, keeping them in my sight at all times. I would stop and fire, drop a few, and then move. But for every one I shot, two or three replaced them. The camp had been infested with the bastards. If I had to put a count to them, I would have guessed three or four hundred. I did not have that many shots.

Any minute now, the guys would come in blazing, flank the mass, and I would make for the shack and kill the green-eyed demons. The .50 caliber would ring out with its pulsating *whump whump whump,* and I would be able to complete my task.

More were on the move, and I had to make a run for it. I came to a clearing and jumped to the side in an attempt to stay out of view. I was behind a copse, but it was overgrown with blackberry bushes. I had to skirt it, and this exposed me to their eyes. They moaned and howled for my blood, and I shivered in the warming day.

Into the woods again. A branch to the face. Eyes closed as I brushed away the dry needles. Into a tree at nearly full speed. I struck it and nearly fell over, so I paused to catch my breath.

On the run again. More undead to my right. I wrapped the rifle strap over my shoulder so I could draw my handgun. A guy broke through the trees with a woman in tow. They were joined at the wrist by handcuffs, and I almost laughed out loud at the sight of them both naked. Must have been an interesting story there--one I wouldn't ever get to hear. One they wouldn't ever tell, either, as I shot them both. The first round pegged the guy and tossed him to the ground like a rag doll. I managed to get the girl in the shoulder as she spun, and a second shot took the side of her head off.

Moving again. There was a horde just ahead, so I unsnapped

another grenade and threw it from my side, arm whipping out from my body. I kept moving as it WHUMPED behind me.

As if in answer, a gunshot called out behind me, far behind me. What kept them so long?

With the cavalry on the way, I decided to risk the open area. If they made speed in the truck, they would break into the open area in less than a minute.

I was twenty or thirty feet from the mass of zombies when I came screaming out of the trees, rifle blazing, popping off as many rounds as I could. All high shots, so I would take the zombies in the head, if possible. Changing magazines on the run was an exercise in patience.

With a fresh round in the chamber, I blasted a couple that came into view ahead of me. One went down, but my second shot went wide, and I nearly ran into the second zombie. A front kick sent it reeling, and I passed the bastard, on my way again.

The shack was ahead, and all around me, the cages rose like a weird circus. Some still had humans in them. We had to have missed them in the craziness of the night before. God, had it only been a day?

More shots sounded behind me--a mix of automatic and single rounds. That did not sound right. Then the big machine gun opened up, and I grinned as I shot another zombie. This bullet took it in the throat and must have passed through the spine because it went down without a sound.

The shack was just ahead. I didn't know what purpose it had before, but now it was my target. I knew it sheltered the ghouls and served as their base, because I had seen people brought to it, and they did not come out. No matter the purpose, I had a surprise for the building. Something I had been saving.

I spun and shot, emptying an entire magazine. The group coming toward me fell, some now missing body parts. The violence of the bullets ripping into the mass was appalling.

I hit the shack and it rattled. I slammed into it again, then peeked around the corner toward the road that led into the compound. Jack and Scott should have been here by now!

It would have been much easier if we had some way to communicate. Even an old pair of cell phones with Bluetooth units, but those hadn't worked in months.

Note to self: Get walkie talkies.

Note to self: Kill everything with green eyes.

The small building was constructed of corrugated steel. In the summer, it would have been a sauna. It was rusted on one side, and the few windows were covered over with wood and paper. I dropped into a crouch near one and tried to peer in by looking over my shoulder, but the coverings made it impossible to see inside.

With my back pressed to the wall, I slid toward the door. The dead were onto me and on the move. They were closing in from all sides, and it looked like I might have just one shot at this.

I ripped the last fragmentation grenade off my shoulder and stopped at the wooden door. When I hit the wall, then door popped open, but shut quickly from the force of my back striking the rickety building.

I pulled the pin and looked up briefly. Not a prayer exactly, just something I had seen done many times. If there was a God, he wasn't here. The only thing here was the dead. Fuck the dead.

Gunfire erupted behind me just as I popped the door open. I poked my head around the corner of the doorway, I could have sworn something splatted across the ground nearby. What the hell was going on out there?

I would have to hope for the best, hope they got here soon. I didn't have much time left.

I tossed the grenade in the shack then ran. The space was small enough that the shrapnel should take it down. It did a good job, all right, lifting the building up slightly with its explosion. The flat roof shifted to one side, and then smoke rose as the building fell on its side.

One wall went over, and the rest followed. A crumpled mass of old metal rang like a bell as it crashed to the ground. I picked myself up and went to the wreckage, hoping the confined space helped finish the job, but if any still lived, I would take them down with a bullet. I wanted this camp shut down and the green-eyed bastards eradicated from it.

The rumble of a giant machine gun called, assuring me that the cavalry had finally arrived.

A horde of zombies was on its way, so I slammed in a fresh magazine and opened up. From behind me came the sound of more groaning. They were calling for my flesh. Spinning, I dropped one that was too close—a woman missing part of her left arm and all of her right. Her ragged flesh hung like a nightmare, and where blood should have flowed, only bugs and maggots dwelled.

After I shot her in the face, I bolted for the remains of the shack. Smoke rose from the fallen walls and made the air reek of explosives. I poked the gun under one sheet of metal that had fallen over a desk. It was bowed in the middle, making a weird little tent. I couldn't help but think that it would have made a much better place to rest than our cage. I would have killed for such a place a few days ago.

Scanning the remains of the walls, I didn't see any legs or hands poking out. There were no bodies to be found.

"Goddammit!" I yelled in frustration.

Shoving aside one of the thin walls, I found the remains of a sparse room built atop a thin wooden floor. I moved more pieces aside, hoping to see bodies squirming around in the wreckage or lying unmoving.

Setting the rifle down, I worked on the edges, but kept one pistol in hand. When one of the dead got too close, I would shoot it.

The chance to escape with my life was fading as they arrived. They closed in from all sides as I worked to slide things aside.

There were no bodies.

The big gun opened fire again, hopefully raining hell down on the dead.

My boot snagged on a ragged section of wood that stuck out of the ground. Stepping over it, I wrestled another piece of metal out of the way. I had to move my foot off the metal, then I stepped back onto the place I had cleared.

Something snapped and I was suddenly sliding. I reached out for purchase, for anything, but there was only the hard wooden floor to grasp at as I went down.

A flight of stairs greeted me as I fell, and I'm pretty sure I crashed into every step on my way down. I tried to stay on my back, but I hit a railing and slid over to smash into the wall about halfway down. Clods of dirt smacked me in the face as my feet hit the ground. I lay for a few seconds just listening. The zombies above me moaned, while chunks of stair and earth fell all around.

My body felt like someone had taken a jackhammer to it. My legs and back were bruised and sore to begin with, but now they were barely able to function when I told them to get me up. I reached for the railing, but it broke in my hand, so I had to sit forward and try to lurch to my feet.

In my current state, I was as close to being one of the dead as I had ever been in my life. If one of them fell on me now, I doubted I would have the strength to resist. Then it would all be over.

Struggling to my feet, I took in the room. It was much larger than the floor above. There were a few bodies here, but none of them moved. I trained the gun around me, sweeping it left and right in the poor light. Nothing rose up to threaten me.

Parts of the walls were shored up with wood. I found a light switch and flipped it a few times, but nothing came on. Idiot. It wasn't like there was electricity to begin with.

I staggered around until I found a shelf in the back. Feeling along it, I came across something round and hard—a flashlight. After I hit the button, a dull light cut into the gloom. Dust fell from above, as did more chunks of earth. What was this room for? Had someone built it as a prison, or just a place to work and escape the heat during the day?

As I scanned the room, a shape moved into my light, and gleaming green eyes transfixed me. My body went cold with shock, and goose bumps rose across my chest. A ghoul stood before me.

"Hello," it hissed, emitting breath as foul as any sewer I had ever smelled.

FORTY-SIX

After I didn't jump out of my skin at the shock of a ghoul standing in front of me, I returned his greeting with lead. I pulled the gun up and shot it twice. Once in the throat—almost a reflex shot—and once in the cheek. I meant to shoot it in the center of its forehead but fired careless in my shock.

At this range, nearly point blank, the ghoul was taken off its feet and fell to the ground. Well, there was my revenge, just as pretty as you please. A ghoul shot down and me the victor. Weep for me, world; the greatest victory I could ever hope for was at my feet, and I still felt empty inside.

Then other bodies on the floor moved. Why didn't I check them when I first tumbled down here? Probably because my brain was addled from the fall.

I don't know how many there were in the room. Three? Ten? Instead of wondering, I started shooting. They howled for my blood as they closed in. I shot one in the forehead, and then rocked my elbow back into someone's face as they grasped at me.

I stepped on something and slipped. Only when my foot slid off it did I look down and recognize the shape. A skull. Another ghoul came from the right, sliding off the ground like a shadow. I barely saw it until the eyes gleamed with intent. Green, angry, and dead, but cunning. I planted the barrel in its face as its hands reached for me. They brushed my shirt, questing for something to hold on to. I fired, but my aim shifted as I was rocked from the rear by another of them.

Gunfire sounded from above, and I hoped it was my friends.

"Down here!" I yelled, lashing my elbow back, but I missed my target. I adjusted my aim and fired again. The shape fell away, but I didn't know if I'd hit it. There was no sound. My ears were completely numb, felt like they were full of cotton. The noise in the room when I fired was overwhelming. Each shot was now muffled, like I was shooting underwater. I hated that I had lost one of my best weapons--my hearing.

I backed up until my legs hit the stairs. A piece of the building had fallen so that it partially blocked my view. Light streamed in from where I'd found the entrance.

My shoulder and back ached from the fall. I had banged my hip pretty hard, and it throbbed to my heartbeat. The pain was refreshing; it reminded me that I was still alive, and it kept me focused.

I shot another one in the chest, and it fell back, then I fired at another shape before the gun jammed. I was surprised it had lasted this long without getting stuck. The weapons were in good shape, but not all that well taken care of. "Way to go, Lee, still fucking me over."

Dropping the rifle, I drew the Desert Eagle from under my arm. It was a heavy gun--big and nasty. When it spoke, it did so with authority. I didn't have time to inspect everything carefully, but I was pretty sure it was a Mark VII. It held eight rounds of the .44 caliber variety instead of the modified .50 I had fired a few times. That gun took even fewer rounds, but it would probably take down a bear. I didn't need to shoot anything that large, but the weight was reassuring.

It was good to know that if I did fire off seven rounds, I had one left with my name on it.

The ghoul behind me got up again, snarling, and drooling blood from a busted lip where my elbow had struck. I spun, leveled the nearly foot-long gun, and shot it. The gas-powered auto-loader worked like a dream as it propelled the massive .44 load down the long barrel. It sounded like someone had tossed an explosive at my feet, and it did the job. The ghoul didn't so much fall back as he was blown into the wall. Not a headshot, but I think the gun did enough damage to justify not aiming.

Fuckers were everywhere. I tried to get up the first step, but missed it and scraped my chin as a hand closed on my ankle. Cold, questing fingers that felt like they were coated in slime wrapped around my leg. I spun and stomped down, missing the wrist but smashing the forearm into the ground. Aiming where I thought the thing was, I fired another load, then another as I shifted the aim based on the flash. If I hit it, the round went in probably near the shoulder. My next shot was right in the brain.

The ghoul's head hit the ground so hard that it recoiled, and a mass of gray splattered the cold wood floor.

"Stop," someone called out. It was soft, but had the telltale dry rasp, signifying it was not human. It sounded like two old pieces of leather rubbing against each other.

The shapes fell away and moved to the side of the room. There were a lot of them--more than I thought possible. Green eyes regarded me from all four walls. I didn't know who had spoken. If I found out, I was looking forward to shooting that one in its glowing orbs.

"Stop killing. We talk like civilized men. You and I. Just put away your gun. I promise you safety."

"You can promise me safety? I believe that about as far as I can spit. Talk fast so I can get back to killing all of you." My lungs hurt from the night before, from running, from being lost in the woods. They hurt from falling, and they ached from the fight. I didn't have much left. Hell, I hadn't had much left when I woke up this morning. Here I was, letting the damned things I came to kill try to talk me out of it.

"You are hurting us, hurting our kind. Go. Leave us. Alone."

"Fuck you and your kind. You're an abortion. I want every one of you dead." Anger seared through me—a hot fuse that was going to explode. If I had a box of C-4, I would have probably set it off just to spite these assholes.

"But we are you. We are human," the ghoul said. Why couldn't I pick him out in the mass? I couldn't even determine where his voice was coming from.

The room swam before my eyes, and I didn't think I could stay on my feet much longer. How many shots had I fired from the big gun? Did I have another one I could use on myself? Rookie mistake, losing count like that. Or the simple mistake of a man driven to the brink of his sanity and exhaustion. The whole last terrible month felt like it was crushing me with an ungodly weight. I wanted to sit down and babble about the evils of the world, find Jesus, slink away to a cave somewhere, and just die.

But if these ghouls had their way, I would join them. It wouldn't take much for them to simply hold me down and force feed me some zombie flesh. Then they could lock me up until I changed.

What did I have? A few bullets? A knife? And I was faced with about fifteen or twenty of the glowing-eyed bastards. A pair of eyes from much farther away than the rest told me a tunnel stretched into the distance. Who knew how far back it went or what it contained? There could be a hundred more of the monsters.

If I only had some last resort. Once again, I yearned for a brick of C-4 explosives; maybe that would shut this place down.

Screams from above accompanied flashes against the dark of the stairs as bullets bounced around. I wished I were up there, able to fight with my friends, but they would do their best to finish the mission. They would kill every last one of the dead in the camp before leaving. They had assured me it would be done. Then they would lead the survivors out of the camp into freedom. Maybe take them to Portland.

Wait. Explosives. These ghouls were mean, but they weren't all that bright. I took one of the bags off my shoulder ever so slowly while trying to keep the gun trained on them. It had a couple of smoke grenades that I wasn't sure what to do with, but the boy scout in me had said they might come in handy. I held it up above my head.

"This explosive can level this place. If I pull the pin, we all go up. You, me, and everything in the room--every last dead one of you. Someone want to start negotiating?"

Silence was their answer, while unblinking green eyes continued watching me. No one moved. It was a start.

"You will die," one of them said in that voice that made me want to rip off my own ears.

"I don't care."

Or did I? I missed Katherine terribly and wanted nothing more than to join her again. For all her problems, she was as close to the perfect woman for me as I had ever met. Allison had been pale and waifish, beautiful, and flighty. She never knew what she wanted, and I never knew where I stood with her. With Katherine, there was never any bullshit.

"Your sacrifice would be for nothing. We are everywhere. We are--as the old line goes--legion."

One of the green-eyed monsters stepped away from the wall with its hands above its head. He was dressed in the rags of his old life—a Hawaiian shirt that now looked ridiculous hanging from his dead body. It was torn and dirty, and I don't think he cared one bit. He wore a pair of jeans that hung low and loose, the bottoms torn and frayed.

"You're dead and you don't seem to understand that."

"You are the one who doesn't understand. We were created in a lab. We are an aberration, but we are alive in our way."

His eyes regarded me in their lifeless way. The others moved around as he stepped toward me, and I expected one of them to pop out and try to take me while my attention was focused on the ghoul moving toward me.

More gunfire from up above. Yelling, but the words were hard to make out. Ripples of fire rocked the ground as the big gun spoke.

"You want to live? Fine, you go first." I gestured toward the stairs.

He picked his way over the broken stairs. I followed close, the Desert Eagle aimed at his head and the 'package of explosives' in my other hand. As we moved upward, I kicked debris over the edge of the stairs.

I squinted as we came into the light above. I worried that Scott or Jack would see the ghoul and shoot on sight, but they seemed to have their attention on taking out zombies.

When I came into the light outside, I looked around. The vehicle was fifty or sixty feet away with Scott on the machine gun, firing toward the entrance of the camp. Jack was on the side of the truck firing in single-shot mode from an automatic. I grabbed the ghoul and thrust him in front of me. He nearly fell, but I didn't help. Touching the thing was repulsive.

"Look at all of your sheep dying."

"There are always more sheep--many more sheep. A whole world of sheep." the ghoul said. "I was one once. My name was Warren. I was much like you, but now I am better."

"And dead."

The thing turned to look at me, his face a nightmare of bruised and mottled flesh around large green eyes that even glowed in the light of day.

"As will you be, someday. I look forward ... to it."

I could just shoot him here and now, be done with it, but then I would lose a bargaining chip. I needed him, but only for the time being.

"Scott, Jack, you ready to roll?" I called out.

Jack looked at me as he changed a magazine. Bullets whizzed by him, and one pinged off the side of the truck. Scott readjusted his aim and fired in the general direction of whoever was shooting. He was smart, for he didn't pound the gun. Instead, he shot a short burst, moved his aim, and shot again.

Who the hell was shooting at them?

"Are there more ghouls out there with guns?"

"Our kind rarely use guns. Mine use a much greater weapon."

"Blah blah. Why don't you stick to simple yes or no answers?" I considered shooting the ghoul again, then I had a better idea. Besides, he was full of shit. I knew one of them had shot Katherine.

I grabbed his cold neck, but shifted the remains of his shirt up so I didn't have to touch his flesh. Then, with the warm barrel dug into his neck, I propelled him ahead of me toward the truck. There were a few hordes coming at us.

Pushing the ghoul ahead of me, I used him as a shield. We walked as fast as he could, but his movement was wooden, stiff, and resistant, like he was on stilts or had boards strapped to his legs. The ground was flat, and I frowned when we passed a cage that was now empty.

A large naked zombie plastered with mud came at us with a pair of them close behind. One was missing a foot and dragged the remains of his leg. I lowered the big gun and fired, but the shot went wide and only hit his shoulder. He spun around as the round ripped a path of destruction along its way. Stumbling, the zombie fell into one of the others, then they all went down like dominoes.

Bullets kicked up clumps of dirt around me, but none struck the ghoul. He stumbled once, over the foot of one of the dead lying discarded on the ground. I stayed with him and guided him back to his feet so we both didn't go down.

Scott tore his gaze away from whatever he was aiming at and scanned the area. I followed his focus as I tried to keep it together. Just a few more feet. Then, once in the truck, I would rearm and shoot everything that moved. That was the plan now.

"New girlfriend?" Scott asked as we slammed into the side of the truck.

"You run off and I'll shoot you in the back of the head. Got that?" I said in the ghoul's ear, but his dead eyes were unreadable. I wanted to smash the gun into his head, wanted to grind the barrel between his lips and blow the back of his neck out. The thing that was once a man disgusted me.

"Who the hell's shooting?" I ducked down as more fire rippled our way. Behind us, several hordes advanced in our direction. Ten shambled into view, then, or so it seemed, hundreds came. There were so many that I couldn't count. They came from the woods, from the buildings. They crawled if they couldn't walk. A couple of them moved faster than the others, in a way that was closer to a normal human gait, and they were snarling. Their eyes were livid as they got a look at us.

Scott leaned down out of sight and came up with a bottle. He applied flame to the piece of cloth that hung out of the top.

"Cover me!" he yelled.

Jack sprayed the area ahead of us, emptying most of his magazine.

Scott stood up and tossed the Molotov at a cluster of dead that had taken a liking to us. It splattered the ground and set their clothing on fire. Soon we would have walking torches that would hopefully set other zombies on fire.

"We need to get the fuck out of here, now!" I yelled.

Scott answered by ripping a blast of machine gun fire into a horde that came in at a fifteen-degree angle. They blew apart as rounds pounded into their mass. The carnage was horrific, but it was what we had come for. We had come to kill these dead and soulless things in their multitudes. I would not rest until I eradicated them.

"That asshole from yesterday followed us," Scott told me. "He waited until we were inside, then pinned us down. He won't poke his head out, and he keeps shooting."

"Ah Christ!" That was just great. Just great!

"What do we have for wares?" I crawled in behind the back seat next to Scott.

"An AK, I think. Looks beat up, but it probably works well enough."

Grabbing the ghoul by his shirt, I pulled him in. He went almost willingly. I grimaced as more of the dead closed in. They were everywhere.

"Fuck it. Charge him," I said as I looked over the mass around us.

"What?" Jack teetered off balance as he slapped a fresh magazine home. His head snapped back, and then he fell flat on his back. A blast tore at the air. It shook like a plane breaking the speed of sound. Part of Jack's head was gone.

"Ah hell. Get ready to fire at anything that moves!" I called to Scott as I crawled over the passenger seat and into the driver's seat. I waited to feel the blast of a bullet any second, wondering if I would see the glass of the windshield break when the bullet took me apart. Lee had a damn accurate rifle, and I didn't want to be his next target.

The truck was rumbling, so I slammed the stick into gear and hit the gas. Rocks shot out as it rocketed forward. Four or five zombies had been heading in our direction, and I angled the big front end, so we side-swiped a pair of them.

Scott went to town with the giant gun. It rattled away, picking off a few of the zombies moving in our direction, but he also shifted aim and sprayed the area that led into the camp. Dirt kicked up as he tried to find a target. It was too hard to see where the shots had come from, but he kept a steady finger on the trigger and sprayed anything that moved.

Hot shells rained down on the hard metal floor, and created a staccato that sounded almost like rain--metal rain. The gun was immensely loud, and it battered away at my hearing.

What a mess this assault had become. What was I thinking? I should have waited and come back with an army. Lee was a wild card, but if we had waited at the farm then moved on later, Jack would still be alive. Another death meant more blood on my hands.

A glance in the rearview mirror showed me the ghoul sitting perfectly serene, as if we were heading to the store for groceries. Was he communicating with his brethren somehow?

A green and tan vehicle lay near the line of trees, and a pair of giant wheels were exposed toward the front of what looked like a Stryker. Our HMMV was a big truck, but that thing was huge by comparison. If I hit the tires, I doubted we would do much more than piss off the guy lying on top of the vehicle. So I aimed for the front.

I felt more than saw the bead of the gun as it drew on the truck. I jerked the wheel to the right, and sure enough, the windshield exploded where a passenger would have taken a bullet. It punched into the empty seat, and I wondered if it struck the ghoul that was cowering in the back.

Fuck it!

"Strap in!" I yelled as loud as I could, gunning the engine as I reached for the seatbelt. I dragged it up and over my lap, reaching awkwardly for the clasp, but it slipped in my hand. Dragging it back up, I tried to snap it in place. Scott dropped into his seat, yelling something at me, but I didn't hear what he said. I tried to concentrate on getting the belt on.

The engine roared. Fifty feet from the giant vehicle. *Please don't draw a bead on me.*

Forty feet. The metal buckle went behind the clasp.

Thirty feet. I jerked the wheel hard to the left.

Twenty feet. *Breathe. Concentrate on the lock.*

Ten feet. A quick glance. *There it is.*

It clicked into place.

Impact!

FORTY-SEVEN

The screech of metal and broken glass filled my ears as we crashed into the military-style vehicle that had a pair of men on the roof. The back of this transport was cracked open and hung like a lip. We hit it at about thirty-five miles an hour, which was more than enough to rattle my bones. I was already sore, but this made me black out for a few seconds. It might have been a few minutes, or hours for all I knew. Except I was still strapped in, and we weren't being consumed by the dead.

Steam shot out from the front of the truck. Probably punctured the radiator. I doubted the truck was ever going to be drivable again, and I wondered if I was going to be able to walk again. My body ached like I was thrown across a room, and my head rang from hitting the other vehicle. A large airbag was deployed in the seat, so I guessed I could thank my lucky stars for that.

I looked in the back to find Scott in bad shape. He leaned forward, a trail of blood streaming from his nose to the floor. The ghoul was in a heap, curled up on the mat like a dog. If he was dead, it was just as well. I felt no pity whatsoever.

A cough from the front of the other vehicle caught my attention. A haze of motion, as something interrupted the steam pouring out of the punctured hood. A shape came into view, and I thought it was a deader at first. I reached for the Desert Eagle, but it was nowhere to be found. The floor seemed like the likeliest place, but when I looked down, all I saw was darkness. I reached under the passenger seat, but the door was hauled open and a blood-splattered face met mine. One hand came in and pulled at me, but the seatbelt kept me in place.

I weakly slapped the hand away and reached under the seat once more, but I couldn't get my hand back far enough. I hit the release on the belt, and it popped without retracting into its shell. When I got my hand farther under the seat, my fingers brushed the gun. I leaned over more, my face pressed to the seat, which smelled like sweat and body odor. I grabbed the gun by the barrel just as I was pulled out of the truck by my shirt.

The zombie was strong, and even though I got a hand on the roof of the truck to stop my momentum, I was dragged out and tossed on the ground, losing the gun in the process.

Getting my hand up stopped an incoming blow. I didn't need this; I couldn't fight back. At least it was a zombie, so it was slow and dumb. I could probably get it off balance and figure out a strategy, like how to crawl under the truck for the gun.

A hand grabbed me and pulled me farther from the vehicle. The person was breathing hard and muttering under their breath. Not the typical undead actions, or so my addled brain told me. I almost giggled when I thought about talking zombies. Then a vision of the ghoul in the back of the truck blossomed in my mind.

A fist blocked out the sun and aimed at my temple. I jerked aside, but it still caught me on the side of the head and made my ears ring. Feebly, I kicked and made contact with something. Then the hand holding me down withdrew, so I grabbed hold and helped myself up. This was no zombie I was fighting.

The sun was bright and high in the sky. When I came to my shaking feet, I couldn't make out the figure. It was like they had a big yellow halo around their head. A fast jab shot toward my head, but my body worked on instinct. My right hand came up close to my side then flattened, palm up to take the blow along my arm and redirect the force along the side of my body.

My other hand snaked over and did a check, felt a shoulder, then I used my close quarters training to raise my right elbow up high and clock the attacker in the head. But it wasn't where I expected it to be, and all I ended up hitting was the side of its neck.

I pivoted on one foot and came around with my hands in the air to block. When the sun was at my back, I got a clean look at his bloody face.

It was Lee, and he was pissed. "I'm gonna shit you into tomorrow."

He grimaced and threw a big haymaker that would have laid me out for the rest of the day, but I crossed my body with my right hand and barely deflected the blow from my head into my arm. My left shoulder went numb, and I staggered to the side. A left hook came next, and it wasn't as strong or accurate as the first. That told me he wasn't used to fighting off-hand. I turned my weary body just a tad to the side, and his punch missed. Then with what little strength I had, I whipped my hand up like a viper striking, first knuckle closed so that my hand formed a half-fist, and drove my hand into his face. Thank you, Katherine.

I struck him below the nose, feeling his lips mash and split around his teeth. He fell back with a groan of pain, and had I been in any kind of fighting condition, I would have followed and finished him off. But I could barely stand, let alone step into his guard and finish him.

"You're an idiot, Lee. You know that?"

"No one fucks me. No one! I'm gonna wear your carcass like a jacket, and then when it's dried out, I'm going to set it on fire."

So much for pleasantries. Here we were, in the middle of a camp full of the zombies we had both sworn to kill, and all we wanted to do was murder each other.

He came in swinging, so I got my hands up, dropped down low, and put a quick right foot into one of his legs. It wasn't much of a strike, but the heel of the foot to a thigh could be devastating. Score one for me. He grunted but got a blow over my guard, smashing it into my cheek. This one made my eye start to water right away. It blurred my vision, and my head rang.

I dropped to my side, and kicked low, hoping for a knee. I must have struck his shin, because he moved away and gasped in reply. He ran at me and stomped his foot toward my face. I rolled toward the truck again, but my attempt to get the gun was pathetic. I could curl up in a ball and hope he got tired of beating on me soon, but I wasn't sure how long it would be before Scott came too. If he had his gun ready, he could drop this jerk for me.

Moans nearby informed me that the dead were closing in. If Lee didn't finish me off soon, they would.

A foot caught the inner side of my calf. If it had been angled, I'm sure it would have broken. I lashed up with my other foot and caught his leg, then hooked and pulled. He went down in a big puff of leaves and debris, and I wanted to turn my head and cough out a mouthful of the stuff. It felt like I was eating it instead of trying to breathe through it.

Dizzy and in pain everywhere, I sat up and tried to get ahold of a pant leg. He kicked out at me again, but I got my hands up in time to keep the blow away from my face. Instead I took the shot on my already sore arms and hands. I balled my fist and hit him hard in the thigh with just two knuckles. A Charlie horse wasn't exactly fair fighting, but I was more interested in living than offering him a chance to take my own life.

I went to work, using every memory of training I had acquired over the years. Ground fighting was tough; one had to keep his balance and work the big muscles in the thighs.

His arm came up as I moved close. I nearly hovered over him. Smashing aside his strike, I drove my straightened fingers into his shoulder, then took a blow on my arm. Turning just in time, I jabbed fingertips at his eyes, almost making contact. He looked away long enough for me to get another strike in, but it brushed his ear, and another knuckle struck close by his nose. He retaliated with a snap punch to my gut. Not much power, but it rocked me back on my heels.

I fell on him and batted aside his hands as he reached for my throat. I weighed about as much as Lee, but my hope was that he was as weak as me.

He bucked his hips up with a grunt and tried to turn to the side. I gathered what I had and smashed his nose with my fist. This time it was a full blow that knocked his head into the dirt.

I didn't stop. I went for his eyes, his throat, then slashed toward his temples, grabbed his hair and smashed his head into the ground. Then I hit him a few more times, even getting a throat strike in that hit his Adam's apple and made him gag. Smashing his already pulped nose, I hit him one more time.

He stopped moving.

A gun started to fire, and I ducked in fear, but one glance told me that Scott had come to his senses and was mowing down the zombies with a purpose. Thank God for Scott! I was going to hug the man if we got out of this alive.

They were everywhere. I hit Lee again and decided to just leave him for the dead to finish off. After diving for the truck, I scrambled around until I found the big handgun and came up shooting. Zombies were all around us, but I dropped a pair, even though they weren't badly wounded.

"Shit shit shit!" I yelled as I made for the truck. The AK was on the floor, and when I picked it up, I caught a glimpse of the ghoul laying still, his eyes ablaze, and I swear he was smiling.

"Just shoot them!" Scott gave the gun a break.

I opened up with the Soviet weapon and dropped several, then I moved into the driver's seat and tried to turn over the engine, but it would have none of that.

"The other truck!" Scott yelled.

"I won't leave you!"

"Just go start the fucking thing and stop acting like a bitch. I got this."

I had to grin as I tried to jump out, nearly falling to the ground in my beaten condition. I limped the short distance to the rear door of the military transport. It was open, thankfully, so I walked up the short ramp and into the warm confines.

Some of the seats were gone. In their place sat a bunch of cardboard boxes filled with all sorts of gear. I maneuvered past them and toward the front. I didn't know anything about this particular transport, so I just hoped for the best.

The driver's seat was hard as I sat down. It might have been cushioned at one time, but someone had ripped out the material and covered it with a blanket that smelled like horseshit.

There was an ignition button with a big smiley face sticker on the top. When I pressed it, the vehicle rumbled to life. I looked all over the inside for a way to release the back door. That would explain the shots from the end of the road. But where were his other men? I was sure he wouldn't have come alone.

I didn't know a hell of a lot about this transport's operation, but I'd been around several them while fighting in the Middle East. While it was top of the line, this one had an awful lot of gear removed. The gunner station was open on top, but a large weapon of some sort was attached. Tubes led down the hole to blue barrels on the floor. I would have expected a big M2 browning .50 machine gun or even a grenade launcher. Who knew where Lee's men got the damn thing to begin with? It was a scary world where weapons like this were just left for the taking.

The command station was also gutted, and none of the electronics were in place. Some variations of this vehicle had sophisticated gear. This one had next to nothing left. Someone had left a plastic drink holder duct taped to a space where electronic readout equipment should have sat.

Scott came hobbling out of the truck, firing as he limped. I hit the side door and kicked it open.

"Here!" I screamed.

He made a beeline for me and slammed into the seat so hard he gasped. He tossed the gun in the back and slammed his door shut. We were safe, for now, as there was no way for the things to get in.

I pulled forward a few feet, jammed the gear in reverse and, with a rending screech, tore free of the beat-up Humvee.

In the side mirror my eyes fell on Lee's body. He jerked and I realized that hands had closed on his ankles, and he was being dragged away. As I pulled forward a pair of glowing green eyes met mine and then Lee was pulled toward the remains if the shack and the space that had contained the hive of ghouls.

Enjoy your snack.

We roared out of the camp and made for the open road. The ride was bumpy, and I felt around for straps or something to hold me in the seat. Before long, we hit pavement and I stopped the Humvee. He leaned back and breathed deep. The air probably tasted like the best champagne in the world.

"What a cluster fuck," I muttered.

"We had it, man, but that asshole had to spoil things."

I stared out the window at the road ahead. Trees had grown here, long and lean, and branches hung over the road, creating a canopy. A power wire had been pushed down.

"What was I thinking? Dragging you guys into this. Now Jack is dead."

"We signed on to help. We knew the risks. It could just as easily have been me back there, dead, with half my fool head gone. But I'm alive, and so are you."

I sighed.

"Look, man. It's done and nothing can undo it. You gonna live with guilt your whole life, or are you going to channel it and make Jack's death count for something? All the deaths, for that matter. We started this thing, so let's figure out a way to finish it."

"Are you crazy? I can barely move. Do you think we can just roll back in there with machine guns and shoot them all? We wouldn't stand a chance."

Was he thinking about a suicide mission? I felt so miserable it almost appealed to me. But that would be a selfish way out. I owed it to Katherine to let her know I had survived. She would wonder for a long time, otherwise.

Scott crawled out of the chair and went in the back of the vehicle, climbed the small ladder, and poked his head out. He was up there for a while, fiddling with the weird gun. Then he dropped back down with a big shit-eating grin on his face.

"I have an idea."

I stared at my bloody hands on the wheel of the vehicle. The knuckles on my right hand were bruised and torn. My left hand shook, and the pinky was bent at an odd angle. Probably broken.

"Erik, we have to go back anyway. The food and water is in the truck. Not to mention the ammo."

I shook my head. I felt like I was coming out of a bad nightmare. "Yeah."

"And the people still in the cages ... Are we going to just leave them?"

Scott put his hand on my shoulder, and I looked back at him. His face was a bloody mess, and his hair was caked with dirt. We made a fine pair. I patted his hand like an affectionate uncle. He grinned and looked at the ladder. Following his gaze, I wondered what he had up his sleeve, and then he told me.

FORTY-EIGHT

Twenty minutes later we roared into the camp the way we had left-- like the devil himself was on our heels. This time we were bringing hell. I had wanted to destroy the base before, but now I would do it for real. Scott maneuvered next to the smashed Humvee. It was surrounded by the dead, but he rolled down his window and went to work with the AK-47.

I turned my unique gun on anything that moved. Scott had worked out the device. He followed the tubes to the blue barrels then back to the weapon. After messing with it, he discovered there was a tiny propane tank on the end that provided the spark. The barrel was nothing less than a flamethrower.

I turned the dial and let a little gas leak out. There was a sparker next to it. I clicked it a few times, and a blue flame appeared. The weapon had a couple of gauges on the side, so I messed with them until I had a good stream, then I triggered the gun. Fire leapt out and consumed the first pair of zombies near the side of the truck. They staggered away, now walking torches. I was hoping to set Lee on fire, but he was gone. They probably dragged his body back to feast on.

A search of the vehicle had turned up a couple of other weapons. I took a worn but well-oiled MP5 and had a few mags lined up near the flamethrower.

I set to clearing the immediate area while Scott dragged boxes from the back of the Humvee to our vehicle. He tossed me a large bottle of Gatorade, so I took the top off and drank warm but clean water out of it, draining it in a few massive swallows.

I turned the gun on one of the dead that had grown interested in Scott. His head exploded backwards, and his body slumped to the side, just like that. Another body to add to the list.

It only took a few minutes to move our supplies. If the rear door had been able to slide down, it would have been faster. The impact of the Humvee had damaged the rear too badly.

I slid down to help move things around, then we took our positions again.

"Ready?"

"Damn right," I said.

WE STARTED at the rear of the camp. Our path was littered with the dead. When we came across them, we ran them down and kept going. I shot the few I had to, but I wanted to work from the rear to the front.

We approached the destroyed hut. The corrugated metal was pushed aside, thanks to my escape. I almost felt a sense of glee when I turned the flamethrower on the opening and set it for full stream. Fire raced down and roared into the space. It was so loud that I couldn't hear any screams from those below. I let the fuel run for a few minutes until I was satisfied the place was sanitized.

It took most of the day to clean house. We worked from the other end of the camp, burning away any of the dead we found. Sometimes they came at us en masse, which made it easy to destroy them. When each section was cleared, Scott jumped out of the truck and freed any prisoners that were still in cages.

The stench of burning flesh tested my gag reflex. It filled the air, and I knew it would haunt my nightmares for years to come.

The survivors sat in what space they could find in the vehicle. A couple of the men took guns from our stash and joined in the massacre. We rescued a few children who couldn't have been older than ten or twelve. I wondered why there were no others in Haley's age range. Then it hit me: they probably took the older ones to convert to ghouls—which I had just destroyed.

The cleansing, as I thought of it, was a success. We left a mountain of scorched bodies in our wake. By the end of the battle, we had a tattered army of a dozen or so men and women.

One thing I didn't find was Lee's corpse, and that bothered me.

The younger members of the crew sat on the floor in the cramped vehicle. What seemed like a huge space before was filled with the wretched remains of the camp. Weary faces munched on the remaining protein bars. They drank what little water we had, and a few even broke into the energy drinks.

I stayed on the ladder for a long time, gun aimed at the opening to the camp so I could kill any stragglers. The flamethrower was just about out of fuel. I would have to work out the formula they used to create the custom device. It had been one of the most effective weapons since I came back to the world.

"Are you going to come down?" Scott called from the front. He popped out of the vehicle with the AK-47 slung down low. "I think I have this thing working."

I crawled on top of the Stryker then slid down inside. It was obvious we had cleaned the camp, as no other zombies wandered out. Flames still rose into the sky. A small section of forest had caught on fire, but it was dying down thanks to all the wet wood. An out-of-control fire in the woods would be a terrible sight. How would it ever be stopped?

Scott sat with his rifle in his lap. He had an old beat-up CB radio with the top off on the ground in front of him. There was a wire running from a car battery to the inside.

I collapsed beside him, my body more tired than it had ever been. Talk drifted from inside the Stryker, but I couldn't make out the words. The refugees had been grateful, but some also wore distrustful looks.

He adjusted something on the inside and, with a crackle, the speaker let out a squawk. He hit a knob then adjusted a dial, and his eyes lit up like a kid at Christmas. Then he turned up the volume a little bit. A flat hiss sounded, but it wasn't so loud it might call any remaining zombies within the vicinity to our camp.

"Now we wait." He grinned and patted the top of the radio.

"Wait for what?"

"Wait for someone to talk to us. A bunch of groups keep in contact with CB's, but we can't run them all the time."

"Let me guess, on a particular channel that requires a decoder ring to gain access too?"

"Something like that." He laughed.

We sat in silence for a few moments, both of us waiting for the radio to speak up.

"Do I need to say it?" Scott's gaze drifted toward our vehicle.

"That we rescued a lot of people?"

"No, man. How many of them are like Haley? About to change ..." He trailed off as he turned his eyes back to the burning camp.

"We don't know that for sure. We don't know if she was one of them."

"Come on, man. She was. Lee was an asshole, and he could have handled it differently. The fact is, we might have learned a lot from her. Maybe she wouldn't have been like the others. Maybe our influence would have kept her on our side."

'Our side." I thought dully, *What is our side?* "People hiding out, waiting for something to happen."

"Better than the alternative."

"It is, but we have to do something about it. I'm sick of running, of being afraid. I'm tired of seeing groups of people divided. We need to find a place to call home and get people organized."

Scott looked thoughtful.

"There are a lot of people out there still. People that want to fight back. I say we head to Portland, find Lisa and her crew, and start the revolution."

"And then what? Make an army of flamethrowers and clean out these camps? Do you know how long that will take?"

"It's better than the alternative. If we let them continue to multiply, we will never win."

Scott sighed, but he had to know I was right.

"What are we going to do now?"

"Go back to the farm, get some rest, and then make a break for Portland. If some of these folks want to go with us, they're welcome. The rest can go their separate ways."

"Works for me. All I want to do is rejoin my old friends. Lisa, I miss her."

"You have something going with her?" I had wondered if she moved on after Devon.

"I don't know. We spent some time together. What do you think? Would we make a good match?" He grinned.

"She is pretty fiery. Good with a gun. She might shoot you if you piss her off. I mainly knew her before the change. I guess that means I didn't really know her at all."

Scott chuckled and stared at the flames.

The day had been exhausting, but I suspected the coming days would be worse. My body was sore, and my face hurt from the fight with Lee. I wished I had found his body so I could finish him off. He would never see reason, no matter how hard I argued. I had to stop and reflect on the fact that I had so glibly decided to kill another human being. Eradicating the dead was making it easy to kill. Was one human life so cheap?

We sat for a long time as the flames died down and smoke continued to rise. As night came on, we decided to make for the farm and call it a day.

As I stood up, a voice came over the speaker. I just about jumped out of my skin.

"News of the world?" A female voice that sounded familiar to me. Deep, but still female.

"Hey. If it ain't the mysterious Lizabeth," Scott said. "You can't believe how happy I am to hear you. It's been a while."

"Well if it isn't the smart-ass. I thought maybe they got you."

"They did, but we escaped. Are you still in town?"

"Nope. We left a few weeks ago. We're camped on the outskirts of Portland."

"That's where we're headed."

Lizabeth. Liz. It had to be her. So they had made it out of town after our distraction. They were safe. I breathed a heavy sigh of relief.

"Liz, it's Tragger." There was a long pause from the other end of the line.

"You." She laughed.

"Me."

"You got us out, you know that? We made it out of town thanks to you. Are Pat and Katherine okay?"

I closed my eyes for a few seconds then spoke.

"Pat didn't make it. He sacrificed himself so Katherine and I could escape. Katherine's with another group of survivors. They left for Portland about a week ago. They're in a huge convoy of trucks. You can't miss them."

"I hope it's not the sorry group of burned out vehicles we found a few days ago. Some of the guys were on a sortie to find some food. It looked like the convoy had been attacked at night. We found bodies but not many. Some may have escaped."

I clenched my fist in fury, slamming it into the hard ground and ignoring the pain.

"She has to be alright," I muttered. "Everyone else is gone. I need her to be okay."

"Maybe she is. We'll send out a party in the morning. Maybe they're hiding in the woods. No guarantees, but we will do our best. It's the least we can do. I didn't care for you much, Tragger. But you done good," Liz said over the airwaves.

"We're coming to you. We'll be on the road first thing in the morning." I wanted to leave right then and there, but what about the other survivors with us? Some might want to return to whatever home they had occupied. I would wait to broach the subject after some rest. We all needed it before making any hasty decisions.

"Lizabeth. If you find them, ask for Lisa. She runs the outfit. Tell her you are a friend of Scott and Erik's. Just tell her that and bring her in. Bring them all in."

"I will. Hey I have to go. We have some activity here."

"Wait!" I yelled at the radio, but it went dead.

PART 4

FORTY-NINE

Night arrived with a burst of comets that reminded me of a time not so long ago when airplanes plied the skies for passage. It elicited cries of dismay from a man at the turret of the striker vehicle. Edward had been a banker at one time. Now he was an emaciated stick figure who had endured the worst the world could throw at him and had come out a spitting viper; but instead of venom, his weapon was flame.

Then it thundered and rained like the devil himself decided to piss on the earth. We left the road, pulled down the long driveway of a home set back in the woods, and parked the vehicle. We remained there for a few hours while the storm blew over. Sounded like howling banshees out there. It put me and our passengers on edge.

When the rain let up and we moved on, lightning still arced across the sky for the rest of the night while thunder barked in the distance.

Next to me perched Scott, who peered out the front turret as the sky lit up. It was possible to drive with it open but, with the rain, he used the thick glass to pick our way across the dilapidated roads.

I had seen a meteor show once a few years ago. Allison and I had traveled to Eugene Oregon and, along the way, the sky had become a silent staccato of racing fireflies just as we were witnessing today.

Years. Was that all it was? It seemed like decades, a lifetime or three ago.

The last four or five months alone had felt like a slow-motion nightmare. One I had been inexorably drawn into.

One of the survivors was a child. A boy of no more than twelve. He lay on his side, his knees drawn up to his chest. He had his thumb in his mouth and I felt pity for him. It radiated from me like a furnace. What had this child endured? Surely something as horrendous as Haley, the girl we had witnessed murdered by the side of the road by a madman named Lee.

I had put an end to Lee just a day ago and the ghouls had dragged his body away for a mid-day feast before we burned their camp to the ground. I had taken him to the ground and damaged him so badly that, when the ghouls and zombies arrived, he could not have lasted long. I hoped they had taken their time in feasting on his flesh while he screamed in pain.

After the assault on the ghoul camp, we'd managed to free as many of the prisoners as possible. The ghouls had collected us to add to their ranks. As I'd come to learn, they were able to turn people by force feeding them the rotted flesh of the undead. Just a few bites and a day or two later the change took place. Whatever had created the zombie epidemic had also created the green-eyed bastards. From the first days when they were semi-mindless automatons, until today, when they were thinking and talking plotters of humanities demise, and we fought them tooth and nail.

I'd missed a lot of the end of the world due to my self-imposed exile up in the mountains. My friend's cabin had sustained me until I'd been forced to come back to the real world and confront the truth. You can only run so long before you must stop and make a stand. I'd made that stand with new friends and learned to hate the ghouls and everything they stood for.

I'd learned to kill both the living and the dead. Now I was an expert at the art of imparting death on those who stood in my way.

We had taken Lee's Stryker vehicle and loaded the survivors from the camp in the back. After sorting out all the gear, I had been happy to find a full set of clothing sporting the United States Army's universal camouflage pattern (UCP) well as a tactical vest to match. It was lined with pockets for magazines. I'd done my best to fill them but, as far as weapons and extra rounds went, the vehicle was light.

I'd dug out a few mags for a Beretta 92F and filled them, too. The desert eagle still rode my hip but I wasn't going to get far with it because there were only about fifteen rounds of .44 ammo.

Scott whistled as I pulled the big vehicle to a stop. The turret let in a fresh whisper of breeze that carried the stench of the refugees. I would have crinkled my nose at it one time, probably turned away or cast my eyes on them with disdain. Now I inhaled and felt glad to be among my fellow survivors no matter the circumstances.

I caught Scott's eye as he turned to regard me.

"Big voodoo magic up there," I said.

"Yeah. For a minute I thought it was nukes. Remember back in the day when they kept us scared of the Russians all the time? I half expected a hundred bombs to destroy my city at any given moment."

"Instead, we got the dead. I wish we had a smart nuke that could destroy them." I turned back to the show in the sky.

"Then what would we do for fun?"

"I don't know. Rebuild, drink, and chase girls. Unless you have a better idea," I said.

"Beer. Lots of beer."

"Tequila?" I arched my eyebrows up.

"I'm Mexican. What do you think?" He half-smiled.

"They aren't that high up. I wonder if they're planes."

"Doubtful. Have you seen a plane in the last few weeks?" he asked.

"Now that you mention it. I did see a plane at the ghoul's camp. One shot over the base and even shook its wings at me. I wondered who was in it," I said.

Scott was all the way forward at the controls of the vehicle. I was still surprised at how like a regular car it was. Then again, what had I expected? Something like a tank?

"Must have been a fan." He grinned over his shoulder.

"I don't have many of those." I thought of Lee. Fuck him and the monstrous company he had kept. They were worse than the ghouls as far as I was concerned. They had turned their back on their humanity and abandoned people to the dead. How many of those had joined the army of the dumb and slow. How many lay at his feet?

"You got that right, *gringo*. For better or for worse. I got your back, and you got my wetback," he said.

It was a worth a chuckle. From the beginning, Scott with his Latino background had become the butt of a few jokes. But he called me white boy once even though his complexion was almost as fair as mine. Since then, the friendly banter had not stopped. It was an escape from our horrible world and we both recognized it as such. The truth of the matter was, there was no one else I would rather have at my back than him. Except Katherine.

I sighed and tried to mentally urge the vehicle to roll faster.

The switch on the radio had to be close to falling off. I had been clicking it through channels all day and most of the night. Whenever I tossed in the little seat, dreams interrupted by how damned uncomfortable I was on the plastic monstrosity, the first thing I did was scan channels on the radio.

Three days and still no word. I thought I was going to climb out of my skin.

Not that long ago, I would have picked up a cell phone and made a call, sent a message or even an email from it. Now I was stuck hoping to get a signal from a group that was still thirty or so miles from us. Might as well be all the way across the country.

Our passengers were stuffed in the back of the tiny truck and they were a sorry lot. They had been in cages for days and some for weeks. The stench of unwashed bodies, too long on the ground, hung like a pallor over the inside of the vehicle. Eyes downcast every time I glanced back at them. Few of them would engage with us no matter how long we peppered them with questions.

Except for Chris.

From the start his eyes followed me wherever I went. If I was in the back cleaning a gun, I was sure he had daggers pointed at me. He was a short man, built like an Auschwitz survivor, which sadly, was how a lot of the others looked. He had a full ragged beard that reminded me of an extremist. Hell, we were all extremists now. I didn't even want to think about how bad I looked. But with his eyes full of fervor, or hate, he reminded me more of the Unabomber.

I didn't understand the dirty looks. It was just a day ago that I had rescued all of the survivors. After being captured by the ghouls, Scott, Haley, and I had sat in a cramped cage for almost a week. It was the girl who got us out. She had been slim and we had managed to lift the cage far enough for her to slither out. I had encouraged her to run but she hadn't listened and, instead, helped to break us out.

It was into the woods, and then an escape that saw Haley killed by Lee. He put a gun to her head and blew her brains all over the side of the road. Just the thought of it, of her pleading eyes, sent me reeling. I couldn't get the scared look out of my mind. There had been no acceptance of her fate. At the time I thought I caught a hint of anger, but it was gone in a flash as her head hit the ground.

But I'd taken care of Lee. We'd shot at each other, resorted to fists, and then, when I'd rendered him nearly unconscious and broken some of his bones, I'd left his sorry ass for the zombies. Good riddance, Lee. You were an asshole.

Whatever the problem with Chris, I was planning to sort it out the next time we stopped. I ached, everywhere, from our ordeal and the fight with Lee, but some little pissant wasn't going to deter me from my goal to find Katherine. I'd beat him senseless, too, if I had to, and leave him to the dead. No one, and I mean no one, was going to stop me.

The other survivors with us were an assorted group of misery. It took a few tries to get everyone's name correct, I had never been good with names, and this was no exception. It didn't help that everyone wore rags and were covered in filth. Even with the water at the barn they were pitiful. As much as I felt for them, I had no intention of taking them any farther than I had to. The first chance we had to drop them off, they were gone.

Maybe sensing my intentions, some had deserted us at the farmhouse and now our miserable lot was down to six.

My goal was to make contact with Lizbeth back at the base and find out where Katherine had gone missing. Then I was going there and, if I had to abandon this truck to do it, so be it.

Sam was the most bright-eyed. She was in her early thirties, if I had to guess, and had a shock of purple hair that hung over her shoulders. More than once, I had caught a glance of some sort of colorful tattoo on her neck.

Jon and Janet were a couple. About a decade of years separated them with her on the older end. They clung to each other whenever we hit a large bump. I suspected they had met in the cage and sought each other for comfort.

Our first night together was tentative at best. We sought shelter in the old farm we had used the day before. We'd holed up in the old slaughterhouse because we had supplies and blankets there. Funny how fast we became accustomed to the smell of blood and guts. The sheer horror of the dead around made the minor horrors seem insignificant by comparison.

No one in our new group grimaced or said a word against our stop. We simply ate what was left of the supplies and passed out. It didn't make sense to attempt rationing the food. They had been too long without rations for us to stop them. And so had we, for that matter. The whole horrible week I was stuck in that cursed cage with Scott and Haley was like a bad dream now. I looked back on it in dread. I looked back on it with a lot of anger, too. I felt despair wash over me at times and, when I met the eyes of another survivor, I saw the same sense of loss. How much of our humanity had we lost while being subject to the will of the dead?

That night, a few of the survivors slipped away. I never saw them again. We'd rescued them but it wasn't like I was responsible for them. Besides, the less people we had to care for, the better.

FIFTY

W e had only made it a few slow miles before we had to come to a stop. The road was an old two-lane that hadn't been repaved in decades, and it was littered with potholes and runnels carved into the pavement by heavy rain.

Scott whistled as he took in the sight. Cars sat in both lanes blocking the road. There was a nice-looking Cadillac sitting across the median. Another driver in a small compact had hit the car, T-boning it. A skeleton hung out the broken front window and lay across the hood. Animals or birds had pecked away most of its flesh, leaving a sad reminder behind in a flannel shirt.

"How far are we from anything major?" I asked.

"Not much. Should be some warehouses and a train depot around here somewhere. We can walk it if we have to," Scott said.

"And give up this fine military vehicle? I say we keep to it as long as possible," I said.

Scott grunted.

I sat back and looked toward the roadblock and wondered how we were going to get around it. A couple of cars had pulled over in an attempt to move around the mass and had become stuck. We could try and push the cars aside but one side of the transport was damaged from our escape a few days ago. Scott had hit the Stryker at a good clip with our own truck, unsettling the guy on top that was taking pot shots at us. Now the front fender hung by a thread and, occasionally, there was a loud pop from that wheel cover, like something was loose. The more we drove the worse it got. We weren't likely to find a full-service garage to go over the damage. I didn't really have a plan except to drive it until we found something more reliable. Maybe we would have to dump this thing after all. For some reason I thought of how I'd taken it from Lee, like it was a trophy, and I didn't want to give it up.

"Shit." Scott echoed my thoughts exactly.

I didn't have time for this. I had to find Katherine, sick with need for her. We had all lost a great deal in the apocalypse that was now our time, but I refused to lose her.

I checked the gun at my side. Among the gear in the truck, I had come across a holster that was for a slightly larger pistol than the Beretta 93F I carried out of the undead camp. Still, the comfort of the weapon at my side was worth the frustration of it bumping across my hip every time I stood up.

I popped the magazine down and slid it back in after assuring it was still loaded just as I had left it a few hours ago. Some habits are hard to break. I slid the chamber back a half inch. The copper jacket caught my eye, so I let it close with a click.

"I'll get Bessie," Scott said. He pulled out a pump action shotgun and slid a leather bag around his shoulder to hang at his side, then he dumped out a box of shells and pushed them into pockets and a sack.

Jon's face betrayed trepidation so I talked to him, but the rest of our refugees had to know I was addressing them as well.

"It's probably no big deal. We're going to check out the roadblock and see if we can figure out how to get around it."

"I got your back." Edward leaned down from the turret and nodded. His hair was long and black but caked in mud. It gave him a crazed look. It didn't help that he had found some kind of face camouflage and painted his cheeks dark green. He wore glasses that were missing one side so they frequently hung low on his right. I liked Edward from the start. The first time I saw him pick up a gun his eyes lit up like it was Christmas. It took very little effort to explain how it worked, how to load on the fly, and how to shoot in a hurry. He took to it with a zeal I couldn't help but appreciate.

We all dealt with things in different ways and if his way was by shooting every dead thing in the state, who was I to say no?

"Just don't set us on fire." Scott grimaced.

Jon left Janet's side along with Chris. They both grabbed weapons and untied the rope that bound the rear door shut. Chris left last. He took an old hunting rifle and looked it over. He held it by the barrel with his hand on top. I could tell he wasn't familiar with guns but that was fine. A little on the job training wasn't a bad thing.

When we first took over Lee's Stryker vehicle, the rear door didn't even work so we had to crawl on top of the vehicle and shimmy down the ladders. One of the men had spent some time playing with the controls and figured out how to get the hydraulics working. Only they barely functioned, so he drained fluid here and there and then, with a *clang* that probably alerted everything in the area to our location, the door struck the ground like a bad day.

Lee's band of idiots must have rigged the door up this way for some reason. Maybe it was to keep interested parties out if they were stopped somewhere for the night. I suspected there had been a camera that showed the back of the vehicle, but all of the electronics had been torn out for some unknown reason. Maybe they needed the room to fit more people. Maybe to make room for weapons or it was due to the failure of electronics in the air, satellites and drones. Not to mention the ever-present AWACS over a typical battlefield. The kind of stuff didn't work worth a shit nowadays.

Jon lowered the door and a few of us stepped out.

I pulled my Beretta and trained it around the location. I stopped to listen for movement but my legs were cramped and demanded a stretch. I felt a knee *pop* and my hip twinge in protest. The fall down the stairs at the ghouls' hideout just a few days ago left a huge bruise.

I was a big, miserable ball of sore. My head hurt from the fight with Lee. My upper body hurt from the week in the prison camp not to mention the fact that we had been on the run for days on end.

My legs unfolded like I was in my eighties. Each step was a groan of pain from my feet to my hips.

I sighed and glanced up at the sky, which was a gray drizzle. Rain fell in a steady staccato. It was light but annoying and I wished I had a rain jacket to wear over my camouflage duds. I was cold, chilled in a matter of moments. The time in the vehicle with air rushing in every time we moved had not helped. Just like the electronics, a lot of the other items were missing as well as a heat source. I hoped the city had something approaching human comforts.

Portland.

It was like a pot of gold at the end of a rainbow. Something you set your sights on knowing full well you won't ever make it. I had my doubts from the moment we gathered the refugees and, as we made it a mere few miles from the farm, I realized just how impossible our dream might be.

FIFTY-ONE

L eaves lay like dead things around the side of the road. A tree had reached out and hung over the road, intruding on the wires and cables that used to carry electricity and phone connections. One of the larger cables had broken loose and lay on the ground like a black snake.

"Erik. We got something," Scott called from inside the vehicle.

I clambered back onboard and only managed to rack my knee in the process.

"What's going on?" I asked.

"We got them back on the radio. Listen," Scott said.

A burst of static, and then the channel clattered to life. We had been on the same channel that Lizbeth had used a few days ago but this was the first time we had been able to reach them.

"Liz? You there?"

Static, then a couple of clicks.

"Tragger?" her voice was scratchy

"Lizbeth. Quick before we lose the connection again. Where was Katherine's last location? I need to find her and the other survivors."

"Two seconds, Tragger."

"Roger that, Liz. Thank you," I said.

I waited. Twenty seconds, then a minute. Nothing. I called for her but she didn't answer.

Goddamnit!

Finally, she came back on the line.

"Sorry about that. Had to get a map and work out the coordinates. Hope you have a pen and paper handy," she said.

"We have a map?" I asked Scott.

"Probably somewhere in this heap." He shrugged.

"Okay, Liz. Go."

She rattled off numbers and Scott jotted them down as quickly as possible. A year ago I would have been able to load Google Maps and find the location in thirty seconds.

"What else can you tell me about the caravan?" I asked.

"It's in bad shape but from the tracks it looks like some escaped. Either that or they were dragged off," she said.

"Christ."

"Sorry, Tragger. Do your best. We're near Portland now. Join us. There's real resistance here. A genuine force. That's why I called you. We need more smart fighters."

"I'll do my best, Liz," I said, "but I have to know Katherine's fate. Hers and the rest of the men and women I knew in my old neighborhood. I'll go crazy if I don't get to the bottom of their disappearance."

"Shit, Tragger. Best of luck, my friend. I have to go. We don't have a lot of juice for the radio but we're working on some generators. I'll call again as soon as I can," she said.

"Thank you, Liz. We liberated some survivors from a ghoul camp. Hope we can all meet up soon," I said, but she was already gone.

I sat back in the chair while Scott dug through pockets and bins. He'd written down the coordinates on a scrap of paper. Jon helped toss the Stryker while I dug around the steering column. Finally, Scott yelled, "Bingo," and came up with a roll out map.

It showed the area of Portland and at least fifty miles around the city. Jon proved his worth by studying the numbers Liz had given me.

"I can convert that to latitude and longitude, but it takes a little math. I don't suppose anyone has a calculator?" Jon said.

"Sorry, man. I left my nerd calculator watch back at the house," Scott said with a wink.

"I didn't see one in the vehicle," I said.

Jon nodded and got to work.

"See. You have to convert the numbers to minutes and seconds. Then cross those against the latitude and longitude on the map. I should be able to pinpoint the location. Gimme about fifteen minutes. I'm rusty at this stuff," Jon said.

"But he's also very good at it," Janet said with affection. She ran her fingers through his hair while he scribbled numbers on the slip of paper.

"Let me guess, used to be a teacher?" Scott said.

"A professor actually. Anthropology. But I remember how to convert thanks to a class I took years ago," Jon said.

I sat back and thought about what Jon had said. We'd lost so much and GPS was the least of it.

I wondered how long it took for electricity to die down once the dead arose. Had it been days, or even a week? Figure there was the panic. People fleeing but nowhere to go. Then the power plants that normally need some kind of human intervention would have triggered alarms and failsafe's would have kicked in. Would the nuclear power plants have gone up in smoke by now? Were there now vast shafts of irradiated land around once proud, hundred-foot-tall chimneys?

I took a quick stroll and found a stump to sit on, pulling out the Desert Eagle to inspect it. I considered digging out a rag and some motor oil to clean the gun, which was the best I could do without a cleaning kit. I didn't need a misfire in the coming days.

Chris crept up beside me. He'd quietly followed me out of the Stryker and approached from my six. I glanced to my left and saw a hard-set jaw below scrunched together eyes. He was looking for something to shoot. I knew the feeling all too well. Not too long ago my body raged against the injustice of all I had been subjected to. I wanted to kill anything that moved. Now I was back to being myself. Back to being centered. I had a goal in mind, and I was determined to reach it no matter the grudge he felt toward me.

On second thought, I decided to get to the bottom of it. It would be easy to ignore for now, watch him stew in a sauce of passive-aggression. But that would just bleed out to the rest of the survivors. We needed to have it out here and now.

"How come you don't like me?" I asked him point blank.

Chris stared at me for a few seconds, his eyebrows going up at my forward question. His lip trembled but no words came out.

"Did I wrong you somehow? For the life of me, I can't remember ever seeing you before the camp."

"It's nothing," he mumbled. His mouth sounded like it was filled with marbles.

"Nothing?" I said and got in his face. "If it's nothing then we don't have an issue now do we? If you do have a problem, I suggest you just walk away right now. Where we're going, I don't have room or time for someone I can't trust."

He stepped back a pace and looked down. I took in his body language with my peripheral vision. His knuckles were white on the gun and he shook although he tried to hide it.

I had to be careful with this one. Every instinct was telling me to distance myself from him. But I also recognized the fact that I needed everyone I could get. Things weren't going to get any easier in the near future.

"Make up your goddamn mind!" I said louder than I had anticipated.

"Don't you take the Lord's name in vain!" He shot back, and then swallowed hard.

I was as tired as I had ever been in my life but I was already marking striking points on his frame. He stood slightly off center and I knew a decent blow would knock him off balance. Then I could take him to the ground. I'd have the gun away from him and pointed at his face in seconds.

Movement to my left drew my attention. A hand broke free of the foliage surrounding the road, followed by another one, and then a head. The thing saw us and moaned.

Chris backed up, fumbling for his weapon. I didn't want to hear a gunshot. It would carry and probably attract more of them. I motioned for him to lower the weapon but he seemed to ignore me and raised it. I reached for the barrel, to bat it down, but I was too slow and a sharp retort tore at the air.

The others stopped what they were doing and dropped to a crouch.

The shot missed and the thing got loose. Unsure what to do now, Chris raised the gun to his shoulder and tried to fire again. This time I was successful in smacking it. I hit it so hard it fell out of his hand and bounced on the ground in a clatter. He glared daggers at me.

"Idiot. You've drawn every undead bastard in the area to our location!" I said, raised the handgun, and shot the dead man in the head. He flopped back into a branch and then fell forward. Rotted brain matter spilled out of a cracked skull and dropped to the ground in front of us.

Chris had seen enough. He tried to turn to leave but ended up throwing up instead.

I left him with his hands on his knees, but not before I took away his hunting rifle and returned it to the vehicle.

FIFTY-TWO

"What the hell?" Scott asked as I approached the wreck he was inspecting. If we could get it out of the way we'd have a chance.

"Chris got antsy." I shot back. I turned to the others. "We may have company soon. Get the rest ready. Load up on whatever weapons there are and keep guard while we figure out how to escape this cluster fuck."

They headed back to the Stryker. Scott joined me as I went to the first car, which was just a rust hulk. From the marks on the side, it looked like someone had tried to force it off the road. In doing so, they had left it blocking the shoulder.

Three of the tires were more or less full of air and the other was flat. I tried the door but it wouldn't budge. Scott took my cue and smashed the window on the passenger side, then backed up with the sight trained on the interior. When nothing jumped out at us except for the smell of rot, he opened the door, leaned in, nose wrinkled, and unlocked my side.

There were no keys, and I didn't feel like going over the car. There was a shape in the back, on the floor, that didn't move. I had no desire to find out what it was. I tried to turn the engine over but it just clicked. On the next try it made a screeching noise, but the engine didn't start.

"You thought it would be that easy?" Scott asked.

"It was worth a shot."

I put the car in neutral, thanking God that it was a manual transmission, and, with the help of a groaning Edward and Jon, we pushed the car forward. There was a line of vehicles lining the road and we didn't really have anywhere to go except into the woods with it. I shouted directions while I tried to crank the steering wheel to the right. The front of the car angled toward the line of trees. The others got the idea and we pushed faster and harder. As we approached the break, I slid free of the wheel and the others gave one last push.

With a groan, the car hit the edge of the tree line and smashed through a six-foot-high grove. It tilted down and kept going. I walked to the edge of the woods and stared down a sharp ravine that ended at a stream. The car bucked over branches and fallen chunks of woods. It hit the stream bed, tilted up in the air, and rolled over until the roof was in the water.

I stared for a moment longer until I was sure there were none of the things down there. I was about to turn and rejoin my comrades when a gunshot broke the silence. The sound made me drop to my knees. My Beretta was halfway tucked into the waist of my pants. I grabbed it, hoping I had remembered to set the safety. It would be embarrassing if I accidentally shot myself in the ass cheek.

Dammit. I'd chastised Chris for making all of that noise, and then gone and pushed a car into a ravine and made enough noise to call every zombie in the area to us. I might as well have stood on top of the Stryker vehicle and shouted, "Come get us!"

A pair of the dead stood on the other side of the road, eyes intent on our military vehicle.

"Get moving!" I called and ran toward the Stryker.

Like a nightmare, they came from the woods. At first there were only a few, then a few more. They came in their ugliness, this destitute horde of broken humanity. They shambled one by one, then by the pair. Soon they poured out a half dozen at a time. Some hissed and others moaned as if they possessed some kind of intelligence.

The range was at least thirty feet so I didn't waste bullets on hoping to make a shot. I ran as fast as I could, which wasn't that quick considering the shape I was in. Air wheezed in and out of my lungs as I struggled to breathe. My legs were on fire within seconds. Luckily it wasn't far to the vehicle.

The rest were piling in, with Chris the last in the back. He looked in my direction and actually reached for the cord as if to close me out of the Stryker. Ungrateful little shit.

Scott grabbed him and pushed him aside. I ran up the tiny ramp and nearly collapsed in the space. The guys pulled the door shut with a *clang* that reverberated inside the vehicle.

Edward slithered up the port with automatic in hand. The smell of fresh oil was thick in the enclosure. Someone had been cleaning the guns while we were out playing pitch the Caddy into the stream. I snatched up a rifle and aimed at the portal as it closed.

Scott slid through the little portal and crawled into the driver seat. He fired up the engine, put it in gear and, with a lurch, we were on our way. I made for the front of the vehicle, ducking so I didn't bang my head on the heavy metal ceiling.

The view outside was bleak. A lot of the dead were on the scene. They came in their lurching masses, their moans and dead eyes fixed on us. If enough got in front of us we would become stuck. The Stryker was large, but it wouldn't take much to stop us in our tracks. Already damaged, I didn't want to test its limits.

Edward must have settled in up top. His machine gun hammered at the air, sounding like a rattling lawnmower from inside. I wanted to see what he was shooting at so I climbed the ladder, hands tight on the rungs as we lurched into motion.

Edward had a strap around his body that connected to a tie on the top of the vehicle. He looked down the sight and took aim with care. He didn't panic. He fired a round, paused, adjusted, and fired again. He hit more than he missed.

Toward the front of the truck, the road was smooth sailing now that the car was out of the way. Scott used the clear road to move with purpose. Like Edward and his rifle, Scott took to the road in a controlled sort of panic. We yawed left and right a few times but he kept it steady and got around the mess of cars a moment later.

Then it was clear for at least a couple of football fields before we came to another mess.

This was not looking good. We needed to make it to Lisa's base and drop the refugees off. At this rate it was going to take all day. I supposed we could hole up in the Stryker if things got rough. I didn't trust the ghouls enough to try it though. They had already proved to be much cleverer than I would ever give them credit for.

"What was your count?" I asked Edward as we pulled away. He had slithered back down out of the turret so he could reload. I was happy he'd seen the sense in not using the flame thrower. If we got trapped and the trees were on fire, we would be stuck in an oven.

Edward's long hair hung around his face. He shook it back and reached into a shirt pocket. Edward took out a rubber band and tied his hair back in a ponytail.

"I didn't keep track. I never do," he said. He didn't look. He concentrated on sliding rounds into a magazine. I took the other magazine and helped him.

"No?"

"Nah, what's the point? It's not like anyone is paying me to do it. I kept score for a while, but this crazy girl named Julie thought it would be fun to constantly one up me. All the men for that matter."

"Sounds like a keeper."

"She was until they got to her. I was in the woods when I watched three of them hold her down and force some disgusting hunk of rotted flesh down her throat. She screamed for a long time after they let her up."

"Christ." I sighed.

"He wasn't there that day. Anyway, I waited until it was almost dark and, when she started to show signs, I shot her in the head. She fell over without a sound, but I wonder if there was a smile on her lips. Isn't that funny? A dead girl smiling?"

"I don't think it's funny at all." I didn't meet his eyes. My thoughts were on my own ghosts. "How did you get away?"

"Oh. I took one down and sort of faded into the woods. I had a lot better camouflage at that point. We were organized, had roles and jobs. It was easier then, but now everything is just a fucking mess."

His hand tightened on the magazine. He slid it into the gun and racked a round in. Then he slithered up the portal. I motioned and he moved on top so I could join him.

We lay down and eyed the title army of the dead. A desiccated man came at us. He was fast mover with a torn-up hat. Might have been something suited for a cowboy at one time. Now it was just a scrap that wasn't fit to piss in.

I lay the gun along the back of the truck and took aim. There was a short sight on the rifle designed for hunting game. The dead man's head came into view. I put the crosshair right on the zombie's forehead but before I could shoot, Edward fired and took the thing in the throat. It fell back legs scrambling at the ground. As it gave up its second life, one leg kept kicking at the road propelling the big guy around in a half circle. His motor skills gave up before he could come all the way around to face us.

"Nice shot."

"I was aiming for his chest. I thought his head would be too much of a small target. But I'll take it," Edward replied.

"How long were you in the camp?" I asked.

"The concentration camp? That's what we called it. It was like some crazy experiment the Nazi's might've tried. These ghouls are smart. They know how to prey on horror. They know how to terrify and how to make you do what they want you to do. Some of the stronger ones even influenced people to do things they didn't want to do. They tried it on me, and I thought I felt a tingling, like a fly was loose in my brain, but I stopped it with a thought. I made them go away. One dude even grabbed his head like he was hurt. I think their tricks don't work on some of us."

"That's good news. I wonder what makes you different."

"Not sure. I think you're different, too. It's like you have immunity to their tricks. Most folks would have gone to them. They would have seen the first sign of zombies coming at them and would have started to go nuts. It's bad in a house when one of your friends starts shooting at anything that moves. Every shadow and flicker becomes an enemy. I saw one guy shoot out a lamp and turn the gun on himself. I pushed it away but he still managed to take of part of his ear and lose his hearing on that side for good."

Edward gave me a lot to think about.

Back in the command seat I settled in for the haul. We had to stop fifteen minutes later for yet another car pileup.

FIFTY-THREE

The new world had showed me a lot of death. I thought I had seen it in all its forms. Before this, I was a soldier. I had fought where they sent me. I had shot at people, and on more than one occasion, I had killed. Some of the guys in my squad liked it. They liked saying they had a kill. They kept count and some even put marks on the stock of their weapons.

I didn't like it, and in some ways, I had distanced myself from the feeling because the things I shot were already dead. Even the ghouls, with their barely functioning systems, were fodder. I could count those in my most welcome daydream and consider each death a blessing.

But nothing in the world had prepared me for this.

The woods opened at last and we were met with the familiar sight of a highway junction. Another five or ten minutes and we'd be well outside of Vesper Lake and near the location of Lisa's caravan. I chewed on my fingernails while I considered what I'd find. I hated to think what I would do if I came across her corpse. Or worse. What if she'd become a ghoul? The best I could do for her was to shoot her but would that be what she wanted? It wasn't my place to decide her fate.

There was no way we could climb its peak to the top and get on a road littered with the husks of cars and trucks. We would have to pick our way along the side of the wide road and hope we didn't run out of places to run along the side of. The once well-kept freeway was anything but. Shrubs grew along the side, and in another year, they would take over the road.

Cars had been abandoned. Most were empty but more than one held a figure that moved. I guess the dead were too stupid to figure out how to use a door handle. I didn't care to get close enough to check on them either. If a ghoul came along, maybe they could help.

A set of railroad tracks ran parallel to the road for a while before fading over the horizon and into a copse of woods.

A few cars lay along the side of the track. Overturned railway cars had spilled their cargo. We edged along the side of the road as much as we could but there wasn't a lot of room between the metal guide rails.

Chatter was brief in the back of the vehicle. The survivors didn't want to talk much. At times they seemed amazed they were alive at all. Other times they were in shock.

Another car pushed to the side of the road blocked us. I got on top of the vehicle, head sticking out, so I could eyeball the way ahead. I called into the hatch, so Scott knew what to anticipate ahead. I did my best, but we still ran into numerous abandoned cars and trucks. Some looked like roadblocks from the way they covered our escape route, like someone had foreseen our path and planned the best way to kill us.

As crazy as the green-eyed ghouls were, I was pretty sure they weren't prescient, but after what Edward had told me, now I wasn't so sure.

Scott and I got out of the vehicle to inspect the pile of shit. Jon and Janet covered us and Chris, his eyes darting around, stood around with his hands in his pockets.

Scott and I set to work on a burned-out wrecker, the ball and hook of which connected, ironically, to another car blocking our path. We had to dig around until we found a hacksaw. No bolt cutters to be seen. I went at the chain for a few minutes with each hand, then Scott took over while I took the watch.

Machine gun pointed everywhere at once, I listened to the wind and the creaking of the trees all around us. The smell was one of decay, rot, ruin. Burned out husks filtered the smell of charcoal. Every time I took a whiff, I thought of how much I would give for a cookout. Oh God, hamburgers on the grill broiled to bloody center perfection.

The next smell that hit me was a different kind of rot. A foul smell that reeked very lightly of old fish. Like someone had left a hunk of cod out in the sun.

The hair on the back of my neck stood at attention. A chill swept down my spine even though the day was hot and getting hotter by the moment. It was so bright that it would be impossible to make out any glowing eyes. But the smell was enough. I knew they were out there. At the last stop I thought I saw movement in the distance, in the woods that lined the freeway. I thought I saw something large but later convinced myself it was just a group of deer.

Now I wasn't so sure. Could the dead be hunting us? Could the ghouls have gotten wind of our location and been looking for revenge?

We were in no condition to make a stand if they surrounded us. We would have to use what little fuel the flamethrower had to make our escape and hope we didn't set the woods around us on fire, creating a pressure cooker. If one or two of us rode on top they could provide fire for anything that got in front of us. If too many piled up we might never make it though. The Stryker was in bad enough shape without it having to withstand a full assault.

The chain came loose and the car dropped the two feet to the ground so we set to pushing it off the road. The wrecker was next and that called for all hands. Even with it in neutral it took us precious minutes to get the beast out of the way.

Now that the road was clear for a few feet, I sent a few of the refugees to repeat the process while Scott and I conferred.

"We need to sweep this area. I can't hear them, but I swear to fucking God I can sense them out there," I said.

Scott nodded. "I hear ya, man. It's like I got a bullseye on the back of my neck. Making me itch."

"Keep an eye on Chris, too. He's been acting weird around me."

"I think I know why. Didn't want to say anything. Homeboy can't take it personal."

"What?" I asked Scott.

"Pretty sure one of those ghouls back at the camp was his dad."

"Son of a bitch," I muttered.

We cleared another pair of cars and piled into the vehicle once more. Bringing it up to speed wasn't so easy because we had a lot of debris on the road to contend with. I took the wheel so Scott could take a break and act as my lookout.

Something bounced off the top of the Stryker. Scott and I looked up at the same time.

Something else hit the side.

"Drive on. Ignore it," Scott advised.

I agreed and kept my foot on the gas.

We came around a bend in the road and found a pile of bodies. Not just a few, but at least a dozen. They'd been strung out in a row and Scott had to slow down. Some of the corpses appeared to have been burned while others simply bore bloody wounds. Limbs had been placed around the mound and I couldn't help but gag at the atrocity.

I slowed again but this time came to a halt. We could drive over it but what in the hell could have possessed someone to create such a thing.

Something else bounced off the roof. I tensed, expecting an attack, or worse, an explosion. We'd probably be safe inside if we buttoned up but the weird flame thrower that had been constructed on top made that nearly impossible.

They came out of the trees. Dozens of the dead and, around them, were many green-eyed ghouls. They moved to surround the vehicle. Scott put it in gear and we lurched forward, nosing through the mass. More things hit the Stryker as we approached the pile of bodies. Maybe my mind was playing tricks on me but I thought for sure one of the faces in the mass belonged to Haley.

Then one of the bodies rose and approached us. The ghoul was covered in gore, but his eyes shone brightly. I accelerated and struck him, and he fell away. The Stryker rolled over the bodies, crested the little hill, and we were over it. Then something exploded and the rear of the big vehicle lifted into the air. I was tossed forward and barely managed to get my hand up in time to keep from smacking into the front dash. Scott sat back in his seat, hard, and cursed. Screams rose from our passengers as we shuddered to a halt. I gunned the engine anyway and we managed to roll forward a few dozen yards before the smell of smoke told me we needed to assess. I didn't want to but we needed to clear this area and quickly. *Christ!*

The goddamn ghouls had set a trap for us.

Something else exploded behind us but I could tell it hadn't struck us. I looked into the cramped confines of the vehicle and found scared faces. A few bore wounds from being thrown around. Chris glared at me as a trickle of blood rolled down his forehead, nose, and then caressed his upper lip.

"Stay calm. We're still mobile. I'm going to get us as far away as possible," I yelled over the cries.

"They're coming for us!" One of the refugees shouted.

"We're all dead," another screamed.

The road had another bend and flames rose into the air, casting the street in eerie shadows. Smoke carried on the wind and found us. I gagged and wished this damn vehicle was battle ready.

I hit the gas again and came around the bend only to find the source of the fire.

Several cars were aflame, and they created a perfect blockade. The sides of the road were narrow and butted up against low walls of rock. This passageway had been cut into the side of a large hill decades ago, and now it was a trap.

I wanted to go for it, but since the explosion the vehicle had started to sheer to the left. We'd probably lost a wheel or two back there.

More objects hit the top as I came to a decision.

"Everyone hold the fuck on," I said.

"If you get us stuck, we'll probably join that barbecue," Scott observed.

"Then pray we don't get stuck," I muttered and punched the pedal all the way to the floor.

The Stryker didn't exactly shoot forward, but it found purchase and we barreled along the street. I fought the steering wheel the whole time as the big military vehicle tried to pull us to the left. We had a good twenty or thirty feet, but I feared it wouldn't be enough to get our momentum up high enough.

I glanced over my shoulder and found everyone clutching at whatever they could. Fear rode their faces as eyes met mine.

We hit the first car and it bounced away. The second car was a lot bigger, an older Buick if I had to make my guess, and like our ride, it was built like a tank. The Stryker, and what remained of its eight wheels, fought for purchase as our already reduced momentum pushed it to the side. Then we were through.

I gasped as the next obstacle came into view.

The flames and smoke had done a good job of hiding it. The flatbed of an eighteen-wheeler, sans tractor and without a load lay in front of us. I slammed on the brakes, but it was too late.

FIFTY-FOUR

If the previous impacts had been a jolt to the system, this was a smack upside the head with a lead bat. I was thrown forward and hit the dash hard enough to see stars. Scott cried out in pain and somehow ended up on the floor. The survivors behind me made their own cries of misery. Smoke. That was all I could see.

I tried to put the beat-up Stryker into reverse but it wasn't having any of that. The gears ground together and seemed to catch before a louder noise, probably the transmission taking a shit, gave up the ghost. I hit the gas, but all the engine did was give a half-hearted revving noise.

We had to get out of there before the flames spread.

I staggered through the little passageway and grabbed Scott by the arm.

"I'm okay, just rattled," he said.

We pushed together into the space the refugees occupied and helped them to their feet. Edward had slid back out of the turret just before we struck and had managed to wedge himself against the opening and the floor. He staggered backward and triggered the lift's release. At least that worked because the door opened and dropped to the ground to create our exit ramp.

The undead were all around us. A pair shrugged away the flames and came at the opening. Something called outside in a keening voice but there were no words to it.

My vision swam but I managed to stay on my feet.

Then we were out in the open. I clamped one hand onto Jon's shoulder and used him to prevent myself from falling over. Janet, his wife, helped us both down the ramp.

Chris staggered past me and into the open. He'd dug out a handgun and used it to shoot at a zombie. The round took the guy in the chest but the undead shrugged it off even though the blast tore through his back with a spectacular exit wound, judging by the spray of blood.

A half dozen of the aimless zombies closed in on us. I whistled for the others and we made a beeline for the eighteen wheeler. I skirted the edge and we found ourselves staring at open road. Familiar road no less. We were minutes from our goal and if I could keep this group together we might actually make it.

Scott, on my left, pointed at a break in the tree line. I nodded and waved at our group to follow.

I felt like I was in a daze and touched my forehead. My fingers came away bloody. Further exploration revealed that I'd suffered a laceration just below my hairline. It didn't feel like it was that bad and a head wound can bleed a lot. Ignoring the pain and throbbing, I led us away from the crash.

That's when a small horde of them came out of the woods. Among them were several green-eyed ghouls. One of them a boy really, moved along on all fours. His hair was a ragged mess that hung in front of his eyes and, in the smoke from the wreck, he looked demonic.

"That dude's having a bad hair day," Scott quipped.

"He can join the club," I muttered.

I drew my big Desert Eagle and lined up a shot, but I was seeing two of the things. It leapt off the ground and landed ten feet away on top of the eighteen wheeler's empty trailer. I fired but it moved with dazzling speed and was gone from sight behind the wreck. The undead came at us en masse. I fired wildly. Probably hit one or two. I was still so dazed I couldn't be sure.

They swam before my eyes and, when one got too close, me or one of the crew shot them in the head or disabled them with a leg shot. Zombies look like they can take any kind of damage you throw at them but take out a limb and you might buy yourself a few precious seconds. Then Scott took one down and we wove away from the wreckage and into the low rise of woods.

An undead came at me. A big guy built like a pro wrestler but missing large pieces of his left thigh. His tan pants were covered in blood and left the wounds open to our eyes. I nearly gagged when I noticed the mass of maggots that clung to his lower half

I staggered right, barely avoiding the big zombie's hand, batting at it wildly. He fell as he reached for me again and landed on his face. Body flat, I had the chance to get away. This confused gang of the dead were a sorry lot, even for zombies. They were so aimless, they walked away from me once I was out of sight.

I crouched for a while behind a big bole and caught my breath. I was so sore it was an effort just to stand back up after the ordeal of the past few days. With dogged persistence, I got my feet under me and made for the road once again.

Scott crouched next to me and took in a few deep breaths. The others gathered around.

Where was that goddamn ghoul?

"You okay, *hombre?*"

"Yeah, man. Just need to rest. Guess there's no time right now."

"No rest for the wicked."

Jon dropped next to us but kept his gun trained toward the rear. Janet kept watch as well. She had a Glock in one hand and a hatchet in the other. Her red hair didn't do much to hide the blood that had splattered her. Janet had split an undead's head like a melon a few minutes ago. Our group had somehow shrunk because I didn't see a few faces. Some must have fled deeper into the woods.

Chris, with his evasive eyes, watched me as he also kept an eye on the advancing dead.

"I see two choices," I told the crew. "We can try to fade back into the woods and circle around this mess, but we'd have to stay close and quiet. Problem is we don't know what's waiting for us once we hit the open road again."

"I say we risk the woods," Scott said.

"Yep." Jon echoed.

Janet and Chris nodded assent so that was the path we chose.

Edward looked pensive, but whatever he was going to say was washed away by peer pressure, so he just nodded.

"Scott, lead the way. I'm still a little woozy," I said.

"Sure thing, boss." Scott led us out.

We moved as quickly as we could, but we were all covered in bumps and bruises. My head was starting to clear but it also throbbed to each beat of my heart, and that was unfortunate because it was beating quickly.

Scott took us diagonal to the road as things beat at the branches behind and to our side. Something snuffled in the woods ahead and I hoped it was an animal but knew it wasn't.

Then we were clear and back on the road where it bisected the old highway. I couldn't remember its name to save my life but I knew that, if we followed it a few more blocks, we'd find the location of the overrun caravan, and then I could finally start looking for Katherine.

The ghoul was having none of that.

He shot out of the woods and went for Janet. She was hanging to the perimeter of our group and the green-eyed jerk snatched her arm and pulled her away from us. Jon went in pursuit without a thought. He was with us one minute and away the next. Scott broke after them and I was left with Chris and a twelve-year-old kid. I didn't even know his name. He just looked scared to damn death and I didn't blame him.

"Keep the kid close and follow me," I said to Chris.

"Whatever." Chris made no move to follow.

I got in his face.

"You and I got a problem. There was no way I could have known your father was in that camp. Even if he had gotten away, would you really want him around? He was one of *them*," I said.

"Fuck you and your problem. They might have found a cure. God works in mysterious ways so just go and get yourself killed," Chris said.

The kid next to him started crying and I couldn't blame him. Not one bit. Chris was being an idiot.

"Fine. He goes with me," I said and extended my hand.

Chris's own hand came up and he had a gun in it. One that was pointed at my face.

"You killed him," he said.

Gunshots sounded to my right. The urge to dash into the woods after my friends, was strong. But I'd probably catch a bullet in my back.

"Listen, Chris, I didn't know he was your dad. I don't even know which one he was! I had a duty to close down that miserable camp once and for all. The ghouls don't want to reason with us. They want us to join them or die," I pleaded. "I was on a mission to free as many people as possible. People is the operative word."

The kid crept away from Chris and me. A hand reached out of the woods for him and got a hold of his shirt collar.

Chris spun to aim at the undead, but I moved faster. I slammed my right hand against the gun, looped my fingers over the barrel, and twisted hard towards Chris's chest. Then I yanked and took the gun away from him. I inspected the piece, a Colt .40, and found that a round hadn't even been chambered. Then I drew the gun back and smashed it into Chris's face.

He stumbled in shock and hit the ground hard. I jacked a round into the chamber and pulled the kid back to me. As the zombie came into view, I shot it in the face. She was an ugly bitch with her black hair covered in little branches and pine needles. Blood covered her from mouth to stomach.

A tiny hole appeared in her forehead, and she was then blown off her feet.

"Chris, follow or stay here and die. I don't fucking care. Make up your own mind." I leaned over and looked him in the eye. "You pull a gun on me again and I'll kill you."

I took the kid's hand in mine and together we fled after our friends.

Scott had come to a stop and crouched down behind a wrecked SUV to fire at a trio of the dead who had sights on them. Janet was back among them and Jon looked no worse for wear. The ghoul had apparently fallen victim to a bullet or fled.

I pounded across the hard ground until I joined them and gave the care of the kid over to the group.

"We were just about to come back for you," Scott said. "Where's Chris?"

"He might join us. Might not. He put a gun in my face and I put him down." I growled.

"Okay, boss. You know I got your six," Scott said.

Jon and Janet exchanged glances.

"Where'd the ghoul go?" I asked.

"Jon knocked his hand loose, and I kicked him as hard as I could. We shot at him but he hightailed it," Janet said.

She pushed her hair back up her forehead. She'd been rattled. I could tell by the way her hand shook uncontrollably.

"Good job," I said.

The trio of zombies arrived, and we made short work of them. I put a round in one's forehead while Jon and Scott beat the other two to the ground and smashed in their heads. Scott's knife got stuck so we left it.

We faded around a few more abandoned cars. I wanted to try a few but was sure that, even if we found one that still had a working battery, the gas would have gone bad a few months ago. No sense in piling into a car just so we can get fifty feet before it backfired loud enough to bring another horde our way. Plus, it would most likely stall and leave us high and dry.

Then the dead began to pour out of the tree line. Not just a few, but dozens. There was no way we stood a chance against so many so we did the only thing we could. We ran.

I glanced over my shoulder, but Chris was nowhere to be seen. I tried to feel pity but couldn't muster up anything more than a sigh.

We ran into the shit a few minutes later.

Scott picked a path that skirted a pair of burned-out duplexes. They'd been built recently but now they were just skeletons of the buildings they used to be. Through a collapsed wall I spotted a couch with two charred corpses. The only thing that was still mostly intact was a glass framed picture of some abstract art. Some of the artwork had been scorched by the flames but the center was still colorful and alive, unlike everything else in the home.

Out of the ruins flowed a stream of undead. They came from behind the house and through a back door. Ten, then twenty. Soon I lost count. We had no choice but to keep running.

We pounded over the pavement, and that's when the ghoul made a reappearance.

The bastard leapt from behind an overturned ice cream truck and landed just to my left. I aimed and squeezed off a shot, but he was already on me. The others in the group closed in to help but the distraction allowed a number of zombies to take us on our right flank.

Edward screamed in pain as one of the zombies got him. The dead guy fell on him and took him to the ground. Edward fought but it wasn't enough to stop the oozing sack of flesh from taking out part of the back of Edward's neck. I yelled for him but there wasn't any way to save the member of our crew.

I had problems of my own.

The ghoul was rancid and reeked of dead fish. I punched at his face but there wasn't a lot behind the blow. My hand and wrist ached from the pounding I'd given that fucker Lee a few days ago and, in my weakened state, I wasn't being smart and locking my wrist straight. It's a wonder I hadn't broken it before now.

The ghoul's breath was horrid. He got a hand around my neck and pulled me in. His lips peeled back to reveal bloodstained teeth that were jagged, gums covered in green rot.

I swung the big desert eagle around and smashed it into his cheek. That got his attention and broke his grip.

"We...come for you," it said in a voice that was flat and sounded like a hissing water hose leak.

"Fuck you," I said back and lined up the gun to blow his brains all over the ground.

He moved swiftly, got a knee under me and, with surprising strength, sent me flying. I tried to regain my balance and land on both feet, but I was already on the way to an impact between my ass and hard pavement. I felt it all the way along my spine. My teeth *clicked* together, and I was lucky I didn't bite through my tongue.

I fired wildly, the gun bucking in my hand, but I didn't hit him.

He was back on his feet and stalking toward me. I aimed but he batted the gun aside.

Another zombie came out of the woodwork and fell on me.

From the corner of my eye I caught sight of Scott fending off two of the undead while Jon and Janet fought alongside him. The kid, didn't know his name, huddled next to a car, and then slid underneath it. His dark eyes found mine and there were tears there.

I managed to kick the undead off me, but the ghoul was still in my face. He got his knee between my legs and nearly ended the fight early. It was only my quick reflexes that threw him to the side again.

Another undead fell onto me. Its mouth clamped onto my lower leg but my pants prevented the teeth from penetrating. I kicked and got a glancing blow in but it was all I had. I was completely spent and about to die. I dug deep for any reserves but my body was completely out of juice.

I grabbed him by his lank and greasy hair and yanked his head close. His green eyes burned hate into mine. I ignored the two zombies scrambling to bite my legs, managed to lift the Desert Eagle, and place the barrel under his chin. My hand drifted as I fought to squeeze the trigger. If I was going to die I was going to take this fucking ghoul with me.

FIFTY-FIVE

Something *boomed* nearby. Then another gun went off with several loud pops. Good, Jon and Janet must have been giving them hell. At least I would be the only one who died here. If they could carve a path, they'd be free in no time.

Something pulled one of the zombies away and my leg was free. I wanted to reach down and touch the place where its teeth had tried to rip away my flesh. I was horrified I'd discover that I'd been bitten.

The ghoul snarled and tried to pull back. I pulled the trigger, but his head darted out of the way, though whether from luck or some freaky preternatural instinct I couldn't say. The gun *boomed* and nearly flew out of my weak grip.

The ghouls shrank away from the explosion, but I didn't let go of his hair. Hands and teeth clawed at my left leg as I tried to shake it loose.

More *pops* around me and splatters as blood and guts hit the ground. Something cold splashed across my face and I wiped it away. Blood. Black and rotten, smelling powerfully of iron.

The ghoul smacked my hand aside and, this time, I lost my grip and the gun slid across the ground.

I managed to get my left hand under his chin and kept him from biting me.

I kicked at his body. My legs, knees, and feet became weapons as I thrashed under the ghoul, but I wasn't going to last more than a few seconds. I was out of energy. Completely spent from the efforts of the last few days.

Someone grabbed the ghoul's hair and ripped upward. The ghoul's head twisted and its eyes went livid with rage. Hair ripped out in a huge chunk; it was flung to the ground.

I punched the ghoul in the nose and it crunched under my knuckles.

The ghoul went on the defensive and disengaged but I wasn't done with him.

Dragging in a ragged breath, head stuffed with cotton and my mind reeling, I refused to let go.

I hit him again even as my would-be rescuer got a hold of the ghoul's shirt collar and pulled the creature off me.

More gunshots echoed around me, and I had the urge to curl up in a ball. I was just as likely to get shot by one of my companions as get bit by a zombie.

Rolling to my side, I took the ghoul with me, then got my knees between us. I lifted my hand as I came upright and drove my fist into the ghoul's face again. Something snapped inside of me and I went at the green-eyed monster. I battered him repeatedly, fists rising and falling until there was something like pulp under me. When he finally stopped twitching, I crawled away and vomited up everything that was in my stomach.

"Jesus Christ, Tragger. Remind me to never piss you off."

Someone touched the back of my neck. A hand that was cool and soft. I looked around and smiled even though the act of drawing my torn lips around my teeth sent fresh spikes of pain through my face.

"Lisa," I said.

She looked harried and glanced around the area as shaped moved around us. I recognized a few from the camp she'd established in my old neighborhood. Men, women, and even a few kids moved among the mass of zombies bashing in heads. Knocking them down and breaking necks. It was an efficient but gory job that they went at with something like gusto.

"You okay, big guy?"

"I'd hug you, but I don't think I can move," I said.

"That's okay. You smell like shit anyway."

I snorted back a laugh and wiped my mouth.

Then I collapsed.

A few minutes later they helped me out of the area. I stayed lucid but I was also in a daze and the world took on a surreal feel as they dragged me away.

I didn't exactly pass out but I was certainly out of it. We moved away from the battleground, leaving piles of bodies. Some still twitched or tried crawling across the ground. But the others, along with Scott and a newly acquired crowbar he wielded with gusto, turned the last few zombies into twice dead corpses.

The morning was gone, and afternoon was setting in. Clouds drifted by, cutting the sun's rays in and out as we staggered away. Lisa stuck to my side, as did Maddy. I recognized the Asian nurse who'd healed Katherine when I brought her to Lisa's collective. Katherine had been shot by a ghoul who'd stalked us at the cabin up in the hills.

Lisa's men and women set up a camp with the remains of the trucks and vehicles from the enclave near my old house and arrayed the vehicles so that, in the event of trouble, they'd be able to make a hasty exit. That came not long after I'd met them. I had been attempting to capture a ghoul so I could understand what they wanted. It had gone sour and an army of the dead had assaulted the location.

As I scanned the new area of operation, I let out a little gasp. There was my armored SUV, and it was mostly in one piece.

"You kept her," I said.

"We did but we repurposed the vehicle. Stick around this time and maybe you can have her back," she said with a smirk.

"Thank you for rescuing us, Lisa."

"Not sure I should have. When you show up, things go to hell fast," she said with a grimace.

"I'm sorry about what happened, Lisa. Genuinely sorry," I said lamely.

"Erik, it wasn't just the ghoul you tried to bring back. We had a patrol out who were on their way to report the mass of undead. You bringing the ghoul back wasn't what set them off. We were about to be surrounded anyway. I guess they'd been planning it for a while, judging by how organized they were."

"Before you showed up, Edward, one of my guys, was bitten. Did he get away?" I asked.

"We took care of him. Scott did. It was quick," Lisa assured me.

I nodded and fought off passing out.

I got a grip and told Lisa about the hellhole we'd been tossed in. I told her about the people who were stuck in cages and forced to eat the flesh of the dead. She didn't speak and, instead, gave me her full attention. I spilled everything about the days we were stuck in there. I talked about Haley and how Lee had executed her in front of us. Then I told her about killing him and liberating the living from the camp.

I explained how we'd hid for a day and licked our wounds. During that time, some of the refugees had left out little group, leaving us with our few remaining friends. I thought of Chris and how he'd made a run for it when we'd been attacked. Where was he now?

Lisa had taken a seat on the ground with her legs crossed in front of me. At one point, she leaned forward and patted my hand. I appreciated the contact, but I didn't want to feel sorry for myself.

A familiar figure approached us and I couldn't help but grin.

"Thomas," I said.

"That's me. And look at you. You're a fucking mess," he said.

Thomas and Pat had been the first people I'd met at the Walmart. They'd allowed me to stay, and it was thanks to them that I'd met Katherine. Pat was dead but the fact that Thomas was here, with Lisa's group, reminded me there still hope in the world.

"They found us in the woods and saved us," Lisa said. "We were attacked by dozens of the green-eyed monsters, along with a small army of the dead. They trashed a lot of our trucks but we managed to escape. The wreckage is a few miles to the east," Lisa said.

"Hey. We're here to help each other our, right?" Thomas said with a wry smirk. "It was Tragger here who told us all about you."

"What happened to Katherine?" I asked.

"She was taken along with a few others," Lisa met my eyes. "We tried to get her back but they dragged her away. They got about half a dozen of our guys and escaped. We've looked day and night for them but it wasn't until yesterday that we found any sign."

I waited, expecting them to tell me that Katherine was dead.

"We think it's them, but there's a problem," Thomas interjected.

"After we escaped, we thought those who had been captured would be killed, but we found signs of something unexpected."

"Very unexpected," Lisa said.

"Just tell me if she's dead," I said.

"Don't know for sure, but there's a place where a bunch of people are being held," Lisa said.

"Great. Another ghoul camp."

"Not quite. It's a camp all right, but it's run by people," Thomas said.

"What do you mean?"

Lisa stood up and stretched her legs. She brushed leaves off her pants, and then looked me in the eye.

"They seem to be helping the ghouls," she said.

"What?" Scott said in shock, beating me to the punch.

"Not only helping, I think they worship the green-eyes."

Just when I thought the world had gone completely insane it did its best to one-up itself.

FIFTY-SIX

Maddy took care of me, but all I wanted to do was get out of the seat.

They'd taken me into a beat up, old silver RV that was stacked from floor to roof with boxes and crates of supplies. A dozen packs of distilled water sat in one corner, covered with a box of old music tapes and magazines. I spotted a stack of comic books and thought about how relaxing it would be to lay down and read one. Didn't matter what it was about, I just wanted to chill for an hour. The past week had been a journey into hell I didn't want to think about.

She treated me with the same methodic and cold precision she'd done before. Salve for abrasions and, in one spot on my left arm, she said she needed to apply stitches to an open wound.

"Ow," I said.

"Don't be such a baby. I haven't even started stitching yet."

"Don't you have any lidocaine or something?"

"This is the end of the world. We save that stuff for the big wounds like Katherine had. Remember the gunshot? Suck it up, Tragger." She scraped dirt out, and then applied straight alcohol.

I remembered Katherine getting shot and how I'd raced back to find help. I remembered it all too well. Maddy had probably saved her life.

I gritted my teeth and clenched the chair arm with my free hand.

Katherine was out there and every moment I waited was another one she grew farther and farther away.

Maybe it was time to consider the fact that she might be dead. For all I knew, she had been killed, or worse, was one of the dead.

The cut burned like it was on fire. I squinted my eyes as Maddy put a piece of string into a sewing needle.

"Won't it heal on its own? Christ, just put some superglue in it and push it together," I said. I'd seen that in a movie once.

"Trust me, Tragger. This is the best way to treat this kind of wound, unless you want to go out and find me some glue. In the meantime, this will probably get infected, and you'll have to get your arm chopped off in a few weeks. Your call," she said with a little smirk.

"This is going to suck," I muttered.

"I'll be quick. I used to sew up a lot of cuts at my old job. I'm a pro."

"Are you Korean?" I asked in an attempt to take my mind off what she was about to do.

"Half. Dad was in the military and my mother is from Pusan," she said as she set the needle next to my skin.

"That's cool."

The needle bit into my skin and she whisked the thread through and into the other side of the wound. She tugged it tight, and then looped it over and pushed again.

"It's better if you don't look," she said.

"Glad you're not following your own advice," I said through clenched teeth.

I tried her idea and looked away, but it was all I could do to sit still while she pushed the needle through again and again. After a minute, she cinched it tight, tied of a knot, and then cut the string. She took the alcohol again and, despite thinking it couldn't hurt any more, I was very wrong. The fresh dab went on cold before pain raced up my arm once again like a lightning bolt.

"Keep it clean. I'm going to put gauze on and tape the wound. Come back tomorrow and I'll clean it just to make sure you don't get an infection," Maddy said.

"Sure, Doc. It will be my first stop."

"Don't whine, Tragger. It's for your own good."

The bandage was cut from an opened package of gauze, which made sense. Conserving supplies was more important than ever.

I left the RV and made my way back into camp, hoping to get more information about Katherine's whereabouts. Weariness dogged my steps as I stumbled across a small group of tents. One of the men who looked familiar from the Walmart days gestured for me. He'd grown out his beard but he had sharp blue eyes surrounded by a layer of crows' feet. He, like most of us now, looked like a mountain man.

"Got an extra sleeping bag. I heard about what you did, Erik. We all did. You saved a lot of people from those things. Least I can do is give you this." He handed me a bundle.

"Thanks. What's your name, man?"

"I'm Neil. We met once, but briefly. I didn't have all of this," he said and touched his facial fur.

"Thanks, Neil. I'll return it later."

"Take your time, brother. Now go find a quiet place and take a short nap. An hour isn't going to kill you," he said.

I thanked him again and wandered off. A section of camp was surrounded by long pine branches. I rolled out the sleeping bag and tried to ignore the smell of old sweat. I crawled inside it, intent on taking his advice and closing my eyes for an hour at most.

I didn't wake up until the next day.

"YOU GONNA LIVE, BOSS?" Scott nudged my leg with his foot.

"The fuck?" I sat up and my head swam.

"Guess the answer's yes," Scott said. He squatted next to my sleeping bag and looked me over.

"How long?"

"How long you been out or how long have you been snoring? Same number of hours. About sixteen," he said.

"Ah hell." I rolled out of my cocoon. The morning chill hit me immediately, so I stretched my arms and legs. The wound Maddy had stitched up throbbed in pain. I peeled the gauze aside and found I'd bled through the stitches. I shifted the dressing to a clean place and pressed it back down. I'd have to go see Maddy after a bite to eat.

Scott took me to an RV that had food. Something like MREs, but for civilians. The packaging was similar to food I'd eaten in the field. My meal today was chili mac. I ripped into mine without even using the heating bag. It came with something claiming to be corn bread. The package I opened had yellow crumble in it. I dumped them into the main pouch and ate like a king. Then wished I had another. Scott surprised me with a can of pork and beans.

"You remembered," I said with a wink.

"Just like old times, eh?" He laughed. "Figured a white boy like you would kill for some pork and beans."

The day we had dragged the ghoul back to Lisa's enclave we'd raided my old house and turned up the food I'd stashed months ago. I'd offered Scott some refried beans and he'd made a joke about being Mexican.

We found a quiet spot and Scott produced a can opener. We took turns digging spoonful's out of the little container while savoring the flavor. Even cold they were the best damn beans I'd ever eaten, and that included the ones my father used to slow cook on the barbecue.

"I feel like I got beat up," I said.

"You did. Then you got beat up again. You're a lucky son of a bitch, that's for sure," Scott said.

"I don't feel lucky. Maybe it would have been better if we all bit it at the start of this mess."

"Bullshit. Staying alive is what we do. Fighting is what we do. If we give up what kind of world are we going to leave?"

"Didn't know you were such a philosopher." I chuckled. "So what's the situation out there today?"

"Nothing's changed. They're antsy to get moving but something in the woods sent a recon team back to ask for assistance. Oh and that asshole Chris turned up last night. Almost got his ass shot off."

"What did they do with him?"

"I don't know. I told Lisa to keep an eye on him but she said she wasn't a jailer. I told her that he has a grudge against you. She said she'd have someone watch but she didn't seem to care much about a grudge. Something about the new world sorting itself out," Scott said. "Anyway, I guess they let him wander away. Heard he was gone this morning."

"He left?"

"Yeah. Guess he didn't like the food," Scott said. "Or maybe he just doesn't like people. Guy's a jerk. Let it go."

We polished off the beans and Scott let me dig out the last of the pork. Chris was gone and that was a plus. I didn't need that kid constantly taking up my peripheral vision. There were enough dangers out there to worry about.

"Are Jon and Janet doing okay?" I asked.

"Seem to be. Jon has already started helping them with logistics."

"What about that little kid that was with us?"

"He didn't make it out of the ambush. Sorry, man."

I sighed and fought the urge to pound the earth with my fist. So many people gone. Innocence didn't matter when the dead came for you.

"What's this situation you were talking about?"

"Don't know. They're having a meeting in a few minutes. That's why I came to wake you up."

"Great," I said. "You know all I want to do is search for Katherine."

"I know, but whatever happened to that recon team, I thought you might want a heads up before we head off again."

"You don't have to go with me, Scott."

"I know, brother. But you got my back and I got yours. Let's see what's up. Sounded to me like they think it will help find the remains of the caravan."

I nodded, grateful he was still willing to stick by my side. The way things were going, I was just as likely to get us killed as find Katherine.

I rose and went to find a latrine.

———

I WANTED to lick my wounds while I headed out to find Katherine. As Scott and I continued to talk, a complete picture of what had occurred in the last few weeks appeared. Lisa and her crew had deserted their location, fully intending to setup a new one. They'd been beset by ghouls who were assisted by humans. They'd fought and some of the trucks had been captured or destroyed. It was only by sheer chance that Thomas's group had stumbled on the remains of the destruction and, a few hours later, ran into Lisa's group. They'd been in a pitched battle with a small army of the dead when Thomas had flanked the zombies and made short work of them.

The ghouls faded into the woods and hadn't been heard from since.

I joined the debriefing and listened in from behind a couple of other men and women who looked familiar.

"Okay, people," Lisa was saying. "We know some of our own were taken a couple of days ago, and this is the first hint we've had so far as to their whereabouts. I need five or six who are willing to investigate. You'll be outfitted with full kits and ammo, food, and water. But this is an extended recon. Not a full assault force. We need to know what the ghouls are doing and where they're going. If you can free the prisoners, then do it. Bring them back here." Lisa said as she looked around the little group.

The group broke up and I approached Lisa. She looked harried. Her hair was done up in a tight bun. She wore a set of hunting camouflage and carried a large caliber handgun on her hip. She was a far cry from the cute housewife I'd known when she and Devon lived down the block from us.

"Tragger. I asked for you because this might help you find Katherine. One of our guys found something strange and we're sending out a full team to investigate. We aren't in the search and rescue business, not normally, but this demands attention. I don't know if Katherine is with them or if it will even lead you to her location. It's what we've got right now. You interested in going along?"

"Count me in, Lisa."

"Do me a favor, Erik." Lisa said. "Don't even think about bringing a ghoul back to camp."

"I wouldn't dream of it. I'm sure I said it before but just in case, I'm sorry I dragged that one back to the old location."

"I have some gear set aside for you. What're you packing?" She nodded at my vacant waist.

"Got a desert eagle and a shotgun. I could use some ammo."

"We have a case of weapons. I know for a fact that there's an M4 without anyone's name on it. You interested?"

"Hell yeah, I am. Got any .44 rounds?"

"See that truck?" She pointed at a big Ford pickup with an older green camper on the back. "Ask for Molly. She'll get you settled."

"Perfect. When do we leave?"

"Fifteen minutes. If you're still hungry I recommend filling up now. We don't have the best food in the world but it's better than going hungry," she said.

My stomach growled again at the thought of food.

"Thanks, Lisa. For thinking of me, and for everything," I said.

"You're a valuable asset, Erik. Do right by us and we'll do right by you," she said, and then went to meet with one of her team members. They leaned over a map and studied red lines that had been drawn on the paper. Jon pointed out landmarks and helped us establish a route.

I set out to find the gunsmith and hopefully a few boxes of ammo. I still hurt just about everywhere, but I was anxious to get back into the woods and start tracking down Katherine. I prayed she was still alive.

FIFTY-SEVEN

We assembled in a small clearing and went over our weapons and gear. True to Lisa's word Molly had provided me with a full load out. The M4 was well worn but it had been maintained and smelled of fresh oil. The action was smooth as I worked the charging handle and tested the gun. It wasn't the A1 variant, so I was stuck with semi-auto and 3 round bursts. That suited me just fine because ammo was not a luxury we had.

Molly handed me a box of 240 grain .44 caliber rounds. I filled my gun and pocketed the rest of ammo. She handed me an extra magazine for the M4, which brought me to sixty rounds of 5.56. I was better equipped than I'd been in some time. The final surprise was a two-point sling for the assault rifle.

We were busy prepping for the next few hours. When I got hungry again I went looking for food and what a luxury that was. For the last few days we'd scraped by on next to nothing. My stomach was like a big hollow pit.

I found the chow line to be busy and was handed a paper plate with a blob of thick, lukewarm oatmeal, a slab of cold SPAM, and a single small green apple that was covered in brown spots and fit in the palm of my hand.

It was like I was eating at a five-star restaurant. I devoured every bite including the apples core, and then proceeded to lick the plate clean.

"Got a little more oatmeal if you want," the cook, a kid no more than sixteen years old, offered. He wore a wool jacket over a flannel shirt and sported tufts of downy hair on his face.

"I'll take it." I said, accepted the blob, and demolished it.

"Got any coffee back there," I joked.

"It's instant but it's got kick. Get it while you can because we're down to our last few cans."

"Christ. I was kidding. Hit me with a full mug," I said. "What's your name?"

"Trey."

"Chef Trey, you're my new favorite person," I said.

He handed over something like eight ounces of brew in a Styrofoam cup. I sipped it, found it to indeed by high octane, and guzzled the rest. It was barely warm. I didn't envy my stomach in the next few hours, or the results once it ran through my system, because I'd have to pop a squat at some point.

"Chef Trey. It's got a cool ring to it," he said.

"What's for dinner, Chef?"

"Probably the same stuff," he said with a crooked smile.

"Shame I'll miss it." I offered him a snap salute before moving out to find Molly.

She was all business, but she knew my name. She handed over a Colt M4 that had seen better days, but at least someone had cleaned it. I tucked an extra magazine into my tactical jacket and a box of rounds into my backpack.

She had a dozen .44 rounds. I pocketed those with a smile.

THE TEAM CONSISTED OF ME, Scott, Thomas, and a woman I hadn't met before, named Sloane McAllister. She had long hair that had gone gray and she wore a pair of glasses that were thick enough to make her eyes bulge. She had a hard face that bore proud age lines. For some reason, I thought of a DMV worker when I saw her but quickly changed my mind. She was sharp and had a quick wit even if her sense of humor was dry.

I'd known Thomas since the first days at the Walmart and knew he was a capable fighter. He'd been a cop back before the change. He'd also been a leader even though he said he didn't want the job. Still, people had listened to him. His wife, Ella, was an auburn haired beauty that doted on him at every chance.

"How's Ella?" I asked Thomas.

"Good. Safe. We have a second location a few miles back. Kept the bulk of the people and supplies separated just in case."

"This whole camp is expeditionary?"

"Something like that," he said. "Since you torched that camp some of them have been acting even weirder than normal. They don't show themselves as much. I think they're planning something but Lisa thinks differently."

"Sounds like ghouls to me," I said.

"I think you took a large slice of them out, Erik," Lisa said as she strode into the circle.

"I hope that's it," Thomas said.

"It was bad down there. They lived like animals in the dark," I said. "No telling how many more of these warrens are around. They want us gone. All of us. We join them or we die."

When we'd returned to the camp with an arsenal I'd managed to fall into some kind of lair. That's where I'd had a conversation with one of them. Then I'd killed everyone I could find. After that, we'd torched the place. I don't know how many ghouls had infested the location but I doubted a single one was still alive.

Scott had slipped away to take a leak but now reappeared. He packed a shotgun over one shoulder and wore his 9mm low on his waist like a gunslinger. He'd slipped two extra magazines into a holder so they were within easy reach.

"We gonna do this thing?" Scott asked.

"Right. Let's move out. I'll lead us to the spot, and then we'll do our best to track them. If we don't make contact within eight hours, we head back," Thomas said.

I nodded because the plan was smart, but I couldn't help but wonder if I'd return with them if there was no sign of Katherine or the other survivors from the camp.

THE TREES CLOSED around us as we dove deeper into them. We'd skirted a side road and made for a wooded area that had been a state park. We weren't far from Portland, but this section of the Pacific Northwest didn't care. As we walked over hard ground and avoided overgrown areas, we developed a marching order. Thomas took the lead and I was behind him. Sloane was quiet the entire time but fell in behind me. Scott stuck to the rear.

We paused at noises and avoided one large clump of undead. They'd become fascinated with some dead wildlife, a pair of deer if I'd had to guess, though it was hard to tell by the blood and mass of broken bones. It was a pile of gore left to rot.

Half an hour later, we came to the spot the recon team had reported.

I moved around the area, inspecting the ground and surroundings. Something big had come to a rest here. There was a lot of blood and, as we pushed aside leaves and branches, I came across a hand. It had been severed and some of the flesh had been chewed off. I shuddered and covered it again. Not much of a burial. I hated to think about who it had been attached to. Were they still alive?

The mass had left a beaten path that led further into the woods before we hit an old road. The street had no signs, and it was barely a two-lane. At one spot, it was clear someone would have had to pull over to let another car pass. We followed blood splatters for half a mile before we came across a house back from the woods.

There was a fence and a gate that was closed. The home was dilapidated, but it was clear someone had recently done work on the location. Windows had fresh boards over them and the front door was completely blocked off with a huge piece of plywood that was nailed over the entryway. I nosed around and found a spot to eyeball the house from cover.

It was clear to me that whoever was living there was smart. There was a dip in the roof and under underneath sat a dark wood dining table that had been knocked over. There were also slits cut into the boarded up top floor windows, which would provide perfect firing angles to anyone trying to assault the location.

We moved out, cautiously, me with a creeping feeling that someone had a gun trained on us the entire time.

A few minutes later, we stumbled out of the woods and into an industrial area. Warehouses and abandoned buildings lay close to the Willamette River. There was a train and a depot. Boxcars had been opened and emptied. A line of low buildings kissed the edge of the river. We could spend all day investigating this area and maybe come up with a lot of supplies. More than likely it had already been picked completely clean. Six plus months into the end of the world meant that almost everything that could be snatched and eaten had been. There was a chance we'd come across a stash of canned food at some point. There had to be some out there. Think about all of the warehouse stores. All of the storage locations that fed those stores. Think about the companies who created the canned goods. They were probably sitting on tons of supplies.

Right now, we didn't have time for that.

Instead of investigating any further, we moved back towards the woods.

A quarter of an hour later, we picked up the trail again. That's when we found the first body.

"What a mess," Scott said.

The man's age was hard to make out because most of his face had been torn off. Little bits of stringy hair still stuck to the side of his head but there wasn't much more of his scalp. Bone shone through the gore and his eyeballs were gone. The rest of his body had been stripped of clothing and most of its skin. His intestines and organs had been pulled out of his midsection and lay in piles around his corpse. Flies buzzed around the mass, and I had no doubts that maggots would soon appear.

"That guy died in agony," Thomas said as he crouched next to me.

I covered my nose with my hand but it did little to alleviate the stench. Blood, guts, and shit, not to mention rot, created a concoction that made me want to forget about ever eating again.

"Think he's from the house back there?" Scott said.

"I think he was dinner," I said.

We moved out a few minutes later and picked up the trail. It was easy—just follow the blood and body parts.

An hour later we ran into a shit show. A clump of undead had found something alive and made short work of it. I had taken the lead and had gotten a little bit lazy. I stumbled out of the trees and smack dab into a drooling rotter who hadn't had a bath in months. My first instinct was to start shooting, but there was no telling how many others were in the vicinity without further scouting. I kicked the creep in the gut and he fell back into one of his companions. This started a domino effect that would have been awesome if not for all the damn squishing and moans.

Thomas strode into the mass with a hand axe and laid into the first undead who set her bloody gaze on him. He hit it with the flat side of the weapon and flipped over the hand axe and cleaved in her skull. Another undead came at him but he slapped it aside and planted the sharp end into the bastard's throat, nearly decapitating him. It was enough to cut his lifeline. He dropped to the ground in a heap.

I went for my knife and pushed one of the undead aside, then slashed another across the throat.

Two undead fell on Scott and took him to the ground. He thrashed under them but managed to roll away from the unlikely threesome. Scott pushed himself to his feet and drove the knife into the man's eye. He stopped twitching a few minutes later. I dragged the other one away by its ankle and put the putrid asshole out of his misery.

After we recovered our cool, we moved out again.

WE'D BEEN on the move for another hour when we ran into something unexpected.

A pair of men sat by the side of the road. They'd built a little fire and were roasting something. Looked like a skinned rabbit. The smell of cooking meat practically made me drool. We skirted their location, keeping to cover, but I was pretty sure one of them had spotted us and was just playing it cool. If we made a sudden appearance, it was likely we'd be looking down the barrel of any weapons they carried.

The one tending the fire was in his fifties and had a long black and white streaked beard that swept down the front of his shirt. He wore a black skullcap and red and brown checkered flannel. The other man was half his age, and similarly dressed, but he had on an olive drab jacket like you'd find at an Army/Navy surplus store.

"What do you think?" I asked.

Thomas didn't take his eyes off them. "I say we avoid them. No telling what they're up to. A little too convenient just sitting out there cooking a meal."

I nodded.

"We see you. Don't want no trouble," the man with the heavy beard said.

"So much for the element of surprise," Scott muttered.

I stood up and showed both of my hands. The M4 was slung in front of me from the two-point harness. I kept my hands away from the gun. Sloane broke away from us and moved backward a few feet before fading into the woods.

"Not looking for trouble," I said.

About twenty-five feet separated us. If one of them went for a gun I'd be able to reach mine faster.

"We're not either. Just cooking a little food before we find a place to sleep for the night," the younger man said.

They'd dug a small pit and put wood in it then gotten a couple of chunks of wood good and hot. There was no flame, just bright red coals to cook the meat. I wondered if they had a bag of charcoal. Damn but I wanted a cookout, and some ribs. While I was fantasizing about food some fresh pineapple and tequila would go a long way toward making my day.

"We'll leave you to it," I said.

"Fine," the older man said.

"Don't go in them woods over there," the younger one said and pointed in the direction we were headed.

"Why not?" I asked.

"Because they went that way. Whole mess of them."

"What did you see?" I asked.

"That's a good question. Why are you asking?" he said.

"We're looking for someone. Some of our friends."

"Might as well mourn them now and be done with it. All you'll find in there is death. They're setup real nice with a camp and everything. They bring people in and send green eyes out," the older man said.

I looked at my companions. Thomas shrugged.

That's when I noticed something. All morning we'd heard the rustling of trees, branches on leaves and a lot of birds chirping away. Now it was quiet.

"Who brings them in?" I asked.

"We do," the older man said.

I barely got my hands on my M4 when they dove for cover. Someone started shooting behind us. I dropped to a crouch, then rolled to my right and kissed the ground. A large branch was the best I could do for cover, so I went for it. Thomas got his handgun out and his radio to his mouth at the same time. He didn't wait for the two men to open fire and, instead, shot at them.

"Five on our six," Sloane called from somewhere behind us.

"Got more at three o'clock," Scott said from somewhere to my left.

I got a bead on the younger guy and could have taken his head off but something stopped me. He looked scared. The older man, who may have been his father, grabbed him by the collar and yanked him into some bushes. I fired over their heads to keep them running.

More guns poked out from the woods on our right flank. I shifted aim but stopped myself from shooting because the new enemy hadn't fired first and they outgunned us quite a bit.

Sloane had moved away and covered our butts. She didn't even hesitate and opened up. Then someone fired at her. She let out a scream and stopped shooting.

"Stop it!" I yelled. "Tell us what you want. No one needs to get killed today."

"Drop 'em and come out with hands over your heads. Way over. You don't and we're gonna wax each and every one of you," a voice said.

Thomas spoke into the radio, then he pushed it into the backpack.

"Helps on the way," he said.

"Can we hold them off long enough?" I asked.

"No. Give up. Lisa is bringing firepower. If we can stay alive, they'll save us," he said.

"Fuck that. I played the prisoner game once and it wasn't any fun," Scott said.

"Don't do anything stupid. We got a sharpshooter with us. He can take you out at any time," the voice called out.

"Bullshit," I called back.

The ground in front of my face exploded as a high-speed round impacted. It threw dirt into my eyes, forcing me to blink rapidly. *Shit!*

"Next one's in your head," a different voice called.

"Sloane, are you hit?" Thomas called.

"Son of a bitch." I said and pushed my rifle away. Someone was a very good shot indeed. I didn't want to find out how good.

"I don't like this, Erik," Scott said next to me. His eyes were pinched up in fear.

"Sloane!" Thomas called again.

"I'm hit, but not bad. I think," she called back from behind our location.

"We didn't kill your friend. Just took her shooting privileges away," the voice again. I wanted to wrap my hands around the owner and throttle them.

"All right!" Thomas yelled.

He was first. He tossed his handgun in front of him and slowly stood up with his hands in the air. I was next, but Scott looked like he was ready to fight. His face was flushed, and he looked as if he was about to do something stupid. Then he must have come to some conclusion because he lifted one hand into the air, and then his other. I breathed a sigh of relief.

Luckily, he didn't take a bullet because the minute we took our hands off our weapons at least a dozen guns came into view, and they were all pointed at us.

FIFTY-EIGHT

They bound my hands in front of my body with a piece of frayed rope and did the same to my companions. The men stripped our weapons, ammo, and supplies. What food we had they passed among them, and it was eagerly eaten. I'd had a few protein bars stashed in the bottom of my backpack, but they disappeared into someone's jacket. The guy took one, ripped the packages open, and devoured it like he hadn't eaten in days. I guess there hadn't been enough rabbit to go around.

Then I took another look at the campfire and realized it wasn't an animal at all. It was someone's arm on a spit. I turned away and fought down bile.

Sloane was in pain but our captors ignored her with the exception of placing a rag inside her shirt sleeve to stop the bleeding. She'd been hit in the upper arm and cried out when they worked on her. She cursed but they ignored her. They kept us in single file and walked us farther into the woods. I tried to engage with the man we'd initially seen, the one with the younger guy I'd taken to be his son. He told me to shut the fuck up.

The men and women were dressed much like him. They wore thick jackets with flannel shirts and jeans or overalls. They'd been doing this for a while because they worked well as a team. Something my new group didn't have experience with yet. The way things were going, we might not get that chance.

One thing that caught my eye was the little symbol each of them had affixed to their clothes. Whether painted or stitched on it made me shiver. When Scott noticed he gave a little gasp and moved closer to me.

"Did you see that?" he whispered.

"Hard to miss," I said.

"Y'all want to make it to our base you need to shut the fuck up," the leader craned his head around and spoke.

Scott looked like he was going to offer a retort, but common sense must have gotten the better of him.

They escorted us down a path until we came across an old road that led to a farmhouse. They cut into the woods and led us deeper and deeper. I was certain this was some kind of a preserve or even a national park, but we hadn't come across any signs. Then we broke out of the foliage to stand in front of a series of streets that led up a hill. Homes, boarded up but mostly ransacked, lay before us. Corpses of long dead people lay in various positions of woe in yards and on the streets. Someone had strung up a man and woman from a signpost and left them to rot. Crows must have gone to work because there was very little left except for rot covered bones.

"Why don't you let us go," Thomas implored the leader.

He didn't say anything. Just stepped in front of Thomas and planted the butt of my M4 into Thomas's midsection.

Thomas keeled over and nearly went to his knees but managed to stay upright.

"Hey!" I yelled in protest and got a cuff across the face.

Someone grabbed Scott before he could surge forward.

That was how the next half hour went. We were hit, prodded, and guided past abandoned buildings, gutted neighborhoods, and a few strip malls that had been cleaned out. Doors busted in. Graffiti paint. And bodies. Always bodies. Then there was the mass of vehicles that had been left behind when people fled the undead.

We came across five cars that had been pushed together in the middle of a cross street and set on fire. Bodies lay on the ground blackened from the flames.

Then we were back into a wooded area again and heading into a park. There was a small stream that was clogged with more bodies. Water had pooled around them and created a small dam. I gagged on the smell but pushed on because if I fell behind, I would likely get a gun stock to the back of my head or back. Not enough to knock me down but enough to ring my bell and consider ways to hurt the person if I ever got loose.

We pushed into another area that was heavily wooded.

I was starting to lose hope and whatever energy reserves I'd had would soon be depleted. My legs were leaden, and my head swam. Still, I struggled on step after step.

We were knee deep in a copse of trees. Our captors pushed us onward while keeping large branches out of our faces. As we came out from around a group of sequoias, I noticed a pair of faces peeking from between a bunch of branches. They studied us and, just as I made eye contact with a white guy, they disappeared. The other man was black, and he had a hard face that was shadowed by a dark blue ball cap. As they faded from view, I caught sight of an assault rifle.

If anyone else noticed the men they didn't say anything.

We were pushed onward until we came to a clearing in the trees. A large duplex was setup next to a well and there were several tool sheds placed around the home. A small fence, which appeared to have been used to hold livestock, held a bunch of shambling undead. They moved from one side to the other, milky white eyes looking dull and lifeless.

Then I noticed the cart and let out a gasp.

It was like something out of an Amish village. Wooden, and clearly built in the last twenty years. It was attached to five people who looked close to death. They were dressed in rags and they knelt on the ground while a guard stood over them. He had a shotgun in one hand and kept it pointed at the bunch. In the back of the cart were about a dozen bodies in various states. Blood dripped from the wooden floor and soaked into the ground. This is what we'd been sent out to investigate.

I felt like throwing up.

The front doors to the duplex were shut and chained. Through the dirty windows I observed a few faces, but they were indistinct.

Of the horror movie that the world had become, this was the most horrifying thing I'd seen yet.

Then it got worse.

Among the men and women who worked the little camp, a couple of ghouls moved. One of them was a large woman who moved around on all fours. Her eyes were bright green, and when they settled on me, my scalp itched.

Anger burned in her gaze as she moved across the ground until she was before the head captor.

He leaned over and waited as she hissed something into his ear.

I waited, hoping against hope that they weren't talking about me. He nodded, and then she was off and moving toward one of the big tool sheds.

The man turned and approached our pitiful group.

"You," he said pointing at my face. "You're first. Bring him."

I struggled as my arms were grabbed. I fought as they dragged me across the ground. Someone hit me in the gut and another guy knocked me across the back of the head.

"No!" I yelled.

"Shut up and this will be over soon," another guy said, then there was another blow.

They took me into the little toolshed and the door slammed closed.

FIFTY-NINE

"**P**ut him on the table," the leader said.

The room reeked of blood and misery. Chains and knives hung from the walls. There were a few limbs tossed in a corner as well as a pile of bloody clothes.

With four of them it wasn't that hard. I was already exhausted, and they'd beaten the shit out of me. I played it safe and pretended like I was giving in. If there was any kind of opening, I was going to take as many of these fuckers out as I could before they killed me so I conserved my energy.

The ghoul stood hunched over the low table waiting. Her eyes burned into me.

They held my arms and dragged me before her.

"Let me tell you what's about to go down, Chief." the leader said.

"Fuck you," I said.

"We're going to strap you down and she's going to change you. I don't know what you did to piss them off, but she wants you bad."

Two men had my arms in a tight grip and they tried to turn me around, presumably to lay me flat on my back. The man on my left was scrawny but strong. The guy on the right was a beast with a huge black beard running down his face so I named him Grizzly Adams. They were efficient with the rope and got my wrists bound tightly together.

Grizzly Adams smelled like a dead bear and I told him as much. When I turned my head to the side and tried to hold my breath, he leaned over and slapped me.

The blow rocked my head to the side. I blinked away tears and thought about what it would be like to press my thumbs into his eye sockets.

"This isn't right!" I protested and tasted blood on my lip. "Why are you working for these fucking things?"

"You'll know soon. Just give it up. You'll either be one of them or you'll be chopped to pieces. We got a whole pen of them out there to feed. Your choice," he said.

I noticed there was a small bucket on the ground and it was filled with rancid chunks of meat. Like the cages we'd been kept in, it had to be the diseased flesh of the twice dead. I knew the score. Once feeding on the meat, whatever virus from hell was contained would change me. I'd join the ranks of the ghouls.

Would I be able to fight it and hold back its effects?

I had a feeling they were going to end up killing me instead because there was no way I was going to ingest that shit.

The lifted me and dropped me on the table. The ghoul leaned over and picked up something that looked like it might have been a tongue.

"Chew and swallow. Easiest thing in the world," the leader said.

She leaned over and proffered the meat.

The guy on my left must have felt cocky because his grip loosened as they deposited me on the table. I used the chance to twist my wrist swiftly while yanking away. My hand came free and I swung my body to the right and hit the Grizzly Adams in the face. One of my digits got a lucky shot and caught him in the eye. He howled and dropped away.

I got my legs up, rolled back, and kicked the ghoul in the face before she could leap away.

The leader fell on me and pressed me back down. He lifted his arm and drove his fist into my side. I tried to roll away, but the blow blew the breath out of my lungs. The guy on my left, who'd been holding my arm, got back on his feet and shook his hand. I slammed my knee upward, and then again, catching my assailant in the thigh. I'd been hoping to get him between his legs, but he slid away.

The ghoul recovered and leaned over me. Her green eyes burned with fury. She lifted her hand to strike but I shoved the guy on top of me into its path. She caught him upside the head and he let out a gasp of pain. I went with it, ignoring the ghoul to concentrate on the greater threat. I wiggled my hand up and shoved it into the guy's throat, trying to crush his windpipe, but he shook the blow aside.

I didn't have much left. My body simply refused to obey my commands to fight back. I was beyond the point of exhaustion, and they were about to win.

There are many places on the human body that can be used as striking points. Elbows, knees, feet, calves, and everything in between. I used one of my last ones by grabbing Grizzly Adams by his hair, then slammed my forehead into his face. His nose cracked and blood poured over my face. He screamed in pain and fell away.

I was free! I pushed myself up, intent on finding a corner to put my back against.

But the ghoul and the other man leapt on me. The leader staggered back against the side of the little building, cursing all the time. His eyes blazed with hatred and he had a knife in one hand. Not just a knife, but a big hulking slice of razor-sharp pain. At least ten inches long, it looked like my death was imminent.

The ghoul shoved the meat into my face trying to get it between my lips.

I fought back as the guy whose wrist I'd snapped struggled to hold me down.

The rancid meat hit my lips again and I clamped them shut like a little kid being force fed creamed peas.

The man with the knife swam into view. The knife rose and I knew I was about to die.

Then a gunshot sounded outside.

The guy spun to seek the sound, as did the ghoul. I grabbed her around the neck, my hand sliding around her cold skin, and squeezed while I dragged her close. She fought but I closed my hand as tight as I could. The thing about ghouls was that, as far as I could tell, they barely breathed. They did need oxygen but they didn't need a lot. The weird virus had altered their bodies so that they were close to dead. No one understood the virus or the altered state it caused in the ghouls.

Still, I was intent on ripping her goddamn throat out.

But she got her hands around my wrist and pulled my hand loose. She was so strong it was freakish.

A full blast of bullets echoed from outside. The leader slammed open the door and suddenly my path was almost clear.

More bullets ripped through the air. Someone screamed in pain outside.

The leader, the guy I'd clawed in the eyes, rubbed at his head but drew a handgun from beneath his jacket. He perched next to the entryway.

"Keep him back. Kill him if you have to," he called over his shoulder.

The ghoul hopped on top of me. I slugged her and she rocked back from the blow.

A round passed overhead and struck the wall. We both looked up and I took the opportunity to buck my back, so she flew off me.

I didn't know how Lisa and her crew had found us so quickly, but I was grateful. If I survived this, I was going to give her a hug.

Bullets hammered through the wall of the little shack, causing us to drop. I landed on the ghoul, and she slithered away. I found a wall shrank into it. Grizzly Adams came at me on his hands and knees. He had that big blade in one hand and hatred in his eyes.

I caught his wrist as he dove in with the blade. The ghoul grabbed me around the waist and pulled me close to her. She got her mouth next to my neck. I freaked out and slammed my head back as I kicked at the knife wielder. If she got a piece of me, I wasn't going to die easily. I was pretty sure I'd become one of the undead within minutes.

"We have need of you in our ranks," she said close to my ear as she pulled herself on top of me.

"Fuck you and your ranks," I said while I gasped for air.

I slammed my head back again, but she slipped aside and held on tight.

Then a huge shape appeared in the doorway. He was at least six foot two and had thick arms. He had a short and badly maintained growth of beard. He wore overalls and a dark jacket. He had a pistol in his left hand and a huge wrench, of all things, in his right. He stormed into the little building and commenced to kicking ass.

The leader of the group who'd captured us came to his feet and swung at the guy. The big man slammed the gun into the side of his head and the guy dropped. The ghoul shrieked in rage and suddenly I was free and could breathe.

She came off the ground and launched herself at my rescuer.

The man on my left side recovered and came at me with a knife. I rolled to the side and barely missed getting slashed before he turned and made for the door.

The ghoul landed on the table and reached for the big man. He wasn't having any of that and hit her with the wrench so hard it turned her head inside out. She dropped to the ground and didn't move again. The smell, like rotted fish and old blood permeated the little room. I backed myself into a corner and hoped the big man wasn't going to kill me next.

"You okay, man?" he crouched in front of me.

"Uh. No. Yeah."

"Shit. I blew it this time. Joel's gonna give me hell. You ready to move?" he said.

I stared at him in confusion. I was sure I was about to die less than a minute ago, and now this guy had suddenly appeared and smashed the ghoul to the ground.

He turned and shot at the guy who was fleeing. The bullet caught him in the leg and he stumbled, screaming in pain as he went down.

More bullets ripped into the camp. I got into a half crouch and fought my swimming head. I needed to sleep for a week but that wasn't going to happen.

"Who are you?"

"Jackson. We didn't plan on a rescue operation. We were just checking things out when one of those shufflers caught wind of me. They came at us and we, well, Joel started shooting. Truth is, I saw them drag you in here and it pissed me off. Gets me into trouble every time. My temper, know what I mean?" Jackson said.

"Thank you," I said, and then stumbled toward the doorway.

I gasped for breath and nearly collapsed.

The camp was in chaos as the men and women who'd captured us ran to different corners of the compound. They probably had no idea what to do so they acted like headless chickens. I spotted Scott, Thomas, and Sloane. They huddled next to a low fence.

"Sure. We need to haul ass. You know how to handle a gun?" Jackson asked me.

"Yep."

He slung a Remington shotgun off his shoulder and handed it to me, but before my hands closed on the stock, he turned to look me in the eye. "I don't know you from Adam, brother. You turn on me or my friends and you're not going to like the results. We cool?"

Jackson was a big man, and his gaze was intimidating. More importantly, I understood where he was coming from. It was hard to trust anyone these days.

"We're cool. We came out here to investigate these guys when they captured us. They want to turn us all into ghouls," I said.

"I know. We were doing the same thing, reconnoitering, when we found this camp. Fuck those guys," he muttered.

I took the gun and checked the load and found it was ready to fire. It was a pump action and I suspected a model 870. If it was fully loaded, I had four rounds plus one in the chamber. I quickly moved to the other side of the doorway to cover Jackson. He didn't seem to like that idea and gestured for me to take the lead. I guess he didn't want to put his back to an armed stranger.

One of our captors ran from the field of battle toward the big house. A pair of ghouls appeared and came toward us. I was too far away for an accurate shot with the Remington, but it didn't matter because a shot rang out from the woods and one of them dropped with a hole in their head. The second ghoul figured out he was in someone's gunsights and dove out of the line of fire.

I moved toward the fence as quickly as I could. Someone opened fire from the house so I lifted the shotgun and fired back. It hammered against my shoulder and nearly took me off balance. I stumbled and almost went down but managed to keep moving. I hit the dirt next to Thomas and put the gun down. The fence was six feet tall and made of Cedar, the kind of thing you see in every other yard in the Pacific Northwest.

It provided threadbare cover, but it was better than nothing. At least we were out of sight.

"Can you cut us loose?" Thomas asked. He turned and showed me his hands. I went to work on untying the knots. I could have dug out a knife but I'd probably cut his hand off in the process. My mind reeled and my body wasn't exactly in the best shape. My hands shook so badly I thought I was having a seizure. Amped up adrenaline will do that to you.

Scott and Sloane were busy, butted back-to-back, on their sides, trying to undo each other's bindings.

I got Thomas free, and he moved over them, using his body as cover.

I closed my eyes and took a couple of steady breaths. When my head stopped spinning I got back in the fight.

I leaned around the side of the fence and fired at a man who'd gotten brave and moved out of the little home. He fired back at me so I got the hell out of his way. I wasn't sure where the shooter in the woods was but my guess was that his line of sight was blocked.

I counted to three, then dropped to the ground and slid out from the behind the fence. I fired the shotgun and the blast went wide but it made the advancing man kiss the ground.

That's when I noticed several faces pressed to a window in the home.

One of them was Katherine.

SIXTY

"Katherine!" I yelled, but of course she couldn't hear me.
Thomas grabbed my shoulder as I lurched forward.

"Wait. You can't storm that place alone. You'll die," he said.

He shouldn't have had to tell me. I knew it was being stupid. I was just reacting on instinct, instinct that would indeed see me slaughtered. Plans formed and fell apart in my mind. There weren't enough of us. The group that had brought us here had numbered at least six and there were still others in the house and possibly more surrounding it. The gunfight had been brief and now everyone would be on alert. Not only that, but every ghoul around would be on its way to kill us. I had no doubt that would be our fate. They weren't dumb enough to try capturing us again. This time we were going to die.

Frontal assault was a bad idea. We could try to set up a flanking maneuver with two of our crew providing a distraction with gunfire. Then Scott and I could sneak around the side. The problem was that we didn't have the manpower for an assault. Plus, we didn't have enough guns. We'd barely be able to escape with our lives. The only choice we had was to regroup.

"You're right. We need to meet up with Lisa and get her involved. With her force we can take the building," I said, convincing myself it was the best option. The truth was I had no intention of leaving until she was safe. Or I was dead.

Someone poked their head out of the compound and bullets erupted from the woods again. The man spun in shock and the flopped to the ground. Christ. The guy with Jackson was a hell of a shot. If I had to guess, I'd say he took the man from fifty to seventy yards.

Jackson picked that moment to make a run for it. He pounded across the ground and dropped behind the fence with us. He's picked up a couple of bags on his way and tossed them to us.

"Let's move, kids. Nothing else to see here," he said.

"One of ours is inside the building," I said.

"Sorry to hear that but we're not here to fight. This rescue was an accident," he said as we pushed away from the fence and toward the surrounding woods.

I dug into the bags and found some of our gear. The food was gone and I cursed the fact that someone had taken the M4 and I was likely never going to see it again.

I helped Scott up while Thomas poked his head over the top of the cedar fence. When it didn't get shot off, he grabbed Sloane's arm under his shoulder and hoisted her to her feet. She grunted with pain. I noticed that blood had seeped through her sleeve from the wound.

Together, the five of us staggered into the woods. When a dozen undead didn't fall on us I almost breathed a sigh of relief.

Goddamit! I wanted to go back for Katherine so badly. I wanted to assault the building and kill everyone inside who'd done her harm.

Rounds passed overhead making us hit the dirt. Jackson nearly dropped his wrench but managed to keep a death grip. I'd never considered using a weapon like that but now that I'd seen him in action, I might have to reconsider. Swinging something that heavy could quickly tire a person.

We wove our way through the forest in the direction we'd initially arrived from. After a few minutes, a new face appeared ahead of us. I lifted the Remington, but Jackson motioned for me to lower it. The guy who approached had to have been the shooter in the woods. He wore a dark ball cap and had ebony skin. As he drew closer, I realized this guy and Jackson were the two men we'd seen earlier in the day as we'd been pushed toward the camp. They'd poked their heads out for the briefest of seconds before disappearing again.

"Jackson. What kind of happy horse shit was that?" the new guy asked.

"My bad. I didn't think the shuffler saw me. Then all hell broke loose."

"I told you we're not in the rescue operation business," the black guy said.

"Yeah, man, but those ghouls had it coming."

Joel looked at his friend and something flashed between them before the other man rolled his eyes.

He was dressed in the remains of some kind of military body armor and wore a light camouflage jacket. Jackson and I did introductions but Joel, the guy with the assault rifle, didn't look too interested in getting to know us. That was cool with me. He and Jackson had saved us and I was grateful but I had no chance of dragging them into my newly forming plans to save Katherine.

"How'd you end up there?" Joel asked us.

"We got captured a few hours ago west of here. Heard rumors of some kind of ghoul activity and we wanted to make sure the way was clear before heading to our final objective," I said.

"Military, huh. What branch?" Joel asked me.

"Ex-Army. Wasn't in long."

Joel and Jackson exchanged another glance.

"Well hell, brother. If we had an air force puke here, we'd have a complete circle jerk. I'm Navy and my friend here was a Marine," Jackson said.

"Still a Marine," Joel said.

"Right. Once a jarhead always a jarhead," Jackson said.

Thomas tended to Sloane while we chatted. He dug around in the bags until he found a small first aid kit and applied some clean gauze.

"I'll need stitches," Sloane said.

I grimaced at the thought because I'd been stitched up the day before and the experience had not been pleasant. My wound itched, and I hadn't had a chance to change the dressing and put fresh salve on as the doc had instructed.

"So you guys just happened to be around and got into the shit?" Scott said. "Thank God for you both. I thought we were dead."

"Didn't mean to rescue you," Joel said, "but I'm glad it worked out."

"Regardless, you have our thanks," Thomas said.

I nodded. Thank God indeed. If they hadn't stumbled on us, I'd probably be a damn ghoul now, or zombie food.

"They have my girlfriend in there," I said and nodded back toward the house we'd fled from.

"Oh hell, brother. I don't know what to tell you. Even if we helped it wouldn't be enough," Jackson said.

"I know. Appreciate you saving us," I said. "We'd be dead. Hey, why don't you guys join us? We have a tight crew and we're going to Portland once we figure out how to get Katherine out of that home."

"Thanks for the offer but we're doing okay," Joel said.

"Wait. What's in Portland? We actually came up here from California and we've heard rumors."

"There's a large group intent on taking this entire area back. They've been building up for the last month. I'm tired of hiding and shitting in holes. I want to take the fight to the dead and those ghouls," I said, and I meant it. From the very beginning I'd wanted to strike back.

"That's an interesting proposition. What do you think, Joel? Bring them to fortress?" Jackson said.

Fortress?

"No offense, but we're flying solo. Don't need more help," Joel said.

Gunshots echoed then, and something exploded from the direction we'd fled. I rose to my feet and found smoke trailing into the air. What in the hell was going on back there? Then more shots were exchanged. I couldn't see a damn thing.

I took a few steps before Scott once again stopped me. "Dude. What are you thinking?"

"I'm thinking that I need to go back. Now."

"Let's just look. Nothing more. Okay?" Scott asked.

"Tragger. Hold up," Thomas called to me.

I turned and found he was on the radio. He'd dug it out of one of the bags and was communicating with someone.

"What?" I asked.

BEYOND THE BARRIERS 363

"It's Lisa. They just engaged with that compound and shit is going south fast," Thomas said.

"Lisa is here?"

"As soon as they heard gunshots from our capture they set off in pursuit. They picked up the path and followed us here."

"Goddamn. We may be able to rescue Katherine after all," I muttered.

Sure enough, more guns sounded near the compound. Like any battle, it was hard to get a feel for what was happening in the distance. I needed to get closer if I was going to get Katherine out. Waiting could mean she died in the fight.

I turned and found Jackson and Joel's eyes on me. I hoped I met their gaze with enough pleading. Regardless, I was about to do something stupid and they could join me or they could go back to wherever they'd come from.

SIXTY-ONE

Evening was fast approaching, and with it came the threat of rain. It was like I could smell it in the air. The other scent was smoke and gunfire. I'd been in this situation before. Too many times, in fact. And here I was, once again, going in headstrong. It was going to be the death of me one of these days.

"Thanks for all the help. Sincerely, but my girl is in that compound, and I need to get her out," I said.

"Shit," Jackson said and hefted his wrench.

"No, man. We don't have time for this. Good way to get killed." Joel told his friend.

"Yeah, but that's his girl, man. I understand," Jackson replied.

"I do too, but we don't know them. After all the shit we've seen, you're telling me you're ready to just jump when someone needs help? Ain't no one helped us in a long time."

Jackson nodded but he was obviously chewing on the things I'd presented.

"I get it," I said, but I was disappointed.

I didn't stick around to come up with a plan. If the others followed, which was looking highly unlikely, then good. If not, well, I'd been in worse situations over the last few weeks. The goal was to get to that compound as quickly as possible, but I had one serious problem. I was at the point of exhaustion and my body might give out at any second.

"I got your back," Scott said.

I clamped my hand over his shoulder and nodded at my friend. Thomas lifted his weapon and pointed at the house.

I broke away from the group and ran toward the duplex, using the cedar fence as cover. As I came to the edge I poked my head around to assess the situation. What I saw caused great concern. I checked over the shotgun and decided I was lucky if there were still two rounds left. I needed more firepower.

The shed.

Scott and Thomas were right on my heels. We came to a stop at the edge of the fence and panted for breath. Leaves crunched under my feet and knees as I dropped to the ground

"We need more firepower. Might be some on the bodies in there. Cover me," I said.

I dashed toward the shed. I barreled through the doorway and found the corpses of the men who'd tried to feed me to the ghoul. I checked bodies and found a Glock chambered for .40 caliber. I dug out an extra mag and stuffed it in my pocket. I also got lucky and found some shotgun shells from one of the dead men's packs. I chambered three rounds.

I rolled his corpse over and found a snub nose revolver in his belt.

Scott had moved to cover the entrance to the shed. He gave a sharp hiss that drew my attention.

"We gotta hurry, man," he said.

"Found you a present," I said and tossed him the little .38 revolver.

"Damn, I didn't get you anything."

Scott found a knapsack one of the men had carried. He tossed the contents and found another handgun and one spare mag.

From the east corner of the dilapidated townhome, smoke rolled out of a window. Someone had smashed the glass allowing for escape. It also let more air in and that would help a fire spread quickly.

Scott and Thomas had moved toward the home. They used what little cover there was, mainly trees and a couple of barrels that were probably used to store rainwater.

I noticed a pen when we were brought into the compound, but it was now empty. The people trapped inside had somehow managed to escape into the woods.

I moved catty-corner to Scott and Thomas but provided hand signals. We moved as a team.

Someone kicked open a top window. The figure appeared and leapt. They landed, rolled, and then were quickly on their feet. My conservative guess was that the distance had to be at least twenty-five feet. How in the world did they do that?

Then the man turned, and I caught green eyes. He snarled at me, so I lifted the shotgun. At fifteen feet the blast was lethal and took off the side of his head.

Someone opened fire from the window and I had to duck. I rolled away and came up behind an old tractor. Rounds *plinke*d off the metal. Thomas fired back and the figure disappeared.

Scott waved me on as he pointed his gun at the side of the building.

More figures appeared in the window I thought I'd seen Katherine in. Now that I was approaching the house, I wondered if it was really her. Just a glimpse, that's all I'd had. Maybe it was my desperation to find her. Maybe it was just my imagination and I had seen someone who looked like her. Maybe I was simply chasing a ghost and Katherine had died a week ago.

A door opened on the west side of the building and out poured a half dozen people. We ducked and took cover, but it was too late. They had spotted us. More figures pounded behind them and fled into the woods.

Another asshole opened fire on us and we had no choice but to make for the side of the building. We were less than a dozen feet away and, if we stayed out in the open, we were sitting ducks. As I hit the side of the home, figures swarmed out of the woods toward the compound. In the lead was Lisa.

I breathed a sigh of relief until someone on the second story opened fire on them. They scattered but one of the men took a hit and went down. I wanted to rush to their side, but Lisa fired back at the shooter while someone helped her man back into the woods.

Her group returned fire and splattered bullets over that side of the house. I wanted to yell at her to stop shooting because one of the bullets might find Katherine.

Fire crackled overhead and that made me cringe. I glanced up from my location and found a window was directly overhead.

"Scott, cover me," I said.

He rolled to the right and trained the gun around. I stood and got a quick look at the interior. The layout was weird. What had probably been some kind of kitchen had been replaced by a prep area complete with card tables. There was something on one of them that looked like a pot filled with blood. Appliances had been ripped away from the wall, leaving gaping holes, and there were shackles bolted to the floor. Someone swam into view and I ducked back down. The man didn't look like a ghoul but he moved like one. Long and lank hair covered his face but there were no green eyes. Luckily, he didn't see me.

"I'm going in through that window," I said to Scott.

"How the hell do you plan to do that?"

"Shoot it a couple of times. I'll hop up, grab the ledge, and smash my way in," I said.

"That's the stupidest fucking plan I've ever heard," Scott said. "It's not going to work because you aren't a stuntman in a movie. What if the room is filled with armed individuals?"

"Got a better suggestion?"

"What if we go around the back. Those guys ran out of a door so it's probably open," Scott said. "It's less than twenty feet. We check it out and if it's not clear we try your plan."

I chewed on that for a few seconds. Scott made sense. I was working on a fierce need to get to Katherine and it was making me stupid.

I finally nodded and we moved together skirting the wall and staying low. Sloane and Thomas poked their heads out from behind their cover, a large stack of wood. I made hand gestures I hoped they understood. Then someone fired on them from the upstairs. They both ducked. Thomas waited a few seconds, and then returned fire.

Scott and I made it to the edge of the building and I peeked around. Sure enough, the back door was open as if in open invitation.

"This is dumb. It's like they're waiting for us," I said.

"Go slow, man. Duck and cover," Scott said.

I snorted and moved out.

I rounded the building and stepped over a pile of leaves someone had raked up. I nearly stepped on the rake head which would have resulted in a comedic yelp from me or Scott. I reached the entryway, which was wide open.

I waited and listened but there was little I could hear over the gunfire on both sides of the house, not to mention the fire that was kicked up far above. Something *popped* and a chunk of the wall fell. I looked up and found flames spreading as they licked out through a shattered window.

I took a chance and glanced inside. Luckily no one blew my face off.

I nodded at Scott and scooted inside, staying low as I entered the building.

The room had been built to hold captives. Chains lay on the ground secured to bolts driven into the floorboards. There were a couple of metal cages large enough to contain people. Christ! They'd been using this location to add to the ghoul ranks.

Scott came in behind me. He covered our back as we moved around the room. Something *popped* overhead and there was movement. Several footsteps as if someone was running. A large *thump* sounded, then yelling.

"Shit. Someone's locked inside up there," Scott said.

The place reeked of human sweat and rot. There was an undercurrent of mold but all of that was about to be obliterated by flame. It was already beginning to permeate the air.

We swept the room but didn't have time to do a full investigation. I knew this was risky. There could be a dozen people or ghouls hiding and we wouldn't know it. The minute we went up the stairs we could be trapped.

The steps were old and, as I planted my foot on the first one, the wood creaked. Scott kept his back to me as he covered my ascent. I took one more stair, and then paused. When no one rushed us, I took them two at a time until I was nearly to the landing. There had been railing but part of the wooden latticework was broken. I poked my head up and found the upper level was cleared of all furniture. There were a couple of cages. One of them contained a person but they didn't move. I rushed to the side, regardless of my safety. Scott hissed in dismay but followed.

"Careful," he whispered.

I waved to him but kept the Glock trained ahead of me.

The woman wasn't Katherine and I breathed a sigh of relief. She was a mess though, covered in wounds and bite marks. One of her eyes glowed with malevolence and a luminous shade of green I immediately recognized. Her other eye was filled with blood. She was dressed in the remains of a pair of shorts and a button up floral print shirt. She smelled of feces and urine.

Her lips pulled back revealing a set of shattered teeth. She tried to say something, but when her mouth opened her tongue was gone.

I choked back bile and moved away.

Someone *pounded* on a door and yelled, "Help!"

Scott patted my shoulder and motioned to the west corner of the big room. There were other doors but they were open and we could make out the fact that they were empty. There was a bed in one and some beat up metal chairs in the other. No one dashed out or aimed guns at us. Whoever had been shooting earlier were either gone or they were deeper inside the building.

I sucked in a breath when I realized we were only seeing about a third of the upper floor. It might take us an hour to search this place. Meanwhile, it would burn to ash around us.

The door *thumped* again. Scott moved toward it as smoke started to fill the room.

I moved away from the woman who was on her way towards being a ghoul, wondering if I should put her out of my misery but she was locked up and wasn't an immediate threat.

We advanced down a hallway that was ten or twelve feet long. Glancing in doorways, we found no one moving. Just chains and rags. There were blood splatters on the walls and floors. It was like a damned slaughterhouse. More smoke rolled into the building and a fresh round of bullets peppered the side of the compound.

The door bulged again as someone hit it.

"Who's in there?" I called out.

"Help us, please. They left us to die," a man yelled.

There was a latch with a combination lock on the door.

"Shoot it off?" Scott asked.

"I don't think that actually works. Better to pry the latch off," I said.

We ducked into side rooms. I tossed items around and pulled the empty drawers out of an old wood dresser. Nothing. I kicked over a trashcan filled with debris and a few body parts. It rolled across the floor and out rolled a strip of metal that appeared to be the broken end of a machete. I gulped when I considered what it had been used for.

Smoke rolled into the hallway and we both coughed. It burned my nose and eyes and before I knew it tears were streaming down my face.

"Can you get it?" Scott asked.

"Working on it," I said and tried again.

This time I pounded the metal strip, but it slipped away from the latch.

"Please get us out." The man's voice sounded from within the room.

"We're working on it," I said.

I tried again but the metal strip was simply too thick to slide between the bolts.

Scott had ducked back into another room and came up behind me.

"Let me try," he said.

I turned and found he had a metal fire extinguisher in his hand. I stepped aside with a grin. Scott lifted the red canister and smashed the end into the lock. The second time he struck it, the metal ring broke and the lock fell to the ground.

Scott stepped back and raised his weapon to cover me. I slammed the latch aside and pushed open the door.

They were a motley assortment of misery. Five or six men and women dressed in rags, covered in blood, and sporting fresh bruises. The man rushed at me with anger blazing in his eyes. I backed up and lifted my pistol. He stopped in his tracks but those behind him pressed close.

"Who are you? Are you with them?" The man croaked.

"I'm not with them, whoever them is," I said.

"They've kept some of us in this building for days. Killed a few. Turned others," he said.

"Is there someone named..." I didn't finish my question.

A woman pushed past him and stopped in her tracks. Her auburn hair had been shoulder length the last time I'd seen her but now it was shorn close to her head. She had a large bruise on the left side of her face and her eye was partially closed. But her other was clear. When she took me in she gave a gasp.

"Erik," she said, and then she was in my arms.

SIXTY-TWO

I ignored the smell of body odor and blood and kissed her. She stank like she'd been kept in a sweat box for a week. But here she was, and I couldn't have been happier.

"Katherine!"

The others pushed past us and fled down the stairs while smoke continued to fill the building. I clung to Katherine, and she clung to me.

"Great. We got her, let's go, man," Scott said from behind me.

I held her and pulled her tightly against my chest.

"Erik. How did you find me?" she asked.

I touched her wounded face and wished I had the person who had done this to her in front of me. I'd take him apart. But now was not the time to go hunting them down. For all I knew, it was one of the assholes who'd tried to turn me. As smoke swirled around us, I shook my head. There was time for *us* now. There would be a moment when we were free of this and we would be able to talk and love.

"Long story, my love. Stay close. We're getting out of here."

"You have to be careful. There's a lot of green-eyes out there," she said.

I tugged her hand and drew her after me.

"I know. We've been dealing with them with extreme prejudice," I said.

"Erik. The ghouls are smart, and they knew there was a large force outside. That's what some of the men were talking about," she said. "They just moved us up to the second floor and locked the room before setting the place on fire."

We moved to the stairs as the people we'd rescued fled before us. They ran into the main room and headed for the door. I refused to let go of Katherine's hand as we descended the steps.

"Shit. What should we do?" Scott asked.

"Stay tight, people. We're getting the hell out of here," I said, hoping my voice carried conviction.

Above us the flames crackled as the fire spread. We'd entered without a problem. There hadn't been a force waiting for us. How long had we been in here? Ten minutes?

With Thomas and Sloane outside, not to mention Lisa's force providing cover fire on the compound, I thought we stood a pretty good chance of making a run for it.

Then I realized the shooting had died down.

"Can we get out that way?" I asked pointing to the other side of the building.

"Maybe," Katherine said. "They usually keep the doors secured on that side. That's where they do a lot of experiments."

"Jesus," Scott breathed.

One of the survivors screamed.

I dashed into the dilapidated main room and through the doorway where I spotted the source of fear.

There were dozens outside. One of the green-eyed bastards went down with a bullet hole in the center of their face. Gunfire rippled again but it sounded like a lone shooter. The group of people we'd freed took cover behind anything they could find as the army advanced on the door. They came en masse, with little regard for themselves. Ghouls surrounded by a small army of the dead.

"I hope Lisa didn't leave before this party got started," I said.

"I can't let them take me again, Erik. Please. If it looks like that's going to happen, you have to take care of it. I can't live that horror again," Katherine pleaded.

I looked her in the eye and nodded even though, in the back of my mind, I doubted I'd be able to kill her.

I moved to the window I'd spotted Katherine through and poked my head out, hoping that Thomas and Sloane didn't shoot it off. I hit the window with the butt of my handgun. It cracked so I hit it again until shards broke and fell to the ground.

"Thomas. You out there?" I yelled.

"Yeah. We're about to make a run for it though. You need to do the same. Meet with Lisa's group on the south side of the compound. Go now," he called back.

The army of ghouls and undead closed in on the doorway. I heard Thomas move away and fire a few more times.

"Grab anything you can and fight back," I yelled.

A man and a woman clamped their hands together and ran past us. I guess Scott decided to try and set an example. He walked into the room with the little revolver held high and stopped in the center of the space. He planted his legs, lifted the gun, and fired three times. One ghoul went down and a guy missing most of his jaw spun into another undead directly behind him.

"Fight back!" he yelled.

Some of the survivors were paralyzed with fear but a couple found makeshift weapons. One was a fold up chair. The survivor held it over his head like he was at a wrestling match. When the first undead appeared he sucked in a breath, ran forward, and hit the zombie so hard it was smashed to the floor.

"Katherine, clear that window and find something to put over the edge. That's how we're getting out," I said.

"How will we get everyone out of that space before we're overrun?"

"Let me handle that. I have an idea," I said even though I had shit.

The doorway was small. With any luck Scott and I, plus one or two survivors, could keep the little entryway clogged with bodies so they couldn't all flood in at once.

Smoke rolled down the stairway and something *cracked* overhead. Then there was a rending sound as a wall caved in above.

Katherine tossed things out of cabinets until she found an old rug, then she started to clear the broken glass. The problem with the window was that it was so small we'd only be able to get one person out at a time.

I strode into the main room and backed up Scott. He aimed and fired again but missed his target. The round took down a zombie in the rear ranks.

"Listen up," I said to the survivors. "We have a way out, but we need to fall back in small groups."

One of the men turned to regard me. He was a teenager and one of his eyes was overtaken by blood under the iris, the skin around it was purple. He wore a pair of sweatpants and a shirt covered in Disney characters. What there was of it had dried bloodstains. He looked like he wanted to jump out of his own skin.

"Man. Shit. What are we going to do?" He said.

"What's your name?" I asked.

"I'm Colin and I'm scared. Is the window ready? Need to get out of here, man!"

"Keep a level head, Colin, and I'll see all of us out of here. Got it?"

He nodded, but then he rushed past me. Several others in the little group took the hint and also moved. They scrambled for the window, knocking Katherine out of the way in the process. She'd gotten most of the glass out but had left a ragged row on the bottom of the frame. Colin didn't care. He leapt upward and shimmied over the windowsill. I didn't see it but I heard skin tear. He screeched in pain but that didn't stop him.

He stopped struggling for a few seconds, and then let out a loud yell. Then his body was pulled out of the window. He *thumped* on the other side and yelled for help. Then his yells turned to screams.

Katherine risked a glance outside and fled back from the window. One of the other survivors popped their head out even as Katherine yelled at him not to. Hands covered in wounds grasped the man's head and pulled. He let out a yelp and tried to tear away but fingers got his shirt and he was pulled out of the window.

"We can't get out that way." Katherine yelled, voice filled with revulsion.

The stairwell *crackled* as the fire finally reached it. Then flames, fed by the open window and door, leapt out to lick the ceiling.

We were trapped.

SIXTY-THREE

The heat from the flames made me want to grab Katherine's hand and run. If we didn't get out of the building, we were going to be roasted alive. Smoke became thick and forced us to drop low. The few survivors from upstairs milled around the open door forcing back the undead as they tried to enter. Ghouls stood in the back of the mass, guiding their minions.

I moved away from the window and stood so I could see outside. At least five of them waited there. I shot one in the head and that made the others duck out of sight. I moved closer to the window and pumped another round into the gun. When one of the ghouls' heads came into view, I shot the top off. It exploded in a mass of bone, brain, and blood. The twice dead corpse fell away.

Scott fired until he was empty, so I tossed him my handgun and extra magazine.

"Katherine. Show me the other way out," I said.

She guided me to a heavy door in the back of the room. I tested the knob and found it was hot.

"Shit," I said.

"What?"

"Fire on the other side."

"That's the only other way out, the rest of the windows are boarded up. We lived like animals in here while they experimented on us."

"Guess we have two ways out. One really. We're going to have to rush them." I said.

Scott turned and looked at me like I was crazy. Katherine and I reached his side, and I immediately saw what the problem was. More of the ghouls and undead had come to bear on our position. They stood in a group that was three or four thick. Even if we ran flat out, we'd never carve a path through them.

I tossed open cabinets, looking in vain for more weapons as I fought the smoke. My throat and lungs burned with the effort. I found chains and not much else. An old wooden spoon had been left next to a pan that was covered in mold.

Scott directed the others in their efforts to beat back the zombies as they came through the door. Before much longer we were going to be blocked in by their corpses.

Flames roared overhead and I started to cough uncontrollably. Katherine's eyes watered and she tugged up the remains of her sweater to cover her mouth and nose.

Scott swayed but fought on.

"Fuck!" I yelled.

"I say we make a run for it," Scott said.

"I'm not getting taken alive again," Katherine said.

I grimaced and contemplated another way out. If I dove out of the window, could I come up behind the ghouls and take them out while Scott shot at them from the window? I wasn't even sure how many rounds we had between us but I doubted it was enough to take them all down. Plus, I wasn't an action hero in a movie. This was all too real.

I dropped into a crouch and considered the shotgun. I ejected shells and found I had three. Three. Scott, Katherine, and me.

I looked at my companions.

Something exploded outside then, and gunfire erupted. I risked a glance and found a pair of men running toward the back door. The black guy, Joel, who'd recommended he and Jackson leave us behind, was in the lead. He shot as he moved, eyes glued to his scope, feet stepping in front of each other as he maintained a classic shooters stance.

Jackson barreled into a pair of ghouls, his wrench swinging wildly, his large frame turning him into a tank.

"We're going out the door. Everyone get ready," I yelled.

There were only four of them left. Heads nodded but there was despair in their eyes. More bullets flew and a pair of ghouls went down. Scott fired as he ran and managed to take one down.

The ceiling *crackled* and started to cave in. Flames rushed into the room so quickly they scorched the hairs on the back of my head and made my shirt steam from the sweat I'd accumulated over the last ten minutes.

Scott leapt through the doorway with me and Katherine close behind. I was hit almost immediately by a green-eyed fuck who reeked of rotten fish. The guy was a lot bigger than me but not all that well coordinated. He carried a pipe and, as he pushed me to the ground, he tried to bash in my head. I got the shotgun between us and fired. The blast lifted him off me and dropped him a few feet away with a gaping hole in his center.

I rolled to my side and came up in a crouch. Katherine had grabbed the moldy pot on her way out the door and applied it to a zombie's head. The hollow ring echoed as the creature went to its knees.

Scott fired until he ran dry, and then used the butt of the gun to cave in a head.

Even with Joel carefully picking off targets, there were still too many of them. We were still trapped and worse, I'd used my last few shotgun shells.

I spun the Remington around, grasped the hot barrel, and came up out of my crouch. The stock connected with a ghoul but another one leapt out of the crowd, and I was on my back again. I tried to exhale and slap my palm to alleviate some of the pressure of hitting the ground, but the old judo move wasn't timed and I lost my breath.

The ghoul pounded on my chest with his fists, and then lowered his head. Rancid breath assaulted my nose as it spoke.

"You will all join us," it said in a voice that sounded like crunching marbles. I looked up and realized who I was fighting. It was Chris. He'd been turned into one of them.

I didn't have room for a full blow, so I used my elbow to smash the side of Chris's head. The ghoul fell to the side, and I managed to sidle away. I got to my hands and knees and retreated from the green-eyed guy. Katherine stepped over me and smashed the side of Chris's head in with her pan. The bastard's glowing eyes rolled up in their sockets. She hit him again for good measure but this time the handle broke. I did not think he was dead, just wounded, and that was a real shame. Too bad I didn't have time to finish the job.

She grabbed my hand and helped me to my feet.

"Thank you, Katherine," I said. I wanted to pull her into my arms but it would have to wait.

"Glad I get to rescue you for a change," she said.

Jackson shouldered aside a zombie and crushed its spine with his wrench. He pointed at a break in the wall of the dead.

"Let's go, folks. Your friends are nearby but about to be overwhelmed. No rest for the goddamn wicked." Jackson grinned.

Katherine grabbed my hand and tugged me away. Scott joined us while Joel Kelly covered our retreat. He fired in a slow and steady manner, carefully taking aim and dropping the army of the dead one headshot at a time. Jackson broke away and smacked a zombie in the back of the neck.

"Wait!" I yelled and ran to the side of the house. Thomas had dropped his pack but he was nowhere to be seen.

I shouldered it and followed our new friends. Scott shot me a wide-eyed look

We fled from the remaining ghouls and zombies, leading them into the woods before circling back around. I gasped for breath and couldn't keep from coughing. The smoke had burned my lungs, and I couldn't seem to fill them with oxygen. The fight had taken a lot out of me, but the searing flames we'd fled hadn't helped at all.

Lisa's group was nowhere to be found but I was sure they'd been made to retreat. If they had faced a force anywhere near the size we had just faced, then they had no choice. With the building on fire, and us trapped inside, I didn't blame them. I just hoped Thomas and Sloane were with them.

We moved through the trees until we came across a small road. Jackson and Joel worked well as a team and took turns covering our retreat. Zombies still pursued us, judging by the sounds, but we stayed well ahead of them.

"Not much farther. We have rides," Jackson assured us.

I nodded, too exhausted to talk. It had taken everything I had to make it this far. I felt like I was going to drop dead from exhaustion at any second.

But I had Katherine and I had new friends. I concentrated on putting one foot in front of the other until we were safe.

EPILOGUE

P eace and quiet for a change.

After our escape from the enemy's compound, our new friends Joel and Jackson got to their ATVs. We crowded onto the vehicles with Katherine being the third passenger behind me, and Joel Kelly. Being so overloaded, the little engine was pushed to the limit as it carried us away.

We ran into trouble almost immediately but with Joel leading the way we were able to put down a small horde of zombies without much effort. He and Jackson Creed worked together like pros. It didn't hurt that they had a lot of weapons and a supply of ammo. I was glad that they didn't require us to help because I wasn't about to let Katherine out of my sight again.

Then, after half an hour of zigzagging around, we finally came to a break in the road that was covered with brush. Jackson hopped down and moved it aside. Once he started pushing branches out of the way, it was easy to see that the barrier was handmade. It provided cover for the little driveway but wouldn't stand up to a close inspection.

They took us to a house they referred to as Fortress. We met a teenage girl named Christy who was happy to help us get settled. There was Anna who wore a dour look on her face the entire time we were doing introductions. Jackson slipped his hand in hers and she relaxed a little bit.

Then a white Labrador named Frosty bounded into the house and raised its hackles at us. Katherine dropped to her knees and talked to him in a baby voice while rubbing her neck. She decided Katherine was the dog's new best friend.

Joel kept to himself. I felt like he was irritated by our presence, and I understood that. Three more mouths to feed hadn't on his to-do list today.

They had an impressive setup at the house. Rainwater was collected in barrels and they sterilized it with tiny amounts of bleach. They had managed to build up a lot of canned goods. In one corner of the kitchen, they had a basket filled with fresh-picked berries.

Joel was very guarded and kept an eye on us.

"I don't know you. I don't know if I can trust you. You fuck us and I'll make sure you regret it," he told me.

"I understand, and I'd feel the same way. I swear to you, I'm one of the good guys," I said.

"I'm really grateful you helped us escape," Scott said.

"Ain't no good guys in the zombie fucking apocalypse," Jackson Creed interjected.

"What my boy said," Joel nodded and went back too stripping and cleaning his weapons.

Scott found a corner and laid out a sleeping bag. He zipped himself up and, within seconds, was snoring like a saw.

It was an hour later before Katherine and I had some time together. I asked for some water and carried a few pails upstairs to what had been a kid's bedroom. We stopped in the bathroom, and I took Katherine's clothes off and put her in the tub. Even with the cold water she let me take care of her. She cried and told me about her ordeal.

"We didn't see it coming. A tree was dropped in our path and the convoy slammed to a halt. Before we knew it, we were swamped by an army led by the ghouls. We fought but a lot of people were captured. They destroyed our vehicles and took a lot of us to that camp," Katherine said as I cleaned blood off her forehead.

"What happened when they got you back to the compound?"

"It was horrible, Erik. They kept us like slaves in pens. I was one of the lucky ones. I was kept inside that building but I was always chained or locked up. They would take us out, one at a time, and do experiments on us. They made some of the men eat rancid meat, and then they judged how quickly it worked. How fast they turned into ghouls. They tried different things. Some of them were terrible because I heard the screams. I waited for my turn, but you showed up and the people in the compound went crazy. How did you even find me?"

"I saw you downstairs through the window. At least I thought it was you."

"That's when they were rounding us up to put in the room upstairs. I wasn't kidding about how smart they are, Erik. They can not only strategize but they communicate with the human servants."

"Why in the hell would anyone want to work with those monsters?" I said in disbelief.

"Food, water, and shelter. They've setup a number of enclaves and the ghouls provide security," she said. "But that's not all of it. Some people seem to now be susceptible to the strange telepathic commands the ghouls use on the dead."

"Christ," I muttered. I had suspected this was the case. Having it confirmed made me feel extreme unease. How were we supposed to fight a world filled with the dead when humans were helping them?

"I'm glad you found me," she smiled.

"I never gave up, Katherine. I met up with Lisa and we went in search of the convoy. Then we managed to get captured," I gave her an abbreviated version of the events since I'd last seen her and explained how we'd ended up in pens ourselves. I spoke of Haley and how Lee had killed her. I talked about freeing the prisoners and erasing the ghoul camp. We talked for as I used the water to help bathe and tend to her wounds.

When she was clean, I took my clothes off and sat with her, shivering in the tub while she tended to my cuts and scrapes. We dried ourselves and retired to our room. I dug out the radio from the backpack and fired it up. The battery was low, but I managed to reach Lisa's group.

"Erik. You're a cat. Nine fucking lives," she said over the crackling radio.

"I guess so," I said. "Scott and I got Katherine out. Glad you all survived. What about Thomas and Sloane?"

"Yeah, they're here. We had to make a run for it. I'm sorry, Erik, once the flames started to appear on the first floor I was sure you were all gone."

"I thought so too," I said. I didn't mention our new friends because they were already antsy about us. "We're safe for now and plan to rest for at least a few days."

"Good to hear. We're making the final push toward Portland tomorrow. We've made contact with a man named Stevens. He's guiding us in. If you can make it, I think you can help us make a difference."

"I plan too, Lisa," I said.

"Stay safe," Lisa said, then she rattled off a frequency I could use to find the people in Portland.

"You too, Lisa. Batteries low so I'm signing off."

"Stay frosty, pal."

Katherine and I folded ourselves into bed and warmed each other. We spoke of other things like life back at the cabin. I inspected the wound where she's been shot but it had partially healed and I could tell it would leave a scar.

For that hour, I mainly listened to her voice and stroked her hair. The bruises on her face and body would fade and I hoped the ones on her soul would as well.

After Katherine drifted off, I lay awake for a long time and listened as our new friends spoke and moved around downstairs. I'd go down later and ask if they wanted me to take a watch. Then I managed to fall asleep and didn't wake until the morning light blazed through the window.

I LEANED over and kissed Katherine awake but we didn't get out of bed for another hour.

It's been a few days since we hooked up with Jackson Creed and Joel Kelly's little crew. I've spent time with them, and they are good people. I think we have gained their trust. I've been out on a few patrols with Jackson, and we hit it off well enough. Joel is cold toward me, but Jackson assured me he was like that with everyone.

Scott has been as chipper as usual. He has been doing a lot of the cooking because he likes it. Said it keeps his mind off the horrors outside. None of us have the heart to tell him he's a terrible cook.

It was early morning, a few days later, and we were sitting around the dining area, eating powdered eggs cooked on a propane stove. Christy had dug up some tubers and fried them in Crisco. Joel had placed a map of the surrounding area on the table.

"It's getting worse out there. A few weeks ago, we had the run of this area. Now we're finding Zs everywhere, and it's just a matter of time before they locate us here," Jackson said.

He drew an outline of the surrounding area and placed little X's to indicate where we'd seen the dead.

"We could find some fuel and fly out of here," Anna suggested.

"Have to be an airport for that," Joel said. "Then getting the fuel back here and hope it hasn't gone bad, sounds like a nightmare. Besides, where would we go?"

"Away from here," Anna suggested.

"You all have a plane?" I asked.

"Yeah, and it's a beaut. Anna knows how to fly," Joel said.

"Not a bad idea. But where to go?"

"Like Anna said, away from here."

So I took a breath and explained to them about the situation in Portland. Joel considered my words carefully. Jackson looked skeptical and Anna shook her head and went to dig some more eggs out of the pan.

"Don't know what it's like in the city. Might be we can help. If we can even get there," Jackson said as he stroked the growth of hair over his lip.

"We have two ideas. Forage for fuel, hope it's good, haul it back here, and then hop in the plane and go fuck knows where," Jackson said. "Or we abandon Fortress and make for the big city where there's a bunch of militants with guns waiting to take back this area."

"About sums it up," I said.

"I don't like either idea," Anna said. "Why don't we just move out and find a safe haven a few miles from here? We can stay on the move. That old truck in the barn can take most of the food and supplies."

"I'm tired of running," Joel said.

I nodded.

"I'll go with you to Portland," Joel said after we'd all grown quiet for a few minutes.

Jackson and Anna exchanged looks but I couldn't read them.

"I'll let you know in the morning if we're going with you," Anna said.

Jackson looked surprised but he nodded after a minute.

We're going to rest up for the day, and tomorrow we'll make our move. I hope we can all go as a team, but Joel doesn't seem like he's going to stop Jackson and Anna if they want to take a different path. Christy stuck to Anna's side most of the time, so I guessed where her loyalty lay.

It's going to be a tense day, but I plan to stay out of everyone's way. Katherine and I are going to find the stream they pull water from and spend some time together. It's going to be a long time before she recovers from her ordeal. I'll be there for her and when she's ready to talk about what happened, I'll listen. Maybe it will bring her peace of mind.

I've kept this journal for half a year and I think it's time to take a break. Maybe I'll pick it up again at some point and continue my recollection of the events I've experienced as humanity faced its greatest threat. The funny thing is, Jackson has also been keeping a log of his life since the apocalypse began. We agreed to share some of our writing with each other later today.

For now, we're safe. I have my friend Scott and my love Katherine by my side. We've fought, escaped horrors no one should have to live through, seen friends die, and we're still here. Now I'm ready to take the fight to the dead and Heaven help anyone or anything that gets in my way.

The End

ALSO BY TIMOTHY W. LONG

Drums of War 1: A Bradley Adams Novel

March to War 2: A Bradley Adams Novel

Casualties of War 3: A Bradley Adams Novel

Forged in the Fires of Heaven

Chicken Dinner

Enter the Realm

Dawn of the Rage Apocalypse

Among the Living

Among the Dead

Beyond the Barriers

At the Behest of the Dead

The Zombie Wilson Diaries

The Apocalypse and Satan's Glory Hole w/Jonathan Moon

Z-Risen 1: Outbreak

Z-Risen 2: Outcasts

Z-Risen 3: Poisoned Earth

Z-Risen 4: Reavers

Z-Risen 5: Barriers

The Front: Screaming Eagles w/David Moody and Craig DiLouie

Impact Earth: Symbiosis

Damaged w/Tim Marquitz

Printed in Great Britain
by Amazon

42430935R00218